JOSEPH CONRAD, a paradox in the history of English literature, became one of England's greatest novelists and prose stylists although h... ...and did not ...fore his firs... ...e was nea... ...s as a merc... ...iction, like ...ircle the world. Some ...nest stories reflect the impact of voyages to Malaya, the Congo and other exotic lands. In settings of fecund jungle, Conrad dramatized the fate of the European in isolation, challenged by primitivism, tempted to meddle in native affairs, left to perish in moral languor.

Here are three tales—two short novels and a story—characterized by similar settings and the same brooding view of disillusionment, deterioration and collapse. All bear the mark of Conrad's unique personal vision of mankind in peril.

ALBERT J. GUERARD, who has written the introduction to *The Laurel Conrad,* is a novelist, a critic, and a Professor of English at Stanford University. He is the author of a critical work on Conrad, *Conrad the Novelist,* and his most recent novel is entitled *The Bystander*.

Heart of Darkness
Almayer's Folly
The Lagoon

By Joseph Conrad

with a general introduction by

Albert J. Guerard

THE LAUREL CONRAD

Published by
DELL PUBLISHING CO., INC.
750 Third Avenue
New York 17, N.Y.

Cover painting by Richard Powers

Reprinted by arrangement with
Doubleday and Company, Inc., New York,
and J. M. Dent & Sons Ltd., London

First printing—August, 1960
Second printing—April, 1962
Third printing—August, 1963
Fourth printing—April, 1964
Fifth printing—December, 1964
Sixth printing—October, 1965
Seventh printing—August, 1966

Printed in U.S.A.

Contents

Introduction

1

There are certain writers who do not improve with acquaintance. But this is not true of Conrad. For the Conrad of the biographers—this austere, aloof, aristocratic, conservative, secretive man with his protective mustache and alert, distrustful eyes—becomes, when we see him through the screen of certain very intimate books, a different and more engaging person. And so too his long novels *Lord Jim* and *Nostromo*—exasperatingly difficult in the first hour we give to them, labyrinthine in structure and dark of allusion —become as familiar to us as anything else of major importance in our lives. The position to take at the outset is that Conrad's best books change upon rereading and were written to be read more than once. And we, as we emerge from these readings and rereadings, discover that we too have changed. The novel has been rightly described as the richest mode of personal communication ever devised: this communication between a man writing at his desk (and often saying things he wouldn't say to his best friends) and another man sitting in a chair. And of great novelists, Conrad is one of the most personal. We enjoy his novels for suspense and adventure and even for exotic glamour. Yet all the while these stories play subtly upon our sensibilities and tamper with our convictions. At the least they demand of us more complex sympathies than we ordinarily need to muster in the everyday business of our lives. This is one reason why they do not leave us as we were.

Joseph Conrad, born Teodor Jozef Konrad Korzeniowski (1857–1924), left his native Poland when he was not quite

seventeen, having most improbably decided on a career at
sea. He made his decision against the urgings of his guardian
and his relatives, who saw it as the action of a man bent on
throwing his life away. The departure from occupied Poland
could even be regarded by them as unpatriotic. For Conrad
was the son of a noted leader in the struggle against Russian oppression, and the deaths of both his parents had been
accelerated by exile. It is safe to say that Conrad's feelings
toward his father and toward Poland were never satisfac-
torily resolved. Surely this has something to do with his
insistent claims to fidelity in his essays and letters, and with
his repeated dramatization (in the novels) of betrayal and
desertion. But it would be another twenty years before Conrad began to publish novels. And if it seems unlikely a Pole
by birth should become one of England's greatest novelists
and prose stylists, it would seem quite as unlikely for such a
man to become a master-mariner in the British merchant
marine.

The first years after leaving Poland were adventurous
enough. There were voyages on French ships to Central and
South America, perhaps involving gun-running. (On one
such trip Conrad was to acquire in a few days those impres-
sions which would help make *Nostromo* the greatest novel
in English about South American politics.) And before he
was twenty-one Conrad was, if we are to believe his statements and listen to his hints, co-owner of a small ship smuggling arms and messages to Spain on behalf of the Pre-
tender Don Carlos. Moreover he may have been the lover
of one "Doña Rita," mistress of the "king." It was largely
for her, Conrad implies, that he made his smuggling voyages on board the *Tremolino,* and for her he fought a duel
with an American adventurer named Blunt. But this period
of his life is still deeply shrouded in ambiguities. No record
of a *Tremolino* has been found, and a recently rediscov-
ered letter suggests Conrad's revolver wound may have
come not from a duel but from attempted suicide, after the
loss of all his money at Monte Carlo. If this is true, Conrad

covered his traces most elaborately. He was to become one
of the most subjective of British novelists, but by no means
one of the most openly confessional. His very evasiveness
of temperament led him to dramatize ambiguities and secre-
cies of spirit, and to use highly involuted forms. The spidery
complexity of his best longer novels is a true reflection of
his temperament.

It has been the fashion in recent years to discount Conrad's long experience as a seaman and officer, and to consider only the probing psychological novelist and lover of
artistic experiment. But a Conrad who had not been to sea
would not be the same writer at all. His career, after those
early voyages, involved no further illegal activities, so far
as we know. Once committed to England (and still only
21) Conrad became more British than the British, and ac-
quired profound respect for the pitiless maritime ethic and
stern tradition of duty. But the man deeply divided between
order and anarchy can seldom leave his conflicts wholly behind. Conrad the officer was, according to one of his
friends, noted both for his risky maneuvers at sea and for
his meticulous care to details of stowage. And it is wholly
characteristic that in a series of fictions Conrad should
have associated several famous crimes at sea with his own
first command of the tiny *Otago*. This long-delayed and
then long-becalmed first voyage on the Gulf of Siam with
a cholera- and dysentery-ridden crew returned repeatedly
to Conrad's imagination as an archetypal experience of self-
testing. In "The Secret Sharer" it invites a story of dark
introspection and loyalty to an outlaw "double," who must
be recognized before full command can be achieved. And
in *The Shadow Line* that first voyage becomes a test of ra-
tionality clung to in the face of extreme bad luck. This
brooding short novel, the last of Conrad's works to possess
any real merit, even seems to reflect or symbolize an effort
to throw off the blackness of immobilizing depression. Conrad the master-mariner had a solid, real knowledge of ships
and seamen. But the sea was even for him "the unstable ele-

ment," and had its part in the experience of guilt and in the act of self-scrutiny, those two foundations of Conrad's fictional world.

Conrad came to novel-writing abnormally late and was almost forty before he published his first novel. Even then he had not wholly abandoned all thoughts of returning to the sea. Nevertheless, most of his best work was done in one great decade, from *Almayer's Folly* of 1895 to *Nostromo* of 1904. This is the period that primarily concerns us, though *The Secret Agent* (1907) and *Under Western Eyes* (1911) have great merit. (Conrad's period of commercial success, beginning with *Chance* in 1913, corresponds fairly exactly with his period of sharp decline in energy and art.) But the work of the first decade offers the essential Conradian dreams and the three great segments of his fictional world. These are, to group very roughly: the *sea*, where both ships and men are tested; the *jungle*, where men deteriorate in solitude, or are corrupted by native intrigue; and *politics*, where dreams and self-delusions become history. The groupings are indeed rough, since certain human traits and obsessive fears may exist anywhere. But there is something to be gained from this roughness, and from looking at the three areas in turn.

2

The line between fact and fiction is a slender and wavering one in Conrad's writings on the sea. *The Mirror of the Sea* (1906) is the work of a professional seaman who does not like to see nautical terms misused, and who evokes ships, seas, rivers, weather, winds with a loving precision. Still, this book of essays and recollections, which claims to hold back nothing, obviously holds back a great deal; its chapters on the Carlist adventure remain distinctly suspect. This is supposed to be non-fiction. The ship *Narcissus* of the famous short novel actually existed, on the other hand, and I have seen the details of its sturdy shipmaking in a Lloyd's Register of the time—a ship on which, because of her beauty, Conrad chose to sail in 1884. Even earlier he sailed on the ill-fated *Palestine*, which became the *Judea* of the short novel *Youth*. And there are the two famous crimes of the summer of 1880 which became attached to very personal narratives—the killing of a sailor aboard the *Cutty Sark* (which went into both "The Secret Sharer" and *Lord Jim*) and that abandonment of the *Jeddah (Patna)* which became the central incident of *Lord Jim*. To them we may add the crime of cannibalism which, in the story "Falk," also became associated with Conrad's first command.

But all this only means that everything Conrad wrote about the sea had its personal accent and undertone. A more useful distinction, it may be, would separate the stories which present life at sea in its own terms from the stories in which such life becomes generalized, visionary, symbolic—would separate, in a word, *The End of the Tether* from *The Nigger of the "Narcissus,"* with *Typhoon* somewhere between the two.

The End of the Tether derives directly enough from voyages Conrad made as first mate on the *Vidar* in 1887 and early 1888, between Singapore and Borneo, trading "among dark islands on a blue-scarred sea." These were the voyages that would give him his closest view of Malayan life and provide him with the settings for four of his novels. We know from the captain of the *Vidar* that Conrad was worried about his eyesight at that time; we know too that this was for him a period of restlessness and undefined spiritual crisis. Yet *The End of the Tether* seems to be one of Conrad's most impersonal works, carefully controlled in overall structure and style. The technical problem of the story— to work very close to Captain Whalley's consciousness yet withhold from the reader the central preoccupation of that consciousness—was a most difficult one, deliberately and successfully solved. This problem was the more severe, too, because Conrad was never wholly comfortable when using the objective, third-person narrative form in writing about the interior life. Still *The End of the Tether*, overlong and perhaps oversimple of plot, and revealing its specific area of guilt only near the end, contains some of Conrad's most pleasing evocations of the sea. The unobsessed writing has the beauty of exactness.

Typhoon too is a simple, controlled and, on the whole, impersonal reflection of Conrad's experience at sea. Other and greater works may profit by the devil's share of unconscious creation. But the rugged strength of *Typhoon* derives from the author's full conscious control of his fiction—Conrad the retired officer supplying the expert knowledge of ship and storm and psychology of command; Conrad the artist carefully planning his effects and wisely omitting the very worst of the storm; Conrad the moralist shrewdly weighing the merits of the three officers, and very exactly exposing his theme of justice triumphing over sentiment.

"MacWhirr is not an acquaintance of a few hours, or of a few weeks, or a few months. He is the product of twenty years of life. My own life." In these prefatory words Conrad suggested that *Typhoon* was a very personal story. But it was so only in a curiously indirect and compensatory way. For Conrad so distrusted imagination and introspection and intellectual complexity (and all the other qualities that made him a great writer) that he came to overvalue the simple men who did not possess them, and who were free from his own anxieties. He could almost idealize, in certain hours and moods, such a stolid, unimaginative, unintellectual man as MacWhirr, untroubled by the past, for whom the future "was not there yet." The typhoon of the story (and the chaotic situation of the coolies tumbling in the hold) puts this extrovert simplicity to the test. MacWhirr substitutes stubbornness and courage for "storm-strategy," will for intellect. And in his ignorance of what such a storm could do and be, he is momentarily demoralized. Significantly he is saved by order and routine: by finding in the darkness a towel in just the place it is supposed to be. (These are the extremes of Conrad's moral world: the perilous night journey into self, and finding a towel in the right place!)

At least MacWhirr proves himself a good officer of his

kind, against whom Mr. Jukes must stand in calculated and shameful contrast. This imaginative and even sentimental officer—who anticipates catastrophe, and in the midst of crisis hopes to be praised—wanted to alter the course of the ship so the coolies could ride more comfortably. This, to Captain MacWhirr, is nonsense. But it is MacWhirr who does the only fair thing with the coolies, by dividing the scattered dollars among them. His unromantic and stolid fairness becomes a kind of heroism.

These are controlled, balanced and eminently readable short novels. *The Nigger of the "Narcissus,"* however, is one of the summits of the art of fiction. It is tempting to read it as the record of a real voyage and a real ship, though Conrad himself left her at Dunkirk, not London, and though the name "Wait" was taken from a Negro on board another ship. And he would be a desecrator indeed who saw here only a symbolic ship and metaphysical seas. This short novel is a tribute to certain remembered "children of the sea" and a memorial to the era of sail. For one of Conrad's aims, as he says in his eloquent Preface, was to seize "a passing phase of life from the remorseless rush of time." These simple men, tested by the storm and tempted by the foul, mutinous Donkin, tested and tempted even more insidiously by James Wait and his debilitating egoism, turn out all right in the end. And the white female ship, with her known weakness, turns out all right: the human protagonist pitted against a storm of seemingly preternatural malevolence. This is truly a substantial sea. The account of the ship's overthrow by that wave "like a wall of green glass topped with snow" is exceeded, as dramatic writing, only by that of the ship's deliberate, human and heroic rising hours later, and her subsequent wild rush along a towering sea, "spouting thick streams of water through every opening of her wounded sides." The lovely *Narcissus*—binding the parts of the novel—is its central figure, to be desecrated at the end by the grime of London and by the feet of alien landsmen, the soiling touch of commerce. But heroic too is the simple, unsentimental Singleton, who still steered with care after thirty hours of storm at the wheel, and with his white beard deliberately tucked under his coat.

Life itself and such writing about it may well be more important than buried subtleties of symbol and theme. But these other interests exist too, and in fact we would hardly care as much as we do for the sea narrative if it did not speak to us on a more personal level. Some themes and symbols in *The Nigger of the "Narcissus"* are perfectly conscious and overt. We see that Conrad clearly intended this voyage as symbolic of life and this ship as a microcosm of the freighted earth. We see too that he intended to express an ultimate skepticism when he makes his equation of God and the immortal sea, in the first paragraph of chapter four. It is evident that Conrad wanted to express his profound distrust of human qualities many people are accustomed to revere—pity, for instance, or intellectual complexity. And surely it is also evident that Conrad intended to represent, in James Watt, a certain *blackness* within human nature, a blackness which the ship must be rid of before she can end her journey. Hence the occult circumstance of a favorable wind rising at the very moment Wait's body is deposited, like Jonah's, in the sea.

There are, in fact, symbols and meanings more elusive than these, though presumably less conscious. A powerful imagination and waking dream may discover, as it were, inadvertently, certain archetypal patterns of the human spirit and universal myths. Thus we say with some assurance that "The Secret Sharer" and *Heart of Darkness* (beneath the level of explicit theme, and far beneath the level of adventure story) dramatize a deep, introspective descent into the half-conscious and unconscious mind. The rescue of James Wait strikes us as suggesting such a descent. But at the very least we can say that these men absurdly strive to save the force that has almost destroyed them; or again, considering all the imagery of difficult childbirth, that we have attended the rebirth of evil on the ship.

Whatever we may feel about the existence of such buried

meanings, we can make no doubt about the concealed yet solid artistry of the novel's structure—the skill with which Conrad juxtaposes the two tests of the crew, that of the storm and that of the demoralizing Wait; or the skill with which he restores our faith in the crew by making the ship herself heroic in that beat up the channel toward home; or the care with which he modulates his narrative downward from the elevated rhetoric of Singleton at the wheel to the prosaic life of everyday; or, centrally, the tact with which he prepares us by tone and imagery to accept the audacious symbolic coincidence of Wait's burial and the wind's rising.

3

The Malayan voyages of 1887 and the Congo journey of 1890 were closely associated in Conrad's imagination and left much the same dark impact on his work. *Almayer's Folly* (with its sequels *An Outcast of the Islands* and *The Rescue*) has interest as a document on Bornean politics, and on the squalid inertia of native life. And *Heart of Darkness* is an unforgettable report on Belgian exploitation and cruelty. But these works, together with such stories as "An Outpost of Progress," "Karain" and "The Lagoon," form a cluster of brooding, pessimistic visions of deterioration and collapse. The same themes and preoccupations appear in these works, and often the same lush and sinuous prose.

The first of these themes involves the fascination and moral peril of involvement in native affairs. Conrad's imagination was caught by the historical figure of James Brooke, the fabulously successful first white Rajah of Sarawak, but also by an enigmatic, obscure personage named Wyndham, who traded with certain natives, became a benevolent despot over them, and in the end could not tear himself away. Conrad himself encountered the prototype of his Kurtz (of *Heart of Darkness*), one Georges-Antoine Klein, who died on the *Roi des Belges*. Kurtz goes further than any of Conrad's other meddlers in native intrigue, since he becomes one of the high devils of the land, worshiped in unspeakable ceremonies. Captain Tom Lingard, many years before the opening action of *Almayer's Folly,* rescued a Malayan prince and his sister and worked to help them recover their kingdom. The nameless white man of "The Lagoon" has also been involved in native intrigue, and the skulking Willems of *An Outcast of the Islands* betrays Lingard's secret for the embraces of a native girl. The implication is that only extraordinary strength of will can survive any traffic with natives, or overcome the languor it invites. In the jungle outpost or native village, and freed from the watching eye of policeman or European neighbor, the white man is threatened with moral collapse.

The second theme or preoccupation concerns the character of the intervening "benevolent despot," this vulnerable, romantic idealist. Captain Tom Lingard is such a romantic meddler, with his indiscriminate rescues of the unfortunate and his bland magisterial control of their lives. And even the Kurtz of unspeakable lusts and gratifications had gone to the Congo with idealistic ardor, to bring enlightenment and progress. The burden of the message is to beware of the sentimental humanitarian, bemused by his generous dreams. The Lord Jim of Patusan is thus intoxicated by his power to do good, and his protection of the community at last brings it ruin. The vain dreamer may be possessed at last by what he thought to possess: "He looked with an owner's eye at the peace of the evening, at the river, at the houses, at the everlasting life of the forests, at the life of the old mankind, at the secrets of the land, at the pride of his own heart: but it was they that possessed him and made him their own to the innermost thought, to the slightest stir of blood, to his last breath."

The third recurring preoccupation, intimately related to the first two, can best be described as a dread of *immobilization.* A menace of sexual failure, or of peril attaching to sexual fulfillment, is repeatedly associated with the fecund jungle of *Almayer's Folly* and *An Outcast of the Islands;* some of Conrad's gloomiest jungle descriptions accompany the clandestine meetings of lovers. But beyond the sexual fear, and perhaps related to it, is fear of an inability to act at all. The dream landscape of "The Lagoon" is "bewitched into an immobility perfect and final," and within it the guilty Arsat is immobilized by remorse over his desertion of his brother, an impulsive, unintended betrayal. And the ship moving toward Kurtz and the Inner Station moves through a fog and silence like a "state of trance." Kurtz himself is once referred to as an enchanted princess, and Marlow's task is to "break the spell." But this immobilized devil does not want to be saved.

This concern with immobilization appears in many of Conrad's novels and stories. Men may be immobilized by sexual bondage but also, as in *Victory,* by sexless intellectual detachment. The Decoud of *Nostromo* is immobilized by skepticism; various characters by guilt, remorse and even by the recognition of one's own guilt in another person. And of course men may be immobilized by deep introspection and self-analysis. Thus "The Secret Sharer" (with its Jungian descent into self) and *The Shadow Line* (with its black and utter calm) seem at the very heart of Conrad's meaning. But so too is *Lord Jim.* For Jim is literally immobilized at the critical moments of his life. As a boy on the training-ship he cannot move and loses his chance to join in the rescue. On board the *Patna* the conscious man stands still for twenty-seven minutes, till something less than consciousness makes him jump . . . into an immobilizing guilt, an everlasting black hole. Thereafter he is paralyzed by all chance reminders of the *Patna* incident. His inability to act —his immobilization by his "double" Gentleman Brown— brings on the catastrophe.

We know that Conrad broke off *Lord Jim* to write *Heart of Darkness,* and we know that a man named Marlow serves as narrator in both works. But their roles are very different. The Marlow of *Heart of Darkness* is the true protagonist of his story, and however we interpret that journey up the Congo, it is unmistakably an inward journey. This is the intimate narrative of a man cut off from his familiar surroundings and habits, and compelled to choose between the mean, flabby rapacity of ordinary exploiters and the legendary, already suspect Kurtz. It would be rash to say dogmatically what the meeting and struggle with Kurtz signify in psychological terms. But at least this confrontation, the "culminating point" in Marlow's experience, involves subtler temptations than a crude reversion to savagery, the urge to have a howl and a dance. Perhaps it is best to say that this, like any richly rendered subjective experience, defies single and simple summation.

So this Marlow is protagonist, the very subject of his own tale. But the Marlow of *Lord Jim*, though he too has his inward debates, is first of all narrator and listener, the chief of several witnesses to Jim's state of being and soul. *Lord Jim* is a moral drama, and the reader's ultimate task is to locate this vulnerable idealist and conscientious failure on a moral spectrum. He must decide whether Jim's is a drama of bruised vanity or a tragedy of conscience. This is the chief question that the novel, through Marlow, asks. "I don't mean to say that I regret my action, nor will I pretend that I can't sleep o' nights in consequence; still the idea obtrudes itself that he made so much of his disgrace while it is the guilt alone that matters." And does Jim redeem himself in Patusan? Can we even categorically say that Jim's final act is one of moral self-repudiation, rather than one last gesture of selfish pride?

Such are the questions asked by this long and circumspect novel. The answers cannot be found in what Jim says about himself, nor even wholly in what Marlow and Stein say. Jim himself would have it that intentions are more important than actions, with the pure heart excusing many an ugly deed. But this is not Conrad's view; his view is that our acts especially matter. Thus the acts of various other characters (or "reflectors") modify our attitude toward Jim. We notice that the French Lieutenant stayed on board the *Patna* for thirty-six hours, concerned less because the ship might sink at any moment than because he had no wine with his meals. There is big Brierly, who commits suicide after recognizing that he too might have committed such a crime as Jim's. There is little Bob Stanton, who drowns trying to save one person while Jim deserted eight hundred. And there is even that heroic native helmsman who never thought of leaving the ship. Conrad, as in most of his books, exhibits deep personal sympathy for his victims of romantic illusion and criminal failures of good intention. But also he presents the grounds for moral condemnation. The emotional appeal of *Lord Jim* largely derives from the interplay of incorrigible sympathy and stern, ironic judgment. This duality, and the need for an ebb and flow of sympathy and for an ever-changing distance, partly account for the novel's involuted form, and for its long withholding of certain facts we need to know. The reader is not permitted easy commitment. Instead, struggling for foothold and lost in the scrambled chronology, bewildered by the conflicting evidence, he must face the issues as he would face them in real life. There is no omniscient author consistently present to help him. He must, instead, explore these ambiguities and arrive at his own moral judgments.

4

Conrad's last important full-length novels—*Nostromo* (1904), *The Secret Agent* (1907) and *Under Western Eyes* (1911)—enter the urban world of politics. The dates of the novels are surprising, since all three seem so contemporary: *Nostromo* as up-to-date as the latest Central or South American revolution. All three, though written in the relatively secure Edwardian days, reflect our own age of moral anarchy and latent violence, of espionage and counter-espionage, of deceptive and self-deceptive propaganda, of growing callousness to atrocity. And all three reflect not so much Conrad's political conservatism as a deep skepticism concerning all political motive and intention, be it conservative, radical or liberal.

We may prefer the interior resonance and minute artistry of *Lord Jim* or the disturbing short novels. But *Nostromo,* though radically defective in its second half, remains Conrad's richest creation of life. His few days in South America a quarter of a century before, the reading of a book about Paraguay, a few stories and personal memories—these seem to be all Conrad needed to bring into existence his Republic of Costaguana, as substantial and real a place as any we can hope to visit. The imagined state and city have, certainly, a greater reality than Bangkok and the Bornean villages Conrad actually knew. And there is a far more impressive range of characters than in any of his other novels—from chiefs of state to the florid person of French extraction and mistress of the Finance Minister who sells her influence; from Father Corbelàn, austere head of the Church and the country's first Cardinal-Archbishop, to Father Roman, great snuff-taker and card-player, who had "shriven many simple souls on the battlefields of the Republic"; from General Barrios and the backwoods General Montero to the craven Colonel Sotillo and the craven Señor Hirsch. Various personages seem entirely new to Conrad's fictional world. The loquacious politicians are always convincing. So too are Mrs. Gould and Antonia Avellanos, the first interesting white women in the work of a man who showed much misogynist distrust. Perhaps the major disappointment of the novel, in terms of characterization, is Nostromo himself, the Capataz de Cargadores and idealizer of his own vanity. Charles Gould, who sacrifices everything to the idealization of his silver mine, is a pallid figure. But such he was intended to be.

The very number of vivid characters and incidents, and the impressionistic structure of the first part, make *Nostromo* the most difficult of Conrad's novels to begin. The narrative flows backward and forward in time with the waywardness of casual memory; only about a tenth of Part

One exists in the present. Thus we have the illusion that events occurring over only a few days actually cover years; so too events long past may be dramatized with intense immediacy. Essential information, moreover, may reach us through a digression within a digression, while matters of no real importance may be given sharp visual emphasis. All this can be exasperating, and on a first reading it is perhaps unwise to try to untangle all the threads. For one desired effect is likely to be enjoyed anyway, by all but the most resistant reader—the effect of being immersed in a bewildering actuality. The reader becomes truly a visitor in Sulaco: one who arrives without guidebook or written history, and who must try to make himself at home in a world of revolution and counter-revolution.

The political realities emerge more clearly after those first rich and difficult chapters. We begin to discern political alignments. And presently a certain political vision and authorial attitude also begin to emerge: a profoundly skeptical "philosophy of history." Corruption and cynicism are rife in Costaguana, which has its long history of venality and brutal dictatorship. But even the idealists pursue a fatality of failure and are corrupted by their generous dreams. The slogans and enthusiasms of the liberals are futile and the pages of Don José's exposé of misrule are used as wadding for guns.

The critique of idealization is particularly incisive in its assessment of industry and capitalism, often referred to as "material interest." It is in the nature of material interest to subvert moral principle, as Dr. Monygham perceives. But the sentimental Charles Gould idealizes his silver mine, the chief political force in the country, and insists on the incorruptible metal's power to bring progress and order. He could not "act or exist without idealizing every simple feeling, desire, or achievement. He could not believe his own motives if he did not make them first a part of some fairy tale." Holroyd too, the San Francisco financier, must moralize his sinister game of power. He "would not drop his idea of introducing, not only justice, industry, peace, to the benighted continents, but also that pet dream of his of a purer form of Christianity." Are Costaguana and Sulaco better off in the end, for the mine and its American financing, for the control of government by capital? The case is by no means clear. Holroyd himself predicts, in any event, what would happen in the coming decades, and suggests history may escape man's reason and will. "We shall run the world's business whether the world likes it or not. The world can't help it—and neither can we, I guess." The best intentions of men are subject to brute chance and inhuman process. And their ideals however generous are undermined by the egoism that fostered them. The magnitude of men is destroyed by their "irremediable littleness."

Nostromo is not yet, entirely, an historical novel. The regular torturing of political opponents was almost a thing of the past in the Costaguana of the novel but was reported from Paraguay on the day I wrote these lines. The dependence of a backward Costaguana is reflected in the present plight of Bolivia. And few Latin American countries have escaped the absurd cycles of reform dictatorship and military junta, proclamation and plebiscite. *Nostromo* suggests, however, that the larger political forces at work in Costaguana may be at work anywhere: the vanities and illusions and secret pulls of power, and especially the easily corrupted force of words, especially man's incorrigible gift for deceiving himself with the words by which he intended to deceive others.

5

Such are some of the interests—psychological, moral, political, artistic—of Conrad's fictional world. *The Secret Agent* (1907), dealing with the underside of political life and international intrigue, represents a new departure in form, a controlled, ironic and suspenseful story not unlike certain "entertainments" of Graham Greene. *Under Western Eyes* (1911) returns us to Conrad's central story of marginal crime and betrayal of the outlaw "brother," with betrayer and betrayed now Russians, and in a European setting. His not unsympathetic portrait of Russia and Russians is an act of high imaginative integrity on the part of a novelist who hated and distrusted both; and *Under Western Eyes* is a great novel.

Otherwise, except for scattered pages and except for the brief *Shadow Line,* Conrad's later novels are inferior. Attempting a more charitable ethic and more generous psychology, and a more affirmative attitude toward love, the late novels succeed only in becoming slack, sentimental, tired. In time they will be forgotten. But the works of the first decade, from *Almayer's Folly* through *Nostromo,* constitute an extraordinary personal vision and creation, dark yet glowingly alive. They are more than enough to assure Conrad his austere and very high place.

ALBERT J. GUERARD

HEART
OF DARKNESS

CHAPTER 1

The *Nellie,* a cruising yawl, swung to her anchor without a flutter of the sails, and was at rest. The flood had made, the wind was nearly calm, and being bound down the river, the only thing for it was to come to and wait for the turn of the tide.

The sea-reach of the Thames stretched before us like the beginning of an interminable waterway. In the offing the sea and the sky were welded together without a joint, and in the luminous space the tanned sails of the barges drifting up with the tide seemed to stand still in red clusters of canvas sharply peaked, with gleams of varnished sprits. A haze rested on the low shores that ran out to sea in vanishing flatness. The air was dark above Gravesend, and farther back still seemed condensed into a mournful gloom, brooding motionless over the biggest, and the greatest, town on earth.

The Director of Companies was our captain and our host. We four affectionately watched his back as he stood in the bows looking to seaward. On the whole river there was nothing that looked half so nautical. He resembled a pilot, which to a seaman is trustworthiness personified. It was difficult to realize his work was not out there in the luminous estuary, but behind him, within the brooding gloom.

Between us there was, as I have already said somewhere, the bond of the sea. Besides holding our hearts together through long periods of separation, it had the effect of making us tolerant of each other's yarns—and even convictions. The Lawyer—the best of old fellows—had, because of his many virtues, the only cushion on deck, and was lying on the only rug. The Accountant had brought out already a box of dominoes, and was toying architecturally with the bones.

Marlow sat cross-legged right aft, leaning against the
mizzen-mast. He had sunken cheeks, a yellow complexion,
a straight back, an ascetic aspect, and, with his arms
dropped, the palms of hands outwards, resembled an idol.
The director, satisfied the anchor had good hold, made his
way aft and sat down amongst us. We exchanged a few
words lazily. Afterwards there was silence on board the
yacht. For some reason or other we did not begin that game
of dominoes. We felt meditative, and fit for nothing but
placid staring. The day was ending in a serenity of still and
exquisite brilliance. The water shone pacifically; the sky,
without a speck, was a benign immensity of unstained
light; the very mist on the Essex marshes was like a gauzy
and radiant fabric, hung from the wooded rises inland, and
draping the low shores in diaphanous folds. Only the gloom
to the west, brooding over the upper reaches, became more
sombre every minute, as if angered by the approach of the
sun.

And at last, in its curved and imperceptible fall, the sun
sank low, and from glowing white changed to a dull red
without rays and without heat, as if about to go out suddenly, stricken to death by the touch of that gloom brooding over a crowd of men.

Forthwith a change came over the waters, and the serenity became less brilliant but more profound. The old river
in its broad reach rested unruffled at the decline of day,
after ages of good service done to the race that peopled its
banks, spread out in the tranquil dignity of a waterway leading to the uttermost ends of the earth. We looked at the
venerable stream not in the vivid flush of a short day that
comes and departs for ever, but in the august light of abid-
ing memories. And indeed nothing is easier for a man who
has, as the phrase goes, "followed the sea" with reverence
and affection, than to evoke the great spirit of the past upon
the lower reaches of the Thames. The tidal current runs to
and fro in its unceasing service, crowded with memories of
men and ships it had borne to the rest of home or to the
battles of the sea. It had known and served all the men of
whom the nation is proud, from Sir Francis Drake to Sir

John Franklin, knights all, titled and untitled—the great knights-errant of the sea. It had borne all the ships whose names are like jewels flashing in the night of time, from the *Golden Hind* returning with her round flanks full of treasure, to be visited by the Queen's Highness and thus pass out of the gigantic tale, to the *Erebus* and *Terror*, bound on other conquests—and that never returned. It had known the ships and the men. They had sailed from Deptford, from Greenwich, from Erith—the adventurers and the settlers; kings' ships and the ships of men on 'Change; captains, admirals, the dark "interlopers" of the Eastern trade, and the commissioned "generals" of East India fleets. Hunters for gold or pursuers of fame, they all had gone out on that stream, bearing the sword, and often the torch, messengers of the might within the land, bearers of a spark from the sacred fire. What greatness had not floated on the ebb of that river into the mystery of an unknown earth! . . . The dreams of men, the seed of commonwealths, the germs of empires.

The sun set; the dusk fell on the stream, and lights began to appear along the shore. The Chapman lighthouse, a three-legged thing erect on a mud-flat, shone strongly. Lights of ships moved in the fairway—a great stir of lights going up and going down. And farther west on the upper reaches the place of the monstrous town was still marked ominously on the sky, a brooding gloom in sunshine, a lurid glare under the stars.

"And this also," said Marlow suddenly, "has been one of the dark places on the earth."

He was the only man of us who still "followed the sea." The worst that could be said of him was that he did not represent his class. He was a seaman, but he was a wanderer, too, while most seamen lead, if one may so express it, a sedentary life. Their minds are of the stay-at-home order, and their home is always with them—the ship; and so is their country—the sea. One ship is very much like another, and the sea is always the same. In the immutability of their surroundings the foreign shores, the foreign faces, the changing immensity of life, glide past, veiled not by a sense of mystery but by a slightly disdainful ignorance; for there is nothing mysterious to a seaman unless it be the sea itself, which is the mistress of his existence and as inscrutable as Destiny. For the rest, after his hours of work, a casual stroll or a casual spree on shore suffices to unfold for him the secret of a whole continent, and generally he finds the secret not worth knowing. The yarns of seamen have a direct simplicity, the whole meaning of which lies within the shell of a cracked nut. But Marlow was not typical (if his propensity to spin yarns be excepted), and to him the meaning of an episode was not inside like a kernel but outside, enveloping the tale which brought it out only as a glow brings out a haze, in the likeness of one of these misty halos that sometimes are made visible by the spectral illumination of moonshine.

His remark did not seem at all surprising. It was just like Marlow. It was accepted in silence. No one took the trouble to grunt even; and presently he said, very slow—

"I was thinking of very old times, when the Romans first came here, nineteen hundred years ago—the other day. . . . Light came out of this river since—you say Knights? Yes; but it is like a running blaze on a plain, like a flash of lightning in the clouds. We live in the flicker—may it last as long as the old earth keeps rolling! But darkness was here yesterday. Imagine the feelings of a commander of a fine—what d'ye call 'em?—trireme in the Mediterranean, ordered suddenly to the north; run overland across the Gauls in a hurry; put in charge of one of these craft the legionaries—a wonderful lot of handy men they must have been, too—used to build, apparently, by the hundred, in a month or two, if we may believe what we read. Imagine him here—the very end of the world, a sea the colour of lead, a sky the colour of smoke, a kind of ship about as rigid as a concertina—and going up this river with stores, or orders, or what you like. Sand-banks, marshes, forests, savages,—precious little to eat fit for a civilized man, nothing but Thames water to drink. No Falernian wine here, no going ashore. Here and there a military camp lost in a wilderness, like a needle in a bundle of hay—cold, fog, tempests, disease, exile, and death,—death skulking in the air, in the water, in the bush. They must have been dying like flies here. Oh, yes—he did it. Did it very well, too, no doubt, and without thinking much about it either, except afterwards to brag of what he had gone through in his time, perhaps. They were men enough to face the darkness. And perhaps he was cheered by keeping his eye on a chance of promotion to the fleet at Ravenna by and by, if he had good friends in Rome and survived the awful climate. Or think of a decent young citizen in a toga—perhaps too much dice, you know—coming out here in the train of some prefect, or tax-gatherer, or trader even, to mend his fortunes. Land in a swamp, march through the woods, and in some inland post feel the savagery, the utter savagery, had closed round him,—all that mysterious life of the wilderness that stirs in the forest, in the jungles, in the hearts of wild men. There's no initiation either into such mysteries. He has to live in the midst of the incomprehensible, which is also detestable. And it has a fascination, too, that goes to work upon him. The fascination of the abomination—you know, imagine the growing regrets, the longing to escape, the powerless disgust, the surrender, the hate."

He paused.

"Mind," he began again, lifting one arm from the elbow, the palm of the hand outwards, so that, with his legs folded before him, he had the pose of a Buddha preaching in European clothes and without a lotus-flower—"Mind, none of us would feel exactly like this. What saves us is efficiency—the devotion to efficiency. But these chaps were not much account, really. They were no colonists; their administration was merely a squeeze, and nothing more, I suspect. They were conquerors, and for that you want only brute force—nothing to boast of, when you have it, since your strength is just an accident arising from the weakness of others. They grabbed what they could get for the sake of what was to be got. It was just robbery with violence, aggravated murder on a great scale, and men going at it blind—as is very proper for those who tackle a darkness. The conquest of the earth, which mostly means the taking it away from those who have a different complexion or slightly flatter noses than ourselves, is not a pretty thing when you look into it too much. What redeems it is the idea only. An idea at the back of it; not a sentimental pretence but an idea; and an unselfish belief in the idea—something you can set up, and bow down before, and offer a sacrifice to. . . ."

He broke off. Flames glided in the river, small green flames, red flames, white flames, pursuing, overtaking, joining, crossing each other—then separating slowly or hastily. The traffic of the great city went on in the deepening night upon the sleepless river. We looked on, waiting patiently—there was nothing else to do till the end of the flood; but it was only after a long silence, when he said, in a hesitating voice, "I suppose you fellows remember I did once turn fresh-water sailor for a bit," that we knew we were fated, before the ebb began to run, to hear about one of Marlow's inconclusive experiences.

"I don't want to bother you much with what happened to me personally," he began, showing in this remark the weakness of many tellers of tales who seem so often unaware of what their audience would best like to hear; "yet to understand the effect of it on me you ought to know how I got out there, what I saw, how I went up that river to the place where I first met the poor chap. It was the farthest point of navigation and the culminating point of my experience. It seemed somehow to throw a kind of light on everything about me—and into my thoughts. It was sombre enough, too—and pitiful—not extraordinary in any way—not very clear either. No, not very clear. And yet it seemed to throw a kind of light.

"I had then, as you remember, just returned to London after a lot of Indian Ocean, Pacific, China Seas—a regular dose of the East—six years or so, and I was loafing about, hindering you fellows in your work and invading your homes, just as though I had got a heavenly mission to civilize you. It was very fine for a time, but after a bit I did get tired of resting. Then I began to look for a ship—I should think the hardest work on earth. But the ships wouldn't even look at me. And I got tired of that game, too.

"Now when I was a little chap I had a passion for maps. I would look for hours at South America, or Africa, or Australia, and lose myself in all the glories of exploration. At that time there were many blank spaces on the earth, and when I saw one that looked particularly inviting on a map (but they all look that) I would put my finger on it and say, When I grow up I will go there. The North Pole was one of these places, I remember. Well, I haven't been there yet, and shall not try now. The glamour's off. Other places were scattered about the Equator, and in every sort of latitude all over the two hemispheres. I have been in some of them, and . . . well, we won't talk about that. But there was one yet—the biggest, the most blank, so to speak—that I had a hankering after.

"True, by this time it was not a blank space any more. It had got filled since my boyhood with rivers and lakes and names. It had ceased to be a blank space of delightful mystery—a white patch for a boy to dream gloriously over. It had become a place of darkness. But there was in it one river especially, a mighty big river, that you could see on the map, resembling an immense snake uncoiled, with its head in the sea, its body at rest curving afar over a vast country, and its tail lost in the depths of the land. And as I looked at the map of it in a shop-window, it fascinated me as a snake would a bird—a silly little bird. Then I remembered there was a big concern, a Company for trade on that river. Dash it all! I thought to myself, they can't trade without using some kind of craft on that lot of fresh water— steamboats! Why shouldn't I try to get charge of one? I went on along Fleet Street, but could not shake off the idea. The snake had charmed me.

"You understand it was a Continental concern, that Trading society; but I have a lot of relations living on the Continent, because it's cheap and not so nasty as it looks, they say.

"I am sorry to own I began to worry them. This was al-

ready a fresh departure for me. I was not used to get things
that way, you know. I always went my own road and on
my own legs where I had a mind to go. I wouldn't have believed it of myself; but, then—you see—I felt somehow I
must get there by hook or by crook. So I worried them. The
men said 'My dear fellow,' and did nothing. Then—would
you believe it?—I tried the women. I, Charlie Marlow, set
the women to work—to get a job. Heavens! Well, you see,
the notion drove me. I had an aunt, a dear enthusiastic
soul. She wrote: 'It will be delightful. I am ready to do anything, anything for you. It is a glorious idea. I know the
wife of a very high personage in the Administration, and
also a man who has lots of influence with,' etc., etc. She was
determined to make no end of fuss to get me appointed
skipper of a river steamboat, if such was my fancy.

"I got my appointment—of course; and I got it very
quick. It appears the Company had received news that one
of their captains had been killed in a scuffle with the natives.
This was my chance, and it made me the more anxious to
go. It was only months and months afterwards, when I
made the attempt to recover what was left of the body, that
I heard the original quarrel arose from a misunderstanding
about some hens. Yes, two black hens. Fresleven—that was
the fellow's name, a Dane—thought himself wronged somehow in the bargain, so he went ashore and started to hammer the chief of the village with a stick. Oh, it didn't surprise me in the least to hear this, and at the same time to
be told that Fresleven was the gentlest, quietest creature
that ever walked on two legs. No doubt he was; but he had
been a couple of years already out there engaged in the
noble cause, you know, and he probably felt the need at last
of asserting his self-respect in some way. Therefore he
whacked the old nigger mercilessly, while a big crowd of his
people watched him, thunderstruck, till some man—I was
told the chief's son—in desperation at hearing the old chap
yell, made a tentative jab with a spear at the white man—
and of course it went quite easy between the shoulder-
blades. Then the whole population cleared into the forest,

expecting all kinds of calamities to happen, while, on the other hand, the steamer Fresleven commanded left also in a bad panic, in charge of the engineer, I believe. Afterwards nobody seemed to trouble much about Fresleven's remains, till I got out and stepped into his shoes. I couldn't let it rest, though; but when an opportunity offered at last to meet my predecessor, the grass growing through his ribs was tall enough to hide his bones. They were all there. The supernatural being had not been touched after he fell. And the village was deserted, the huts gaped black, rotting, all askew within the fallen enclosures. A calamity had come to it, sure enough. The people had vanished. Mad terror had scattered them, men, women, and children, through the bush, and they had never returned. What became of the hens I don't know either. I should think the cause of progress got them, anyhow. However, through this glorious affair I got my appointment, before I had fairly begun to hope for it.

"I flew around like mad to get ready, and before forty-eight hours I was crossing the Channel to show myself to my employers, and sign the contract. In a very few hours I arrived in a city that always makes me think of a whited sepulchre. Prejudice no doubt. I had no difficulty in finding the Company's offices. It was the biggest thing in the town, and everybody I met was full of it. They were going to run an over-sea empire, and make no end of coin by trade.

"A narrow and deserted street in deep shadow, high houses, innumerable windows with venetian blinds, a dead silence, grass sprouting between the stones, imposing carriage archways right and left, immense double doors standing ponderously ajar. I slipped through one of these cracks, went up a swept and ungarnished staircase, as arid as a desert, and opened the first door I came to. Two women, one fat and the other slim, sat on straw-bottomed chairs, knitting black wool. The slim one got up and walked straight at me—still knitting with down-cast eyes—and only just as I began to think of getting out of her way, as you would for a somnambulist, stood still, and looked up. Her dress was as plain as an umbrella-cover, and she turned round without a word and preceded me into a waiting-room. I gave my name and looked about. Deal table in the middle, plain chairs all round the walls, on one end a large shining map, marked with all the colours of a rainbow. There was a vast amount of red—good to see at any time, because one knows that some real work is done in there, a deuce of a lot of blue, a little green, smears of orange, and, on the East Coast, a purple patch, to show where the jolly pioneers of progress drink the jolly lager-beer. However, I wasn't going into any of these. I was going into the yellow. Dead in the centre. And the river was there—fascinating—deadly—like a snake. Ough! A door opened, a white-haired secretarial head, but wearing a compassionate expression, appeared, and a skinny forefinger beckoned me into the sanctuary. Its light was dim, and a heavy writing-desk squatted in the middle. From behind that structure came out an impression of pale plumpness in a frock-coat. The great man himself. He was five feet six, I should judge, and had his grip on the handle-end of ever so many millions. He shook hands, I fancy, murmured vaguely, was satisfied with my French. *Bon voyage.*

"In about forty-five seconds I found myself again in the waiting-room with the compassionate secretary, who, full of desolation and sympathy, made me sign some document. I believe I undertook amongst other things not to disclose any trade secrets. Well, I am not going to.

"I began to feel slightly uneasy. You know I am not used to such ceremonies, and there was something ominous in the atmosphere. It was just as though I had been let into some conspiracy—I don't know—something not quite right; and I was glad to get out. In the outer room the two women knitted black wool feverishly. People were arriving, and the younger one was walking back and forth introducing them. The old one sat on her chair. Her flat cloth slippers were propped up on a foot-warmer, and a cat reposed on her lap. She wore a starched white affair on her head, had a wart on one cheek, and silver-rimmed spectacles hung on the top of her nose. She glanced at me above the glasses. The swift and indifferent placidity of that look troubled me. Two youths with foolish and cheery countenances were being piloted over, and she threw at them the same quick glance of unconcerned wisdom. She seemed to know all about them and about me, too. An eerie feeling came over me. She seemed uncanny and fateful. Often far away there I thought of these two, guarding the door of Darkness, knitting black wool as for a warm pall, one introducing, introducing continuously to the unknown, the other scrutinizing the cheery and foolish faces with unconcerned old eyes. *Ave!* Old knitter of black wool. *Morituri te salutant.* Not many of those she looked at ever saw her again— not half, by a long way.

"There was yet a visit to the doctor. 'A simple formality,' assured me the secretary, with an air of taking an immense part in all my sorrows. Accordingly a young chap wearing his hat over the left eyebrow, some clerk I suppose,— there must have been clerks in the business, though the house was as still as a house in a city of the dead—came from somewhere up-stairs, and led me forth. He was shabby and careless, with ink-stains on the sleeves of his jacket, and his cravat was large and billowy, under a chin shaped like the toe of an old boot. It was a little too early for the doctor, so I proposed a drink, and thereupon he developed a vein of joviality. As we sat over our vermouths he glorified the Company's business, and by and by I expressed casually my surprise at him not going out there. He became very cool and collected all at once. 'I am not such a fool as I look, quoth Plato to his disciples,' he said sententiously, emptied his glass with great resolution, and we rose.

"The old doctor felt my pulse, evidently thinking of something else the while. 'Good, good for there,' he mumbled, and then with a certain eagerness asked me whether I would let him measure my head. Rather surprised, I said Yes, when he produced a thing like calipers and got the dimensions back and front and every way, taking notes carefully. He was an unshaven little man in a threadbare coat

like a gaberdine, with his feet in slippers, and I thought him
a harmless fool. 'I always ask leave, in the interests of
science, to measure the crania of those going out there,' he
said. 'And when they come back, too?' I asked. 'Oh, I never
see them,' he remarked; 'and, moreover, the changes take
place inside, you know.' He smiled, as if at some quiet joke.
'So you are going out there. Famous. Interesting, too.' He
gave me a searching glance, and made another note. 'Ever
any madness in your family?' he asked, in a matter-of-fact
tone. I felt very annoyed. 'Is that question in the interests
of science, too?' 'It would be,' he said, without taking notice of my irritation, 'interesting for science to watch the
mental changes of individuals, on the spot, but . . .' 'Are you
an alienist?' I interrupted. 'Every doctor should be—a little,'
answered that original, imperturbably. 'I have a little theory
which you Messieurs who go out there must help me to
prove. This is my share in the advantages my country shall
reap from the possession of such a magnificent depend-
ency. The mere wealth I leave to others. Pardon my questions, but you are the first Englishman coming under my
observation . . .' I hastened to assure him I was not in the
least typical. 'If I were,' said I, 'I wouldn't be talking like
this with you.' 'What you say is rather profound, and probably erroneous,' he said, with a laugh. 'Avoid irritation
more than exposure to the sun. Adieu. How do you English say, eh? Good-bye. Ah! Good-bye. Adieu. In the tropics
one must before everything keep calm.' . . . He lifted a
warning forefinger. . . . '*Du calme, du calme. Adieu.*'

"One thing more remained to do—say good-bye to my
excellent aunt. I found her triumphant. I had a cup of tea
—the last decent cup of tea for many days—and in a room
that most soothingly looked just as you would expect a
lady's drawing-room to look, we had a long quiet chat by
the fireside. In the course of these confidences it became
quite plain to me I had been represented to the wife of the
high dignitary, and goodness knows to how many more
people besides, as an exceptional and gifted creature—a
piece of good fortune for the Company—a man you don't

get hold of every day. Good heavens! and I was going to
take charge of a two-penny-half-penny river-steamboat with
a penny whistle attached! It appeared, however, I was also
one of the Workers, with a capital—you know. Something
like an emissary of light, something like a lower sort of
apostle. There had been a lot of such rot let loose in print
and talk just about that time, and the excellent woman,
living right in the rush of all that humbug, got carried off
her feet. She talked about 'weaning those ignorant millions
from their horrid ways,' till, upon my word, she made me
quite uncomfortable. I ventured to hint that the Company
was run for profit.

" 'You forget, dear Charlie, that the labourer is worthy of
his hire,' she said, brightly. It's queer how out of touch with
truth women are. They live in a world of their own, and
there has never been anything like it, and never can be. It
is too beautiful altogether, and if they were to set it up it
would go to pieces before the first sunset. Some confounded
fact we men have been living contentedly with ever since
the day of creation would start up and knock the whole
thing over.

"After this I got embraced, told to wear flannel, be sure
to write often, and so on—and I left. In the street—I don't
know why—a queer feeling came to me that I was an im-
poster. Odd thing that I, who used to clear out for any part
of the world at twenty-four hours' notice, with less thought
than most men give to the crossing of a street, had a moment—I won't say of hesitation, but of startled pause, before this common-place affair. The best way I can explain it
to you is by saying that, for a second or two, I felt as
though, instead of going to the centre of a continent, I were
about to set off for the centre of the earth.

"I left in a French steamer, and she called in every
blamed port they have out there, for, as far as I could see,
the sole purpose of landing soldiers and custom-house officers. I watched the coast. Watching a coast as it slips by
the ship is like thinking about an enigma. There it is before
you—smiling, frowning, inviting, grand, mean, insipid, or

savage, and always mute with an air of whispering. Come
and find out. This one was almost featureless, as if still in
the making, with an aspect of monotonous grimness. The
edge of a colossal jungle, so dark-green as to be almost
black, fringed with white surf, ran straight, like a ruled
line, far, far away along a blue sea whose glitter was blurred
by a creeping mist. The sun was fierce, the land seemed to
glisten and drip with steam. Here and there grayish-whitish
specks showed up clustered inside the white surf, with a flag
flying above them perhaps. Settlements some centuries old,
and still no bigger than pinheads on the untouched expanse of their background. We pounded along, stopped,
landed soldiers; went on, landed custom-house clerks to
levy toll in what looked like a God-forsaken wilderness,
with a tin shed and a flag-pole lost in it; landed more soldiers—to take care of the custom-house clerks, presumably.
Some, I heard, got drowned in the surf; but whether they
did or not, nobody seemed particularly to care. They were
just flung out there, and on we went. Every day the coast
looked the same, as though we had not moved; but we
passed various places—trading places—with names like
Gran' Bassam, Little Popo; names that seemed to belong to
some sordid farce acted in front of a sinister back-cloth.
The idleness of a passenger, my isolation amongst all these
men with whom I had no point of contact, the oily and
languid sea, the uniform sombreness of the coast, seemed
to keep me away from the truth of things, within the toil of
a mournful and senseless delusion. The voice of the surf
heard now and then was a positive pleasure, like the speech
of a brother. It was something natural, that had its reason,
that had a meaning. Now and then a boat from the shore
gave one a momentary contact with reality. It was paddled
by black fellows. You could see from afar the white of their
eyeballs glistening. They shouted, sang; their bodies
streamed with perspiration; they had faces like grotesque
masks—these chaps; but they had bone, muscle, a wild vi-
tality, an intense energy of movement, that was as natural
and true as the surf along their coast. They wanted no ex-

cuse for being there. They were a great comfort to look at.
For a time I would feel I belonged still to a world of
straight-forward facts; but the feeling would not last long.
Something would turn up to scare it away. Once, I remember, we came upon a man-of-war anchored off the coast.
There wasn't even a shed there, and she was shelling the
bush. It appears the French had one of their wars going
on thereabouts. Her ensign dropped limp like a rag; the
muzzles of the long six-inch guns stuck out all over the
low hull; the greasy, slimy swell swung her up lazily and
let her down, swaying her thin masts. In the empty immensity of earth, sky, and water, there she was, incomprehensible, firing into a continent. Pop, would go one of the six-
inch guns; a small flame would dart and vanish, a little
white smoke would disappear, a tiny projectile would give a
feeble screech—and nothing happened. Nothing could happen. There was a touch of insanity in the proceeding, a
sense of lugubrious drollery in the sight; and it was not dissipated by somebody on board assuring me earnestly there
was a camp of natives—he called them enemies!—hidden
out of sight somewhere.

"We gave her her letters (I heard the men in that lonely
ship were dying of fever at the rate of three a day) and
went on. We called at some more places with farcical names,
where the merry dance of death and trade goes on in a
still and earthy atmosphere as of an overheated catacomb;
all along the formless coast bordered by dangerous surf, as
if Nature herself had tried to ward off intruders; in and out
of rivers, streams of death in life, whose banks were rotting
into mud, whose waters, thickened into slime, invaded the
contorted mangroves, that seemed to writhe at us in the
extremity of an impotent despair. Nowhere did we stop
long enough to get a particularized impression, but the
general sense of vague and oppressive wonder grew upon
me. It was like a weary pilgrimage amongst hints for nightmares.

"It was upward of thirty days before I saw the mouth of
the big river. We anchored off the seat of the government.

But my work would not begin till some two hundred miles farther on. So as soon as I could I made a start for a place thirty miles higher up.

"I had my passage on a little sea-going steamer. Her captain was a Swede, and knowing me for a seaman, invited me on the bridge. He was a young man, lean, fair, and morose, with lanky hair and a shuffling gait. As we left the miserable little wharf, he tossed his head contemptuously at the shore. 'Been living there?' he asked. I said, 'Yes.' 'Fine lot these government chaps—are they not?' he went on, speaking English with great precision and considerable bitterness. 'It is funny what some people will do for a few francs a month. I wonder what becomes of that kind when it goes up country?' I said to him I expected to see that soon. 'So-o-o!' he exclaimed. He shuffled athwart, keeping one eye ahead vigilantly. 'Don't be too sure,' he continued. 'The other day I took up a man who hanged himself on the road. He was a Swede, too.' 'Hanged himself! Why, in God's name?' I cried. He kept on looking out watchfully. 'Who knows? The sun too much for him, or the country perhaps.'

"At last we opened a reach. A rocky cliff appeared, mounds of turned-up earth by the shore, houses on a hill, others with iron roofs, amongst a waste of excavations, or hanging to the declivity. A continuous noise of the rapids above hovered over this scene of inhabited devastation. A lot of people, mostly black and naked, moved about like ants. A jetty projected into the river. A blinding sunlight drowned all this at times in a sudden recrudescence of glare. 'There's your Company's station,' said the Swede, pointing to three wooden barrack-like structures on the rocky slope. 'I will send your things up. Four boxes did you say? So. Farewell.'

"I came upon a boiler wallowing in the grass, then found a path leading up the hill. It turned aside for the boulders, and also for an undersized railway-truck lying on its back with its wheels in the air. One was off. The thing looked as dead as the carcass of some animal. I came upon more pieces of decaying machinery, a stack of rusty rails. To the left a clump of trees made a shady spot, where dark things seemed to stir feebly. I blinked, the path was steep. A horn tooted to the right, and I saw the black people run. A heavy and dull detonation shook the ground, a puff of smoke came out of the cliff, and that was all. No change appeared on the face of the rock. They were building a railway. The cliff was not in the way or anything; but this objectless blasting was all the work going on.

"A slight clinking made me turn my head. Six black men advanced in a file, toiling up the path. They walked erect and slow, balancing small baskets full of earth on their heads, and the clink kept time with their footsteps. Black rags were wound round their loins, and the short ends behind waggled to and fro like tails. I could see every rib, the joints of their limbs were like knots in a rope; each had an iron collar on his neck, and all were connected together with a chain whose bights swung between them, rhythmically clinking. Another report from the cliff made me think suddenly of that ship of war I had seen firing into a continent. It was the same kind of ominous voice; but these men could by no stretch of imagination be called enemies. They were called criminals, and the outraged law, like the bursting shells, had come to them, an insoluble mystery from the sea. All their meagre breasts panted together, the violently dilated nostrils quivered, the eyes stared stonily up-hill. They passed me within six inches, without a glance, with that complete, deathlike indifference of unhappy savages. Behind this raw matter one of the reclaimed, the product of the new forces at work, strolled despondently, carrying a rifle by its middle. He had a uniform jacket with one button off, and seeing a white man on the path, hoisted his weapon to his shoulder with alacrity. This was simple prudence, white men being so much alike at a distance that he could not tell who I might be. He was speedily reassured, and with a large, white, rascally grin, and a glance at his charge, seemed to take me into partnership in his exalted trust. After all, I also was a part of the great cause of these high and just proceedings.

"Instead of going up, I turned and descended to the left. My idea was to let that chain-gang get out of sight before I climbed the hill. You know I am not particularly tender; I've had to strike and to fend off. I've had to resist and to attack sometimes—that's only one way of resisting—without counting the exact cost, according to the demands of such sort of life as I had blundered into. I've seen the devil of violence, and the devil of greed, and the devil of hot desire; but, by all the stars! these were strong, lusty, red-eyed devils, that swayed and drove men—men, I tell you. But as I stood on this hillside, I foresaw that in the blinding sunshine of that land I would become acquainted with a flabby, pretending, weak-eyed devil of a rapacious and pitiless folly. How insidious he could be, too, I was only to find out several months later and a thousand miles farther. For a moment I stood appalled, as though by a warning. Finally I descended the hill, obliquely, towards the trees I had seen.

"I avoided a vast artificial hole somebody had been digging on the slope, the purpose of which I found it impossible to divine. It wasn't a quarry or a sandpit, anyhow. It was just a hole. It might have been connected with the philanthropic desire of giving the criminals something to do. I don't know. Then I nearly fell into a very narrow ravine, almost no more than a scar in the hillside. I discovered that a lot of imported drainage-pipes for the settlement had been tumbled in there. There wasn't one that was not broken. It was a wanton smash-up. At last I got under the trees. My purpose was to stroll into the shade for a moment; but no sooner within than it seemed to me I had stepped into the gloomy circle of some Inferno. The rapids were near, and an uninterrupted, uniform, headlong, rushing noise filled the mournful stillness of the grove, where not a breath stirred, not a leaf moved, with a mysterious sound—as though the tearing pace of the launched earth had suddenly become audible.

"Black shapes crouched, lay, sat between the trees leaning against the trunks, clinging to the earth, half coming out, half effaced within the dim light, in all the attitudes of pain, abandonment, and despair. Another mine on the cliff went off, followed by a slight shudder of the soil under my feet. The work was going on. The work! And this was the place where some of the helpers had withdrawn to die.

"They were dying slowly—it was very clear. They were not enemies, they were not criminals, they were nothing earthly now,—nothing but black shadows of disease and starvation, lying confusedly in the greenish gloom. Brought from all the recesses of the coast in all the legality of time contracts, lost in uncongenial surroundings, fed on unfamiliar food, they sickened, became inefficient, and were then allowed to crawl away and rest. These moribund shapes were free as air—and nearly as thin. I began to distinguish the gleam of the eyes under the trees. Then, glancing down, I saw a face near my hand. The black bones reclined at full length with one shoulder against the tree, and slowly the eyelids rose and the sunken eyes looked up at me, enormous and vacant, a kind of blind, white flicker in the depths of the orbs, which died out slowly. The man seemed young—almost a boy—but you know with them it's hard to tell. I found nothing else to do but to offer him one of my good Swede's ship's biscuits I had in my pocket. The fingers closed slowly on it and held—there was no other movement and no other glance. He had tied a bit of white worsted round his neck—Why? Where did he get it? Was it a badge—an ornament—a charm—a propitiatory act? Was there any idea at all connected with it? It looked startling round his black neck, this bit of white thread from beyond the seas.

"Near the same tree two more bundles of acute angles sat with their legs drawn up. One, with his chin propped on his knees, stared at nothing, in an intolerable and appalling manner: his brother phantom rested its forehead, as if overcome with a great weariness; and all about others were scattered in every pose of contorted collapse, as in some picture of a massacre or a pestilence. While I stood horror-struck, one of these creatures rose to his hands and knees, and went off on all-fours towards the river to drink. He lapped out of his hand, then sat up in the sunlight, crossing his shins in front of him, and after a time let his woolly head fall on his breastbone.

"I didn't want any more loitering in the shade, and I made haste towards the station. When near the buildings I met a white man, in such an unexpected elegance of get-up that in the first moment I took him for a sort of vision. I saw a high starched collar, white cuffs, a light alpaca jacket, snowy trousers, a clean necktie, and varnished boots. No hat. Hair parted, brushed, oiled, under a green-lined parasol held in a big white hand. He was amazing, and had a pen-holder behind his ear.

"I shook hands with this miracle, and I learned he was the Company's chief accountant, and that all the book-keeping was done at this station. He had come out for a moment, he said, 'to get a breath of fresh air.' The expression sounded wonderfully odd, with its suggestion of sedentary desk-life. I wouldn't have mentioned the fellow to you at all, only it was from his lips that I first heard the name of the man who is so indissolubly connected with the memories of that time. Moreover, I respected the fellow. Yes; I respected his collars, his vast cuffs, his brushed hair. His appearance was certainly that of a hairdresser's dummy; but in the great demoralization of the land he kept up his appearance. That's backbone. His starched collars and got-up shirt-fronts were achievements of character. He had been out nearly three years; and, later, I could not help asking him how he managed to sport such linen. He had just the faintest blush, and said modestly, 'I've been teaching one of the native women about the station. It was difficult. She had a distaste for the work.' Thus this man had verily accomplished something. And he was devoted to his books, which were in apple-pie order.

"Everything else in the station was in a muddle,—heads, things, buildings. Strings of dusty niggers with splay feet arrived and departed; a stream of manufactured goods, rubbishy cottons, beads, and brass-wire set into the depths of darkness, and in return came a precious trickle of ivory.

"I had to wait in the station for ten days—an eternity. I lived in a hut in the yard, but to be out of the chaos I would sometimes get into the accountant's office. It was built of horizontal planks, and so badly put together that, as he bent over his high desk, he was barred from neck to heels with narrow strips of sunlight. There was no need to open the big shutter to see. It was hot there, too; big flies buzzed fiendishly, and did not sting, but stabbed. I sat generally on the floor, while, of faultless appearance (and even slightly scented), perching on a high stool, he wrote, he wrote. Sometimes he stood up for exercise. When a trucklebed with a sick man (some invalid agent from upcountry) was put in there, he exhibited a gentle annoyance. 'The groans of this sick person,' he said, 'distract my attention. And without that it is extremely difficult to guard against clerical errors in this climate.'

"One day he remarked without lifting his head, 'In the interior you will no doubt meet Mr. Kurtz.' On my asking who Mr. Kurtz was, he said he was a first-class agent; and seeing my disappointment at this information, he added slowly, laying down his pen, 'He is a very remarkable person.' Further questions elicited from him that Mr. Kurtz was at present in charge of a trading post, a very important one, in the true ivory-country, at 'the very bottom of there. Sends in as much ivory as all the others put together . . .' He began to write again. The sick man was too ill to groan. The flies buzzed in a great peace.

"Suddenly there was a growing murmur of voices and a great tramping of feet. A caravan had come in. A violent babble of uncouth sounds burst out on the other side of the planks. All the carriers were speaking together, and in the midst of the uproar the lamentable voice of the chief agent was heard 'giving it up' tearfully for the twentieth time that day. . . . He rose slowly. 'What a frightful row,' he said. He crossed the room gently to look at the sick man, and returning, said to me, 'He does not hear.' 'What! Dead?' I asked, startled. 'No, not yet,' he answered, with great composure. Then, alluding with a toss of the head to the tumult

in the station-yard, 'When one has got to make correct entries, one comes to hate those savages—hate them to the
death.' He remained thoughtful for a moment. 'When you
see Mr. Kurtz,' he went on, 'tell him for me that everything
here'—he glanced at the desk—'is very satisfactory. I don't
like to write to him—with those messengers of ours you
never know who may get hold of your letter—at that Central Station.' He stared at me for a moment with his mild,
bulging eyes. 'Oh, he will go far, very far,' he began again.
'He will be a somebody in the Administration before long.
They, above—the Council in Europe, you know—mean
him to be.'

"He turned to his work. The noise outside had ceased,
and presently in going out I stopped at the door. In the
steady buzz of flies the homeward-bound agent was lying
flushed and insensible; the other, bent over his books, was
making correct entries of perfectly correct transactions;
and fifty feet below the doorstep I could see the still tree-
tops of the grove of death.

"Next day I left that station at last, with a caravan of
sixty men, for a two-hundred-mile tramp.

"No use telling you much about that. Paths, paths, everywhere; a stamped-in network of paths spreading over the
empty land, through long grass, through burnt grass,
through thickets, down and up chilly ravines, up and down
stony hills ablaze with heat; and a solitude, a solitude, nobody, not a hut. The population had cleared out a long
time ago. Well, if a lot of mysterious niggers armed with all
kinds of fearful weapons suddenly took to travelling on the
road between Deal and Gravesend, catching the yokels
right and left to carry heavy loads for them, I fancy every
farm and cottage thereabouts would get empty very soon.
Only here the dwellings were gone, too. Still I passed
through several abandoned villages. There's something pa-
thetically childish in the ruins of grass walls. Day after day,
with the stamp and shuffle of sixty pair of bare feet behind
me, each pair under a 60-lb. load. Camp, cook, sleep, strike
camp, march. Now and then a carrier dead in harness, at

rest in the long grass near the path, with an empty water-gourd and his long staff lying by his side. A great silence around and above. Perhaps on some quiet night the tremor of far-off drums, sinking, swelling, a tremor vast, faint; a sound weird, appealing, suggestive, and wild—and perhaps with as profound a meaning as the sound of bells in a Christian country. Once a white man in an unbuttoned uniform, camping on the path with an armed escort of lank Zanzibaris, very hospitable and festive—not to say drunk. Was looking after the upkeep of the road, he declared. Can't say I saw any road or any upkeep, unless the body of a middle-aged negro, with a bullet-hole in the forehead, upon which I absolutely stumbled three miles farther on, may be considered as a permanent improvement. I had a white companion, too, not a bad chap, but rather too fleshy and with the exasperating habit of fainting on the hot hillsides, miles away from the least bit of shade and water. Annoying, you know, to hold your own coat like a parasol over a man's head while he is coming-to. I couldn't help asking him once what he meant by coming there at all. 'To make money, of course. What do you think?' he said, scornfully. Then he got fever, and had to be carried in a hammock slung under a pole. As he weighed sixteen stone I had no end of rows with the carriers. They jibbed, ran away, sneaked off with their loads in the night—quite a mutiny. So, one evening, I made a speech in English with gestures, not one of which was lost to the sixty pairs of eyes before me, and the next morning I started the hammock off in front all right. An hour afterwards I came upon the whole concern wrecked in a bush—man, hammock, groans, blankets, horrors. The heavy pole had skinned his poor nose. He was very anxious for me to kill somebody, but there wasn't the shadow of a carrier near. I remembered the old doctor—'It would be interesting for science to watch the mental changes of individuals, on the spot.' I felt I was becoming scientifically interesting. However, all that is to no purpose. On the fifteenth day I came in sight of the big river again, and hobbled into the Central Station. It was on a back water surrounded by scrub and forest, with a pretty border of smelly mud on one side, and on the three others enclosed by a crazy fence of rushes. A neglected gap was all the gate it had, and the first glance at the place was enough to let you see the flabby devil was running that show. White men with long staves in their hands appeared languidly from amongst the buildings, strolling up to take a look at me, and then retired out of sight somewhere. One of them, a stout, excitable chap with black moustaches, informed me with great volubility and many digressions, as soon as I told him who I was, that my steamer was at the bottom of the river. I was thunderstruck. What, how, why? Oh, it was 'all right.' The 'manager himself' was there. All quite correct. 'Everybody had behaved splendidly! splendidly!'—'you must,' he said in agitation, 'go and see the general manager at once. He is waiting!'

"I did not see the real significance of that wreck at once. I fancy I see it now, but I am not sure—not at all. Certainly the affair was too stupid—when I think of it—to be altogether natural. Still . . . But at the moment it presented itself simply as a confounded nuisance. The steamer was sunk. They had started two days before in a sudden hurry up the river with the manager on board, in charge of some volunteer skipper, and before they had been out three hours they tore the bottom out of her on stones, and she sank near the south bank. I asked myself what I was to do there, now my boat was lost. As a matter of fact, I had plenty to do in fishing my command out of the river. I had to set about it the very next day. That, and the repairs when I brought the pieces to the station, took some months.

"My first interview with the manager was curious. He did not ask me to sit down after my twenty-mile walk that morning. He was commonplace in complexion, in feature, in manners, and in voice. He was of middle size and of ordinary build. His eyes, of the usual blue, were perhaps remarkably cold, and he certainly could make his glance fall on one as trenchant and heavy as an axe. But even at these times the rest of his person seemed to disclaim the

intention. Otherwise there was only an indefinable, faint
expression of his lips, something stealthy—a smile—not a
smile—I remember it, but I can't explain. It was unconscious, this smile was, though just after he had said something it got intensified for an instant. It came at the end of
his speeches like a seal applied on the words to make the
meaning of the commonest phrase appear absolutely inscrutable. He was a common trader, from his youth up employed in these parts—nothing more. He was obeyed, yet he
inspired neither love nor fear, nor even respect. He inspired
uneasiness. That was it! Uneasiness. Not a definite mistrust
—just uneasiness—nothing more. You have no idea how ef-
fective such a . . . a . . . faculty can be. He had no genius for
organizing, for initiative, or for order even. That was evident in such things as the deplorable state of the station. He
had no learning, and no intelligence. His position had come
to him—why? Perhaps because he was never ill . . . He had
served three terms of three years out there . . . Because triumphant health in the general rout of constitutions is a
kind of power in itself. When he went home on leave he
rioted on a large scale—pompously. Jack ashore—with a
difference—in externals only. This one could gather from
his casual talk. He originated nothing, he could keep the
routine going—that's all. But he was great. He was great
by this little thing that it was impossible to tell what could
control such a man. He never gave that secret away. Perhaps there was nothing within him. Such a suspicion made
one pause—for out there there were no external checks.
Once when various tropical diseases had laid low almost
every 'agent' in the station, he was heard to say, 'Men who
come out here should have no entrails.' He sealed the utterance with that smile of his, as though it had been a door
opening into a darkness he had in his keeping. You fancied
you had seen things—but the seal was on. When annoyed
at meal-times by the constant quarrels of the white men
about precedence, he ordered an immense round table to be
made, for which a special house had to be built. This was
the station's mess-room. Where he sat was the first place—

the rest were nowhere. One felt this to be his unalterable conviction. He was neither civil nor uncivil. He was quiet. He allowed his 'boy'—an overfed young negro from the coast—to treat the white men, under his very eyes, with provoking insolence.

"He began to speak as soon as he saw me. I had been very long on the road. He could not wait. Had to start without me. The up-river stations had to be relieved. There had been so many delays already that he did not know who was dead and who was alive, and how they got on—and so on, and so on. He paid no attention to my explanations, and, playing with a stick of sealing-wax, repeated several times that the situation was 'very grave, very grave.' There were rumours that a very important station was in jeopardy, and its chief, Mr. Kurtz, was ill. Hoped it was not true. Mr. Kurtz was . . . I felt weary and irritable. Hang Kurtz, I thought. I interrupted him by saying I had heard of Mr. Kurtz on the coast. 'Ah! So they talk of him down there,' he murmured to himself. Then he began again, assuring me Mr. Kurtz was the best agent he had, an exceptional man, of the greatest importance to the Company; therefore I could understand his anxiety. He was, he said, 'very, very uneasy.' Certainly he fidgeted on his chair a good deal, exclaimed, 'Ah, Mr. Kurtz!' broke the stick of sealing-wax and seemed dumfounded by the accident. Next thing he wanted to know 'how long it would take to' . . . I interrupted him again. Being hungry, you know, and kept on my feet too, I was getting savage. 'How can I tell?' I said. 'I haven't even seen the wreck yet—some months, no doubt.' All this talk seemed to me so futile. 'Some months,' he said. 'Well, let us say three months before we can make a start. Yes. That ought to do the affair.' I flung out of his hut (he lived all alone in a clay hut with a sort of verandah) muttering to myself my opinion of him. He was a chattering idiot. Afterwards I took it back when it was borne in upon me startlingly with what extreme nicety he had estimated the time requisite for the 'affair.'

"I went to work the next day, turning, so to speak, my

back on that station. In that way only it seemed to me I
could keep my hold on the redeeming facts of life. Still,
one must look about sometimes; and then I saw this station,
these men strolling aimlessly about in the sunshine of the
yard. I asked myself sometimes what it all meant. They
wandered here and there with their absurd long staves in
their hands, like a lot of faithless pilgrims bewitched inside
a rotten fence. The word 'ivory' rang in the air, was whispered, was sighed. You would think they were praying to it.
A taint of imbecile rapacity blew through it all, like a whiff
from some corpse. By Jove! I've never seen anything so unreal in my life. And outside, the silent wilderness surrounding this cleared speck on the earth struck me as something
great and invincible, like evil or truth, waiting patiently for
the passing away of this fanstastic invasion.

"Oh, these months! Well, never mind. Various things
happened. One evening, a grass shed full of calico, cotton
prints, beads, and I don't know what else, burst into a blaze
so suddenly that you would have thought the earth had
opened to let an avenging fire consume all that trash. I was
smoking my pipe quietly by my dismantled steamer, and
saw them all cutting capers in the light, with their arms
lifted high, when the stout man with moustaches came tearing down to the river, a tin pail in his hand, assured me that
everybody was 'behaving splendidly, splendidly,' dipped
about a quart of water and tore back again. I noticed there
was a hole in the bottom of his pail.

"I strolled up. There was no hurry. You see the thing
had gone off like a box of matches. It had been hopeless
from the very first. The flame had leaped high, driven everybody back, lighted up everything—and collapsed. The shed
was already a heap of embers glowing fiercely. A nigger
was being beaten near by. They said he had caused the fire
in some way; be that as it may, he was screeching most horribly. I saw him, later, for several days, sitting in a bit of
shade looking very sick and trying to recover himself:
afterwards he arose and went out—and the wilderness without a sound took him into its bosom again. As I approached

the glow from the dark I found myself at the back of two
men, talking. I heard the name of Kurtz pronounced, then
the words, 'take advantage of this unfortunate accident.'
One of the men was the manager. I wished him a good evening. 'Did you ever see anything like it—eh? it is incredible,'
he said, and walked off. The other man remained. He was
a first-class agent, young, gentlemanly, a bit reserved, with
a forked little beard and a hooked nose. He was stand-
offish with the other agents, and they on their side said he
was the manager's spy upon them. As to me, I had hardly
ever spoken to him before. We got into talk, and by and by
we strolled away from the hissing ruins. Then he asked me
to his room, which was in the main building of the station.
He struck a match, and I perceived that this young aristo-
crat had not only a silver-mounted dressing-case but also
a whole candle all to himself. Just at that time the manager
was the only man supposed to have any right to candles.
Native mats covered the clay walls; a collection of spears,
assegais, shields, knives was hung up in trophies. The
business intrusted to this fellow was the making of bricks—
so I had been informed; but there wasn't a fragment of a
brick anywhere in the station, and he had been there more
than a year—waiting. It seems he could not make bricks
without something, I don't know what—straw maybe. Any-
ways, it could not be found there, and as it was not likely
to be sent from Europe, it did not appear clear to me what
he was waiting for. An act of special creation perhaps.
However, they were all waiting—all the sixteen or twenty
pilgrims of them—for something; and upon my word it did
not seem an uncongenial occupation, from the way they
took it, though the only thing that ever came to them was
disease—as far as I could see. They beguiled the time by
backbiting and intriguing against each other in a foolish
kind of way. There was an air of plotting about that station,
but nothing came of it, of course. It was as unreal as everything else—as the philanthropic pretence of the whole
concern, as their talk, as their government, as their show
of work. The only real feeling was a desire to get appointed

to a trading-post where ivory was to be had, so that they could earn percentages. They intrigued and slandered and hated each other only on that account,—but as to effectually lifting a little finger—oh, no. By heavens! there is something after all in the world allowing one man to steal a horse while another must not look at a halter. Steal a horse straight out. Very well. He has done it. Perhaps he can ride. But there is a way of looking at a halter that would provoke the most charitable of saints into a kick.

"I had no idea why he wanted to be sociable, but as we chatted in there it suddenly occurred to me the fellow was trying to get at something—in fact, pumping me. He alluded constantly to Europe, to the people I was supposed to know there—putting leading questions as to my acquaintances in the sepulchral city, and so on. His little eyes glittered like mica discs—with curiosity—though he tried to keep up a bit of superciliousness. At first I was astonished, but very soon I became awfully curious to see what he would find out from me. I couldn't possibly imagine what I had in me to make it worth his while. It was very pretty to see how he baffled himself, for in truth my body was full only of chills, and my head had nothing in it but that wretched steamboat business. It was evident he took me for a perfectly shameless prevaricator. At last he got angry, and, to conceal a movement of furious annoyance, he yawned. I rose. Then I noticed a small sketch in oils, on a panel, representing a woman, draped and blindfolded, carrying a lighted torch. The background was sombre— almost black. The movement of the woman was stately, and the effect of the torch-light on the face was sinister.

"It arrested me, and he stood by civilly, holding an empty half-pint champagne bottle (medical comforts) with the candle stuck in it. To my question he said Mr. Kurtz had painted this—in this very station more than a year ago —while waiting for means to go to his trading-post. 'Tell me, pray,' said I, 'who is this Mr. Kurtz?'

" 'The chief of the Inner Station,' he answered in a short tone, looking away. 'Much obliged,' I said, laughing. 'And

you are the brickmaker of the Central Station. Everyone
knows that.' He was silent for a while. 'He is a prodigy,' he
said at last. 'He is an emissary of pity, and science, and
progress, and devil knows what else. We want,' he began to
declaim suddenly, 'for the guidance of the cause intrusted
to us by Europe, so to speak, higher intelligence, wide sympathies, a singleness of purpose.' 'Who says that?' I asked.
'Lots of them,' he replied. 'Some even write that; and so
he comes here, a special being, as you ought to know.'
'Why ought I to know?' I interrupted, really surprised. He
paid no attention. 'Yes. To-day he is chief of the best station, next year he will be assistant-manager, two years
more and ... but I daresay you know what he will be in
two years' time. You are of the new gang—the gang of virtue. The same people who sent him specially also recom-
mended you. Oh, don't say no. I've my own eyes to trust.'
Light dawned upon me. My dear aunt's influential acquaintances were producing an unexpected effect upon that young
man. I nearly burst into a laugh. 'Do you read the Company's confidential correspondence?' I asked. He hadn't a
word to say. It was great fun. 'When Mr. Kurtz,' I continued, severely, 'is General Manager, you won't have the
opportunity.'

"He blew the candle out suddenly, and we went outside. The moon had risen. Black figures strolled about listlessly, pouring water on the glow, whence proceeded a
sound of hissing; steam ascended in the moonlight, the
beaten nigger groaned somewhere. 'What a row the brute
makes!' said the indefatigable man with the moustaches,
appearing near us. 'Serve him right. Transgression—punishment—bang! Pitiless, pitiless. That's the only way. This will
prevent all conflagrations for the future. I was just telling the
manager ...' He noticed my companion, and became crestfallen all at once. 'Not in bed yet,' he said, with a kind of
servile heartiness; 'it's so natural. Ha! Danger—agitation.'
He vanished. I went on to the river-side, and the other followed me. I heard a scathing murmur at my ear, 'Heap of
muffs—go to.' The pilgrims could be seen in knots gesticu-

lating, discussing. Several had still their staves in their
hands. I verily believe they took these sticks to bed with
them. Beyond the fence the forest stood up spectrally in the
moonlight, and through the dim stir, through the faint
sounds of that lamentable courtyard, the silence of the land
went home to one's very heart—its mystery, its greatness,
the amazing reality of its concealed life. The hurt nigger
moaned feebly somewhere near by, and then fetched a deep
sigh that made me mend my pace away from there. I felt a
hand introducing itself under my arm. 'My dear sir,' said
the fellow, 'I don't want to be misunderstood, and especially by you, who will see Mr. Kurtz long before I can
have that pleasure. I wouldn't like him to get a false idea of
my disposition. . . .'

"I let him run on, this papier-mâché Mephistopheles, and
it seemed to me that if I tried I could poke my forefinger
through him, and would find nothing inside but a little loose
dirt, maybe. He, don't you see, had been planning to be
assistant-manager by and by under the present man, and I
could see that the coming of that Kurtz had upset them both
not a little. He talked precipitately, and I did not try to stop
him. I had my shoulders against the wreck of my steamer,
hauled up on the slope like a carcass of some big river animal. The smell of mud, of primeval mud, by Jove! was in
my nostrils, the high stillness of primeval forest was before
my eyes; there were shiny patches on the black creek. The
moon had spread over everything a thin layer of silver—
over the rank grass, over the mud, upon the wall of matted
vegetation standing higher than the wall of a temple, over
the great river I could see through a sombre gap glittering,
glittering, as it flowed broadly by without a murmur. All this
was great, expectant, mute, while the man jabbered about
himself. I wondered whether the stillness on the face of the
immensity looking at us two were meant as an appeal or as
a menace. What were we who had strayed in here? Could
we handle that dumb thing, or would it handle us? I felt
how big, how confoundedly big, was that thing that couldn't
talk, and perhaps was deaf as well. What was in there? I

could see a little ivory coming out from there, and I had heard Mr. Kurtz was in there. I had heard enough about it, too—God knows! Yet somehow it didn't bring any image with it—no more than if I had been told an angel or a fiend was in there. I believed it in the same way one of you might believe there are inhabitants in the planet Mars. I knew once a Scotch sailmaker who was certain, dead sure, there were people in Mars. If you asked him for some idea how they looked and behaved, he would get shy and mutter something about 'walking on all-fours.' If you as much as smiled, he would—though a man of sixty—offer to fight you. I would not have gone so far as to fight for Kurtz, but I went for him near enough to a lie. You know I hate, detest, and can't bear a lie, not because I am straighter than the rest of us, but simply because it appalls me. There is a taint of death, a flavour of mortality in lies—which is exactly what I hate and detest in the world—what I want to forget. It makes me miserable and sick, like biting something rotten would do. Temperament, I suppose. Well, I went near enough to it by letting the young fool there believe anything he liked to imagine as to my influence in Europe. I became in an instant as much of a pretence as the rest of the bewitched pilgrims. This simply because I had a notion it somehow would be of help to that Kurtz whom at the time I did not see—you understand. He was just a word for me. I did not see the man in the name any more than you do. Do you see him? Do you see the story? Do you see anything? It seems to me I am trying to tell you a dream—making a vain attempt, because no relation of a dream can convey the dream-sensation, that commingling of absurdity, surprise, and bewilderment in a tremor of struggling revolt, that notion of being captured by the incredible which is of the very essence of dreams. . . ."

He was silent for a while.

". . . No, it is impossible; it is impossible to convey the life-sensation of any given epoch of one's existence—that which makes its truth, its meaning—its subtle and penetrating essence. It is impossible. We live, as we dream—alone. . . ."

He paused again as if reflecting, then added—

"Of course in this you fellows see more than I could then. You see me, whom you know. . . ."

It had become so pitch dark that we listeners could hardly see one another. For a long time already he, sitting apart, had been no more to us than a voice. There was not a word from anybody. The others might have been asleep, but I was awake. I listened, I listened on the watch for the sentence, for the word, that would give me the clue to the faint uneasiness inspired by this narrative that seemed to shape itself without human lips in the heavy night-air of the river.

". . . Yes—I let him run on," Marlow began again, "and think what he pleased about the powers that were behind me. I did! And there was nothing behind me! There was nothing but that wretched, old, mangled steamboat I was leaning against, while he talked fluently about 'the necessity for every man to get on.' 'And when one comes out here, you conceive, it is not to gaze at the moon.' Mr. Kurtz was a 'universal genius,' but even a genius would find it easier to work with 'adequate tools—intelligent men.' He did not make bricks—why, there was a physical impossibility in the way—as I was well aware; and if he did secretarial work for the manager, it was because 'no sensible man rejects wantonly the confidence of his superiors.' Did I see it? I saw it. What more did I want? What I really wanted was rivets, by heaven! Rivets. To get on with the work—to stop the hole. Rivets I wanted. There were cases of them down at the coast—cases—piled up—burst—split! You kicked a loose rivet at every second step in that station yard on the hillside. Rivets had rolled into the grove of death. You could fill your pockets with rivets for the trouble of stooping down—and there wasn't one rivet to be found where it was wanted. We had plates that would do, but nothing to fasten them with. And every week the messenger, a lone negro, letter-bag on shoulder and staff in hand, left our station for the coast. And several times a week a coast caravan came in with trade goods—ghastly glazed calico that made you shudder only to look at it,

glass beads value about a penny a quart, confounded spotted cotton handkerchiefs. And no rivets. Three carriers
could have brought all that was wanted to set that steamboat afloat.

"He was becoming confidential now, but I fancy my
unresponsive attitude must have exasperated him at last,
for he judged it necessary to inform me he feared neither
God nor devil, let alone any mere man. I said I could see
that very well, but what I wanted was a certain quantity of
rivets—and rivets were what really Mr. Kurtz wanted, if he
had only known it. Now letters went to the coast every
week. . . . 'My dear sir,' he cried, 'I write from dictation.' I
demanded rivets. There was a way—for an intelligent man.
He changed his manner; became very cold, and suddenly began to talk about a hippopotamus; wondered whether sleeping on board the steamer (I stuck to my salvage night and
day) I wasn't disturbed. There was an old hippo that had
the bad habit of getting out on the bank and roaming at
night over the station grounds. The pilgrims used to turn out
in a body and empty every rifle they could lay hands on at
him. Some even had sat up o' nights for him. All this energy was wasted, though. 'That animal has a charmed life,'
he said; 'but you can say this only of brutes in this country. No man—you apprehend me?—no man here bears a
charmed life.' He stood there for a moment in the moonlight with his delicate hooked nose set a little askew, and
his mica eyes glittering without a wink, then, with a curt
Good-night, he strode off. I could see he was disturbed and
considerably puzzled, which made me feel more hopeful
than I had been for days. It was a great comfort to turn
from that chap to my influential friend, the battered,
twisted, ruined, tin-pot steamboat. I clambered on board.
She rang under my feet like an empty Huntley & Palmer
biscuit-tin kicked along a gutter; she was nothing so solid
in make, and rather less pretty in shape, but I had ex-
pended enough hard work on her to make me love her. No
influential friend would have served me better. She had
given me a chance to come out a bit—to find out what I

could do. No, I don't like work. I had rather laze about and think of all the fine things that can be done. I don't like work—no man does—but I like what is in the work,— the chance to find yourself. Your own reality—for yourself, not for others—what no other man can ever know. They can only see the mere show, and never can tell what it really means.

"I was not surprised to see somebody sitting aft, on the deck, with his legs dangling over the mud. You see I rather chummed with the few mechanics there were in that station, whom the other pilgrims naturally despised—on account of their imperfect manners, I suppose. This was the foreman—a boiler-maker by trade—a good worker. He was a lank, bony, yellow-faced man, with big intense eyes. His aspect was worried, and his head was as bald as the palm of my hand; but his hair in falling seemed to have stuck to his chin, and had prospered in the new locality, for his beard hung down to his waist. He was a widower with six young children (he had left them in charge of a sister of his to come out there), and the passion of his life was pigeon-flying. He was an enthusiast and a connoisseur. He would rave about pigeons. After work hours he used sometimes to come over from his hut for a talk about his children and his pigeons; at work, when he had to crawl in the mud under the bottom of the steamboat, he would tie up that beard of his in a kind of white serviette he brought for the purpose. It had loops to go over his ears. In the evening he could be seen squatted on the bank rinsing that wrapper in the creek with great care, then spreading it solemnly on a bush to dry.

"I slapped him on the back and shouted, 'We shall have rivets!' He scrambled to his feet exclaiming, 'No! Rivets!' as though he couldn't believe his ears. Then in a low voice, 'You . . . eh?' I don't know why we behaved like lunatics. I put my finger to the side of my nose and nodded mysteriously. 'Good for you!' he cried, snapped his fingers above his head, lifting one foot. I tried a jig. We capered on the iron deck. A frightful clatter came out of that hulk, and the virgin forest on the other bank of the creek sent it back in a thundering roll upon the sleeping station. It must have made some of the pilgrims sit up in their hovels. A dark figure obscured the lighted doorway of the manager's hut, vanished, then, a second or so after, the doorway itself vanished, too. We stopped, and the silence driven away by the stamping of our feet flowed back again from the recesses of the land. The great wall of vegetation, an exuberant and entangled mass of trunks, branches, leaves, boughs, festoons, motionless in the moonlight, was like a rioting invasion of soundless life, a rolling wave of plants, piled up, crested, ready to topple over the creek, to sweep every little man of us out of his little existence. And it moved not. A deadened burst of mighty splashes and snorts reached us from afar, as though an ichthyosaurus had been taking a bath of glitter in the great river. 'After all,' said the boiler-maker in a reasonable tone, 'why shouldn't we get the rivets?' Why not, indeed! I did not know of any reason why we shouldn't. 'They'll come in three weeks,' I said, confidently.

"But they didn't. Instead of rivets there came an invasion, an infliction, a visitation. It came in sections during the next three weeks, each section headed by a donkey carrying a white man in new clothes and tan shoes, bowing from that elevation right and left to the impressed pilgrims. A quarrelsome band of footsore sulky niggers trod on the heels of the donkey; a lot of tents, camp-stools, tin boxes, white cases, brown bales would be shot down in the courtyard, and the air of mystery would deepen a little over the muddle of the station. Five such instalments came, with their absurd air of disorderly flight with the loot of innumerable outfit shops and provision stores, that, one would think, they were lugging, after a raid, into the wilderness for equitable division. It was an inextricable mess of things decent in themselves but that human folly made look like the spoils of thieving.

"This devoted band called itself the Eldorado Exploring Expedition, and I believe they were sworn to secrecy. Their talk, however, was the talk of sordid buccaneers: it was reckless without hardihood, greedy without audacity, and cruel without courage; there was not an atom of foresight or of serious intention in the whole batch of them, and they did not seem aware these things are wanted for the work of the world. To tear treasure out of the bowels of the land was their desire, with no more moral purpose at the back of it than there is in burglars breaking into a safe. Who paid the expenses of the noble enterprise I don't know; but the uncle of our manager was leader of that lot.

"In exterior he resembled a butcher in a poor neighbourhood, and his eyes had a look of sleepy cunning. He carried his fat paunch with ostentation on his short legs, and during the time his gang infested the station spoke to no one but his nephew. You could see these two roaming about all day long with their heads close together in an everlasting confab.

"I had given up worrying myself about the rivets. One's capacity for that kind of folly is more limited than you would suppose. I said Hang!—and let things slide. I had plenty of time for meditation, and now and then I would give some thought to Kurtz. I wasn't very interested in him. No. Still, I was curious to see whether this man, who had come out equipped with moral ideas of some sort, would climb to the top after all and how he would set about his work when there."

CHAPTER 2

"One evening as I was lying flat on the deck of my steamboat, I heard voices approaching—and there were the nephew and the uncle strolling along the bank. I laid my head on my arm again, and had nearly lost myself in a doze, when somebody said in my ear, as it were: 'I am as

harmless as a little child, but I don't like to be dictated to.
Am I the manager—or am I not? I was ordered to send him
there. It's incredible.' . . . I became aware that the two were
standing on the shore alongside the forepart of the steamboat, just below my head. I did not move; it did not occur
to me to move: I was sleepy. 'It *is* unpleasant,' grunted the
uncle. 'He has asked the Administration to be sent there,'
said the other, 'with the idea of showing what he could do;
and I was instructed accordingly. Look at the influence that
man must have. Is it not frightful?' They both agreed it was
frightful, then made several bizarre remarks: 'Make rain
and fine weather—one man—the Council—by the nose'—
bits of absurd sentences that got the better of my drowsi-
ness, so that I had pretty near the whole of my wits about
me when the uncle said, 'The climate may do away with
this difficulty for you. Is he alone there?' 'Yes,' answered
the manager; 'he sent his assistant down the river with a
note to me in these terms: "Clear this poor devil out of the
country, and don't bother sending more of that sort. I had
rather be alone than have the kind of men you can dispose
of with me." It was more than a year ago. Can you imagine
such impudence!' 'Anything since then?' asked the other,
hoarsely. 'Ivory,' jerked the nephew; 'lots of it—prime sort
—lots—most annoying, from him.' 'And with that?' questioned the heavy rumble. 'Invoice,' was the reply fired out,
so to speak. Then silence. They had been talking about
Kurtz.

"I was broad awake by this time, but, lying perfectly at
ease, remained still, having no inducement to change my
position. 'How did that ivory come all this way?' growled
the elder man, who seemed very vexed. The other explained that it had come with a fleet of canoes in charge
of an English half-caste clerk Kurtz had with him; that
Kurtz had apparently intended to return himself, the station
being by that time bare of goods and stores, but after coming three hundred miles, had suddenly decided to go back,
which he started to do alone in a small dugout with four
paddlers, leaving the half-caste to continue down the river

with the ivory. The two fellows there seemed astounded
at anybody attempting such a thing. They were at a loss for
an adequate motive. As to me, I seemed to see Kurtz for the
first time. It was a distinct glimpse: the dugout, four paddling savages, and the lone white man turning his back suddenly on the headquarters, on relief, on thoughts of home—
perhaps; setting his face towards the depths of the wilderness, towards his empty and desolate station. I did not know
the motive. Perhaps he was just simply a fine fellow who
stuck to his work for its own sake. His name, you understand, had not been pronounced once. He was 'that man.'
The half-caste, who, as far as I could see, had conducted
a difficult trip with great prudence and pluck, was invariably
alluded to as 'that scoundrel.' The 'scoundrel' had reported
that the 'man' had been very ill—had recovered imperfectly.
. . . The two below me moved away then a few paces, and
strolled back and forth at some little distance. I heard:
'Military post—doctor—two hundred miles—quite alone
now—unavoidable delays—nine months—no news—
strange rumours.' They approached again, just as the manager was saying, 'No one, as far as I know, unless a species
of wandering trader—a pestilential fellow, snapping ivory
from the natives.' Who was it they were talking about now?
I gathered in snatches that this was some man supposed
to be in Kurtz's district, and of whom the manager did not
approve. 'We will not be free from unfair competition till
one of these fellows is hanged for an example,' he said.
'Certainly,' grunted the other; 'get him hanged! Why not?
Anything—anything can be done in this country. That's
what I say; nobody here, you understand, *here,* can en-
danger your position. And why? You stand the climate—
you outlast them all. The danger is in Europe; but there
before I left I took care to—' They moved off and whispered, then their voices rose again. 'The extraordinary
series of delays is not my fault. I did my best.' The fat man
sighed. 'Very sad.' 'And the pestiferous absurdity of his
talk,' continued the other; 'he bothered me enough when
he was here. "Each station should be like a beacon on the

road towards better things, a centre for trade of course, but
also for humanizing, improving, instructing." Conceive
you—that ass! And he wants to be manager! No, it's—'
Here he got choked by excessive indignation, and I lifted
my head the least bit. I was surprised to see how near they
were—right under me. I could have spat upon their hats.
They were looking on the ground, absorbed in thought. The
manager was switching his leg with a slender twig: his saga-
cious relative lifted his head. 'You have been well since you
came out this time?' he asked. The other gave a start. 'Who?
I? Oh! Like a charm—like a charm. But the rest—oh, my
goodness! All sick. They die so quick, too, that I haven't the
time to send them out of the country—it's incredible!'
'H'm. Just so,' grunted the uncle. 'Ah! my boy, trust to this
—I say, trust to this.' I saw him extend his short flipper of
an arm for a gesture that took in the forest, the creek, the
mud, the river,—seemed to beckon with a dishonouring
flourish before the sunlit face of the land a treacherous appeal to the lurking death, to the hidden evil, to the profound darkness of its heart. It was so startling that I leaped
to my feet and looked back at the edge of the forest, as
though I had expected an answer of some sort to that black
display of confidence. You know the foolish notions that
come to one sometimes. The high stillness confronted these
two figures with its ominous patience, waiting for the passing away of a fantastic invasion.

"They swore aloud together—out of sheer fright, I believe—then pretending not to know anything of my existence, turned back to the station. The sun was low; and
leaning forward side by side, they seemed to be tugging
painfully uphill their two ridiculous shadows of unequal
length, that trailed behind them slowly over the tall grass
without bending a single blade.

"In a few days the Eldorado Expedition went into the
patient wilderness, that closed upon it as the sea closes
over a diver. Long afterwards the news came that all the
donkeys were dead. I know nothing as to the fate of the
less valuable animals. They, no doubt, like the rest of us,

found what they deserved. I did not inquire. I was then
rather excited at the prospect of meeting Kurtz very soon.
When I say very soon I mean it comparatively. It was
just two months from the day we left the creek when we
came to the bank below Kurtz's station.

"Going up that river was like travelling back to the
earliest beginnings of the world, when vegetation rioted
on the earth and the big trees were kings. An empty
stream, a great silence, an impenetrable forest. The air
was warm, thick, heavy, sluggish. There was no joy in
the brilliance of sunshine. The long stretches of the
waterway ran on, deserted, into the gloom of overshadowed distances. On silvery sandbanks hippos and
alligators sunned themselves side by side. The broad-
ening waters flowed through a mob of wooded islands;
you lost your way on that river as you would in a desert, and
butted all day long against shoals, trying to find the channel, till you thought yourself bewitched and cut off for
ever from everything you had known once—somewhere—
far away—in another existence perhaps. There were moments when one's past came back to one, as it will sometimes when you have not a moment to spare to yourself;
but it came in the shape of an unrestful and noisy dream,
remembered with wonder amongst the overwhelming realities of this strange world of plants, and water, and
silence. And this stillness of life did not in the least re-
semble a peace. It was the stillness of an implacable force
brooding over an inscrutable intention. It looked at you
with a vengeful aspect. I got used to it afterwards; I did
not see it any more; I had no time. I had to keep guessing
at the channel; I had to discern, mostly by inspiration, the
signs of hidden banks; I watched for sunken stones; I was
learning to clap my teeth smartly before my heart flew out,
when I shaved by a fluke some infernal sly old snag that
would have ripped the life out of the tin-pot steamboat and
drowned all the pilgrims; I had to keep a look-out for the
signs of dead wood we could cut up in the night for next
day's steaming. When you have to attend to things of that
sort, to the mere incidents of the surface, the reality—the

reality, I tell you—fades. The inner truth is hidden—luckily,
luckily. But I felt it all the same; I felt often its mysterious
stillness watching me at my monkey tricks, just as it
watches you fellows performing on your respective tight-
ropes for—what is it? half-a-crown a tumble—"

"Try to be civil, Marlow," growled a voice, and I knew
there was at least one listener awake besides myself.

"I beg your pardon. I forgot the heartache which makes
up the rest of the price. And indeed what does the price
matter, if the trick be well done? You do your tricks very
well. And I didn't do badly either, since I managed not to
sink that steamboat on my first trip. It's a wonder to me yet.
Imagine a blindfolded man set to drive a van over a bad
road. I sweated and shivered over that business considerably, I can tell you. After all, for a seaman, to scrape the
bottom of the thing that's supposed to float all the time
under his care is the unpardonable sin. No one may know
of it, but you never forget the thump—eh? A blow on the
very heart. You remember it, you dream of it, you wake
up at night and think of it—years after—and go hot and
cold all over. I don't pretend to say that steamboat floated
all the time. More than once she had to wade for a bit, with
twenty cannibals splashing around and pushing. We had
enlisted some of these chaps on the way for a crew. Fine
fellows—cannibals—in their place. They were men one
could work with, and I am grateful to them. And, after all,
they did not eat each other before my face: they had
brought along a provision of hippo-meat which went rotten, and made the mystery of the wilderness stink in my
nostrils. Phoo! I can sniff it now. I had the manager on
board and three or four pilgrims with their staves—all
complete. Sometimes we came upon a station close by the
bank, clinging to the skirts of the unknown, and the white
men rushing out of a tumble-down hovel, with great gestures of joy and surprise and welcome, seemed very
strange—had the appearance of being held there captive by
a spell. The word ivory would ring in the air for a while—
and on we went again into the silence, along empty reaches,

round the still bends, between the high walls of our winding way, reverberating in hollow claps the ponderous beat of the stern-wheel. Trees, trees, millions of trees, massive, immense, running up high; and at their foot, hugging the bank against the stream, crept the little begrimed steamboat, like a sluggish beetle crawling on the floor of a lofty portico. It made you feel very small, very lost, and yet it was not altogether depressing, that feeling. After all, if you were small, the grimy beetle crawled on—which was just what you wanted it to do. Where the pilgrims imagined it crawled to I don't know. To some place where they expected to get something, I bet! For me it crawled towards Kurtz—exclusively; but when the steam-pipes started leaking we crawled very slow. The reaches opened before us and closed behind, as if the forest had stepped leisurely across the water to bar the way for our return. We penetrated deeper and deeper into the heart of darkness. It was very quiet there. At night sometimes the roll of drums behind the curtain of trees would run up the river and remain sustained faintly, as if hovering in the air high over our heads, till the first break of day. Whether it meant war, peace, or prayer we could not tell. The dawns were heralded by the descent of a chill stillness; the wood-cutters slept, their fires burned low; the snapping of a twig would make you start. We were wanderers on a prehistoric earth, on an earth that wore the aspect of an unknown planet. We could have fancied ourselves the first of men taking possession of an accursed inheritance, to be subdued at the cost of profound anguish and of excessive toil. But suddenly, as we struggled round a bend, there would be a glimpse of rush walls, of peaked grass-roofs, a burst of yells, a whirl of black limbs, a mass of hands clapping, of feet stamping, of bodies swaying, of eyes rolling, under the droop of heavy and motionless foliage. The steamer toiled along slowly on the edge of a black and incomprehensible frenzy. The prehistoric man was cursing us, praying to us, welcoming us—who could tell? We were cut off from the comprehension of our surroundings; we glided past like phantoms, wondering and secretly appalled, as sane men would be before an enthusiastic outbreak in a madhouse. We could not understand because we were too far and could not remember, because we were traveling in the night of first ages, of those ages that are gone, leaving hardly a sign—and no memories.

"The earth seemed unearthly. We are accustomed to look upon the shackled form of a conquered monster, but there—there you could look at a thing monstrous and free. It was unearthly, and the men were— No, they were not inhuman. Well, you know, that was the worst of it—this suspicion of their not being inhuman. It would come slowly to one. They howled and leaped, and spun, and made horrid faces; but what thrilled you was just the thought of their humanity—like yours—the thought of your remote kinship with this wild and passionate uproar. Ugly. Yes, it was ugly enough; but if you were man enough you would admit to yourself that there was in you just the faintest trace of a response to the terrible frankness of that noise, a dim suspicion of there being a meaning in it which you—you so remote from the night of first ages—could comprehend. And why not? The mind of man is capable of anything—because everything is in it, all the past as well as all the future. What was there after all? Joy, fear, sorrow, devotion, valour, rage—who can tell?—but truth—truth stripped of its cloak of time. Let the fool gape and shudder—the man knows, and can look on without a wink. But he must at least be as much of a man as these on the shore. He must meet that truth with his own true stuff—with his own inborn strength. Principles won't do. Acquisitions, clothes, pretty rags—rags that would fly off at the first good shake. No; you want a deliberate belief. An appeal to me in this fiendish row—is there? Very well; I hear; I admit, but I have a voice, too, and for good or evil mine is the speech that cannot be silenced. Of course, a fool, what with sheer fright and fine sentiments, is always safe. Who's that grunting? You wonder I didn't go ashore for a howl and a dance? Well, no—I didn't. Fine sentiments, you

say? Fine sentiments, be hanged! I had no time. I had to
mess about with white-lead and strips of woollen blanket
helping to put bandages on those leaky steampipes—I tell
you. I had to watch the steering, and circumvent those
snags, and get the tin-pot along by hook or by crook. There
was surface-truth enough in these things to save a wiser
man. And between whiles I had to look after the savage
who was fireman. He was an improved specimen; he could
fire up a vertical boiler. He was there below me, and, upon
my word, to look at him was as edifying as seeing a dog in
a parody of breeches and a feather hat, walking on his
hind-legs. A few months of training had done for that really
fine chap. He squinted at the steam-gauge and at the water-
gauge with an evident effort of intrepidity—and he had
filed teeth, too, the poor devil, and the wool of his pate
shaved into queer patterns, and three ornamental scars on
each of his cheeks. He ought to have been clapping his
hands and stamping his feet on the bank, instead of which
he was hard at work, a thrall to strange witchcraft, full of
improving knowledge. He was useful because he had been
instructed; and what he knew was this—that should the
water in that transparent thing disappear, the evil spirit
inside the boiler would get angry through the greatness of
his thirst, and take a terrible vengeance. So he sweated
and fired up and watched the glass fearfully (with an im-
promptu charm, made of rags, tied to his arm, and a piece
of polished bone, as big as a watch, stuck flat-ways through
his lower lip), while the wooded banks slipped past us
slowly, the short noise was left behind, the interminable
miles of silence—and we crept on, towards Kurtz. But the
snags were thick, the water was treacherous and shallow,
the boiler seemed indeed to have a sulky devil in it, and
thus neither that fireman nor I had any time to peer into
our creepy thoughts.

"Some fifty miles below the Inner Station we came
upon a hut of reeds, an inclined and melancholy pole,
with the unrecognizable tatters of what had been a flag of
some sort flying from it, and a neatly stacked wood-pile.

This was unexpected. We came to the bank, and on the
stack of firewood found a flat piece of board with some
faded pencil-writing on it. When deciphered it said: 'Wood
for you. Hurry up. Approach cautiously.' There was a sig-
nature, but it was illegible—not Kurtz—a much longer
word. 'Hurry up.' Where? Up the river? 'Approach cautiously.' We had not done so. But the warning could not
have been meant for the place where it could be only found
after approach. Something was wrong above. But what—
and how much? That was the question. We commented ad-
versely upon the imbecility of that telegraphic style. The
bush around said nothing, and would not let us look very
far, either. A torn curtain of red twill hung in the doorway
of the hut, and flapped sadly in our faces. The dwelling was
dismantled; but we could see a white man had lived there
not very long ago. There remained a rude table—a plank
on two posts; a heap of rubbish reposed in a dark corner,
and by the door I picked up a book. It had lost its covers,
and the pages had been thumbed into a state of extremely
dirty softness; but the back had been lovingly stitched
afresh with white cotton thread, which looked clean yet.
It was an extraordinary find. Its title was, *An Inquiry into
some Points of Seamanship,* by a man Towser, Towson—
some such name—Master in his Majesty's Navy. The matter looked dreary reading enough, with illustrative diagrams
and repulsive tables of figures, and the copy was sixty years
old. I handled this amazing antiquity with the greatest
possible tenderness, lest it should dissolve in my hands.
Within, Towson or Towser was inquiring earnestly into
the breaking strain of ships' chains and tackle, and other
such matters. Not a very enthralling book; but at the first
glance you could see there a singleness of intention, an honest concern for the right way of going to work, which made
these humble pages, thought out so many years ago, luminous with another than a professional light. The simple old
sailor, with his talk of chains and purchases, made me forget the jungle and the pilgrims in a delicious sensation of
having come upon something unmistakably real. Such a
book being there was wonderful enough; but still more

astounding were the notes pencilled in the margin, and plainly referring to the text. I couldn't believe my eyes! They were in cipher! Yes, it looked like cipher. Fancy a man lugging with him a book of that description into this nowhere and studying it—and making notes—in cipher at that! It was an extravagant mystery.

"I had been dimly aware for some time of a worrying noise, and when I lifted my eyes I saw the wood-pile was gone, and the manager, aided by all the pilgrims, was shouting at me from the river-side. I slipped the book into my pocket. I assure you to leave off reading was like tearing myself away from the shelter of an old and solid friendship.

"I started the lame engine ahead. 'It must be this miserable trader—this intruder,' exclaimed the manager, looking back malevolently at the place we had left. 'He must be English,' I said. 'It will not save him from getting into trouble if he is not careful,' muttered the manager darkly. I observed with assumed innocence that no man was safe from trouble in this world.

"The current was more rapid now, the steamer seemed at her last gasp, the stern-wheel flopped languidly, and I caught myself listening on tiptoe for the next beat of the boat, for in sober truth I expected the wretched thing to give up every moment. It was like watching the last flickers of a life. But still we crawled. Sometimes I would pick out a tree a little way ahead to measure our progress towards Kurtz by, but I lost it invariably before we got abreast. To keep the eyes so long on one thing was too much for human patience. The manager displayed a beautiful resignation. I fretted and fumed and took to arguing with myself whether or no I would talk openly with Kurtz; but before I could come to any conclusion it occurred to me that my speech or my silence, indeed any action of mine, would be a mere futility. What did it matter what any one knew or ignored? What did it matter who was manager? One gets sometimes such a flash of insight. The essentials of this affair lay deep under the surface, beyond my reach, and beyond my power of meddling.

"Towards the evening of the second day we judged our-

selves about eight miles from Kurtz's station. I wanted
to push on; but the manager looked grave, and told me the
navigation up there was so dangerous that it would be ad-
visable, the sun being very low already, to wait where we
were till next morning. Moreover, he pointed out that if
the warning to approach cautiously were to be followed,
we must approach in daylight—not at dusk, or in the dark.
This was sensible enough. Eight miles meant nearly three
hours' steaming for us, and I could also see suspicious ripples at the upper end of the reach. Nevertheless, I was annoyed beyond expression at the delay, and most unreason-
ably, too, since one night more could not matter much
after so many months. As we had plenty of food, and cau-
tion was the word, I brought up in the middle of the stream.
The reach was narrow, straight, with high sides like a railway cutting. The dusk came gliding into it long before
the sun had set. The current ran smooth and swift, but a
dumb immobility sat on the banks. The living trees, lashed
together by the creepers and every living bush of the undergrowth, might have been changed into stone, even to the
slenderest twig, to the lightest leaf. It was not sleep—it
seemed unnatural, like a state of trance. Not the faintest
sound of any kind could be heard. You looked on amazed,
and began to suspect yourself of being deaf—then the night
came suddenly, and struck you blind as well. About three
in the morning some large fish leaped, and the loud splash
made me jump as though a gun had been fired. When the
sun rose there was a white fog, very warm and clammy, and
more blinding than the night. It did not shift or drive; it
was just there, standing all round you like something solid.
At eight or nine, perhaps, it lifted as a shutter lifts. We had
a glimpse of the towering multitude of trees, of the immense
matted jungle, with the blazing little ball of the sun hanging over it—all perfectly still—and then the white shutter
came down again, smoothly, as if sliding in greased grooves.
I ordered the chain, which we had begun to heave in, to be
paid out again. Before it stopped running with a muffled rattle, a cry, a very loud cry, as of infinite desolation, soared
slowly in the opaque air. It ceased. A complaining clamour,

modulated in savage discords, filled our ears. The sheer un-
expectedness of it made my hair stir under my cap. I don't
know how it struck the others: to me it seemed as though
the mist itself had screamed, so suddenly, and apparently
from all sides at once, did this tumultuous and mournful
uproar arise. It culminated in a hurried outbreak of almost
intolerably excessive shrieking, which stopped short, leaving us stiffened in a variety of silly attitudes, and obsti-
nately listening to the nearly as appalling and excessive silence. 'Good God! What is the meaning—' stammered at
my elbow one of the pilgrims,—a little fat man, with sandy
hair and red whiskers, who wore side-spring boots, and pink
pyjamas tucked into his socks. Two others remained open-
mouthed a whole minute, then dashed into the little cabin,
to rush out incontinently and stand darting scared glances,
with Winchesters at 'ready' in their hands. What we could
see was just the steamer we were on, her outlines blurred
as though she had been on the point of dissolving, and a
misty strip of water, perhaps two feet broad, around her—
and that was all. The rest of the world was nowhere, as
far as our eyes and ears were concerned. Just nowhere.
Gone, disappeared; swept off without leaving a whisper or a
shadow behind.

"I went forward, and ordered the chain to be hauled in
short, so as to be ready to trip the anchor and move the
steamboat at once if necessary. 'Will they attack?' whispered
an awed voice. 'We will be all butchered in this fog,' murmured another. The faces twitched with the strain, the
hands trembled slightly, the eyes forgot to wink. It was
very curious to see the contrast of expressions of the white
men and of the black fellows of our crew, who were as
much strangers to that part of the river as we, though their
homes were only eight hundred miles away. The whites, of
course greatly discomposed, had besides a curious look of
being painfully shocked by such an outrageous row. The
others had an alert, naturally interested expression; but
their faces were essentially quiet, even those of the one or
two who grinned as they hauled at the chain. Several exchanged short, grunting phrases, which seemed to settle the

matter to their satisfaction. Their headman, a young, broad-
chested black, severely draped in dark-blue fringed cloths,
with fierce nostrils and his hair all done up artfully in
oily ringlets, stood near me. 'Aha!' I said, just for good
fellowship's sake. 'Catch 'im,' he snapped, with a bloodshot
widening of his eyes and a flash of sharp teeth—'catch 'im.
Give 'im to us.' 'To you, eh?' I asked; 'what would you do
with them?' 'Eat 'im!' he said, curtly, and, leaning his elbow
on the rail, looked out into the fog in a dignified and profoundly pensive attitude. I would no doubt have been
properly horrified, had it not occurred to me that he and his
chaps must be very hungry: that they must have been
growing increasingly hungry for at least this month past.
They had been engaged for six months (I don't think a
single one of them had any clear idea of time, as we at the
end of countless ages have. They still belonged to the
beginnings of time—had no inherited experience to teach
them as it were), and of course, as long as there was a
piece of paper written over in accordance with some farcical
law or other made down the river, it didn't enter anybody's
head to trouble how they would live. Certainly they had
brought with them some rotten hippo-meat, which couldn't
have lasted very long, anyway, even if the pilgrims hadn't,
in the midst of a shocking hullabaloo, thrown a considerable quantity of it overboard. It looked like a high-handed
proceeding; but it was really a case of legitimate self-de-
fence. You can't breathe dead hippo waking, sleeping, and
eating, and at the same time keep your precarious grip on
existence. Besides that, they had given them every week
three pieces of brass wire, each about nine inches long;
and the theory was they were to buy their provisions with
that currency in river-side villages. You can see how *that*
worked. There were either no villages, or the people were
hostile, or the director, who like the rest of us fed out of
tins, with an occasional old he-goat thrown in, didn't want
to stop the steamer for some more or less recondite reason. So, unless they swallowed the wire itself, or made
loops of it to snare the fishes with, I don't see what good
their extravagant salary could be to them. I must say it was

paid with a regularity worthy of a large and honourable trading company. For the rest, the only thing to eat— though it didn't look eatable in the least—I saw in their possession was a few lumps of some stuff like half-cooked dough, of a dirty lavender colour, they kept wrapped in leaves, and now and then swallowed a piece of, but so small that it seemed done more for the looks of the thing than for any serious purpose of sustenance. Why in the name of all the gnawing devils of hunger they didn't go for us—they were thirty to five—and have a good tuck-in for once, amazes me now when I think of it. They were big powerful men, with not much capacity to weigh the consequences, with courage, with strength, even yet, though their skins were no longer glossy and their muscles no longer hard. And I saw that something restraining, one of those human secrets that baffle probability, had come into play there. I looked at them with a swift quickening of interest—not because it occurred to me I might be eaten by them before very long, though I own to you that just then I perceived— in a new light, as it were—how unwholesome the pilgrims looked, and I hoped, yes I positively hoped, that my aspect was not so—what shall I say?—so—unappetizing: a touch of fantastic vanity which fitted well with the dream-sensation that pervaded all my days at that time. Perhaps I had a little fever, too. One can't live with one's finger everlastingly on one's pulse. I had often 'a little fever,' or a little touch of other things—the playful paw-strokes of the wilderness, the preliminary trifling before the more serious onslaught which came in due course. Yes; I looked at them as you would on any human being, with a curiosity of their impulses, motives, capacities, weaknesses, when brought to the test of an inexorable physical necessity. Restraint! What possible restraint? Was it superstition, disgust, patience, fear —or some kind of primitive honour? No fear can stand up to hunger, no patience can wear it out, disgust simply does not exist where hunger is; and as to superstition, beliefs, and what you may call principles, they are less than chaff in a breeze. Don't you know the devilry of lingering starvation, its exasperating torment, its black thoughts, its sombre and brooding ferocity? Well, I do. It takes a man all his inborn strength to fight hunger properly. It's really easier to face bereavement, dishonour, and the perdition of one's soul—than this kind of prolonged hunger. Sad, but true. And these chaps, too, had no earthly reason for any kind of scruple. Restraint! I would just as soon have expected restraint from a hyena prowling amongst the corpses of a battlefield. But there was the fact facing me—the fact dazzling, to be seen, like the foam on the depths of the sea, like a ripple on an unfathomable enigma, a mystery greater —when I thought of it—than the curious, inexplicable note of desperate grief in this savage clamour that had swept by us on the river-bank, behind the blind whiteness of the fog.

"Two pilgrims were quarrelling in hurried whispers as to which bank. 'Left.' 'No, no; how can you? Right, right, of course.' 'It is very serious,' said the manager's voice behind me; 'I would be desolated if anything should happen to Mr. Kurtz before we came up.' I looked at him, and had not the slightest doubt he was sincere. He was just the kind of man who would wish to preserve appearances. That was his restraint. But when he muttered something about going on at once, I did not even take the trouble to answer him. I knew, and he knew, that it was impossible. Were we to let go our hold of the bottom, we would be absolutely in the air—in space. We wouldn't be able to tell where we were going to—whether up or down stream, or across—till we fetched against one bank or the other,—and then we wouldn't know at first which it was. Of course I made no move. I had no mind for a smash-up. You couldn't imagine a more deadly place for a shipwreck. Whether drowned at once or not, we were sure to perish speedily in one way or another. 'I authorize you to take all the risks,' he said, after a short silence. 'I refuse to take any,' I said, shortly; which was just the answer he expected, though its tone might have surprised him. 'Well, I must defer to your judgment. You are captain,' he said, with marked civility. I turned my shoulder to him in sign of my appreciation, and looked into the fog. How long would it last? It was the most hopeless look-out. The approach to this Kurtz grubbing for ivory in the wretched bush was beset by as many dangers as though he had been an enchanted princess sleeping in a fabulous castle. 'Will they attack, do you think?' asked the manager, in a confidential tone.

"I did not think they would attack, for several obvious reasons. The thick fog was one. If they left the bank in their canoes they would get lost in it, as we would be if we attempted to move. Still, I had also judged the jungle of both banks quite impenetrable—and yet eyes were in it, eyes that had seen us. The river-side bushes were certainly very thick; but the undergrowth behind was evidently penetrable. However, during the short lift I had seen no canoes anywhere in the reach—certainly not abreast of the steamer. But what made the idea of attack inconceivable to me was the nature of the noise—of the cries we had heard. They had not the fierce character boding immediate hostile intention. Unexpected, wild, and violent as they had been, they had given me an irresistible impression of sorrow. The glimpse of the steamboat had for some reason filled those savages with unrestrained grief. The danger, if any, I expounded, was from our proximity to a great human passion let loose. Even extreme grief may ultimately vent itself in violence—but more generally takes the form of apathy. . . .

"You should have seen the pilgrims stare! They had no heart to grin, or even to revile me: but I believe they thought me gone mad—with fright, maybe. I delivered a regular lecture. My dear boys, it was no good bothering. Keep a look-out? Well, you may guess I watched the fog for the signs of lifting as a cat watches a mouse; but for anything else our eyes were of no more use to us than if we had been buried miles deep in a heap of cotton-wool. It felt like it, too—choking, warm, stifling. Besides, all I said, though it sounded extravagant, was absolutely true to fact. What we afterwards alluded to as an attack was really an attempt at repulse. The action was very far from being aggressive—it was not even defensive, in the usual sense: it was undertaken under the stress of desperation, and in its essence was purely protective.

"It developed itself, I should say, two hours after the fog lifted, and its commencement was at a spot, roughly speaking, about a mile and a half below Kurtz's station. We had just floundered and flopped round a bend, when I saw an islet, a mere grassy hummock of bright green, in the middle of the stream. It was the only thing of the kind; but as we opened the reach more, I perceived it was the head of a long sandbank, or rather of a chain of shallow patches stretching down the middle of the river. They were discoloured, just awash, and the whole lot was seen just under the water, exactly as a man's backbone is seen running down the middle of his back under the skin. Now, as far as I did see, I could go to the right or to the left of this. I didn't know either channel, of course. The banks looked pretty well alike, the depth appeared the same; but as I had been informed the station was on the west side, I naturally headed for the western passage.

"No sooner had we fairly entered it than I became aware it was much narrower than I had supposed. To the left of us there was the long uninterrupted shoal, and to the right a high, steep bank heavily overgrown with bushes. Above the bush the trees stood in serried ranks. The twigs overhung the current thickly, and from distance to distance a large limb of some tree projected rigidly over the stream. It was then well on in the afternoon, the face of the forest was gloomy, and a broad strip of shadow had already fallen on the water. In this shadow we steamed up—very slowly, as you may imagine. I sheered her well inshore—the water being deepest near the bank, as the sounding-pole informed me.

"One of my hungry and forbearing friends was sounding in the bows just below me. This steamboat was exactly like a decked scow. On the deck, there were two little teak-wood houses, with doors and windows. The boiler was in the fore-end, and the machinery right astern. Over the whole there was a light roof, supported on stanchions. The funnel projected through that roof, and in front of the funnel a small cabin built of light planks served for a pilot-house. It contained a couch, two camp-stools, a loaded Martini-Henry leaning in one corner, a tiny table, and the steering-wheel. It had a wide door in front and a broad shutter at each side. All these were always thrown open, of course. I spent my days perched up there on the extreme fore-end of that roof, before the door. At night I slept, or tried to, on the couch. An athletic black belonging to some coast tribe, and educated by my poor predecessor, was the helmsman. He sported a pair of brass earrings, wore a blue cloth wrapper from the waist to the ankles, and thought all the world of himself. He was the most unstable kind of fool I had ever seen. He steered with no end of a swagger while you were by; but if he lost sight of you, he became instantly the prey of an abject funk, and would let that cripple of a steamboat get the upper hand of him in a minute.

"I was looking down at the sounding-pole, and feeling much annoyed to see at each try a little more of it stick out of that river, when I saw my poleman give up the business suddenly, and stretch himself flat on the deck, without even taking the trouble to haul his pole in. He kept hold on it though, and it trailed in the water. At the same time the fireman, whom I could also see below me, sat down abruptly before his furnace and ducked his head. I was amazed. Then I had to look at the river mighty quick, because there was a snag in the fairway. Sticks, little sticks, were flying about—thick: they were whizzing before my nose, dropping below me, striking behind me against my pilot-house. All this time the river, the shore, the woods, were very quiet—perfectly quiet. I could only hear the heavy splashing thump of the stern-wheel and the patter of these things. We cleared the snag clumsily. Arrows, by Jove! We were being shot at! I stepped in quickly to close the shutter on the land-side. That fool-helmsman, his hands on the spokes, was lifting his knees high, stamping his feet, champing his mouth, like a reined-in horse. Con-

found him! And we were staggering within ten feet of the
bank. I had to lean right out to swing the heavy shutter, and
I saw a face amongst the leaves on the level with my own,
looking at me very fierce and steady; and then suddenly, as
though a veil had been removed from my eyes, I made
out, deep in the tangled gloom, naked breasts, arms, legs,
glaring eyes,—the bush was swarming with human limbs
in movement, glistening, of bronze colour. The twigs shook,
swayed, and rustled, the arrows flew out of them, and then
the shutter came to. 'Steer her straight,' I said to the helmsman. He held his head rigid, face forward; but his eyes
rolled, he kept on lifting and setting down his feet gently,
his mouth foamed a little. 'Keep quiet!' I said in a fury. I
might just as well have ordered a tree not to sway in the
wind. I darted out. Below me there was a great scuffle of
feet on the iron deck; confused exclamations; a voice
screamed, 'Can you turn back?' I caught sight of a V-shaped
ripple on the water ahead. What? Another snag! A fusillade
burst out under my feet. The pilgrims had opened with
their Winchesters, and were simply squirting lead into
that bush. A deuce of a lot of smoke came up and drove
slowly forward. I swore at it. Now I couldn't see the ripple
or the snag either. I stood in the doorway, peering, and the
arrows came in swarms. They might have been poisoned,
but they looked as though they wouldn't kill a cat. The bush
began to howl. Our wood-cutters raised a warlike whoop;
the report of a rifle just at my back deafened me. I glanced
over my shoulder, and the pilot-house was yet full of noise
and smoke when I made a dash at the wheel. The fool-
nigger had dropped everything, to throw the shutter open
and let off that Martini-Henry. He stood before the wide
opening, glaring, and I yelled at him to come back, while
I straightened the sudden twist out of that steamboat. There
was no room to turn even if I had wanted to, the snag
was somewhere very near ahead in that confounded smoke,
there was no time to lose, so I just crowded her into the
bank—right into the bank, where I knew the water was
deep.

"We tore slowly along the overhanging bushes in a whirl of broken twigs and flying leaves. The fusillade below stopped short, as I had foreseen it would when the squirts got empty. I threw my head back to a glinting whizz that traversed the pilot-house, in at one shutter-hole and out at the other. Looking past that mad helmsman, who was shaking the empty rifle and yelling at the shore, I saw vague forms of men running bent double, leaping, gliding, distinct, incomplete, evanescent. Something big appeared in the air before the shutter, the rifle went overboard, and the man stepped back swiftly, looked at me over his shoulder in an extraordinary, profound, familiar manner, and fell upon my feet. The side of his head hit the wheel twice, and the end of what appeared a long cane clattered round and knocked over a little camp-stool. It looked as though after wrenching that thing from somebody ashore he had lost his balance in the effort. The thin smoke had blown away, we were clear of the snag, and looking ahead I could see that in another hundred yards or so I would be free to sheer off, away from the bank; but my feet felt so very warm and wet that I had to look down. The man had rolled on his back and stared straight up at me; both his hands clutched that cane. It was the shaft of a spear that, either thrown or lunged through the opening, had caught him in the side just below the ribs; the blade had gone in out of sight, after making a frightful gash; my shoes were full; a pool of blood lay very still, gleaming dark-red under the wheel; his eyes shone with an amazing lustre. The fusillade burst out again. He looked at me anxiously, gripping the spear like something precious, with an air of being afraid I would try to take it away from him. I had to make an effort to free my eyes from his gaze and attend to the steering. With one hand I felt above my head for the line of the steam whistle, and jerked out screech after screech hurriedly. The tumult of angry and warlike yells was checked instantly, and then from the depths of the woods went out such a tremulous and prolonged wail of mournful fear and utter despair as may be imagined to follow the flight of the last hope from

the earth. There was a great commotion in the bush; the
shower of arrows stopped, a few dropping shots rang out
sharply—then silence, in which the languid beat of the
stern-wheel came plainly to my ears. I put the helm hard
a-starboard at the moment when the pilgrim in pink
pyjamas, very hot and agitated, appeared in the doorway.
'The manager sends me—' he began in an official tone, and
stopped short. 'Good God!' he said, glaring at the wounded
man.

"We two whites stood over him, and his lustrous and
inquiring glance enveloped us both. I declare it looked
as though he would presently put to us some question in an
understandable language; but he died without uttering a
sound, without moving a limb, without twitching a muscle.
Only in the very last moment, as though in response to
some sign we could not see, to some whisper we could not
hear, he frowned heavily, and that frown gave to his black
death-mask an inconceivably sombre, brooding, and menacing expression. The lustre of inquiring glance faded swiftly
into vacant glassiness. 'Can you steer?' I asked the agent
eagerly. He looked very dubious; but I made a grab at his
arm, and he understood at once I meant him to steer
whether or no. To tell you the truth, I was morbidly anxious
to change my shoes and socks. 'He is dead,' murmured the
fellow, immensely impressed. 'No doubt about it,' said I,
tugging like mad at the shoe-laces. 'And by the way, I suppose Mr. Kurtz is dead as well by this time.'

"For the moment that was the dominant thought. There
was a sense of extreme disappointment, as though I had
found out I had been striving after something altogether
without a substance. I couldn't have been more disgusted
if I had travelled all this way for the sole purpose of talking with Mr. Kurtz. Talking with . . . I flung one shoe
overboard, and became aware that that was exactly what
I had been looking forward to—a talk with Kurtz. I made
the strange discovery that I had never imagined him as
doing, you know, but as discoursing. I didn't say to myself,
'Now I will never see him,' or 'Now I will never shake him

by the hand,' but, 'now I will never hear him.' The man presented himself as a voice. Not of course that I did not connect him with some sort of action. Hadn't I been told in all the tones of jealousy and admiration that he had collected, bartered, swindled, or stolen more ivory than all the other agents together? That was not the point. The point was in his being a gifted creature, and that of all his gifts the one that stood out preëminently, that carried with it a sense of real presence, was his ability to talk, his words—the gift of expression, the bewildering, the illuminating, the most exalted and the most contemptible, the pulsating stream of light, or the deceitful flow from the heart of an impenetrable darkness.

"The other shoe went flying unto the devil-god of that river. I thought, By Jove! it's all over. We are too late; he has vanished—the gift has vanished, by means of some spear, arrow, or club. I will never hear that chap speak after all,—and my sorrow had a startling extravagance of emotion, even such as I had noticed in the howling sorrow of these savages in the bush. I couldn't have felt more of lonely desolation somehow, had I been robbed of a belief or had missed my destiny in life.... Why do you sigh in this beastly way, somebody? Absurd? Well, absurd. Good Lord! mustn't a man ever— Here, give me some tobacco." ...

There was a pause of profound stillness, then a match flared, and Marlow's lean face appeared, worn, hollow, with downward folds and dropped eyelids, with an aspect of concentrated attention; and as he took vigorous draws at his pipe, it seemed to retreat and advance out of the night in the regular flicker of the tiny flame. The match went out.

"Absurd!" he cried. "This is the worst of trying to tell. ... Here you all are, each moored with two good addresses, like a hulk with two anchors, a butcher round one corner, a policeman round another, excellent appetites, and temperature normal—you hear—normal from year's end to year's end. And you say, Absurd! Absurd be—exploded! Absurd!

My dear boys, what can you expect from a man who out
of sheer nervousness had just flung overboard a pair of
new shoes! Now I think of it, it is amazing I did not shed
tears. I am, upon the whole, proud of my fortitude. I was
cut to the quick at the idea of having lost the inestimable
privilege of listening to the gifted Kurtz. Of course I was
wrong. The privilege was waiting for me. Oh, yes, I heard
more than enough. And I was right, too. A voice. He was
very little more than a voice. And I heard—him—it—this
voice—other voices—all of them were so little more than
voices—and the memory of that time itself lingers around
me, impalpable, like a dying vibration of one immense jab-
ber, silly, atrocious, sordid, savage, or simply mean, without any kind of sense. Voices, voices—even the girl herself
—now—"

He was silent for a long time.

"I laid the ghost of his gifts at last with a lie," he began,
suddenly. "Girl! What? Did I mention a girl? Oh, she is out
of it—completely. They—the women I mean—are out of it
—should be out of it. We must help them to stay in that
beautiful world of their own, lest ours gets worse. Oh, she
had to be out of it. You should have heard the disinterred
body of Mr. Kurtz saying, 'My Intended.' You would have
perceived directly then how completely she was out of it.
And the lofty frontal bone of Mr. Kurtz! They say the
hair goes on growing sometimes, but this—ah—specimen,
was impressively bald. The wilderness had patted him on
the head, and, behold, it was like a ball—an ivory ball; it
had caressed him, and—lo!—he had withered; it had taken
him, loved him, embraced him, got into his veins, consumed
his flesh, and sealed his soul to its own by the inconceivable
ceremonies of some devilish initiation. He was its spoiled
and pampered favourite. Ivory? I should think so. Heaps
of it, stacks of it. The old mud shanty was bursting with it.
You would think there was not a single tusk left either
above or below the ground in the whole country. 'Mostly
fossil,' the manager had remarked, disparagingly. It was
no more fossil than I am; but they call it fossil when it is

dug up. It appears these niggers do bury the tusks sometimes —but evidently they couldn't bury this parcel deep enough to save the gifted Mr. Kurtz from his fate. We filled the steamboat with it, and had to pile a lot on the deck. Thus he could see and enjoy as long as he could see, because the appreciation of this favour had remained with him to the last. You should have heard him say, 'My ivory.' Oh yes, I heard him. 'My Intended, my ivory, my station, my river, my—' everything belonged to him. It made me hold my breath in expectation of hearing the wilderness burst into a prodigious peal of laughter that would shake the fixed stars in their places. Everything belonged to him—but that was a trifle. The thing was to know what he belonged to, how many powers of darkness claimed him for their own. That was the reflection that made you creepy all over. It was impossible—it was not good for one either—trying to imagine. He had taken a high seat amongst the devils of the land—I mean literally. You can't understand. How could you?—with solid pavement under your feet, surrounded by kind neighbours ready to cheer you or to fall on you, stepping delicately between the butcher and the policeman, in the holy terror of scandal and gallows and lunatic asylums—how can you imagine what particular region of the first ages a man's untrammelled feet may take him into by the way of solitude—utter solitude without a policeman—by the way of silence—utter silence, where no warning voice of a kind neighbour can be heard whispering of public opinion? These little things make all the great difference. When they are gone you must fall back upon your own innate strength, upon your own capacity for faithfulness. Of course you may be too much of a fool to go wrong—too dull even to know you are being assaulted by the powers of darkness. I take it, no fool ever made a bargain for his soul with the devil: the fool is too much of a fool, or the devil too much of a devil—I don't know which. Or you may be such a thunderingly exalted creature as to be altogether deaf and blind to anything but heavenly sights and sounds. Then the earth for you is only a standing place—and whether to

be like this is your loss or your gain I won't pretend to say.
But most of us are neither one nor the other. The earth for
us is a place to live in, where we must put up with sights,
with sounds, with smells, too, by Jove!—breathe dead hippo,
so to speak, and not be contaminated. And there, don't you
see? your strength comes in, the faith in your ability for
the digging of unostentatious holes to bury the stuff in—
your power of devotion, not to yourself, but to an obscure,
back-breaking business. And that's difficult enough. Mind,
I am not trying to excuse or even explain—I am trying to
account to myself for—for—Mr. Kurtz—for the shade of
Mr. Kurtz. This initiated wraith from the back of Nowhere honoured me with its amazing confidence before it
vanished altogether. This was because it could speak English to me. The original Kurtz had been educated partly
in England, and—as he was good enough to say himself—
his sympathies were in the right place. His mother was
half-English, his father was half-French. All Europe contributed to the making of Kurtz; and by and by I learned
that, most appropriately, the International Society for the
Suppression of Savage Customs had intrusted him with
the making of a report, for its future guidance. And he had
written it, too. I've seen it. I've read it. It was eloquent,
vibrating with eloquence, but too high-strung, I think. Seventeen pages of close writing he had found time for! But
this must have been before his—let us say—nerves, went
wrong, and caused him to preside at certain midnight
dances ending with unspeakable rites, which—as far as I reluctantly gathered from what I heard at various times—
were offered up to him—do you understand?—to Mr. Kurtz
himself. But it was a beautiful piece of writing. The opening paragraph, however, in the light of later information,
strikes me now as ominous. He began with the argument
that we whites, from the point of development we had arrived at, 'must necessarily appear to them [savages] in the
nature of supernatural beings—we approach them with the
might as of a deity,' and so on, and so on. 'By the simple
exercise of our will we can exert a power for good prac-

tically unbounded,' etc. etc. From that point he soared and took me with him. The peroration was magnificent, though difficult to remember, you know. It gave me the notion of an exotic Immensity ruled by an august Benevolence. It made me tingle with enthusiasm. This was the unbounded power of eloquence—of words—of burning noble words. There were no practical hints to interrupt the magic current of phrases, unless a kind of note at the foot of the last page, scrawled evidently much later, in an unsteady hand, may be regarded as the exposition of a method. It was very simple, and at the end of that moving appeal to every altruistic sentiment it blazed at you, luminous and terrifying, like a flash of lightning in a serene sky: 'Exterminate all the brutes!' The curious part was that he had apparently forgotten all about that valuable postscriptum, because, later on, when he in a sense came to himself, he repeatedly entreated me to take good care of 'my pamphlet' (he called it), as it was sure to have in the future a good influence upon his career. I had full information about all these things, and, besides, as it turned out, I was to have the care of his memory. I've done enough for it to give me the indisputable right to lay it, if I choose, for an everlasting rest in the dust-bin of progress amongst all the sweepings and, figuratively speaking, all the dead cats of civilization. But then, you see, I can't choose. He won't be forgotten. Whatever he was, he was not common. He had the power to charm or frighten rudimentary souls into an aggravated witch-dance in his honour; he could also fill the small souls of the pilgrims with bitter misgivings: he had one devoted friend at least, and he had conquered one soul in the world that was neither rudimentary nor tainted with self-seeking. No; I can't forget him, though I am not prepared to affirm the fellow was exactly worth the life we lost in getting to him. I missed my late helmsman awfully,— I missed him even while his body was still lying in the pilot-house. Perhaps you will think it passing strange this regret for a savage who was no more account than a grain of sand in a black Sahara. Well, don't you see, he had done something, he had steered; for months I had him at my back—a help—an instrument. It was a kind of partnership. He steered for me—I had to look after him, I worried about his deficiencies, and thus a subtle bond had been created, of which I only became aware when it was suddenly broken. And the intimate profundity of that look he gave me when he received his hurt remains to this day in my memory— like a claim of distant kinship affirmed in a supreme moment.

"Poor fool! If he had only left that shutter alone. He had no restraint, no restraint—just like Kurtz—a tree swayed by the wind. As soon as I had put on a dry pair of slippers, I dragged him out, after first jerking the spear out of his side, which operation I confess I performed with my eyes shut tight. His heels leaped together over the little door-step; his shoulders were pressed to my breast; I hugged him from behind desperately. Oh! he was heavy, heavy; heavier than any man on earth, I should imagine. Then without more ado I tipped him overboard. The current snatched him as though he had been a wisp of grass, and I saw the body roll over twice before I lost sight of it for ever. All the pilgrims and the manager were then congregated on the awning-deck about the pilot-house, chattering at each other like a flock of excited magpies, and there was a scandalized murmur at my heartless promptitude. What they wanted to keep that body hanging about for I can't guess. Embalm it, maybe. But I had also heard another, and a very ominous, murmur on the deck below. My friends the wood-cutters were likewise scandalized, and with a better show of reason—though I admit that the reason itself was quite inadmissible. Oh, quite! I had made up my mind that if my late helmsman was to be eaten, the fishes alone should have him. He had been a very second-rate helmsman while alive, but now he was dead he might have become a first-class temptation, and possibly cause some startling trouble. Besides, I was anxious to take the wheel, the man in pink pyjamas showing himself a hopeless duffer at the business.

"This I did directly the simple funeral was over. We were going half-speed, keeping right in the middle of the stream, and I listened to the talk about me. They had given up Kurtz, they had given up the station; Kurtz was dead, and the station had been burnt—and so on—and so on. The red-haired pilgrim was beside himself with the thought that at least this poor Kurtz had been properly avenged. 'Say! We must have made a glorious slaughter of them in the bush. Eh? What do you think? Say?' He positively danced, the bloodthirsty little gingery beggar. And he had nearly fainted when he saw the wounded man! I could not help saying, 'You made a glorious lot of smoke, anyhow.' I had seen, from the way the tops of the bushes rustled and flew, that almost all the shots had gone too high. You can't hit anything unless you take aim and fire from the shoulder; but these chaps fired from the hip with their eyes shut. The retreat, I maintained—and I was right—was caused by the screeching of the steam-whistle. Upon this they forgot Kurtz, and began to howl at me with indignant protests.

"The manager stood by the wheel murmuring confidentially about the necessity of getting well away down the river before dark at all events, when I saw in the distance a clearing on the river-side and the outlines of some sort of building. 'What's this?' I asked. He clapped his hands in wonder. 'The station!' he cried. I edged in at once, still going half-speed.

"Through my glasses I saw the slope of a hill interspersed with rare trees and perfectly free from undergrowth. A long decaying building on the summit was half buried in the high grass; the large holes in the peaked roof gaped black from afar; the jungle and the woods made a background. There was no enclosure or fence of any kind; but there had been one apparently, for near the house half-a-dozen slim posts remained in a row, roughly trimmed, and with their upper ends ornamented with round carved balls. The rails, or whatever there had been between, had disappeared. Of course the forest surrounded all that. The river-bank was clear, and on the water-side I saw a white

man under a hat like a cart-wheel beckoning persistently
with his whole arm. Examining the edge of the forest above
and below, I was almost certain I could see movements—
human forms gliding here and there. I steamed past pru-
dently, then stopped the engines and let her drift down.
The man on the shore began to shout, urging us to land.
'We have been attacked,' screamed the manager. 'I know—
I know. It's all right,' yelled back the other, as cheerful as
you please. 'Come along. It's all right. I am glad.'

"His aspect reminded me of something I had seen—
something funny I had seen somewhere. As I manœuvred to
get alongside, I was asking myself, 'What does this fellow
look like?' Suddenly I got it. He looked like a harlequin.
His clothes had been made of some stuff that was brown
holland probably, but it was covered with patches all over,
with bright patches, blue, red, and yellow,—patches on the
back, patches on the front, patches on elbows, on knees;
coloured binding around his jacket, scarlet edging at the
bottom of his trousers; and the sunshine made him look
extremely gay and wonderfully neat withal, because you
could see how beautifully all this patching had been done. A
beardless, boyish face, very fair, no features to speak of,
nose peeling, little blue eyes, smiles and frowns chasing
each other over that open countenance like sunshine and
shadow on a wind-swept plain. 'Look out, captain!' he
cried; 'there's a snag lodged in here last night.' What!
Another snag? I confess I swore shamefully. I had nearly
holed my cripple, to finish off that charming trip. The
harlequin on the bank turned his little pug-nose up to me.
'You English?' he asked, all smiles. 'Are you?' I shouted
from the wheel. The smiles vanished, and he shook his head
as if sorry for my disappointment. Then he brightened up.
'Never mind!' he cried, encouragingly. 'Are we in time?'
I asked. 'He is up there,' he replied, with a toss of the head
up the hill, and becoming gloomy all of a sudden. His face
was like the autumn sky, overcast one moment and bright
the next.

"When the manager, escorted by the pilgrims, all of them

armed to the teeth, had gone to the house this chap came
on board. 'I say, I don't like this. These natives are in the
bush,' I said. He assured me earnestly it was all right.
'They are simple people,' he added; 'well, I am glad you
came. It took me all my time to keep them off.' 'But you
said it was all right,' I cried. 'Oh, they meant no harm,' he
said; and as I stared he corrected himself, 'Not exactly.'
Then vivaciously, 'My faith, your pilot-house wants a
clean-up!' In the next breath he advised me to keep enough
steam on the boiler to blow the whistle in case of any trouble.
'One good screech will do more for you than all your rifles.
They are simple people,' he repeated. He rattled away
at such a rate he quite overwhelmed me. He seemed to be
trying to make up for lots of silence, and actually hinted,
laughing, that such was the case. 'Don't you talk with Mr.
Kurtz?' I said. 'You don't talk with that man—you listen
to him,' he exclaimed with severe exaltation. 'But now—'
He waved his arm, and in the twinkling of an eye was in
the uttermost depths of despondency. In a moment he
came up again with a jump, possessed himself of both my
hands, shook them continuously, while he gabbled: 'Brother
sailor ... honour ... pleasure ... delight ... introduce myself ... Russian ... son of an arch-priest ... Government
of Tambov ... What? Tobacco! English tobacco; the excellent English tobacco! Now, that's brotherly. Smoke?
Where's a sailor that does not smoke?'

"The pipe soothed him, and gradually I made out he
had run away from school, had gone to sea in a Russian
ship; ran away again; served some time in English ships;
was now reconciled with the arch-priest. He made a point
of that. 'But when one is young one must see things, gather
experience, ideas; enlarge the mind.' 'Here!' I interrupted.
'You can never tell! Here I met Mr. Kurtz,' he said, youth-
fully solemn and reproachful. I held my tongue after that.
It appears he had persuaded a Dutch trading-house on the
coast to fit him out with stores and goods, and had started
for the interior with a light heart, and no more idea of what
would happen to him than a baby. He had been wandering

about that river for nearly two years alone, cut off from everybody and everything. 'I am not so young as I look. I am twenty-five,' he said. 'At first old Van Shuyten would tell me to go to the devil,' he narrated with keen enjoyment; 'but I stuck to him, and talked and talked, till at last he got afraid I would talk the hind-leg off his favourite dog, so he gave me some cheap things and a few guns, and told me he hoped he would never see my face again. Good old Dutchman, Van Shuyten. I've sent him one small lot of ivory a year ago, so that he can't call me a little thief when I get back. I hope he got it. And for the rest I don't care. I had some wood stacked for you. That was my old house. Did you see?'

"I gave him Towson's book. He made as though he would kiss me, but restrained himself. 'The only book I had left, and I thought I had lost it,' he said, looking at it ecstatically. 'So many accidents happen to a man going about alone, you know. Canoes get upset sometimes—and sometimes you've got to clear out so quick when the people get angry.' He thumbed the pages. 'You made notes in Russian?' I asked. He nodded. 'I thought they were written in cipher,' I said. He laughed, then became serious. 'I had lots of trouble to keep these people off,' he said. 'Did they want to kill you?' I asked. 'Oh, no!' he cried, and checked himself. 'Why did they attack us?' I pursued. He hesitated, then said shamefacedly, 'They don't want him to go.' 'Don't they?' I said, curiously. He nodded a nod full of mystery and wisdom. 'I tell you,' he cried, 'this man has enlarged my mind.' He opened his arms wide, staring at me with his little blue eyes that were perfectly round."

CHAPTER 3

"I looked at him, lost in astonishment. There he was before me, in motley, as though he had absconded from a troupe of mimes, enthusiastic, fabulous. His very existence was improbable, inexplicable, and altogether bewildering. He was an insoluble problem. It was inconceivable how he had existed, how he had succeeded in getting so far, how he had managed to remain—why he did not instantly disappear. 'I went a little farther,' he said, 'then still a little farther—till I had gone so far that I don't know how I'll ever get back. Never mind. Plenty time. I can manage. You take Kurtz away quick—quick—I tell you.' The glamour of youth enveloped his particoloured rags, his destitution, his loneliness, the essential desolation of his futile wanderings. For months—for years—his life hadn't been worth a day's purchase; and there he was gallantly, thoughtlessly alive, to all appearance indestructible solely by the virtue of his few years and of his unreflecting audacity. I was seduced into something like admiration—like envy. Glamour urged him on, glamour kept him unscathed. He surely wanted nothing from the wilderness but space to breathe in and to push on through. His need was to exist, and to move onwards at the greatest possible risk, and with a maximum of privation. If the absolutely pure, uncalculating, unpractical spirit of adventure had ever ruled a human being, it ruled this be-patched youth. I almost envied him the possession of this modest and clear flame. It seemed to have consumed all thought of self so completely, that even while he was talking to you, you forgot that it was he—the man before your eyes—who had gone through these things. I did

not envy him his devotion to Kurtz, though. He had not
meditated over it. It came to him, and he accepted it with
a sort of eager fatalism. I must say that to me it appeared
about the most dangerous thing in every way he had come
upon so far.

"They had come together unavoidably, like two ships
becalmed near each other, and lay rubbing sides at last.
I suppose Kurtz wanted an audience, because on a certain
occasion, when encamped in the forest, they had talked all
night, or more probably Kurtz had talked. 'We talked of
everything,' he said, quite transported at the recollection.
'I forgot there was such a thing as sleep. The night did
not seem to last an hour. Everything! Everything! . . . Of
love, too.' 'Ah, he talked to you of love!' I said, much
amused. 'It isn't what you think,' he cried, almost pas-
sionately. 'It was in general. He made me see things—
things.'

"He threw his arms up. We were on deck at the time, and
the headman of my wood-cutters, lounging near by, turned
upon him his heavy and glittering eyes. I looked around,
and I don't know why, but I assure you that never, never
before, did this land, this river, this jungle, the very arch
of this blazing sky, appear to me so hopeless and so dark,
so impenetrable to human thought, so pitiless to human
weakness. 'And, ever since, you have been with him, of
course?' I said.

"On the contrary. It appears their intercourse had been
very much broken by various causes. He had, as he informed me proudly, managed to nurse Kurtz through two
illnesses (he alluded to it as you would to some risky feat),
but as a rule Kurtz wandered alone, far in the depths of the
forest. 'Very often coming to this station, I had to wait
days and days before he would turn up,' he said. 'Ah, it
was worth waiting for!—sometimes.' 'What was he doing?
exploring or what?' I asked. 'Oh, yes, of course;' he had
discovered lots of villages, a lake, too—he did not know
exactly in what direction; it was dangerous to inquire too
much—but mostly his expeditions had been for ivory. 'But
he had no goods to trade with by that time,' I objected.

'There's a good lot of cartridges left even yet,' he answered, looking away. 'To speak plainly, he raided the country,' I said. He nodded. 'Not alone, surely!' He muttered something about the villages round that lake. 'Kurtz got the tribe to follow him, did he?' I suggested. He fidgeted a little. 'They adored him,' he said. The tone of these words was so extraordinary that I looked at him searchingly. It was curious to see his mingled eagerness and reluctance to speak of Kurtz. The man filled his life, occupied his thoughts, swayed his emotions. 'What can you expect?' he burst out; 'he came to them with thunder and lightning, you know— and they had never seen anything like it—and very terrible. He could be very terrible. You can't judge Mr. Kurtz as you would an ordinary man. No, no, no! Now—just to give you an idea—I don't mind telling you, he wanted to shoot me, too, one day—but I don't judge him.' 'Shoot you!' I cried. 'What for?' 'Well, I had a small lot of ivory the chief of that village near my house gave me. You see I used to shoot game for them. Well, he wanted it, and wouldn't hear reason. He declared he would shoot me unless I gave him the ivory and then cleared out of the country, because he could do so, and had a fancy for it, and there was nothing on earth to prevent him killing whom he jolly well pleased. And it was true, too. I gave him the ivory. What did I care! But I didn't clear out. No, no. I couldn't leave him. I had to be careful, of course, till we got friendly again for a time. He had his second illness then. Afterwards I had to keep out of the way; but I didn't mind. He was living for the most part in those villages on the lake. When he came down to the river, sometimes he would take to me, and sometimes it was better for me to be careful. This man suffered too much. He hated all this, and somehow he couldn't get away. When I had a chance I begged him to try and leave while there was time; I offered to go back with him. And he would say yes, and then he would remain; go off on another ivory hunt; disappear for weeks; forget himself amongst these people—forget himself—you know.' 'Why! he's mad,' I said. He protested indignantly. Mr. Kurtz couldn't be mad. If I had heard him talk, only two days ago,

I wouldn't dare hint at such a thing. . . . I had taken up my binoculars while we talked, and was looking at the shore, sweeping the limit of the forest at each side and at the back of the house. The consciousness of there being people in that bush, so silent, so quiet—as silent and quiet as the ruined house on the hill—made me uneasy. There was no sign on the face of nature of this amazing tale that was not so much told as suggested to me in desolate exclamations, completed by shrugs, in interrupted phrases, in hints ending in deep sighs. The woods were unmoved, like a mask—heavy, like the closed door of a prison—they looked with their air of hidden knowledge, of patient expectation, of unapproachable silence. The Russian was explaining to me that it was only lately that Mr. Kurtz had come down to the river, bringing along with him all the fighting men of that lake tribe. He had been absent for several months— getting himself adored, I suppose—and had come down un-expectedly, with the intention to all appearance of making a raid either across the river or down stream. Evidently the appetite for more ivory had got the better of the—what shall I say?—less material aspirations. However, he had got much worse suddenly. 'I heard he was lying helpless, and so I came up—took my chance,' said the Russian. 'Oh, he is bad, very bad.' I directed my glass to the house. There were no signs of life, but there was the ruined roof, the long mud wall peeping above the grass, with three little square window-holes, no two of the same size; all this brought within reach of my hand, as it were. And then I made a brusque movement, and one of the remaining posts of that vanished fence leaped up in the field of my glass. You remember I told you I had been struck at the distance by certain attempts at ornamentation, rather remarkable in the ruinous aspect of the place. Now I had suddenly a nearer view, and its first result was to make me throw my head back as if before a blow. Then I went carefully from post to post with my glass, and I saw my mistake. These round knobs were not ornamental but symbolic; they were expressive and puzzling, striking and disturbing—food for

thought and also for vultures if there had been any looking
down from the sky; but at all events for such ants as were
industrious enough to ascend the pole. They would have
been even more impressive, those heads on the stakes, if
their faces had not been turned to the house. Only one, the
first I had made out, was facing my way. I was not so
shocked as you may think. The start back I had given was
really nothing but a movement of surprise. I had expected
to see a knob of wood there, you know. I returned deliberately to the first I had seen—and there it was, black, dried,
sunken, with closed eyelids,—a head that seemed to sleep
at the top of that pole, and with the shrunken dry lips showing a narrow white line of the teeth, was smiling, too, smiling continuously at some endless and jocose dream of that
eternal slumber.

"I am not disclosing any trade secrets. In fact, the manager said afterwards that Mr. Kurtz's methods had ruined
the district. I have no opinion on that point, but I want you
clearly to understand that there was nothing exactly profitable in these heads being there. They only showed that Mr.
Kurtz lacked restraint in the gratification of his various
lusts, that there was something wanting in him—some small
matter which, when the pressing need arose, could not be
found under his magnificent eloquence. Whether he knew
of this deficiency himself I can't say. I think the knowledge
came to him at last—only at the very last. But the wilderness had found him out early, and had taken on him a terrible vengeance for the fantastic invasion. I think it had
whispered to him things about himself which he did not
know, things of which he had no conception till he took
counsel with this great solitude—and the whisper had
proved irresistibly fascinating. It echoed loudly within him
because he was hollow at the core. . . . I put down the glass,
and the head that had appeared near enough to be spoken
to seemed at once to have leaped away from me into inac-
cessible distance.

"The admirer of Mr. Kurtz was a bit crestfallen. In a
hurried, indistinct voice he began to assure me he had not

dared to take these—say, symbols—down. He was not afraid of the natives; they would not stir till Mr. Kurtz gave the word. His ascendancy was extraordinary. The camps of these people surrounded the place, and the chiefs came every day to see him. They would crawl. . . . 'I don't want to know anything of the ceremonies used when approaching Mr. Kurtz,' I shouted. Curious, this feeling that came over me that such details would be more intolerable than those heads drying on the stakes under Mr. Kurtz's windows. After all, that was only a savage sight, while I seemed at one bound to have been transported into some lightless region of subtle horrors, where pure, uncomplicated savagery was a positive relief, being something that had a right to exist—obviously—in the sunshine. The young man looked at me with surprise. I suppose it did not occur to him that Mr. Kurtz was no idol of mine. He forgot I hadn't heard any of these splendid monologues on, what was it? on love, justice, conduct of life—or what not. If it had come to crawling before Mr. Kurtz, he crawled as much as the veriest savage of them all. I had no idea of the conditions, he said: these heads were the heads of rebels. I shocked him excessively by laughing. Rebels! What would be the next definition I was to hear? There had been enemies, criminals, workers—and these were rebels. Those rebellious heads looked very subdued to me on their sticks. 'You don't know how such a life tries a man like Kurtz,' cried Kurtz's last disciple. 'Well, and you?' I said. 'I! I! I am a simple man. I have no great thoughts. I want nothing from anybody. How can you compare me to . . . ?' His feelings were too much for speech, and suddenly he broke down. 'I don't understand,' he groaned. 'I've been doing my best to keep him alive, and that's enough. I had no hand in all this. I have no abilities. There hasn't been a drop of medicine or a mouthful of invalid food for months here. He was shamefully abandoned. A man like this, with such ideas. Shamefully! Shamefully! I—I—haven't slept for the last ten nights . . .'

"His voice lost itself in the calm of the evening. The long

shadows of the forest had slipped down hill while we talked, had gone far beyond the ruined hovel, beyond the symbolic row of stakes. All this was in the gloom, while we down there were yet in the sunshine, and the stretch of the river abreast of the clearing glittered in a still and dazzling splendour, with a murky and overshadowed bend above and below. Not a living soul was seen on the shore. The bushes did not rustle.

"Suddenly round the corner of the house a group of men appeared, as though they had come up from the ground. They waded waist-deep in the grass, in a compact body, bearing an improvised stretcher in their midst. Instantly, in the emptiness of the landscape, a cry arose whose shrillness pierced the still air like a sharp arrow flying straight to the very heart of the land; and, as if by enchantment, streams of human beings—of naked human beings—with spears in their hands, with bows, with shields, with wild glances and savage movements, were poured into the clearing by the dark-faced and pensive forest. The bushes shook, the grass swayed for a time, and then everything stood still in attentive immobility.

" 'Now, if he does not say the right thing to them we are all done for,' said the Russian at my elbow. The knot of men with the stretcher had stopped, too, halfway to the steamer, as if petrified. I saw the man on the stretcher sit up, lank and with an uplifted arm, above the shoulders of the bearers. 'Let us hope that the man who can talk so well of love in general will find some particular reason to spare us this time,' I said. I resented bitterly the absurd danger of our situation, as if to be at the mercy of that atrocious phantom had been a dishonouring necessity. I could not hear a sound, but through my glasses I saw the thin arm extended commandingly, the lower jaw moving, the eyes of that apparition shining darkly far in its bony head that nodded with grotesque jerks. Kurtz—Kurtz—that means short in German—don't it? Well, the name was as true as everything else in his life—and death. He looked at least seven feet long. His covering had fallen off, and his body emerged from it pitiful and appalling as from a winding-sheet. I could see the cage of his ribs all astir, the bones of his arm waving. It was as though an animated image of death carved out of old ivory had been shaking its hand with menaces at a motionless crowd of men made of dark and glittering bronze. I saw him open his mouth wide—it gave him a weirdly voracious aspect, as though he had wanted to swallow all the air, all the earth, all the men before him. A deep voice reached me faintly. He must have been shouting. He fell back suddenly. The stretcher shook as the bearers staggered forward again, and almost at the same time I noticed that the crowd of savages was vanishing without any perceptible movement of retreat, as if the forest that had ejected these beings so suddenly had drawn them in again as the breath is drawn in a long aspiration.

"Some of the pilgrims behind the stretcher carried his arms—two shot-guns, a heavy rifle, and a light revolver-carbine—the thunderbolts of that pitiful Jupiter. The manager bent over him murmuring as he walked beside his head. They laid him down in one of the little cabins—just a room for a bedplace and a camp-stool or two, you know. We had brought his belated correspondence, and a lot of torn envelopes and open letters littered his bed. His hand roamed feebly amongst these papers. I was struck by the fire of his eyes and the composed languor of his expression. It was not so much the exhaustion of disease. He did not seem in pain. This shadow looked satiated and calm, as though for the moment it had had its fill of all the emotions.

"He rustled one of the letters, and looking straight in my face said, 'I am glad.' Somebody had been writing to him about me. These special recommendations were turning up again. The volume of tone he emitted without effort, almost without the trouble of moving his lips, amazed me. A voice! It was grave, profound, vibrating, while the man did not seem capable of a whisper. However, he had enough strength in him—factitious no doubt—to very nearly make an end of us, as you shall hear directly.

"The manager appeared silently in the doorway; I stepped out at once and he drew the curtain after me. The Russian, eyed curiously by the pilgrims, was staring at the shore. I followed the direction of his glance.

"Dark human shapes could be made out in the distance, flitting indistinctly against the gloomy border of the forest, and near the river two bronze figures, leaning on tall spears, stood in the sunlight under fantastic head-dresses of spotted skins, warlike and still in statuesque repose. And from right to left along the lighted shore moved a wild and gorgeous apparition of a woman.

"She walked with measured steps, draped in striped and fringed cloths, treading the earth proudly, with a slight jingle and flash of barbarous ornaments. She carried her head high; her hair was done in the shape of a helmet; she had brass leggings to the knee, brass wire gauntlets to the elbow, a crimson spot on her tawny cheek, innumerable necklaces of glass beads on her neck; bizarre things, charms, gifts of witch-men, that hung about her, glittered and trembled at every step. She must have had the value of several elephant tusks upon her. She was savage and superb, wild-eyed and magnificent; there was something ominous and stately in her deliberate progress. And in the hush that had fallen suddenly upon the whole sorrowful land, the immense wilderness, the colossal body of the fecund and mysterious life seemed to look at her, pensive, as though it had been looking at the image of its own tenebrous and passionate soul.

"She came abreast of the steamer, stood still, and faced us. Her long shadow fell to the water's edge. Her face had a tragic and fierce aspect of wild sorrow and of dumb pain mingled with the fear of some struggling, half-shaped resolve. She stood looking at us without a stir, and like the wilderness itself, with an air of brooding over an inscrutable purpose. A whole minute passed, and then she made a step forward. There was a low jingle, a glint of yellow metal, a sway of fringed draperies, and she stopped as if her heart had failed her. The young fellow by my side growled. The pilgrims murmured at my back. She looked at us all as if her life had depended upon the unswerving steadiness of her glance. Suddenly she opened her bared arms and threw them up rigid above her head, as though in an uncontrollable desire to touch the sky, and at the same time the swift shadows darted out on the earth, swept around on the river, gathering the steamer into a shadowy embrace. A formidable silence hung over the scene.

"She turned away slowly, walked on, following the bank, and passed into the bushes to the left. Once only her eyes gleamed back at us in the dusk of the thickets before she disappeared.

"'If she had offered to come aboard I really think I would have tried to shoot her,' said the man of patches, nervously. 'I have been risking my life every day for the last fortnight to keep her out of the house. She got in one day and kicked up a row about those miserable rags I picked up in the storeroom to mend my clothes with. I wasn't decent. At least it must have been that, for she talked like a fury to Kurtz for an hour, pointing at me now and then. I don't understand the dialect of this tribe. Luckily for me, I fancy Kurtz felt too ill that day to care, or there would have been mischief. I don't understand. . . . No—it's too much for me. Ah, well, it's all over now.'

"At this moment I heard Kurtz's deep voice behind the curtain: 'Save me!—save the ivory, you mean. Don't tell me. Save *me!* Why, I've had to save you. You are interrupting my plans now. Sick! Sick! Not so sick as you would like to believe. Never mind. I'll carry my ideas out yet—I will return. I'll show you what can be done. You with your little peddling notions—you are interfering with me. I will return. I. . . .'

"The manager came out. He did me the honour to take me under the arm and lead me aside. 'He is very low, very low,' he said. He considered it necessary to sigh, but neglected to be consistently sorrowful. 'We have done all we could for him—haven't we? But there is no disguising the fact, Mr. Kurtz has done more harm than good to the Company. He did not see the time was not ripe for vigorous action. Cautiously, cautiously—that's my principle. We must be cautious yet. The district is closed to us for a time. Deplorable! Upon the whole, the trade will suffer. I don't deny there is a remarkable quantity of ivory—mostly fossil. We must save it, at all events—but look how precarious the position is—and why? Because the method is unsound.' 'Do you,' said I, looking at the shore, 'call it "unsound method?" ' 'Without doubt,' he exclaimed, hotly. 'Don't you?' ... 'No method at all,' I murmured after a while. 'Exactly,' he exulted. 'I anticipated this. Shows a complete want of judgment. It is my duty to point it out in the proper quarter.' 'Oh,' said I, 'that fellow—what's his name?—the brickmaker, will make a readable report for you.' He appeared confounded for a moment. It seemed to me I had never breathed an atmosphere so vile, and I turned mentally to Kurtz for relief—positively for relief. 'Nevertheless I think Mr. Kurtz is a remarkable man,' I said with emphasis. He started, dropped on me a cold heavy glance, said very quietly, 'he *was*,' and turned his back on me. My hour of favour was over; I found myself lumped along with Kurtz as a partisan of methods for which the time was not ripe: I was unsound! Ah! but it was something to have at least a choice of nightmares.

"I had turned to the wilderness really, not to Mr. Kurtz, who, I was ready to admit, was as good as buried. And for a moment it seemed to me as if I also were buried in a vast grave full of unspeakable secrets. I felt an intolerable weight oppressing my breast, the smell of the damp earth, the unseen presence of victorious corruption, the darkness of an impenetrable night. ... The Russian tapped me on the shoulder. I heard him mumbling and stammering something about 'brother seaman—couldn't conceal—knowledge of matters that would affect Mr. Kurtz's reputation.' I waited. For him evidently Mr. Kurtz was not in his grave; I suspect that for him Mr. Kurtz was one of the immortals. 'Well!' said I at last, 'speak out. As it happens, I am Mr. Kurtz's friend—in a way.'

"He stated with a good deal of formality that had we not been 'of the same profession,' he would have kept the matter to himself without regard to consequences. 'He suspected there was an active ill will towards him on the part of these white men that—' 'You are right,' I said, remembering a certain conversation I had overheard. 'The manager thinks you ought to be hanged.' He showed a concern at this intelligence which amused me at first. 'I had better get out of the way quietly,' he said, earnestly. 'I can do no more for Kurtz now, and they would soon find some excuse. What's to stop them? There's a military post three hundred miles from here.' 'Well, upon my word,' said I, 'perhaps you had better go if you have any friends amongst the savages near by.' 'Plenty,' he said. 'They are simple people —and I want nothing, you know.' He stood biting his lip, then: 'I don't want any harm to happen to these whites here, but of course I was thinking of Mr. Kurtz's reputation—but you are a brother seaman and—' 'All right,' said I, after a time. 'Mr. Kurtz's reputation is safe with me.' I did not know how truly I spoke.

"He informed me, lowering his voice, that it was Kurtz who had ordered the attack to be made on the steamer. 'He hated sometimes the idea of being taken away—and then again. . . . But I don't understand these matters. I am a simple man. He thought it would scare you away—that you would give it up, thinking him dead. I could not stop him. Oh, I had an awful time of it this last month.' 'Very well,' I said. 'He is all right now.' 'Ye-e-es,' he muttered, not very convinced apparently. 'Thanks,' said I; 'I shall keep my eyes open.' 'But quiet—eh?' he urged, anxiously. 'It would be awful for his reputation if anybody here—' I promised a complete discretion with great gravity. 'I have a canoe and three black fellows waiting not very far. I am off. Could you give me a few Martini-Henry cartridges?' I could, and did, with proper secrecy. He helped himself, with a wink at me, to a handful of my tobacco. 'Between sailors—you know—good English tobacco.' At the door of the pilot-house he turned round—'I say, haven't you a pair of shoes you could spare?' He raised one leg. 'Look.' The soles were tied with knotted strings sandal-wise under his bare feet. I rooted out an old pair, at which he looked with admiration before tucking it under his left arm. One of his pockets (bright red) was bulging with cartridges, from the other (dark blue) peeped 'Towson's Inquiry,' etc., etc. He seemed to think himself excellently well equipped for a renewed encounter with the wilderness. 'Ah! I'll never, never meet such a man again. You ought to have heard him recite poetry—his own, too, it was, he told me. Poetry!' He rolled his eyes at the recollection of these delights. 'Oh, he enlarged my mind!' 'Good-bye,' said I. He shook hands and vanished in the night. Sometimes I ask myself whether I had ever really seen him—whether it was possible to meet such a phenomenon! ...

"When I woke up shortly after midnight his warning came to my mind with its hint of danger that seemed, in the starred darkness, real enough to make me get up for the purpose of having a look round. On the hill a big fire burned, illuminating fitfully a crooked corner of the station-house. One of the agents with a picket of a few of our blacks, armed for the purpose, was keeping guard over the ivory; but deep within the forest, red gleams that wavered, that seemed to sink and rise from the ground amongst confused columnar shapes of intense blackness, showed the exact position of the camp where Mr. Kurtz's adorers were keeping their uneasy vigil. The monotonous beating of a big drum filled the air with muffled shocks and a lingering vibration. A steady droning sound of many men chanting each to himself some weird incantation came out from the black, flat wall of the woods as the humming of bees comes out of a hive, and had a strange narcotic effect upon my half-awake senses. I believe I dozed off leaning over the rail, till an abrupt burst of yells, an overwhelming outbreak of a pent-up and mysterious frenzy, woke me up in a bewildered wonder. It was cut short all at once, and the low droning went on with an effect of audible and soothing silence. I glanced casually into the little cabin. A light was burning within, but Mr. Kurtz was not there.

"I think I would have raised an outcry if I had believed my eyes. But I didn't believe them at first—the thing seemed so impossible. The fact is I was completely unnerved by a sheer blank fright, pure abstract terror, unconnected with any distinct shape of physical danger. What made this emotion so overpowering was—how shall I define it?—the moral shock I received, as if something altogether monstrous, intolerable to thought and odious to the soul, had been thrust upon me unexpectedly. This lasted of course the merest fraction of a second, and then the usual sense of commonplace, deadly danger, the possibility of a sudden onslaught and massacre, or something of the kind, which I saw impending, was positively welcome and composing. It pacified me, in fact, so much, that I did not raise an alarm.

"There was an agent buttoned up inside an ulster and sleeping on a chair on deck within three feet of me. The yells had not awakened him; he snored very slightly; I left him to his slumbers and leaped ashore. I did not betray Mr. Kurtz—it was ordered I should never betray him—it was written I should be loyal to the nightmare of my choice. I was anxious to deal with this shadow by myself alone,—and to this day I don't know why I was so jealous of sharing with any one the peculiar blackness of that experience.

"As soon as I got on the bank I saw a trail—a broad trail through the grass. I remember the exultation with which I said to myself, 'He can't walk—he is crawling on all-fours—I've got him.' The grass was wet with dew. I strode rapidly with clenched fists. I fancy I had some vague notion of falling upon him and giving him a drubbing. I don't know. I had some imbecile thoughts. The knitting old woman with the cat obtruded herself upon my memory as a most improper person to be sitting at the other end of such an affair. I saw a row of pilgrims squirting lead in the air out of Winchesters held to the hip. I thought I would never get back to the steamer, and imagined myself living alone and unarmed in the woods to an advanced age. Such silly things—you know. And I remember I confounded the beat of the drum with the beating of my heart, and was pleased at its calm regularity.

"I kept to the track though—then stopped to listen. The night was very clear; a dark blue space, sparkling with dew and starlight, in which black things stood very still. I thought I could see a kind of motion ahead of me. I was strangely cocksure of everything that night. I actually left the track and ran in a wide semicircle (I verily believe chuckling to myself) so as to get in front of that stir, of that motion I had seen—if indeed I had seen anything. I was circumventing Kurtz as though it had been a boyish game.

"I came upon him, and, if he had not heard me coming, I would have fallen over him, too, but he got up in time. He rose, unsteady, long, pale, indistinct, like a vapour exhaled by the earth, and swayed slightly, misty and silent before me; while at my back the fires loomed between the trees, and the murmur of many voices issued from the forest. I had cut him off cleverly; but when actually confronting him I seemed to come to my senses, I saw the danger in its right proportion. It was by no means over yet. Suppose he began to shout? Though he could hardly stand, there was still plenty of vigour in his voice. 'Go away—hide yourself,' he said, in that profound tone. It was very awful. I glanced back. We were within thirty yards from the nearest fire. A black figure stood up, strode on long black legs, waving long black arms, across the glow. It had horns—antelope horns, I think—on its head. Some sorcerer, some witch-man, no doubt: it looked fiend-like enough. 'Do you know what you are doing?' I whispered. 'Perfectly,' he answered, raising his voice for that single word: it sounded to me far off and yet loud, like a hail through a speaking-trumpet. If he makes a row we are lost, I thought to myself. This clearly was not a case for fisticuffs, even apart from the very natural aversion I had to beat that Shadow—this wandering and tormented thing. 'You will be lost,' I said—'utterly lost.' One gets sometimes such a flash of inspiration, you know. I did say the right thing, though indeed he could not have been more irretrievably lost than he was at this very moment, when the foundations of our intimacy were being laid—to endure—to endure—even to the end—even beyond.

" 'I had immense plans,' he muttered irresolutely. 'Yes,' said I; 'but if you try to shout I'll smash your head with—'

There was not a stick or stone near. 'I will throttle you for good,' I corrected myself. 'I was on the threshold of great things,' he pleaded, in a voice of longing, with a wistfulness of tone that made my blood run cold. 'And now for this stupid scoundrel—' 'Your success in Europe is assured in any case,' I affirmed, steadily. I did not want to have the throttling of him, you understand—and indeed it would have been very little use for any practical purpose. I tried to break the spell—the heavy, mute spell of the wilderness —that seemed to draw him to its pitiless breast by the awakening of forgotten and brutal instincts, by the memory of gratified and monstrous passions. This alone, I was convinced, had driven him out to the edge of the forest, to the bush, towards the gleam of fires, the throb of drums, the drone of weird incantations; this alone had beguiled his unlawful soul beyond the bounds of permitted aspirations. And, don't you see, the terror of the position was not in being knocked on the head—though I had a very lively sense of that danger, too—but in this, that I had to deal with a being to whom I could not appeal in the name of anything high or low. I had, even like the niggers, to invoke him— himself—his own exalted and incredible degradation. There was nothing either above or below him, and I knew it. He had kicked himself loose of the earth. Confound the man! he had kicked the very earth to pieces. He was alone, and I before him did not know whether I stood on the ground or floated in the air. I've been telling you what we said—repeating the phrases we pronounced—but what's the good? They were common everyday words—the familiar, vague sounds exchanged on every waking day of life. But what of that? They had behind them, to my mind, the terrific suggestiveness of words heard in dreams, of phrases spoken in nightmares. Soul! If anybody had ever struggled with a soul, I am the man. And I wasn't arguing with a lunatic either. Believe me or not, his intelligence was perfectly clear—concentrated, it is true, upon himself with horrible intensity, yet clear; and therein was my only chance—barring, of course, the killing him there and then, which wasn't so good, on account of unavoidable noise. But his soul was mad. Being alone in the wilderness, it had looked within itself, and, by heavens! I tell you, it had gone mad. I had—for my sins, I suppose—to go through the ordeal of looking into it myself. No eloquence could have been so withering to one's belief in mankind as his final burst of sincerity. He struggled with himself, too. I saw it,—I heard it. I saw the inconceivable mystery of a soul that knew no restraint, no faith, and no fear, yet struggling blindly with itself. I kept my head pretty well; but when I had him at last stretched on the couch, I wiped my forehead, while my legs shook under me as though I had carried half a ton on my back down that hill. And yet I had only supported him, his bony arm clasped round my neck—and he was not much heavier than a child.

"When next day we left at noon, the crowd, of whose presence behind the curtain of trees I had been acutely conscious all the time, flowed out of the woods again, filled the clearing, covered the slope with a mass of naked, breathing, quivering, bronze bodies. I steamed up a bit, then swung downstream, and two thousand eyes followed the evolutions of the splashing, thumping, fierce, river-demon beating the water with its terrible tail and breathing black smoke into the air. In front of the first rank, along the river, three men, plastered with bright red earth from head to foot, strutted to and fro restlessly. When we came abreast again, they faced the river, stamped their feet, nodded their horned heads, swayed their scarlet bodies; they shook towards the fierce river-demon a bunch of black feathers, a mangy skin with a pendent tail—something that looked like a dried gourd; they shouted periodically together strings of amazing words that resembled no sounds of human language; and the deep murmurs of the crowd, interrupted suddenly, were like the responses of some satanic litany.

"We had carried Kurtz into the pilot-house: there was more air there. Lying on the couch, he stared through the open shutter. There was an eddy in the mass of human bodies, and the woman with helmeted head and tawny cheeks rushed out to the very brink of the stream. She put out her hands, shouted something, and all that wild mob took up the shout in a roaring chorus of articulated, rapid, breathless utterance.

" 'Do you understand this?' I asked.

"He kept on looking out past me with fiery, longing eyes, with a mingled expression of wistfulness and hate. He made no answer, but I saw a smile, a smile of indefinable meaning, appear on his colourless lips that a moment after twitched convulsively. 'Do I not?' he said slowly, gasping, as if the words had been torn out of him by a supernatural power.

"I pulled the string of the whistle, and I did this because I saw the pilgrims on deck getting out their rifles with an air of anticipating a jolly lark. At the sudden screech there was a movement of abject terror through that wedged mass of bodies. 'Don't! don't you frighten them away,' cried someone on deck disconsolately. I pulled the string time after time. They broke and ran, they leaped, they crouched, they swerved, they dodged the flying terror of the sound. The three red chaps had fallen flat, face down on the shore, as though they had been shot dead. Only the barbarous and superb woman did not so much as flinch, and stretched tragically her bare arms after us over the sombre and glittering river.

"And then that imbecile crowd down on the deck started their little fun, and I could see nothing more for smoke.

"The brown current ran swiftly out of the heart of darkness, bearing us down towards the sea with twice the speed of our upward progress; and Kurtz's life was running swiftly, too, ebbing, ebbing out of his heart into the sea of inexorable time. The manager was very placid, he had no vital anxieties now, he took us both in with a comprehensive and satisfied glance: the 'affair' had come off as well as could be wished. I saw the time approaching when I would be left alone of the party of 'unsound method.' The pilgrims looked upon me with disfavour. I was, so to speak, numbered with the dead. It is strange how I accepted this unforeseen partnership, this choice of nightmares forced upon me in the tenebrous land invaded by these mean and greedy phantoms.

"Kurtz discoursed. A voice! a voice! It rang deep to the very last. It survived his strength to hide in the magnificent folds of eloquence the barren darkness of his heart. Oh, he struggled! he struggled! The wastes of his weary brain were haunted by shadowy images now—images of wealth and fame revolving obsequiously round his unextinguishable gift of noble and lofty expression. My Intended, my station, my career, my ideas—these were the subjects for the occasional utterances of elevated sentiments. The shade of the original Kurtz frequented the bedside of the hollow sham, whose fate it was to be buried presently in the mould of primeval earth. But both the diabolic love and the unearthly hate of the mysteries it had penetrated fought for the possession of that soul satiated with primitive emotions, avid of lying fame, of sham distinction, of all the appearances of success and power.

"Sometimes he was contemptibly childish. He desired to have kings meet him at railway-stations on his return from some ghastly Nowhere, where he intended to accomplish great things. 'You show them you have in you something that is really profitable, and then there will be no limits to the recognition of your ability,' he would say. 'Of course you must take care of the motives—right motives—always.' The long reaches that were like one and the same reach, monotonous bends that were exactly alike, slipped past the steamer with their multitude of secular trees looking patiently after this grimy fragment of another world, the forerunner of change, of conquests, of trade, of massacres, of blessings. I looked ahead—piloting. 'Close the shutter,' said Kurtz suddenly one day; 'I can't bear to look at this.' I did so. There was a silence. 'Oh, but I will wring your heart yet!' he cried at the invisible wilderness.

"We broke down—as I had expected—and had to lie up for repairs at the head of an island. This delay was the first thing that shook Kurtz's confidence. One morning he gave me a packet of papers and a photograph—the lot tied together with a shoe-string. 'Keep this for me,' he said. 'This noxious fool' (meaning the manager) 'is capable of prying into my boxes when I am not looking.' In the afternoon I saw him. He was lying on his back with closed eyes, and I withdrew quietly, but I heard him mutter, 'Live rightly, die, die . . .' I listened. There was nothing more. Was he rehearsing some speech in his sleep, or was it a fragment of a phrase from some newspaper article? He had been writing for the papers and meant to do so again, 'for the furthering of my ideas. It's a duty.'

"His was an impenetrable darkness. I looked at him as you peer down at a man who is lying at the bottom of a precipice where the sun never shines. But I had not much time to give him, because I was helping the engine-driver to take to pieces the leaky cylinders, to straighten a bent connecting-rod, and in other such matters. I lived in an infernal mess of rust, filings, nuts, bolts, spanners, hammers, ratchet-drills—things I abominate, because I don't get on with them. I tended the little forge we fortunately had aboard; I toiled wearily in a wretched scrap-heap—unless I had the shakes too bad to stand.

"One evening coming in with a candle I was startled to hear him say a little tremulously, 'I am lying here in the dark waiting for death.' The light was within a foot of his eyes. I forced myself to murmur, 'Oh, nonsense!' and stood over him as if transfixed.

"Anything approaching the change that came over his features I have never seen before, and hope never to see again. Oh, I wasn't touched. I was fascinated. It was as though a veil had been rent. I saw on that ivory face the expression of sombre pride, of ruthless power, of craven terror—of an intense and hopeless despair. Did he live his life again in every detail of desire, temptation, and surrender during that supreme moment of complete knowledge? He cried in a whisper at some image, at some vision —he cried out twice, a cry that was no more than a breath—

" 'The horror! The horror!'

"I blew the candle out and left the cabin. The pilgrims were dining in the mess-room, and I took my place opposite the manager, who lifted his eyes to give me a questioning glance, which I successfully ignored. He leaned back, se-

rene, with that peculiar smile of his sealing the unexpressed
depths of his meanness. A continuous shower of small flies
streamed upon the lamp, upon the cloth, upon our hands
and faces. Suddenly the manager's boy put his insolent
black head in the doorway, and said in a tone of scathing
contempt—

" 'Mistah Kurtz—he dead.'

"All the pilgrims rushed out to see. I remained, and went
on with my dinner. I believe I was considered brutally cal-
lous. However, I did not eat much. There was a lamp in
there—light, don't you know—and outside it was so beastly,
beastly dark. I went no more near the remarkable man who
had pronounced a judgment upon the adventures of his
soul on this earth. The voice was gone. What else had been
there? But I am of course aware that next day the pilgrims
buried something in a muddy hole.

"And then they very nearly buried me.

"However, as you see, I did not go to join Kurtz there
and then. I did not. I remained to dream the nightmare out
to the end, and to show my loyalty to Kurtz once more.
Destiny. My destiny! Droll thing life is—that mysterious
arrangement of merciless logic for a futile purpose. The
most you can hope from it is some knowledge of yourself
—that comes too late—a crop of unextinguishable regrets.
I have wrestled with death. It is the most unexciting contest
you can imagine. It takes place in an impalpable grayness,
with nothing underfoot, with nothing around, without spectators, without clamour, without glory, without the great desire of victory, without the great fear of defeat, in a sickly
atmosphere of tepid scepticism, without much belief in
your own right, and still less in that of your adversary. If
such is the form of ultimate wisdom, then life is a greater
riddle than some of us think it to be. I was within a hair's
breadth of the last opportunity for pronouncement, and I
found with humiliation that probably I would have nothing
to say. This is the reason why I affirm that Kurtz was a remarkable man. He had something to say. He said it. Since
I had peeped over the edge myself, I understand better the
meaning of his stare, that could not see the flame of the

candle, but was wide enough to embrace the whole universe, piercing enough to penetrate all the hearts that beat in the darkness. He had summed up—he had judged. 'The horror!' He was a remarkable man. After all, this was the expression of some sort of belief; it had candour, it had conviction, it had a vibrating note of revolt in its whisper, it had the appalling face of a glimpsed truth—the strange commingling of desire and hate. And it is not my own extremity I remember best—a vision of grayness without form filled with physical pain, and a careless contempt for the evanescence of all things—even of this pain itself. No! It is his extremity that I seem to have lived through. True, he had made that last stride, he had stepped over the edge, while I had been permitted to draw back my hesitating foot. And perhaps in this is the whole difference; perhaps all the wisdom, and all truth, and all sincerity, are just compressed into that inappreciable moment of time in which we step over the threshold of the invisible. Perhaps! I like to think my summing-up would not have been a word of careless contempt. Better his cry—much better. It was an affirmation, a moral victory paid for by innumerable defeats, by abominable terrors, by abominable satisfactions. But it was a victory! That is why I have remained loyal to Kurtz to the last, and even beyond, when a long time after I heard once more, not his own voice, but the echo of his magnificent eloquence thrown to me from a soul as translucently pure as a cliff of crystal.

"No, they did not bury me, though there is a period of time which I remember mistily, with a shuddering wonder, like a passage through some inconceivable world that had no hope in it and no desire. I found myself back in the sepulchral city resenting the sight of people hurrying through the streets to filch a little money from each other, to devour their infamous cookery, to gulp their unwholesome beer, to dream their insignificant and silly dreams. They trespassed upon my thoughts. They were intruders whose knowledge of life was to me an irritating pretence, because I felt so sure they could not possibly know the things I knew. Their bearing, which was simply the bearing of commonplace individuals going about their business in the as-

surance of perfect safety, was offensive to me like the outrageous flauntings of folly in the face of a danger it is unable to comprehend. I had no particular desire to enlighten
them, but I had some difficulty in restraining myself from
laughing in their faces, so full of stupid importance. I daresay I was not very well at that time. I tottered about the
streets—there were various affairs to settle—grinning
bitterly at perfectly respectable persons. I admit my behaviour was inexcusable, but then my temperature was seldom normal in these days. My dear aunt's endeavours to
'nurse up my strength' seemed altogether beside the mark.
It was not my strength that wanted nursing, it was my imagination that wanted soothing. I kept the bundle of papers
given me by Kurtz, not knowing exactly what to do with it.
His mother had died lately, watched over, as I was told, by
his Intended. A clean-shaved man, with an official manner
and wearing gold-rimmed spectacles, called on me one day
and made inquiries, at first circuitous, afterwards suavely
pressing, about what he was pleased to denominate certain
'documents.' I was not surprised, because I had had two
rows with the manager on the subject out there. I had refused to give up the smallest scrap out of that package, and
I took the same attitude with the spectacled man. He became darkly menacing at last, and with much heat argued
that the Company had the right to every bit of information
about its 'territories.' And said he, 'Mr. Kurtz's knowledge
of unexplored regions must have been necessarily extensive
and peculiar—owing to his great abilities and to the deplorable circumstances in which he had been placed: therefore—' I assured him Mr. Kurtz's knowledge, however extensive, did not bear upon the problems of commerce or administration. He invoked then the name of science. 'It
would be an incalculable loss if,' etc., etc. I offered him the
report on the 'Suppression of Savage Customs,' with the
postscriptum torn off. He took it up eagerly, but ended by
sniffing at it with an air of contempt. 'This is not what we
had a right to expect,' he remarked. 'Expect nothing else,' I
said. 'There are only private letters.' He withdrew upon
some threat of legal proceedings, and I saw him no more;

but another fellow, calling himself Kurtz's cousin, appeared two days later, and was anxious to hear all the details about his dear relative's last moments. Incidentally he gave me to understand that Kurtz had been essentially a great musician. 'There was the making of an immense success,' said the man, who was an organist, I believe, with lank gray hair flowing over a greasy coat-collar. I had no reason to doubt his statement; and to this day I am unable to say what was Kurtz's profession, whether he ever had any—which was the greatest of his talents. I had taken him for a painter who wrote for the papers, or else for a journalist who could paint —but even the cousin (who took snuff during the interview) could not tell me what he had been—exactly. He was a universal genius—on that point I agreed with the old chap, who thereupon blew his nose noisily into a large cotton handkerchief and withdrew in senile agitation, bearing off some family letters and memoranda without importance. Ultimately a journalist anxious to know something of the fate of his 'dear colleague' turned up. This visitor informed me Kurtz's proper sphere ought to have been politics 'on the popular side.' He had furry straight eyebrows, bristly hair cropped short, an eye-glass on a broad ribbon, and, becoming expansive, confessed his opinion that Kurtz really couldn't write a bit—'but heavens! how that man could talk. He electrified large meetings. He had faith—don't you see?—he had the faith. He could get himself to believe anything—anything. He would have been a splendid leader of an extreme party.' 'What party?' I asked. 'Any party,' answered the other. 'He was an—an—extremist.' Did I not think so? I assented. Did I know, he asked, with a sudden flash of curiosity, 'what it was that had induced him to go out there?' 'Yes,' said I, and forthwith handed him the famous Report for publication, if he thought fit. He glanced through it hurriedly, mumbling all the time, judged 'it would do,' and took himself off with this plunder.

"Thus I was left at last with a slim packet of letters and the girl's portrait. She struck me as beautiful—I mean she had a beautiful expression. I know that the sunlight can be made to lie, too, yet one felt that no manipulation of light and pose could have conveyed the delicate shade of truthfulness upon those features. She seemed ready to listen without mental reservation, without suspicion, without a thought for herself. I concluded I would go and give her back her portrait and those letters myself. Curiosity? Yes; and also some other feelings perhaps. All that had been Kurtz's had passed out of my hands: his soul, his body, his station, his plans, his ivory, his career. There remained only his memory and his Intended—and I wanted to give that up, too, to the past, in a way—to surrender personally all that remained of him with me to that oblivion which is the last word of our common fate. I don't defend myself. I had no clear perception of what it was I really wanted. Perhaps it was an impulse of unconscious loyalty, or the fulfilment of one of those ironic necessities that lurk in the facts of human existence. I don't know. I can't tell. But I went.

"I thought his memory was like the other memories of the dead that accumulate in every man's life—a vague impress on the brain of shadows that had fallen on it in their swift and final passage; but before the high and ponderous door, between the tall houses of a street as still and decorous as a well-kept alley in a cemetery, I had a vision of him on the stretcher, opening his mouth voraciously, as if to devour all the earth with all its mankind. He lived then before me; he lived as much as he had ever lived—a shadow insatiable of splendid appearances, of frightful realities! a shadow darker than the shadow of the night, and draped nobly in the folds of a gorgeous eloquence. The vision seemed to enter the house with me—the stretcher, the phantom-bearers, the wild crowd of obedient worshippers, the gloom of the forests, the glitter of the reach between the murky bends, the beat of the drum, regular and muffled like the beating of a heart—the heart of a conquering darkness. It was a moment of triumph for the wilderness, an invading and vengeful rush which, it seemed to me, I would have to keep back alone for the salvation of another soul. And the memory of what I had heard him say afar there, with the horned shapes stirring at my back, in the glow of fires, within the patient woods, those broken phrases came back to me, were heard again in their ominous and terrifying simplicity. I remembered his abject pleading, his abject threats, the colossal scale of his vile desires, the meanness, the torment, the tempestuous anguish of his soul. And later on I seemed to see his collected languid manner, when he said one day, 'This lot of ivory now is really mine. The Company did not pay for it. I collected it myself at a very great personal risk. I am afraid they will try to claim it as theirs though. H'm. It is a difficult case. What do you think I ought to do—resist? Eh? I want no more than justice.' . . . He wanted no more than justice—no more than justice. I rang the bell before a mahogany door on the first floor, and while I waited he seemed to stare at me out of the glassy panel—stare with that wide and immense stare embracing, condemning, loathing all the universe. I seemed to hear the whispered cry, 'The horror! The horror!'

"The dusk was falling. I had to wait in a lofty drawing-room with three long windows from floor to ceiling that were like three luminous and bedraped columns. The bent gilt legs and backs of the furniture shone in indistinct curves. The tall marble fireplace had a cold and monumental whiteness. A grand piano stood massively in a corner; with dark gleams on the flat surfaces like a sombre and polished sarcophagus. A high door opened—closed. I rose.

"She came forward, all in black, with a pale head, floating towards me in the dusk. She was in mourning. It was more than a year since his death, more than a year since the news came; she seemed as though she would remember and mourn for ever. She took both my hands in hers and murmured, 'I had heard you were coming.' I noticed she was not very young—I mean not girlish. She had a mature capacity for fidelity, for belief, for suffering. The room seemed to have grown darker, as if all the sad light of the cloudy evening had taken refuge on her forehead. This fair hair, this pale visage, this pure brow, seemed surrounded by an ashy halo from which the dark eyes looked out at me. Their glance was guileless, profound, confident, and trustful. She carried her sorrowful head as though she were

proud of that sorrow, as though she would say, I—I alone
know how to mourn for him as he deserves. But while we
were still shaking hands, such a look of awful desolation
came upon her face that I perceived she was one of those
creatures that are not the playthings of Time. For her he
had died only yesterday. And, by Jove! the impression was
so powerful that for me, too, he seemed to have died only
yesterday—nay, this very minute. I saw her and him in the
same instant of time—his death and her sorrow—I saw her
sorrow in the very moment of his death. Do you understand? I saw them together—I heard them together. She
had said, with a deep catch of the breath, 'I have survived'
while my strained ears seemed to hear distinctly, mingled
with her tone of despairing regret, the summing up whisper
of his eternal condemnation. I asked myself what I was doing there, with a sensation of panic in my heart as though
I had blundered into a place of cruel and absurd mysteries
not fit for a human being to behold. She motioned me to a
chair. We sat down. I laid the packet gently on the little
table, and she put her hand over it. . . . 'You knew him well,'
she murmured, after a moment of mourning silence.

" 'Intimacy grows quickly out there,' I said. 'I knew him
as well as it is possible for one man to know another.'

" 'And you admired him,' she said. 'It was impossible to
know him and not to admire him. Was it?'

" 'He was a remarkable man,' I said, unsteadily. Then
before the appealing fixity of her gaze, that seemed to watch
for more words on my lips, I went on, 'It was impossible
not to—'

" 'Love him,' she finished eagerly, silencing me into an
appalled dumbness. 'How true! how true! But when you
think that no one knew him so well as I! I had all his noble
confidence. I knew him best.'

" 'You knew him best,' I repeated. And perhaps she did.
But with every word spoken the room was growing darker,
and only her forehead, smooth and white, remained
illumined by the unextinguishable light of belief and love.

" 'You were his friend,' she went on. 'His friend,' she repeated, a little louder. 'You must have been, if he had given

you this, and sent you to me. I feel I can speak to you—and oh! I must speak. I want you—you who have heard his last words—to know I have been worthy of him.... It is not pride.... Yes! I am proud to know I understood him better than any one on earth—he told me so himself. And since his mother died I have had no one—no one—to—to—'

"I listened. The darkness deepened. I was not even sure whether he had given me the right bundle. I rather suspect he wanted me to take care of another batch of his papers which, after his death, I saw the manager examining under the lamp. And the girl talked, easing her pain in the certitude of my sympathy; she talked as thirsty men drink. I had heard that her engagement with Kurtz had been disapproved by her people. He wasn't rich enough or something. And indeed I don't know whether he had not been a pauper all his life. He had given me some reason to infer that it was his impatience of comparative poverty that drove him out there.

" '... Who was not his friend who had heard him speak once?' she was saying. 'He drew men towards him by what was best in them.' She looked at me with intensity. 'It is the gift of the great,' she went on, and the sound of her low voice seemed to have the accompaniment of all the other sounds, full of mystery, desolation, and sorrow, I had ever heard—the ripple of the river, the soughing of the trees swayed by the wind, the murmurs of the crowds, the faint ring of incomprehensible words cried from afar, the whisper of a voice speaking from beyond the threshold of an eternal darkness. 'But you have heard him! You know!' she cried.

" 'Yes, I know,' I said with something like despair in my heart, but bowing my head before the faith that was in her, before that great and saving illusion that shone with an unearthly glow in the darkness, in the triumphant darkness from which I could not have defended her—from which I could not even defend myself.

" 'What a loss to me—to us!'—she corrected herself with beautiful generosity; then added in a murmur, 'To the world.' By the last gleams of twilight I could see the glitter of her eyes, full of tears—of tears that would not fall.

" 'I have been very happy—very fortunate—very proud,' she went on. 'Too fortunate. Too happy for a little while. And now I am unhappy for—for life.'

"She stood up; her fair hair seemed to catch all the remaining light in a glimmer of gold. I rose, too.

" 'And of all this,' she went on, mournfully, 'of all his promise, and of all his greatness, of his generous mind, of his noble heart, nothing remains—nothing but a memory. You and I—'

" 'We shall always remember him,' I said, hastily.

" 'No!' she cried. 'It is impossible that all this should be lost—that such a life should be sacrificed to leave nothing —but sorrow. You know what vast plans he had. I knew of them, too—I could not perhaps understand—but others knew of them. Something must remain. His words, at least, have not died.'

" 'His words will remain,' I said.

" 'And his example,' she whispered to herself. 'Men looked up to him—his goodness shone in every act. His example—'

" 'True,' I said; 'his example, too. Yes, his example. I forgot that.'

" 'But I do not. I cannot—I cannot believe—not yet. I cannot believe that I shall never see him again, that nobody will see him again, never, never, never.'

"She put out her arms as if after a retreating figure, stretching them black and with clasped pale hands across the fading and narrow sheen of the window. Never see him! I saw him clearly enough then. I shall see this eloquent phantom as long as I live, and I shall see her, too, a tragic and familiar Shade, resembling in this gesture another one, tragic also, and bedecked with powerless charms, stretching bare brown arms over the glitter of the infernal stream, the stream of darkness. She said suddenly very low, 'He died as he lived.'

" 'His end,' said I, with dull anger stirring in me, 'was in every way worthy of his life.'

" 'And I was not with him,' she murmured. My anger subsided before a feeling of infinite pity.

" 'Everything that could be done—' I mumbled.

" 'Ah, but I believed in him more than any one on earth —more than his own mother, more than—himself. He needed me! Me! I would have treasured every sigh, every word, every sign, every glance.'

"I felt like a chill grip on my chest. 'Don't,' I said, in a muffled voice.

" 'Forgive me. I—I—have mourned so long in silence— in silence. . . . You were with him—to the last? I think of his loneliness. Nobody near to understand him as I would have understood. Perhaps no one to hear. . . .'

" 'To the very end,' I said, shakily. 'I heard his very last words. . . .' I stopped in a fright.

" 'Repeat them,' she murmured in a heart-broken tone. 'I want—I want—something—something—to—to live with.'

"I was on the point of crying at her, 'Don't you hear them?' The dusk was repeating them in a persistent whisper all around us, in a whisper that seemed to swell menacingly like the first whisper of a rising wind. 'The horror! the horror!'

" 'His last word—to live with,' she insisted. 'Don't you understand I loved him—I loved him—I loved him!'

"I pulled myself together and spoke slowly.

" 'The last word he pronounced was—your name.'

"I heard a light sigh and then my heart stood still, stopped dead short by an exulting and terrible cry, by the cry of inconceivable triumph and of unspeakable pain. 'I knew it—I was sure!' . . . She knew. She was sure. I heard her weeping; she had hidden her face in her hands. It seemed to me that the house would collapse before I could escape, that the heavens would fall upon my head. But nothing happened. The heavens do not fall for such a trifle. Would they have fallen, I wonder, if I had rendered Kurtz that justice which was his due? Hadn't he said he wanted only justice? But I couldn't. I could not tell her. It would have been too dark—too dark altogether. . . ."

Marlow ceased, and sat apart, indistinct, and silent, in the pose of a meditating Buddha. Nobody moved for a time. "We have lost the first of the ebb," said the Director, suddenly. I raised my head. The offing was barred by a black bank of clouds, and the tranquil waterway leading to the uttermost ends of the earth flowed sombre under an overcast sky—seemed to lead into the heart of an immense darkness.

ALMAYER'S
FOLLY

CHAPTER 1

"Kaspar! Makan!"

The well-known shrill voice startled Almayer from his dream of splendid future into the unpleasant realities of the present hour. An unpleasant voice too. He had heard it for many years, and with every year he liked it less. No matter; there would be an end to all this soon.

He shuffled uneasily, but took no further notice of the call. Leaning with both his elbows on the balustrade of the verandah, he went on looking fixedly at the great river that flowed—indifferent and hurried—before his eyes. He liked to look at it about the time of sunset; perhaps because at that time the sinking sun would spread a glowing gold tinge on the waters of the Pantai, and Almayer's thoughts were often busy with gold; gold he had failed to secure; gold the others had secured—dishonestly, of course—or gold he meant to secure yet, through his own honest exertions, for himself and Nina. He absorbed himself in his dream of wealth and power away from this coast where he had dwelt for so many years, forgetting the bitterness of toil and strife in the vision of a great and splendid reward. They would live in Europe, he and his daughter. They would be rich and respected. Nobody would think of her mixed blood in the presence of her great beauty and of his immense wealth. Witnessing her triumphs he would grow young again, he would forget the twenty-five years of heart-breaking struggle on this coast where he felt like a prisoner. All this was nearly within his reach. Let only Dain return! And return soon he must—in his own interest, for his own share. He was now more than a week late! Perhaps he would return to-night.

Such were Almayer's thoughts as, standing on the verandah of his new but already decaying house—that last failure of his life—he looked on the broad river. There was no tinge of gold on it this evening, for it had been swollen by the rains, and rolled an angry and muddy flood under his inattentive eyes, carrying small drift-wood and big dead logs, and whole uprooted trees with branches and foliage, amongst which the water swirled and roared angrily.

One of those drifting trees grounded on the shelving shore, just by the house, and Almayer, neglecting his dream, watched it with languid interest. The tree swung slowly round, amid the hiss and foam of the water, and soon getting free of the obstruction began to move down stream again, rolling slowly over, raising upwards a long, denuded branch, like a hand lifted in mute appeal to heaven against the river's brutal and unnecessary violence. Almayer's interest in the fate of that tree increased rapidly. He leaned over to see if it would clear the low point below. It did; then he drew back, thinking that now its course was free down to the sea, and he envied the lot of that inanimate thing now growing small and indistinct in the deepening darkness. As he lost sight of it altogether he began to wonder how far out to sea it would drift. Would the current carry it north or south? South, probably, till it drifted in sight of Celebes, as far as Macassar, perhaps!

Macassar! Almayer's quickened fancy distanced the tree on its imaginary voyage, but his memory lagging behind some twenty years or more in point of time saw a young and slim Almayer, clad all in white and modest-looking, landing from the Dutch mail-boat on the dusty jetty of Macassar, coming to woo fortune in the godowns of old Hudig. It was an important epoch in his life, the beginning of a new existence for him. His father, a subordinate official employed in the Botanical Gardens of Buitenzorg, was no doubt delighted to place his son in such a firm. The young man himself too was nothing loth to leave the poisonous shores of Java, and the meagre comforts of the parental bungalow, where the father grumbled all day at the stupidity of native gardeners, and the mother from the depths of her long easy-chair bewailed the lost glories of Amsterdam, where she had been brought up, and of her position as the daughter of a cigar dealer there.

Almayer had left his home with a light heart and a lighter pocket, speaking English well, and strong in arithmetic; ready to conquer the world, never doubting that he would.

After those twenty years, standing in the close and stifling heat of a Bornean evening, he recalled with pleasurable regret the image of Hudig's lofty and cool warehouses with their long and straight avenues of gin cases and bales of Manchester goods; the big door swinging noiselessly; the dim light of the place, so delightful after the glare of the streets; the little railed-off spaces amongst piles of merchandise where the Chinese clerks, neat, cool, and sad-eyed, wrote rapidly and in silence amidst the din of the working gangs rolling casks or shifting cases to a muttered song, ending with a desperate yell. At the upper end, facing the great door, there was a larger space railed off, well lighted; there the noise was subdued by distance, and above it rose the soft and continuous clink of silver guilders which other discreet Chinamen were counting and piling up under the supervision of Mr. Vinck, the cashier, the genius presiding in the place—the right hand of the Master.

In that clear space Almayer worked at his table not far from a little green painted door, by which always stood a Malay in a red sash and turban, and whose hand, holding a small string dangling from above, moved up and down with the regularity of a machine. The string worked a punkah on the other side of the green door, where the so-called private office was, and where old Hudig—the Master—sat enthroned, holding noisy receptions. Sometimes the little door would fly open disclosing to the outer world, through the bluish haze of tobacco smoke, a long table loaded with bottles of various shapes and tall water pitchers, rattan easy-chairs occupied by noisy men in sprawling attitudes, while the Master would put his head through and, holding by the handle, would grunt confidentially to Vinck; perhaps send

an order thundering down the warehouse, or spy a hesitating stranger and greet him with a friendly roar, "Welcome, Gapitan! ver' you gome vrom? Bali, eh? Got bonies?
I vant bonies! Vant all you got; ha! ha! ha! Gome in!" Then
the stranger was dragged in, in a tempest of yells, the door
was shut, and the usual noises refilled the place; the song of
the workmen, the rumble of barrels, the scratch of rapid
pens; while above all rose the musical chink of broad silver
pieces streaming ceaselessly through the yellow fingers of
the attentive Chinamen.

At that time Macassar was teeming with life and commerce. It was the point in the islands where tended all those
bold spirits who, fitting out schooners on the Australian
coast, invaded the Malay Archipelago in search of money
and adventure. Bold, reckless, keen in business, not disin-
clined for a brush with the pirates that were to be found on
many a coast as yet, making money fast, they used to have
a general "rendezvous" in the bay for purposes of trade
and dissipation. The Dutch merchants called those men
English pedlars; some of them were undoubtedly gentlemen for whom that kind of life had a charm; most were seamen; the acknowledged king of them all was Tom Lingard,
he whom the Malays, honest or dishonest, quiet fishermen
or desperate cut-throats, recognized as "the Rajah-Laut"—
the King of the Sea.

Almayer had heard of him before he had been three days
in Macassar, had heard the stories of his smart business
transactions, his loves, and also of his desperate fights with
the Sulu pirates, together with the romantic tale of some
child—a girl—found in a piratical prau by the victorious
Lingard, when, after a long contest, he boarded the craft,
driving the crew overboard. This girl, it was generally
known, Lingard had adopted, was having her educated in
some convent in Java, and spoke of her as "my daughter."
He had sworn a mighty oath to marry her to a white man
before he went home and to leave her all his money. "And
Captain Lingard has lots of money," would say Mr. Vinck
solemnly, with his head on one side, "lots of money; more

than Hudig!" And after a pause—just to let his hearers recover from their astonishment at such an incredible assertion—he would add in an explanatory whisper, "You know, he has discovered a river."

That was it! He had discovered a river! That was the fact placing old Lingard so much above the common crowd of sea-going adventurers who traded with Hudig in the daytime and drank champagne, gambled, sang noisy songs, and made love to half-caste girls under the broad verandah of the Sunda Hotel at night. Into that river, whose entrances himself only knew, Lingard used to take his assorted cargo of Manchester goods, brass gongs, rifles and gunpowder. His brig *Flash*, which he commanded himself, would on those occasions disappear quietly during the night from the roadstead while his companions were sleeping off the effects of the midnight carouse, Lingard seeing them drunk under the table before going on board, himself unaffected by any amount of liquor. Many tried to follow him and find that land of plenty for gutta-percha and rattans, pearl shells and birds' nests, wax and gum-dammar, but the little *Flash* could outsail every craft in those seas. A few of them came to grief on hidden sandbanks and coral reefs, losing their all and barely escaping with life from the cruel grip of this sunny and smiling sea; others got discouraged; and for many years the green and peaceful-looking islands guarding the entrances to the promised land kept their secret with all the merciless serenity of tropical nature. And so Lingard came and went on his secret or open expeditions, becoming a hero in Almayer's eyes by the boldness and enormous profits of his ventures, seeming to Almayer a very great man indeed as he saw him marching up to the warehouse, grunting a "how are you?" to Vinck, or greeting Hudig, the Master, with a boisterous "Hallo, old pirate! Alive yet?" as a preliminary to transacting business behind the little green door. Often of an evening, in the silence of the then deserted warehouse, Almayer putting away his papers before driving home with Mr. Vinck, in whose household he lived, would pause listening to the noise of a hot discussion in the private office, would hear the deep and monotonous growl of the Master, and the roared-out interruptions of Lingard—two mastiffs fighting over a marrowy bone. But to Almayer's ears it sounded like a quarrel of Titans—a battle of the gods.

After a year or so Lingard, having been brought often in contact with Almayer in the course of business, took a sudden and, to the onlookers, a rather inexplicable fancy to the young man. He sang his praises, late at night, over a convivial glass to his cronies in the Sunda Hotel, and one fine morning electrified Vinck by declaring that he must have "that young fellow for a supercargo. Kind of captain's clerk. Do all my quill-driving for me." Hudig consented. Almayer, with youth's natural craving for change, was nothing loth, and packing his few belongings, started in the *Flash* on one of those long cruises when the old seaman was wont to visit almost every island in the archipelago. Months slipped by, and Lingard's friendship seemed to increase. Often pacing the deck with Almayer, when the faint night breeze, heavy with aromatic exhalations of the islands, shoved the brig gently along under the peaceful and sparkling sky, did the old seaman open his heart to his entranced listener. He spoke of his past life, of escaped dangers, of big profits in his trade, of new combinations that were in the future to bring profits bigger still. Often he had mentioned his daughter, the girl found in the pirate prau, speaking of her with a strange assumption of fatherly tenderness. "She must be a big girl now," he used to say. "It's nigh unto four years since I have seen her! Damme, Almayer, if I don't think we will run into Sourabaya this trip." And after such a declaration he always dived into his cabin muttering to himself, "Something must be done—must be done." More than once he would astonish Almayer by walking up to him rapidly, clearing his throat with a powerful "Hem!" as if he intended to say something, and then turning abruptly away to lean over the bulwarks in silence, and watch, motionless, for hours, the gleam and sparkle of the phosphorescent sea along the ship's side. It was the night before arriving in

Sourabaya when one of those attempts at confidential communication succeeded. After clearing his throat he spoke. He spoke to some purpose. He wanted Almayer to marry his adopted daughter. "And don't you kick because you're white!" he shouted, suddenly, not giving the surprised young man the time to say a word. "None of that with me! Nobody will see the colour of your wife's skin. The dollars are too thick for that, I tell you! And mind you, they will be thicker yet before I die. There will be millions, Kaspar! Millions I say! And all for her—and for you, if you do what you are told."

Startled by the unexpected proposal, Almayer hesitated, and remained silent for a minute. He was gifted with a strong and active imagination, and in that short space of time he saw, as in a flash of dazzling light, great piles of shining guilders, and realized all the possibilities of an opulent existence. The consideration, the indolent ease of life— for which he felt himself so well fitted—his ships, his warehouses, his merchandise (old Lingard would not live for ever), and, crowning all, in the far future gleamed like a fairy palace the big mansion in Amsterdam, that earthly paradise of his dreams, where made king amongst men by old Lingard's money, he would pass the evening of his days in inexpressible splendour. As to the other side of the picture—the companionship for life of a Malay girl, that legacy of a boatful of pirates—there was only within him a confused consciousness of shame that he a white man— Still, a convent education of four years—and then she may mercifully die. He was always lucky, and money is powerful! Go through it. Why not? He had a vague idea of shutting her up somewhere, anywhere, out of his gorgeous future. Easy enough to dispose of a Malay woman, a slave, after all, to his Eastern mind, convent or no convent, ceremony or no ceremony.

He lifted his head and confronted the anxious yet irate seaman.

"I—of course—anything you wish, Captain Lingard."

"Call me father, my boy. She does," said the mollified old

adventurer. "Damme, though, if I didn't think you were going to refuse. Mind you, Kaspar, I always get my way, so it would have been no use. But you are no fool."

He remembered well that time—the look, the accent, the words, the effect they produced on him, his very surroundings. He remembered the narrow slanting deck of the brig, the silent sleeping coast, the smooth black surface of the sea with a great bar of gold laid on it by the rising moon. He remembered it all, and he remembered his feelings of mad exultation at the thought of that fortune thrown into his hands. He was no fool then, and he was no fool now. Circumstances had been against him; the fortune was gone, but hope remained.

He shivered in the night air, and suddenly became aware of the intense darkness which, on the sun's departure, had closed in upon the river, blotting out the outlines of the opposite shore. Only the fire of dry branches lit outside the stockade of the Rajah's compound called fitfully into view the ragged trunks of the surrounding trees, putting a stain of glowing red halfway across the river where the drifting logs were hurrying toward the sea through the impenetrable gloom. He had a hazy recollection of having been called some time during the evening by his wife. To his dinner probably. But a man busy contemplating the wreckage of his past in the dawn of new hopes cannot be hungry whenever his rice is ready. Time he went home, though; it was getting late.

He stepped cautiously on the loose planks towards the ladder. A lizard, disturbed by the noise, emitted a plaintive note and scurried through the long grass growing on the bank. Almayer descended the ladder carefully, now thoroughly recalled to the realities of life by the care necessary to prevent a fall on the uneven ground where the stones, decaying planks, and half-sawn beams were piled up in inextricable confusion. As he turned towards the house where he lived—"my old house" he called it—his ear detected the splash of paddles away in the darkness of the river. He stood still in the path, attentive and surprised at anybody being on the river at this late hour during such a heavy freshet. Now he could hear the paddles distinctly, and even a rapidly exchanged word in low tones, the heavy breathing of men fighting with the current, and hugging the bank on which he stood. Quite close, too, but it was too dark to distinguish anything under the overhanging bushes.

"Arabs, no doubt," muttered Almayer to himself, peering into the solid blackness. "What are they up to now? Some of Abdulla's business; curse him!"

The boat was very close now.

"Oh, ya! Man!" hailed Almayer.

The sound of voices ceased but the paddles worked as furiously as before. Then the bush in front of Almayer shook, and the sharp sound of the paddles falling into the canoe rang in the quiet night. They were holding on to the bush now; but Almayer could hardly make out an indistinct dark shape of a man's head and shoulders above the bank.

"You Abdulla?" said Almayer, doubtfully.

A grave voice answered—

"Tuan Almayer is speaking to a friend. There is no Arab here."

Almayer's heart gave a great leap.

"Dain!" he exclaimed. "At last! at last! I have been waiting for you every day and every night. I had nearly given you up."

"Nothing could have stopped me from coming back here," said the other, almost violently. "Not even death," he whispered to himself.

"This is a friend's talk, and is very good," said Almayer, heartily. "Drop down to the jetty and let your men cook their rice in my campong while we talk in the house."

There was no answer to that invitation.

"What is it?" asked Almayer, uneasily. "There is nothing wrong with the brig, I hope?"

"The brig is where no Orang Blanda can lay his hands on her," said Dain, with a gloomy tone in his voice, which Almayer, in his elation, failed to notice.

"Right," he said. "But where are all your men? There are only two with you."

"Listen, Tuan Almayer," said Dain. "To-morrow's sun shall see me in your house, and then we will talk. Now I must go to the Rajah."

"To the Rajah! Why? What do you want with Lakamba?"

"Tuan, to-morrow we talk like friends. I must see Lakamba to-night."

"Dain, you are not going to abandon me now, when all is ready?" asked Almayer, in a pleading voice.

"Have I not returned? But I must see Lakamba first for your good and mine."

The shadowy head disappeared abruptly. The bush, released from the grasp of the bowman, sprung back with a swish, scattering a shower of muddy water over Almayer, as he bent forward, trying to see.

In a little while the canoe shot into the streak of light that streamed on the river from the big fire on the opposite shore, disclosing the outline of two men bending to their work, and a third figure in the stern flourishing the steering paddle, his head covered with an enormous round hat, like a fantastically exaggerated mushroom.

Almayer watched the canoe till it passed out of the line of light. Shortly after the murmur of many voices reached him across the water. He could see the torches being snatched out of the burning pile, and rendering visible for a moment the gate in the stockade round which they crowded. Then they went in; the torches disappeared, and the scattered fire sent out only a dim and fitful glare.

Almayer stepped homewards with long strides and mind uneasy. Surely Dain was not thinking of playing him false. It was absurd. Dain and Lakamba were both too much interested in the success of his scheme. Trusting to Malays was poor work; but then even Malays have some sense and understand their own interest. All would be well—must be well. At this point in his meditation he found himself at the foot of the steps leading to the verandah of his home. From the low point of land where he stood he could see both branches of the river. The main stream of the Pantai was lost in complete darkness, for the fire at the Rajah's had gone out altogether; but up the Sambir reach his eye could follow the long line of Malay houses crowding the bank, with here and there a dim light twinkling through bamboo walls, or a smoky torch burning on the platforms built out over the river. Further away, where the island ended in a low cliff, rose a dark mass of buildings towering above the Malay structures. Founded solidly on a firm ground with plenty of space, starred by many lights burning strong and white, with a suggestion of paraffin and lamp-glasses, stood the house and the godowns of Abdulla bin Selim, the great trader of Sambir. To Almayer the sight was very distasteful, and he shook his fist towards the buildings that in their evident prosperity looked to him cold and insolent, and contemptuous of his own fallen fortunes.

He mounted the steps of his house slowly.

In the middle of the verandah there was a round table. On it a paraffin lamp without a globe shed a hard glare on the three inner sides. The fourth side was open, and faced the river. Between the rough supports of the high-pitched roof hung torn rattan screens. There was no ceiling, and the harsh brilliance of the lamp was toned above into a soft half-light that lost itself in the obscurity amongst the rafters. The front wall was cut in two by the doorway of a central passage closed by a red curtain. The women's room opened into that passage, which led to the back court-yard and to the cooking shed. In one of the side walls there was a doorway. Half obliterated words—"Office: Lingard and Co."—were still legible on the dusty door, which looked as if it had not been opened for a very long time. Close to the other side wall stood a bent-wood rocking chair, and by the table and about the verandah four wooden armchairs straggled forlornly, as if ashamed of their shabby sur-roundings. A heap of common mats lay in one corner, with an old hammock slung diagonally above. In the other cor-ner, his head wrapped in a piece of red calico, huddled into a shapeless heap, slept a Malay, one of Almayer's domestic

slaves—"my own people," he used to call them. A numerous and representative assembly of moths were holding high
revels round the lamp to the spirited music of swarming
mosquitoes. Under the palm-leaf thatch lizards raced on
the beams calling softly. A monkey, chained to one of the
verandah supports—retired for the night under the eaves—
peered and grinned at Almayer, as it swung to one of the
bamboo roof sticks and caused a shower of dust and bits
of dried leaves to settle on the shabby table. The floor was
uneven, with many withered plants and dried earth scattered about. A general air of squalid neglect pervaded the
place. The light breeze from the river swayed gently the
tattered blinds, sending from the woods opposite a faint and
sickly perfume as of decaying flowers.

Under Almayer's heavy tread the boards of the verandah
creaked loudly. The sleeper in the corner moved uneasily,
muttering indistinct words. There was a slight rustle behind
the curtained doorway, and a soft voice asked in Malay, "Is
it you, father?"

"Yes, Nina. I am hungry. Is everybody asleep in this
house?"

Almayer spoke jovially and dropped with a contented
sigh into the armchair nearest to the table. Nina Almayer
came through the curtained doorway followed by an old
Malay woman, who busied herself in setting upon the table
a plateful of rice and fish, a jar of water and a bottle half
full of genever. After carefully placing before her master a
cracked glass tumbler and a tin spoon she went away noiselessly. Nina stood by the table, one hand lightly resting on
its edge, the other hanging listlessly by her side. Her face
turned towards the outer darkness, through which her
dreamy eyes seemed to see some entrancing picture, wore a
look of impatient expectancy. She was tall for a half-caste,
with the correct profile of the father, modified and strength-
ened by the squareness of the lower part of the face inherited from her maternal ancestors—the Sulu pirates. Her
firm mouth, with the lips slightly parted and disclosing a
gleam of white teeth, put a vague suggestion of ferocity into
the impatient expression of her features. And yet her dark

and perfect eyes had all the tender softness common to Malay women, but with a gleam of superior intelligence; they looked out gravely, wide open and steady, as if facing something invisible to all other eyes. She stood there all in white, straight, flexible, graceful, unconscious of herself, her low but broad forehead crowned with a shining mass of long black hair that fell in heavy tresses over her shoulders, and made her pale olive complexion look paler still by the contrast of its coal-black hue.

Almayer attacked his rice greedily, but after a few mouthfuls he paused, spoon in hand, and looked at his daughter curiously.

"Did you hear a boat pass about half an hour ago, Nina?" he asked.

The girl gave him a quick glance, and moving away from the light stood with her back to the table.

"I heard nothing," she said, slowly.

"There was a boat. At last! Dain himself; and he went on to Lakamba. I know it, for he told me so. I spoke to him, but he would not come here to-night. Promised to come to-morrow."

He swallowed another spoonful, then said—

"I am almost happy to-night, Nina. I can see the end of a long road, and it leads us away from this miserable swamp. We shall soon get away from here, I and you, my dear little girl, and then—"

He rose from the table and stood looking fixedly before him as if contemplating some enchanting vision.

"And then," he went on, "we shall be happy, you and I. Live rich and respected far from here, and forget this life, and all this struggle, and all this misery."

He approached his daughter and passed his hand caressingly over her hair.

"It is bad to have to trust a Malay," he said, "but I must own that this Dain is a perfect gentleman—a perfect gentleman," he repeated.

"Did you ask him to come here, father?" inquired Nina, not looking at him.

"Well, of course. We shall start on the day after to-morrow," said Almayer, joyously. "We must not lose any time. Are you glad, little girl?"

She was as tall as himself, but he liked to recall the time when she was little and they were all in all to each other.

"I am glad," she said, very low.

"Of course," said Almayer, vivaciously, "you cannot imagine what is before you. I myself have not been to Europe, but I have heard my mother talk so often that I seem to know all about it. We shall live a—a glorious life. You shall see."

Again he stood silent by his daughter's side looking at that enchanting vision. After a while he shook his fist towards the sleeping settlement.

"Ah! my friend Abdulla," he cried, "we shall see who will have the best of it after all these years!"

He looked up the river and remarked calmly:

"Another thunderstorm. Well! No thunder will keep me awake to-night, I know! Good-night, little girl," he whispered tenderly, kissing her cheek. "You do not seem to be very happy to-night, but to-morrow you will show a brighter face. Eh?"

Nina had listened to her father, unmoved, with her half-closed eyes still gazing into the night now made more intense by a heavy thunder-cloud that had crept down from the hills blotting out the stars, merging sky, forest, and river into one mass of almost palpable blackness. The faint breeze had died out, but the distant rumble of thunder and pale flashes of lightning gave warning of the approaching storm. With a sigh the girl turned towards the table.

Almayer was in his hammock now, already half asleep.

"Take the lamp, Nina," he muttered, drowsily. "This place is full of mosquitoes. Go to sleep, daughter."

But Nina put the lamp out and turned back again towards the balustrade of the verandah. She stood with her arm round the wooden support looking eagerly towards the Pantai reach. And motionless there in the oppressive calm of the tropical night she could see at each flash of lightning the forest lining both banks up the river, bending before the furious blast of wind the upper reach of the river whipped into white foam, and the black clouds torn into fantastic shapes trailing low over the swaying trees. Round her all was as yet stillness and peace, but she could hear afar off the driving roar, and hiss of heavy rain, the wash of the waves on the tormented river. It came nearer and nearer, with loud thunder-claps and long flashes of vivid lightning, followed by short periods of appalling blackness. When the storm reached the low point dividing the river, the whole house shook while the rain pattered loudly on the palm-leaf roof. The thunder spoke in one prolonged roll, and the incessant lightning disclosed a turmoil of leaping waters, driving logs, and the big trees bending before a brutal and merciless force.

Undisturbed by the nightly event of the rainy monsoon, the father slept quietly, oblivious alike of his hopes, his misfortunes, his friends, and his enemies; and the daughter stood motionless, at each flash of lightning eagerly scanning the broad river with a steady and anxious gaze.

CHAPTER 2

When, in compliance with Lingard's abrupt demand, Almayer consented to wed the Malay girl, no one knew that on the day when the interesting young convert had lost all her natural relations and found a white father, she had been fighting desperately like the rest of them on board the prau, and was only prevented from leaping overboard, like the few other survivors, by a severe wound in the leg. There, on the fore-deck of the prau, old Lingard found her under a heap of dead and dying pirates, and had her carried on the poop of the *Flash* before the Malay craft was set on fire and sent adrift. She was conscious, and in the great peace and stillness of the tropical evening succeeding the turmoil of the battle, she watched all she held dear on earth after her own savage manner, drift away into the gloom in a great roar of flame and smoke. She lay there unheeding the careful hands attending to her wound, silent and absorbed in gazing at the funeral pile of those brave men she had so much admired and so well helped in their contest with the redoubtable "Rajah-Laut."

The light night breeze fanned the brig gently to the southwards, and the great blaze of light got smaller and smaller till it twinkled only on the horizon like a setting star. It set: the heavy canopy of smoke reflected the glare of hidden flames for a short time and then disappeared also.

She realized that with this vanishing gleam her old life departed too. Thenceforth there was slavery in the far countries, amongst strangers, in unknown and perhaps terrible surroundings. There was in her the dread of the unknown; but otherwise she accepted her position calmly, for was she not a daughter of warriors, conquered in battle, and did she not belong rightfully to the victorious Rajah? Even the evident kindness of the terrible old man must spring, she thought, from admiration for his captive, and the flattered vanity eased for her the pangs of sorrow after such an awful calamity. Perhaps had she known of the high walls, the quiet gardens, and the silent nuns of the Samarang convent, where her destiny was leading her, she would have sought death in her dread and hate of such a restraint. But in imagination she pictured to herself the usual life of a Malay girl—the usual succession of heavy work and fierce love, of intrigues, gold ornaments, of domestic drudgery, and of that great but occult influence which is one of the few rights of half-savage womankind. But her destiny in the rough hands of the old sea-dog, acting under unreasoning impulses of the heart, took a strange and to her a terrible shape. She bore it all—the restraint and the teaching and the new faith—with calm submission, concealing her hate and contempt for all that new life. She learned the language very easily, yet understood but little of the new faith the good sisters taught her, assimilating quickly only the superstitious elements of the religion. She called Lingard father, gently and caressingly, at each of his short and noisy visits, under the clear impression that he was a great and dangerous power it was good to propitiate. Was he not now her master? And during those long four years she nourished a hope of finding favour in his eyes and ultimately becoming his wife, counsellor, and guide.

Those dreams of the future were dispelled by the Rajah Laut's "fiat," which made Almayer's fortune, as that young man fondly hoped. And dressed in the hateful finery of Europe, the young convert stood before the altar with an unknown and sulky-looking white man. For Almayer was uneasy, a little disgusted, and greatly inclined to run away. A judicious fear of the adopted father-in-law and a just regard for his own material welfare prevented him from making a scandal; yet, while swearing fidelity, he was concocting plans for getting rid of the pretty Malay girl in a more or less distant future. She, however, had retained enough of conventual teaching to understand well that according to white men's law she was going to be Almayer's companion and not his slave, and promised to herself to act accordingly.

So when the *Flash* freighted with materials for building a new house left the harbour of Batavia, taking away the young couple into the unknown Borneo, she did not carry on her deck so much love and happiness as old Lingard was wont to boast of before his casual friends in the verandahs of various hotels. The old seaman himself was perfectly happy. Now he had done his duty by the girl. "You know I made her an orphan," he often concluded solemnly, when talking about his own affairs to a scratch audience of shore loafers—as it was his habit to do. And the approbative shouts of his half-intoxicated auditors filled his simple soul with delight and pride. "I carry everything right through," was another of his sayings, and in pursuance of that principle he pushed the building of house and godowns on the

Pantai River with feverish haste. The house for the young
couple; the godowns for the big trade Almayer was going
to develop while he (Lingard) would be able to give himself up to some mysterious work which was only spoken of
in hints, but was understood to relate to gold and diamonds
in the interior of the island. Almayer was impatient too.
Had he known what was before him he might not have been
so eager and full of hope as he stood watching the last canoe
of the Lingard expedition disappear in the bend up the
river. When, turning round, he beheld the pretty little house,
the godowns built neatly by an army of Chinese carpenters,
the new jetty round which were clustered the trading canoes,
he felt a sudden elation in the thought that the world was
his.

But the world had to be conquered first, and its conquest
was not so easy as he thought. He was very soon made to
understand that he was not wanted in that corner of it where
old Lingard and his own weak will placed him, in the midst
of unscrupulous intrigues and of a fierce trade competition.
The Arabs had found out the river, had established a trading post in Sambir, and where they traded they would be
masters and suffer no rival. Lingard returned unsuccessful
from his first expedition, and departed again spending all
the profits of the legitimate trade on his mysterious journeys. Almayer struggled with the difficulties of his position,
friendless and unaided, save for the protection given to
him for Lingard's sake by the old Rajah, the predecessor
of Lakamba. Lakamba himself, then living as a private individual on a rice clearing, seven miles down the river, exer-
cised all his influence towards the help of the white man's
enemies, plotting against the old Rajah and Almayer with
a certainty of combination, pointing clearly to a profound
knowledge of their most secret affairs. Outwardly friendly,
his portly form was often to be seen on Almayer's verandah;
his green turban and gold-embroidered jacket shone in the
front rank of the decorous throng of Malays coming to
greet Lingard on his returns from the interior; his salaams
were of the lowest, and his handshakings of the heartiest,

when welcoming the old trader. But his small eyes took in the signs of the times, and he departed from those interviews with a satisfied and furtive smile to hold long consultations with his friend and ally, Syed Abdulla, the chief of the Arab trading post, a man of great wealth and of great influence in the islands.

It was currently believed at that time in the settlement that Lakamba's visits to Almayer's house were not limited to those official interviews. Often on moonlight nights the belated fishermen of Sambir saw a small canoe shooting out from the narrow creek at the back of the white man's house, and the solitary occupant paddle cautiously down the river in the deep shadows of the bank; and those events, duly reported, were discussed round the evening fires far into the night with the cynicism of expression common to Malays. Almayer went on struggling desperately, but with a feebleness of purpose depriving him of all chance of success against men so unscrupulous and resolute as his rivals the Arabs. The trade fell away from the large godowns, and the godowns themselves rotted piecemeal. The old man's banker, Hudig of Macassar, failed, and with this went the whole available capital. The profits of past years had been swallowed up in Lingard's exploring craze. Lingard was in the interior—perhaps dead—at all events giving no sign of life. Almayer stood alone in the midst of those adverse circumstances, deriving only a little comfort from the companionship of his little daughter, born two years after the marriage, and at the time some six years old. His wife had soon commenced to treat him with a savage contempt expressed by sulky silence, only occasionally varied by outbursts of savage invective. He felt she hated him, and saw her jealous eyes watching himself and the child with almost an expression of hate. She was jealous of the little girl's evident preference for the father, and Almayer felt he was not safe with that woman in the house. While she was burning the furniture, and tearing down the pretty curtains in her unreasoning hate of those signs of civilization, Almayer, cowed by these outbursts of savage nature, meditated in silence on the best way of getting rid of her. He thought of everything; even planned murder in an undecided and feeble sort of way, but dared do nothing—expecting every day the return of Lingard with news of some immense good fortune. Lingard returned indeed, but aged, ill, a ghost of his former self, with the fire of fever burning in his sunken eyes, almost the only survivor of the numerous expedition. But he was successful at last! Untold riches were in his grasp; he wanted more money—only a little more to realize a dream of fabulous fortune. And Hudig had failed! Almayer scraped all he could together, but the old man wanted more. If Almayer could not get it he would go to Singapore—to Europe even, but before all to Singapore; and he would take the little Nina with him. The child must be brought up decently. He had good friends in Singapore who would take care of her and have her taught properly. All would be well, and that girl, upon whom the old seaman seemed to have transferred all his former affection for the mother, would be the richest woman in the East—in the world even. So old Lingard shouted, pacing the verandah with his heavy quarter-deck step, gesticulating with a smouldering cheroot; ragged, dishevelled, enthusiastic; and Almayer, sitting huddled up on a pile of mats, thought with dread of the separation from the only human being he loved—with greater dread still, perhaps, of the scene with his wife, the savage tigress deprived of her young. She will poison me, thought the poor wretch, well aware of that easy and final manner of solving the social, political, or family problems in Malay life.

To his great surprise she took the news very quietly, giving only him and Lingard a furtive glance, and saying not a word. This, however, did not prevent her the next day from jumping into the river and swimming after the boat in which Lingard was carrying away the nurse with the screaming child. Almayer had to give chase with his whale-boat and drag her in by the hair in the midst of cries and curses enough to make heaven fall. Yet after two days spent in wailing, she returned to her former mode of life, chewing betel-nut, and sitting all day amongst her women in stupefied idleness. She aged very rapidly after that, and only roused herself from her apathy to acknowledge by a scathing remark or an insulting exclamation the accidental presence of her husband. He had built for her a riverside hut in the compound where she dwelt in perfect seclusion. Lakamba's visits had ceased when, by a convenient decree of Providence the old ruler of Sambir departed this life. Lakamba reigned in his stead now, having been well served by his Arab friends with the Dutch authorities. Syed Abdulla was the great man and trader of the Pantai. Almayer lay ruined and helpless under the close-meshed net of their intrigues, owing his life only to his supposed knowledge of Lingard's valuable secret. Lingard had disappeared. He wrote once from Singapore saying the child was well, and under the care of a Mrs. Vinck, and that he himself was going to Europe to raise money for the great enterprise. He was coming back soon. There would be no difficulties, he wrote. People would rush in with their money. Evidently they did not, for there was only one letter more from him saying he was ill, had found no relation living, but little else besides. Then came a complete silence. Europe had smallowed up the Rajah Laut apparently, and Almayer looked vainly westward for a ray of light out of the gloom of his shattered hopes. Years passed, and the rare letters from Mrs. Vinck, later from the girl herself, were the only thing to be looked to to make life bearable amongst the triumphant savagery of the river. Almayer lived now alone, having even ceased to visit his debtors who would not pay, sure of Lakamba's protection. The faithful Sumatrese Ali cooked his rice and made his coffee, for he dared not trust any one else, and least of all his wife. He killed time wandering sadly in the overgrown paths round the house, visiting the ruined godowns where a few brass guns covered with verdigris and only a few broken cases of mouldering Manchester goods reminded him of the good early times when all this was full of life and merchandise, and he overlooked a busy scene on the river bank, his little daughter by his side. Now the upcountry canoes glided past the little rotten wharf of Lingard and Co., to paddle up the Pantai branch, and cluster round the new jetty belonging to Abdulla. Not that they loved Abdulla, but they dared not trade with the man whose star had set. Had they done so they knew there was no mercy to be expected from Arab or Rajah; no rice to be got on credit in times of scarcity from either; and Almayer could not help them, having at times hardly enough for himself. Almayer, in his isolation and despair, often envied his near neighbour the Chinaman, Jim-Eng, whom he could see stretched on a pile of cool mats, a wooden pillow under his head, an opium pipe in his nerveless fingers. He did not seek, however, consolation in opium—perhaps it was too expensive—perhaps his white man's pride saved him from that degradation; but most likely it was the thought of his little daughter in the far-off Straits Settlements. He heard from her oftener since Abdulla bought a steamer, which ran now between Singapore and the Pantai settlement every three months or so. Almayer felt himself nearer his daughter. He longed to see her, and planned a voyage to Singapore, but put off his departure from year to year, always expecting some favourable turn of fortune. He did not want to meet her with empty hands and with no words of hope on his lips. He could not take her back into that savage life to which he was condemned himself. He was also a little afraid of her. What would she think of him? He reckoned the years. A grown woman. A civilized woman, young and hopeful; while he felt old and hopeless, and very much like those savages round him. He asked himself what was going to be her future. He could not answer that question yet, and he dared not face her. And yet he longed after her. He hesitated for years.

His hesitation was put an end to by Nina's unexpected appearance in Sambir. She arrived in the steamer under the captain's care. Almayer beheld her with surprise not unmixed with wonder. During those ten years the child had changed into a woman, black-haired, olive-skinned,

tall, and beautiful, with great sad eyes, where the startled
expression common to Malay womankind was modified
by a thoughtful tinge inherited from her European ancestry.
Almayer thought with dismay of the meeting of his wife
and daughter, of what this grave girl in European clothes
would think of her betel-nut chewing mother, squatting in
a dark hut, disorderly, half naked, and sulky. He also feared
an outbreak of temper on the part of that pest of a woman
he had hitherto managed to keep tolerably quiet, thereby
saving the remnants of his dilapidated furniture. And he
stood there before the closed door of the hut in the blazing
sunshine listening to the murmur of voices, wondering what
went on inside, wherefrom all the servant-maids had been
expelled at the beginning of the interview, and now stood
clustered by the palings with half-covered faces in a chatter
of curious speculation. He forgot himself there trying to
catch a stray word through the bamboo walls, till the captain of the steamer (who had walked up with the girl) fearing a sunstroke, took him under the arm and led him into
the shade of his own verandah where Nina's trunk stood
already, having been landed by the steamer's men. As soon
as Captain Ford had his glass before him and his cheroot
lighted, Almayer asked for the explanation of his daughter's unexpected arrival. Ford said little beyond generaliz-
ing in vague but violent terms upon the foolishness of
women in general, and of Mrs. Vinck in particular.

"You know, Kaspar," said he, in conclusion, to the excited Almayer, "it is deucedly awkward to have a half-caste
girl in the house. There's such a lot of fools about. There
was that young fellow from the bank who used to ride to
the Vinck bungalow early and late. That old woman
thought it was for that Emma of hers. When she found out
what he wanted exactly, there was a row, I can tell you.
She would not have Nina—not an hour longer—in the
house. Fact is, I heard of this affair and took the girl to my
wife. My wife is a pretty good woman—as women go—
and upon my word we would have kept the girl for you,
only she would not stay. Now, then! Don't flare up, Kaspar.

Sit still. What can you do? It is better so. Let her stay with you. She was never happy over there. Those two Vinck girls are no better than dressed-up monkeys. They slighted her. You can't make her white. It's no use you swearing at me. You can't. She is a good girl for all that, but she would not tell my wife anything. If you want to know, ask her yourself; but if I was you I would leave her alone. You are welcome to her passage money, old fellow, if you are short now." And the skipper, throwing away his cigar, walked off to "wake them up on board," as he expressed it.

Almayer vainly expected to hear of the cause of his daughter's return from his daughter's lips. Not that day, not on any other day did she ever allude to her Singapore life. He did not care to ask, awed by the calm impassiveness of her face, by those solemn eyes looking past him on the great, still forests sleeping in majestic repose to the murmur of the broad river. He accepted the situation, happy in the gentle and protecting affection the girl showed him, fitfully enough, for she had (as he called it) her bad days when she used to visit her mother and remain long hours in the riverside hut, coming out as inscrutable as ever, but with a contemptuous look and a short word ready to answer any of his speeches. He got used even to that, and on those days kept quiet, although greatly alarmed by his wife's influence upon the girl. Otherwise Nina adapted herself wonderfully to the circumstances of a half-savage and miserable life. She accepted without question or apparent disgust the neglect, the decay, the poverty of the household, the absence of furniture, and the preponderance of rice diet on the family table. She lived with Almayer in the little house (now sadly decaying) built originally by Lingard for the young couple. The Malays discussed eagerly her arrival. There were at the beginning crowded levées of Malay women with their children, seeking eagerly after "Ubat" for all the ills of the flesh from the young Mem Putih. In the cool of the evening grave Arabs in long white shirts and yellow sleeveless jackets walked slowly on the dusty path by the riverside towards Almayer's gate, and made solemn calls upon that Unbeliever under shallow pretences of business, only to get a glimpse of the young girl in a highly decorous manner. Even Lakamba came out of his stockade in a great pomp of war canoes and red umbrellas, and landed on the rotten little jetty of Lingard and Co. He came, he said, to buy a couple of brass guns as a present to his friend the chief of Sambir Dyaks; and while Almayer, suspicious but polite, busied himself in unearthing the old popguns in the godowns, the Rajah sat in an armchair on the verandah, surrounded by his respectful retinue waiting in vain for Nina's appearance. She was in one of her bad days, and remained in her mother's hut watching with her the ceremonious proceedings on the verandah. The Rajah departed, baffled but courteous, and soon Almayer began to reap the benefit of improved relations with the ruler in the shape of the recovery of some debts, paid to him with many apologies and many a low salaam by debtors till then considered hopelessly insolvent. Under these improving circumstances Almayer brightened up a little. All was not lost perhaps. Those Arabs and Malays saw at last that he was a man of some ability, he thought. And he began, after his manner, to plan great things, to dream of great fortunes for himself and Nina. Especially for Nina! Under these vivifying impulses he asked Captain Ford to write to his friends in England making inquiries after Lingard. Was he alive or dead? If dead, had he left any papers, documents; any indications or hints as to his great enterprise? Meantime he had found amongst the rubbish in one of the empty rooms a notebook belonging to the old adventurer. He studied the crabbed handwriting of its pages and often grew meditative over it. Other things also woke him up from his apathy. The stir made in the whole of the island by the establishment of the British Borneo Company affected even the sluggish flow of the Pantai life. Great changes were expected; annexation was talked of; the Arabs grew civil. Almayer began building his new house for the use of the future engineers, agents, or settlers of the new Company. He spent every available guilder on it with a confiding heart. One thing only disturbed his happiness; his wife came out of her seclusion, importing her green jacket, scant sarongs, shrill voice, and witch-like appearance, into his quiet life in the small bungalow. And his daughter seemed to accept that savage intrusion into their daily existence with wonderful equanimity. He did not like it, but dared say nothing.

CHAPTER 3

The deliberations conducted in London have a far-reaching importance, and so the decision issued from the fog-veiled offices of the Borneo Company darkened for Almayer the brilliant sunshine of the Tropics, and added another drop of bitterness to the cup of his disenchantments. The claim to that part of the East Coast was abandoned, leaving the Pantai river under the nominal power of Holland. In Sambir there was joy and excitement. The slaves were hurried out of sight into the forest and jungle, and the flags were run up to tall poles in the Rajah's compound in expectation of a visit from Dutch man-of-war boats.

The frigate remained anchored outside the mouth of the river, and the boats came up in tow of the steam launch, threading their way cautiously amongst a crowd of canoes filled with gaily dressed Malays. The officer in command listened gravely to the loyal speeches of Lakamba, returned the salaams of Abdulla, and assured those gentlemen in choice Malay of the great Rajah's—down in Batavia—friendship and good-will towards the ruler and inhabitants of this model state of Sambir.

Almayer from his verandah watched across the river the festive proceedings, heard the report of brass guns saluting the new flag presented to Lakamba, and the deep murmur

of the crowd of spectators surging round the stockade. The
smoke of the firing rose in white clouds on the green background of the forests, and he could not help comparing his
own fleeting hopes to the rapidly disappearing vapour. He
was by no means patriotically elated by the event, yet he
had to force himself into a gracious behaviour when, the
official reception being over, the naval officers of the Commission crossed the river to pay a visit to the solitary white
man of whom they had heard, no doubt wishing also to
catch a glimpse of his daughter. In that they were disappointed, Nina refusing to show herself; but they seemed
easily consoled by the gin and cheroots set before them
by the hospitable Almayer; and sprawling comfortably on
the lame armchairs under the shade of the verandah, while
the blazing sunshine outside seemed to set the great river
simmering in the heat, they filled the little bungalow with
the unusual sounds of European languages, with noise and
laughter produced by naval witticisms at the expense of the
fat Lakamba whom they had been complimenting so much
that very morning. The younger men in an access of good
fellowship made their host talk, and Almayer, excited by
the sight of European faces, by the sound of European
voices, opened his heart before the sympathizing strangers,
unaware of the amusement the recital of his many misfortunes caused to those future admirals. They drank his
health, wished him many big diamonds and a mountain of
gold, expressed even an envy of the high destinies awaiting
him yet. Encouraged by so much friendliness, the grey-
headed and foolish dreamer invited his guests to visit his
new house. They went there through the long grass in a
straggling procession while their boats were got ready for
the return down the river in the cool of the evening. And
in the great empty rooms where the tepid wind entering
through the sashless windows whirled gently the dried leaves
and the dust of many days of neglect, Almayer in his white
jacket and flowered sarong, surrounded by a circle of glittering uniforms, stamped his foot to show the solidity of the
neatly-fitting floors and expatiated upon the beauties and

convenience of the building. They listened and assented, amazed by the wonderful simplicity and the foolish hopefulness of the man, till Almayer, carried away by his excitement, disclosed his regret at the non-arrival of the English, "who knew how to develop a rich country," as he expressed it. There was a general laugh amongst the Dutch officers at that unsophisticated statement, and a move was made towards the boats; but when Almayer, stepping cautiously on the rotten boards of the Lingard jetty, tried to approach the chief of the Commission with some timid hints anent the protection required by the Dutch subject against the wily Arabs, that salt water diplomat told him significantly that the Arabs were better subjects than Hollanders who dealt illegally in gunpowder with the Malays. The innocent Almayer recognized there at once the oily tongue of Abdulla and the solemn persuasiveness of Lakamba, but ere he had time to frame an indignant protest the steam launch and the string of boats moved rapidly down the river leaving him on the jetty, standing open-mouthed in his surprise and anger. There are thirty miles of river from Sambir to the gem-like islands of the estuary where the frigate was awaiting the return of the boats. The moon rose long before the boats had traversed half that distance, and the black forest sleeping peacefully under her cold rays woke up that night to the ringing laughter in the small flotilla provoked by some reminiscence of Almayer's lamentable narrative. Salt-water jests at the poor man's expense were passed from boat to boat, the non-appearance of his daughter was commented upon with severe displeasure, and the half-finished house built for the reception of Englishmen received on that joyous night the name of "Almayer's Folly" by the unanimous vote of the lighthearted seamen.

For many weeks after this visit life in Sambir resumed its even and uneventful flow. Each day's sun shooting its morning rays above the tree-tops lit up the usual scene of daily activity. Nina walking on the path that formed the only street in the settlement saw the accustomed sight of men lolling on the shady side of the houses, on the high

platforms; of women busily engaged in husking the daily
rice; of naked brown children racing along the shady and
narrow paths leading to the clearings. Jim-Eng, strolling
before his house, greeted her with a friendly nod before
climbing up indoors to seek his beloved opium pipe. The
elder children clustered round her, daring from long acquaintance, pulling the skirts of her white robe with their
dark fingers, and showing their brilliant teeth in expectation of a shower of glass beads. She greeted them with a
quiet smile, but always had a few friendly words for a
Siamese girl, a slave owned by Bulangi, whose numerous
wives were said to be of a violent temper. Well-founded
rumour said also that the domestic squabbles of that industrious cultivator ended generally in a combined assault of
all his wives upon the Siamese slave. The girl herself never
complained—perhaps from dictates of prudence, but more
likely through the strange, resigned apathy of half-savage
womankind. From early morning she was to be seen on the
paths amongst the houses—by the riverside or on the jet-
ties, the tray of pastry, it was her mission to sell, skilfully
balanced on her head. During the great heat of the day she
usually sought refuge in Almayer's campong, often finding
shelter in a shady corner of the verandah, where she squatted with her tray before her, when invited by Nina. For
"Mem Putih" she had always a smile, but the presence of
Mrs. Almayer, the very sound of her shrill voice, was the
signal for a hurried departure.

To this girl Nina often spoke; the other inhabitants of
Sambir seldom or never heard the sound of her voice. They
got used to the silent figure moving in their midst calm and
white-robed, a being from another world and incomprehensible to them. Yet Nina's life for all her outward composure, for all the seeming detachment from the things
and people surrounding her, was far from quiet, in consequence of Mrs. Almayer being much too active for the happiness and even safety of the household. She had resumed
some intercourse with Lakamba, not personally, it is true
(for the dignity of that potentate kept him inside his stock-

ade), but through the agency of that potentate's prime minister, harbour master, financial adviser, and general factotum. That gentleman—of Sulu origin—was certainly endowed with statesmanlike qualities, although he was totally devoid of personal charms. In truth he was perfectly repulsive, possessing only one eye and a pock-marked face, with nose and lips horribly disfigured by the smallpox. This unengaging individual often strolled into Almayer's garden in unofficial costume, composed of a piece of pink calico round his waist. There at the back of the house, squatting on his heels on scattered embers, in close proximity to the great iron boiler, where the family daily rice was being cooked by the women under Mrs. Almayer's superintendence, did that astute negotiator carry on long conversations in Sulu language with Almayer's wife. What the subject of their discourses was might have been guessed from the subsequent domestic scenes by Almayer's hearthstone.

Of late Almayer had taken to excursions up the river. In a small canoe with two paddlers and the faithful Ali for a steersman he would disappear for a few days at a time. All his movements were no doubt closely watched by Lakamba and Abdulla, for the man once in the confidence of Rajah Laut was supposed to be in possession of valuable secrets. The coast population of Borneo believes implicity in diamonds of fabulous value, in gold mines of enormous richness in the interior. And all those imaginings are heightened by the difficulty of penetrating far inland, especially on the northeast coast, where the Malays and the river tribes of Dyaks or Head-hunters are eternally quarrelling. It is true enough that some gold reaches the coast in the hands of those Dyaks when, during short periods of truce in the desultory warfare, they visit the coast settlements of Malays. And so the wildest exaggerations are built up and added to on the slight basis of that fact.

Almayer in his quality of white man—as Lingard before him—had somewhat better relations with the upriver tribes. Yet even his excursions were not without danger, and his returns were eagerly looked for by the impatient Lakamba.

But every time the Rajah was disappointed. Vain were the conferences by the rice-pot of his factotum Babalatchi with the white man's wife. The white man himself was impenetrable—impenetrable to persuasion, coaxing, abuse; to soft words and shrill revilings; to desperate beseechings or murderous threats; for Mrs. Almayer, in her extreme desire to persuade her husband into an alliance with Lakamba, played upon the whole gamut of passion. With her soiled robe wound tightly under the armpits across her lean bosom, her scant greyish hair tumbled in disorder over her projecting cheek-bones, in suppliant attitude, she depicted with shrill volubility the advantages of close union with a man so good and so fair dealing.

"Why don't you go to the Rajah?" she screamed. "Why do you go back to those Dyaks in the great forest? They should be killed. You cannot kill them, you cannot; but our Rajah's men are brave! You tell the Rajah where the old white man's treasure is. Our Rajah is good! He is our very grandfather. He will kill those wretched Dyaks, and you shall have half the treasure. Oh, Kaspar, tell where the treasure is! Tell me! Tell me out of the old man's surat where you read so often at night."

On those occasions Almayer sat with rounded shoulders bending to the blast of this domestic tempest, accentuating only each pause in the torrent of his wife's eloquence by an angry growl, "There is no treasure! Go away, woman!" Exasperated by the sight of his patiently bent back, she would at last walk round so as to face him across the table, and clasping her robe with one hand she stretched the other lean arm and clawlike hand to emphasize, in a passion of anger and contempt, the rapid rush of scathing remarks and bitter cursings heaped on the head of the man unworthy to associate with brave Malay chiefs. It ended generally by Almayer rising slowly, his long pipe in hand, his face set into a look of inward pain, and walking away in silence. He descended the steps and plunged into the long grass on his way to the solitude of his new house, dragging his feet in a state of physical collapse from disgust and fear before that fury. She followed to the head of the steps, and sent the shafts of indiscriminate abuse after the retreating form. And each of those scenes was concluded by a piercing shriek, reaching him far away. "You know, Kaspar, I am your wife! your own Christian wife after your own Blanda law!" For she knew that this was the bitterest thing of all; the greatest regret of that man's life.

All these scenes Nina witnessed unmoved. She might have been deaf, dumb, without any feeling as far as any expression of opinion went. Yet oft when her father had sought the refuge of the great dusty rooms of "Almayer's Folly," and her mother, exhausted by rhetorical efforts, squatted wearily on her heels with her back against the leg of the table, Nina would approach her curiously, guarding her skirts from betel juice besprinkling the floor, and gaze down upon her as one might look into the quiescent crater of a volcano after a destructive eruption. Mrs. Almayer's thoughts after these scenes were usually turned into a channel of childhood reminiscences, and she gave them utterance in a kind of monotonous recitative—slightly disconnected, but generally describing the glories of the Sultan of Sulu, his great splendour, his power, his great prowess, the fear which benumbed the hearts of white men at the sight of his swift piratical praus. And these muttered statements of her grandfather's might were mixed up with bits of later recollections, where the great fight with the "White Devil's" brig and the convent life in Samarang occupied the principal place. At that point she usually dropped the thread of her narrative, and pulling out the little brass cross, always suspended round her neck, she contemplated it with superstitious awe. That superstitious feeling connected with some vague talismanic properties of the little bit of metal and the still more hazy but terrible notion of some bad Djinns and horrible torments invented, as she thought, for her especial punishment by the good Mother Superior in case of the loss of the above charm, were Mrs. Almayer's only theological outfit for the stormy road of life. Mrs. Almayer had at least something tangible to cling to, but Nina,

brought up under the Protestant wing of the proper Mrs.
Vinck, had not even a little piece of brass to remind her of
past teaching. And listening to the recital of those savage
glories, those barbarous fights and savage feasting, to the
story of deeds valorous, albeit somewhat bloodthirsty,
where men of her mother's race shone far above the Orang
Blanda, she felt herself irresistibly fascinated, and saw with
vague surprise the narrow mantle of civilized morality, in
which good-meaning people had wrapped her young soul,
fall away and leave her shivering and helpless as if on the
edge of some deep and unknown abyss. Strangest of all, this
abyss did not frighten her when she was under the influence
of the witch-like being she called her mother. She seemed
to have forgotten in civilized surroundings her life before
the time when Lingard had, so to speak, kidnapped her
from Brow. Since then she had had Christian teaching, social education, and a good glimpse of civilized life. Unfor-
tunately her teachers did not understand her nature, and the
education ended in a scene of humiliation, in an outburst of
contempt from white people for her mixed blood. And now
she had lived on the river for three years with a savage
mother and a father walking about amongst pitfalls, with
his head in the clouds, weak, irresolute, and unhappy. She
had lived a life devoid of all the decencies of civilization,
in miserable domestic conditions; she had breathed the atmosphere of sordid plottings for gain, of the no less disgust-
ing intrigues and crimes for lust or money; and those things,
together with the domestic quarrels, were the only events
of her three years' existence. She did not die from despair
and disgust the first month, as she expected and almost
hoped for. On the contrary, at the end of half a year it had
seemed to her that she had known no other life. Her young
mind having been unskilfully permitted to glance at better
things, and then thrown back again into the hopeless quag-
mire of barbarism, full of strong and uncontrolled passions,
had lost the power to discriminate. It seemed to Nina that
there was no change and no difference. Whether they traded
in brick godowns or on the muddy river bank; whether

they reached after much or little; whether they made love
under the shadows of the great trees or in the shadow of
the cathedral on the Singapore promenade; whether they
plotted for their own ends under the protection of laws and
according to the rules of Christian conduct, or whether
they sought the gratification of their desires with the savage
cunning and the unrestrained fierceness of natures as innocent of culture as their own immense and gloomy forests,
Nina saw only the same manifestations of love and hate and
of sordid greed chasing the uncertain dollar in all its multi-
farious and vanishing shapes. To her resolute nature, however, after all these years, the savage and uncompromising
sincerity of purpose shown by her Malay kinsmen seemed
at last preferable to the sleek hypocrisy, to the polite dis-
guises, to the virtuous pretences of such white people as she
had had the misfortune to come in contact with. After all
it was her life; it was going to be her life, and so thinking
she fell more and more under the influence of her mother.
Seeking, in her ignorance, a better side to that life, she listened with avidity to the old woman's tales of the departed
glories of the Rajahs, from whose race she had sprung, and
she became gradually more indifferent, more contemptuous of the white side of her descent represented by a feeble
and traditionless father.

Almayer's difficulties were by no means diminished by
the girl's presence in Sambir. The stir caused by her arrival
had died out, it is true, and Lakamba had not renewed his
visits; but about a year after the departure of the man-of-
war boats the nephew of Abdulla, Syed Reshid, returned
from his pilgrimage to Mecca, rejoicing in a green jacket
and the proud title of Hadji. There was a great letting off of
rockets on board the steamer which brought him in, and a
great beating of drums all night in Abdulla's compound,
while the feast of welcome was prolonged far into the small
hours of the morning. Reshid was the favourite nephew and
heir of Abdulla, and that loving uncle, meeting Almayer
one day by the riverside, stopped politely to exchange civili-
ties and to ask solemnly for an interview. Almayer sus-

pected some attempt at a swindle, or at any rate something unpleasant, but of course consented with a great show of rejoicing. Accordingly the next evening, after sunset, Abdulla came, accompanied by several other grey-beards and by his nephew. That young man—of a very rakish and dissipated appearance—affected the greatest indifference as to the whole of the proceedings. When the torch-bearers had grouped themselves below the steps, the visitors had seated themselves on various lame chairs, Reshid stood apart in the shadow, examining his aristocratically small hands with great attention. Almayer, surprised by the great solemnity of his visitors, perched himself on the corner of the table with a characteristic want of dignity quickly noted by the Arabs with grave disapproval. But Abdulla spoke now, looking straight past Almayer at the red curtain hanging in the doorway, where a slight tremor disclosed the presence of women on the other side. He began by neatly complimenting Almayer upon the long years they had dwelt together in cordial neighbourhood, and called upon Allah to give him many more years to gladden the eyes of his friends by his welcome presence. He made a polite allusion to the great consideration shown him (Almayer) by the Dutch "Commissie," and drew thence the flattering inference of Almayer's great importance amongst his own people. He— Abdulla—was also important amongst all the Arabs, and his nephew Reshid would be heir of that social position and of great riches. Now Reshid was a Hadji. He was possessor of several Malay women, went on Abdulla, but it was time he had a favourite wife, the first of the four allowed by the Prophet. And, speaking with well-bred politeness, he explained further to the dumbfounded Almayer that, if he would consent to the alliance of his offspring with that true believer and virtuous man Reshid, she would be mistress of all the splendours of Reshid's house, the first wife of the first Arab in the Islands, when he—Abdulla—had been called to the joys of Paradise by Allah the All-merciful. "You know, Tuan," he said, in conclusion, "the other women would be her slaves, and Reshid's house is great.

From Bombay he has brought great divans, and costly carpets, and European furniture. There is also a great looking-glass in a frame shining like gold. What could a girl want more?" And while Almayer looked upon him in silent dismay Abdulla spoke in a more confidential tone, waving his attendants away, and finished his speech by pointing out the material advantages of such an alliance, and offering to settle upon Almayer three thousand dollars as a sign of his sincere friendship and the price of the girl.

Poor Almayer was nearly having a fit. Burning with the desire of taking Abdulla by the throat, he had but to think of his helpless position in the midst of lawless men to comprehend the necessity of diplomatic conciliation. He mastered his impulses, and spoke politely and coldly, saying the girl was young and was the apple of his eye. Tuan Reshid, a Faithful and a Hadji, would not want an infidel woman in his harem; and, seeing Abdulla smile sceptically at that last objection, he remained silent, not trusting himself to speak more, not daring to refuse point-blank, nor yet to say anything compromising. Abdulla understood the meaning of that silence, and rose to take leave with a grave salaam. He wished his friend Almayer "a thousand years," and moved down the steps, helped dutifully by Reshid. The torch-bearers shook their torches, scattering a shower of sparks into the river, and the cortège moved off, leaving Almayer agitated but greatly relieved by their departure. He dropped into a chair and watched the glimmer of the lights amongst the tree trunks till they disappeared and complete silence succeeded the tramp of feet and the murmur of voices. He did not move till the curtain rustled and Nina came out on the verandah and sat in the rocking-chair, where she used to spend many hours every day. She gave a slight rocking motion to her seat, leaning back with half-closed eyes, her long hair shading her face from the smoky light of the lamp on the table. Almayer looked at her furtively, but the face was as impassible as ever. She turned her head slightly towards her father, and, speaking, to his great surprise, in English, asked—

"Was that Abdulla here?"

"Yes," said Almayer—"just gone."

"And what did he want, father?"

"He wanted to buy you for Reshid," answered Almayer, brutally, his anger getting the better of him, and looking at the girl as if in expectation of some outbreak of feeling. But Nina remained apparently unmoved, gazing dreamily into the black night outside.

"Be careful, Nina," said Almayer, after a short silence and rising from his chair, "when you go paddling alone into the creeks in your canoe. That Reshid is a violent scoundrel, and there is no saying what he may do. Do you hear me?"

She was standing now, ready to go in, one hand grasping the curtain in the doorway. She turned round, throwing her heavy tresses back by a sudden gesture.

"Do you think he would dare?" she asked, quickly, and then turned again to go in, adding in a lower tone, "He would not dare. Arabs are all cowards."

Almayer looked after her, astonished. He did not seek the repose of his hammock. He walked the floor absently, sometimes stopping by the balustrade to think. The lamp went out. The first streak of dawn broke over the forest; Almayer shivered in the damp air. "I give it up," he muttered to himself, lying down wearily. "Damn those women! Well! If the girl did not look as if she wanted to be kidnapped!"

And he felt a nameless fear creep into his heart, making him shiver again.

CHAPTER 4

That year, towards the breaking up of the southwest monsoon, disquieting rumours reached Sambir. Captain Ford,

coming up to Almayer's house for an evening's chat,
brought late numbers of the *Straits Times* giving the news
of Acheen war and of the unsuccessful Dutch expedition.
The Nakhodas of the rare trading praus ascending the river
paid visits to Lakamba, discussing with that potentate the
unsettled state of affairs, and wagged their heads gravely
over the recital of Orang Blanda exaction, severity, and
general tyranny, as exemplified in the total stoppage of
gunpowder trade and the rigorous visiting of all suspicious
craft trading in the straits of Macassar. Even the loyal soul
of Lakamba was stirred into a state of inward discontent by
the withdrawal of his licence for powder and by the abrupt
confiscation of one hundred and fifty barrels of that com-
modity by the gunboat *Princess Amelia*, when, after a
hazardous voyage, it had almost reached the mouth of the
river. The unpleasant news was given him by Reshid, who,
after the unsuccessful issue of his matrimonial projects, had
made a long voyage amongst the islands for trading purposes; had bought the powder for his friend, and was over-
hauled and deprived of it on his return when actually con-
gratulating himself on his acuteness in avoiding detection.
Reshid's wrath was principally directed against Almayer,
whom he suspected of having notified the Dutch authorities
of the desultory warfare carried on by the Arabs and the
Rajah with the up-river Dyak tribes.

To Reshid's great surprise the Rajah received his com-
plaints very coldly, and showed no signs of vengeful disposition towards the white man. In truth, Lakamba knew
very well that Almayer was perfectly innocent of any meddling in state affairs; and besides, his attitude towards that
much persecuted individual was wholly changed in consequence of a reconciliation effected between him and his old
enemy by Almayer's newly-found friend, Dain Maroola.

Almayer had now a friend. Shortly after Reshid's departure on his commercial journey, Nina, drifting slowly with
the tide in the canoe on her return home after one of her
solitary excursions, heard in one of the small creeks a

splashing of heavy ropes dropping in the water and the prolonged song of Malay seamen when some heavy pulling is to be done. Through the thick fringe of bushes hiding the mouth of the creek she saw the tall spars of some European-rigged sailing vessel overtopping the summits of the Nipa palms. A brig was being hauled out of the small creek into the main stream. The sun had set, and during the short moments of twilight Nina saw the brig, aided by the evening breeze and the flowing tide, head towards Sambir under her set foresail. The girl turned her canoe out of the main river into one of the many narrow channels amongst the wooded islets, and paddled vigorously over the black and sleepy backwaters towards Sambir. Her canoe brushed the water-palms, skirted the short spaces of muddy bank where sedate alligators looked at her with lazy unconcern, and, just as darkness was setting in, shot out into the broad junction of the two main branches of the river, where the brig was already at anchor with sails furled, yards squared, and decks seemingly untenanted by any human being. Nina had to cross the river and pass pretty close to the brig in order to reach home on the low promontory between the two branches of the Pantai. Up both branches, in the houses built on the banks and over the water, the lights twinkled already, reflected in the still waters below. The hum of voices, the occasional cry of a child, the rapid and abruptly interrupted roll of a wooden drum, together with some distant hailing in the darkness by the returning fishermen, reached her over the broad expanse of the river. She hesitated a little before crossing, the sight of such an unusual object as an European-rigged vessel causing her some uneasiness, but the river in its wide expansion was dark enough to render a small canoe invisible. She urged her small craft with swift strokes of her paddle, kneeling in the bottom and bending forward to catch any suspicious sound while she steered towards the little jetty of Lingard and Co., to which the strong light of the paraffin lamp shining on the whitewashed verandah of Almayer's bungalow served as a convenient guide. The jetty itself, under the shadow of the bank overgrown by drooping bushes, was hidden in darkness. Before even she could see it she heard the hollow bumping of a large boat against its rotten posts, and heard also the murmur of whispered conversation in that boat whose white paint and great dimensions, faintly visible on nearer approach, made her rightly guess that it belonged to the brig just anchored. Stopping her course by a rapid motion of her paddle, with another swift stroke she sent it whirling away from the wharf and steered for a little rivulet which gave access to the back courtyard of the house. She landed at the muddy head of the creek and made her way towards the house over the trodden grass of the courtyard. To the left, from the cooking shed, shone a red glare through the banana plantation she skirted, and the noise of feminine laughter reached her from there in the silent evening. She rightly judged her mother was not near, laughter and Mrs. Almayer not being close neighbours. She must be in the house, thought Nina, as she ran lightly up the inclined plane of shaky planks leading to the back door of the narrow passage dividing the house in two. Outside the doorway, in the black shadow, stood the faithful Ali.

"Who is there?" asked Nina.

"A great Malay man has come," answered Ali, in a tone of suppressed excitement. "He is a rich man. There are six men with lances. Real Soldat, you understand. And his dress is very brave. I have seen his dress. It shines! What jewels! Don't go there, Mem Nina. Tuan said not; but the old Mem is gone. Tuan will be angry. Merciful Allah! what jewels that man has got!"

Nina slipped past the outstretched hand of the slave into the dark passage where, in the crimson glow of the hanging curtain, close by its other end, she could see a small dark form crouching near the wall. Her mother was feasting her eyes and ears with what was taking place on the front verandah, and Nina approached to take her share in the rare pleasure of some novelty. She was met by her mother's extended arm and by a low murmured warning not to make a noise.

"Have you seen them, mother?" asked Nina, in a breathless whisper.

Mrs. Almayer turned her face towards the girl, and her sunken eyes shone strangely in the red half-light of the passage.

"I saw him," she said, in an almost inaudible tone, pressing her daughter's hand with her bony fingers. "A great Rajah has come to Sambir—a Son of Heaven," muttered the old woman to herself. "Go away, girl!"

The two women stood close to the curtain, Nina wishing to approach the rent in the stuff, and her mother defending the position with angry obstinacy. On the other side there was a lull in the conversation, but the occasional light tinkling of some ornaments, the clink of metal scabbards, or of brass siri-vessels passed from hand to hand, was audible during the short pause. The women struggled silently, when there was a shuffling noise and the shadow of Almayer's burly form fell on the curtain.

The women ceased struggling and remained motionless. Almayer had stood up to answer his guest, turning his back to the doorway, unaware of what was going on on the other side. He spoke in a tone of regretful irritation.

"You have come to the wrong house, Tuan Maroola, if you want to trade as you say. I was a trader once, not now, whatever you may have heard about me in Macassar. And if you want anything, you will not find it here; I have nothing to give, and want nothing myself. You should go to the Rajah here; you can see in the daytime his houses across the river, there, where those fires are burning on the shore. He will help you and trade with you. Or, better still, go to the Arabs over there," he went on bitterly, pointing with his hand towards the houses of Sambir. "Abdulla is the man you want. There is nothing he would not buy, and there is nothing he would not sell; believe me, I know him well."

He waited for an answer a short time, then added—

"All that I have said is true, and there is nothing more."

Nina, held back by her mother, heard a soft voice reply

with a calm evenness of intonation peculiar to the better class Malays—

"Who would doubt a white Tuan's words? A man seeks his friends where his heart tells him. Is this not true also? I have come, although so late, for I have something to say which you may be glad to hear. To-morrow I shall go to the Sultan; a trader wants the friendship of great men. Then I shall return here to speak serious words, if Tuan permits. I shall not go to the Arabs; their lies are very great! What are they? Chelakka!"

Almayer's voice sounded a little more pleasantly in reply.

"Well, as you like. I can hear you to-morrow at any time if you have anything to say. Bah! After you have seen the Sultan Lakamba you will not want to return here, Inchi Dain. You will see. Only mind, I will have nothing to do with Lakamba. You may tell him so. What is your business with me, after all?"

"To-morrow we talk, Tuan, now I know you," answered the Malay. "I speak English a little, so we can talk and nobody will understand, and then—"

He interrupted himself suddenly, asking surprised, "What's that noise, Tuan?"

Almayer had also heard the increasing noise of the scuffle recommenced on the women's side of the curtain. Evidently Nina's strong curiosity was on the point of overcoming Mrs. Almayer's exalted sense of social proprieties. Hard breathing was distinctly audible, and the curtain shook during the contest, which was mainly physical, although Mrs. Almayer's voice was heard in angry remonstrance with its usual want of strictly logical reasoning, but with the well-known richness of invective.

"You shameless woman! Are you a slave?" shouted shrilly the irate matron. "Veil your face, abandoned wretch! You white snake, I will not let you!"

Almayer's face expressed annoyance and also doubt as to the advisability of interfering between mother and daughter. He glanced at his Malay visitor, who was waiting silently for the end of the uproar in an attitude of amused expectation, and waving his hand contemptuously he murmured—

"It is nothing. Some women."

The Malay nodded his head gravely, and his face assumed an expression of serene indifference, as etiquette demanded after such an explanation. The contest was ended behind the curtain, and evidently the younger will had its way, for the rapid shuffle and click of Mrs. Almayer's high-heeled sandals died away in the distance. The tranquillized master of the house was going to resume the conversation when, struck by an unexpected change in the expression of his guest's countenance, he turned his head and saw Nina standing in the doorway.

After Mrs. Almayer's retreat from the field of battle, Nina, with a contemptuous exclamation, "It's only a trader," had lifted the conquered curtain and now stood in full light, framed in the dark background of the passage, her lips slightly parted, her hair in disorder after the exertion, the angry gleam not yet faded out of her glorious and sparkling eyes. She took in at a glance the group of white-clad lancemen standing motionless in the shadow of the far-off end of the verandah, and her gaze rested curiously on the chief of that imposing cortège. He stood, almost facing her, a little on one side, and struck by the beauty of the unexpected apparition had bent low, elevating his joint hands above his head in a sign of respect accorded by Malays only to the great of this earth. The crude light of the lamp shone on the gold embroidery of his black silk jacket, broke in a thousand sparkling rays on the jeweled hilt of his kriss protruding from under the many folds of the red sarong gathered into a sash round his waist, and played on the precious stones of the many rings on his dark fingers. He straightened himself up quickly after the low bow, putting his hand with a graceful ease on the hilt of his heavy short sword ornamented with brilliantly dyed fringes of horsehair. Nina, hesitating on the threshold, saw an erect lithe figure of medium height with a breadth of shoulder suggesting great power. Under the folds of a blue turban, whose fringed ends hung gracefully over the left shoulder, was a face full of determination and expressing a reckless good-humour, not devoid, however, of some dignity. The squareness of lower jaw, the full red lips, the mobile nostrils, and the proud carriage of the head gave the impression of a being half-savage, untamed, perhaps cruel, and corrected the liquid softness of the almost feminine eye, that general characteristic of the race. Now, the first surprise over, Nina saw those eyes fixed upon her with such an uncontrolled expression of admiration and desire that she felt a hitherto unknown feeling of shyness, mixed with alarm and some delight, enter and penetrate her whole being. Confused by those unusual sensations she stopped in the doorway and instinctively drew the lower part of the curtain across her face, leaving only half a rounded cheek, a stray tress, and one eye exposed, wherewith to contemplate the gorgeous and bold being so unlike in appearance to the rare specimens of traders she had seen before on that same verandah.

Dain Maroola, dazzled by the unexpected vision, forgot the confused Almayer, forgot his brig, his escort staring in open-mouthed admiration, the object of his visit and all things else, in his overpowering desire to prolong the contemplation of so much loveliness met so suddenly in such an unlikely place—as he thought.

"It is my daughter," said Almayer, in an embarrassed manner. "It is of no consequence. White women have their customs, as you know, Tuan, having travelled much, as you say. However, it is late; we will finish our talk to-morrow."

Dain bent low trying to convey in a last glance towards the girl the bold expression of his overwhelming admiration. The next minute he was shaking Almayer's hand with grave courtesy, his face wearing a look of stolid unconcern as to any feminine presence. His men filed off, and he followed them quickly, closely attended by a thick-set, savage-looking Sumatrese he had introduced before as the commander of his brig. Nina walked to the balustrade of the verandah and saw the sheen of moonlight on the steel spear-heads and heard the rhythmic jingle of brass anklets as the men moved in single file towards the jetty. The boat shoved off after a little while, looming large in the full light of the moon, a black shapeless mass in the slight haze hanging over the water. Nina fancied she could distinguish the graceful figure of the trader standing erect in the stern sheets, but in a little while all the outlines got blurred, con-fused, and soon disappeared in the folds of white vapour shrouding the middle of the river.

Almayer had approached his daughter, and leaning with both arms over the rail, was looking moodily down on the heap of rubbish at the foot of the verandah.

"What was all that noise just now?" he growled peevishly, without looking up. "Confound you and your mother! What did she want? What did you come out for?"

"She did not want to let me come out," said Nina. "She is angry. She says the man just gone is some Rajah. I think she is right now."

"I believe all you women are crazy," snarled Almayer. "What's that to you, to her, to anybody? The man wants to collect trepang and birds' nests on the islands. He told me so, that Rajah of yours. He will come to-morrow. I want you both to keep away from the house, and let me attend to my business in peace."

Dain Maroola came the next day and had a long con-versation with Almayer. This was the beginning of a close and friendly intercourse which, at first, was much remarked in Sambir, till the population got used to the frequent sight of many fires burning in Almayer's campong, where Ma-roola's men were warming themselves during the cold nights of the northeast monsoon, while their master had long conferences with the Tuan Putih—as they styled Al-mayer amongst themselves. Great was the curiosity in Sam-bir on the subject of the new trader. Had he seen the Sul-tan? What did the Sultan say? Had he given any presents? What would he sell? What would he buy? Those were the questions broached eagerly by the inhabitants of bamboo

houses built over the river. Even in more substantial buildings, in Abdulla's house, in the residences of principal
traders, Arab, Chinese, and Bugis, the excitement ran high,
and lasted many days. With inborn suspicion they would
not believe the simple account of himself the young trader
was always ready to give. Yet it had all the appearance of
truth. He said he was a trader, and sold rice. He did not
want to buy gutta-percha or beeswax, because he intended
to employ his numerous crew in collecting trepang on the
coral reefs outside the river, and also in seeking for birds'
nests on the mainland. Those two articles he professed
himself ready to buy if there were any to be obtained in
that way. He said he was from Bali, and a Brahmin, which
last statement he made good by refusing all food during
his often repeated visits to Lakamba's and Almayer's
houses. To Lakamba he went generally at night and had
long audiences. Babalatchi, who was always a third party
at those meetings of potentate and trader, knew how to
resist all attempts on the part of the curious to ascertain
the subject of so many long talks. When questioned with
languid courtesy by the grave Abdulla he sought refuge
in a vacant stare of his one eye, and in the affectation of
extreme simplicity.

"I am only my master's slave," murmured Babalatchi, in
a hesitating manner. Then as if making up his mind suddenly for a reckless confidence he would inform Abdulla
of some transaction in rice, repeating the words, "A hundred big bags the Sultan bought; a hundred, Tuan!" in a
tone of mysterious solemnity. Abdulla, firmly persuaded of
the existence of some more important dealings, received,
however, the information with all the signs of respectful astonishment. And the two would separate, the Arab cursing
inwardly the wily dog, while Babalatchi went on his way
walking on the dusty path, his body swaying, his chin with
its few grey hairs pushed forward, resembling an inquisitive goat bent on some unlawful expedition. Attentive eyes
watched his movements. Jim-Eng, descrying Babalatchi far
away, would shake off the stupor of an habitual opium

smoker and, tottering on to the middle of the road, would await the approach of that important person ready with hospitable invitation. But Babalatchi's discretion was proof even against the combined assaults of good fellowship and of strong gin generously administered by the openhearted Chinaman. Jim-Eng, owning himself beaten, was left uninformed with the empty bottle, and gazed sadly after the departing form of the statesman of Sambir pursuing his devious and unsteady way, which, as usual, led him to Almayer's compound. Ever since a reconciliation had been effected by Dain Maroola between his white friend and the Rajah, the one-eyed diplomatist had again become a frequent guest in the Dutchman's house. To Almayer's great disgust he was to be seen there at all times, strolling about in an abstracted kind of way on the verandah, skulking in the passages, or else popping round unexpected corners, always willing to engage Mrs. Almayer in confidential conversation. He was very shy of the master himself, as if suspicious that the pent-up feelings of the white man towards his person might find vent in a sudden kick. But the cooking shed was his favourite place, and he became an habitual guest there, squatting for hours amongst the busy women, with his chin resting on his knees, his lean arms clasped round his legs, and his one eye roving uneasily— the very picture of watchful ugliness. Almayer wanted more than once to complain to Lakamba of his Prime Minister's intrusion, but Dain dissuaded him. "We cannot say a word here that he does not hear," growled Almayer.

"Then come and talk on board the brig," retorted Dain, with a quiet smile. "It is good to let the man come here. Lakamba thinks he knows much. Perhaps the Sultan thinks I want to run away. Better let the one-eyed crocodile sun himself in your campong, Tuan."

And Almayer assented unwillingly muttering vague threats of personal violence, while he eyed malevolently the aged statesman sitting with quiet obstinacy by his domestic rice-pot.

CHAPTER 5

At last the excitement had died out in Sambir. The inhabitants got used to the sight of comings and goings between Almayer's house and the vessel, now moored to the
opposite bank, and speculation as to the feverish activity
displayed by Almayer's boatmen in repairing old canoes
ceased to interfere with the due discharge of domestic duties
by the women of the Settlement. Even the baffled Jim-Eng
left off troubling his muddled brain with secrets of trade,
and relapsed by the aid of his opium pipe into a state of
stupefied bliss, letting Babalatchi pursue his way past his
house uninvited and seemingly unnoticed.

So on that warm afternoon, when the deserted river
sparkled under the vertical sun, the statesman of Sambir
could, without any hindrance from friendly inquirers, shove
off his little canoe from under the bushes, where it was
usually hidden during his visits to Almayer's compound.
Slowly and languidly Babalatchi paddled, crouching low
in the boat, making himself small under his enormous sun
hat to escape the scorching heat reflected from the water.
He was not in a hurry; his master, Lakamba, was surely
reposing at this time of the day. He would have ample time
to cross over and greet him on his waking with important
news. Will he be displeased? Will he strike his ebony wood
staff angrily on the floor, frightening him by the incoherent
violence of his exclamations; or will he squat down with
a good-humoured smile, and, rubbing his hands gently
over his stomach with a familiar gesture, expectorate copi-
ously into the brass siri-vessel, giving vent to a low, approbative murmur? Such were Babalatchi's thoughts as he

skilfully handled his paddle, crossing the river on his way to the Rajah's campong, whose stockades showed from behind the dense foliage of the bank just opposite to Almayer's bungalow.

Indeed, he had a report to make. Something certain at last to confirm the daily tale of suspicions, the daily hints of familiarity, of stolen glances he had seen, of short and burning words he had overheard exchanged between Dain Maroola and Almayer's daughter. Lakamba had, till then, listened to it all, calmly and with evident distrust; now he was going to be convinced, for Babalatchi had the proof; had it this very morning, when fishing at break of day in the creek over which stood Bulangi's house. There from his skiff he saw Nina's long canoe drift past, the girl sitting in the stern bending over Dain, who was stretched in the bottom with his head resting on the girl's knees. He saw it. He followed them, but in a short time they took to the paddles and got away from under his observant eye. A few minutes afterwards he saw Bulangi's slave-girl paddling in a small dug-out to the town with her cakes for sale. She also had seen them in the grey dawn. And Babalatchi grinned confidentially to himself at the recollection of the slave-girl's discomposed face, of the hard look in her eyes, of the tremble in her voice, when answering his questions. That little Taminah evidently admired Dain Maroola. That was good! And Babalatchi laughed aloud at the notion; then becoming suddenly serious, he began by some strange association of ideas to speculate upon the price for which Bulangi would, possibly, sell the girl. He shook his head sadly at the thought that Bulangi was a hard man, and had refused one hundred dollars for that same Taminah only a few weeks ago; then he became suddenly aware that the canoe had drifted too far down during his meditation. He shook off the despondency caused by the certitude of Bulangi's mercenary disposition, and, taking up his paddle, in a few strokes sheered alongside the water-gate of the Rajah's house.

That afternoon Almayer, as was his wont lately, moved

about on the water-side, overlooking the repairs to his boats. He had decided at last. Guided by the scraps of information contained in old Lingard's pocket-book, he was going to seek for the rich gold-mine, for that place where he had only to stoop to gather up an immense fortune and realize the dream of his young days. To obtain the necessary help he had shared his knowledge with Dain Maroola, he had consented to be reconciled with Lakamba, who gave his support to the enterprise on condition of sharing the profits; he had sacrificed his pride, his honour, and his loyalty in the face of the enormous risk of his undertaking, dazzled by the greatness of the results to be achieved by this alliance so distasteful yet so necessary. The dangers were great, but Maroola was brave; his men seemed as reckless as their chief, and with Lakamba's aid success seemed assured.

For the last fortnight Almayer was absorbed in the preparations, walking amongst his workmen and slaves in a kind of waking trance, where practical details as to the fitting out of the boats were mixed up with vivid dreams of untold wealth, where the present misery of burning sun, of the muddy and malodorous river bank disappeared in a gorgeous vision of a splendid future existence for himself and Nina. He hardly saw Nina during these last days, although the beloved daughter was ever present in his thoughts. He hardly took notice of Dain, whose constant presence in his house had become a matter of course to him now they were connected by a community of interests. When meeting the young chief he gave him an absent greeting and passed on, seemingly wishing to avoid him, bent upon forgetting the hated reality of the present by absorbing himself in his work, or else by letting his imagination soar far above the tree-tops into the great white clouds away to the westward, where the paradise of Europe was awaiting the future Eastern millionaire. And Maroola, now the bargain was struck and there was no more business to be talked over, evidently did not care for the white man's company. Yet Dain was always about the house, but he sel-

dom stayed long by the riverside. On his daily visits to the
white man the Malay chief preferred to make his way
quietly through the central passage of the house, and would
come out into the garden at the back, where the fire was
burning in the cooking shed, with the rice kettle swinging
over it, under the watchful supervision of Mrs. Almayer.
Avoiding that shed, with its black smoke and the warbling
of soft, feminine voices, Dain would turn to the left. There,
on the edge of a banana plantation, a clump of palms and
mango trees formed a shady spot, a few scattered bushes
giving it a certain seclusion into which only the serving
women's chatter or an occasional burst of laughter could
penetrate. Once in, he was invisible; and hidden there, leaning against the smooth trunk of a tall palm, he waited with
gleaming eyes and an assured smile to hear the faint rustle
of dried grass under the light footsteps of Nina.

From the very first moment when his eyes beheld this—to
him—perfection of loveliness he felt in his inmost heart the
conviction that she would be his; he felt the subtle breath of
mutual understanding passing between their two savage
natures, and he did not want Mrs. Almayer's encouraging
smiles to take every opportunity of approaching the girl;
and every time he spoke to her, every time he looked into
her eyes, Nina, although averting her face, felt as if this
bold-looking being who spoke burning words into her willing ear was the embodiment of her fate, the creature of her
dreams—reckless, ferocious, ready with flashing kriss for
his enemies, and with passionate embrace for his beloved—
the ideal Malay chief of her mother's tradition.

She recognized with a thrill of delicious fear the mysterious consciousness of her identity with that being. Listening
to his words, it seemed to her she was born only then to a
knowledge of a new existence, that her life was complete
only when near him, and she abandoned herself to a feeling of dreamy happiness, while with half-veiled face and in
silence—as became a Malay girl—she listened to Dain's
words giving up to her the whole treasure of love and passion his nature was capable of with all the unrestrained

enthusiasm of a man totally untrammelled by any influence of civilized self-discipline.

And they used to pass many a delicious and fast fleeting hour under the mango trees behind the friendly curtain of bushes till Mrs. Almayer's shrill voice gave the signal of unwilling separation. Mrs. Almayer had undertaken the easy task of watching her husband lest he should interrupt the smooth course of her daughter's love affair, in which she took a great and benignant interest. She was happy and proud to see Dain's infatuation, believing him to be a great and powerful chief, and she found also a gratification of her mercenary instincts in Dain's open-handed generosity.

On the eve of the day when Babalatchi's suspicions were confirmed by ocular demonstration, Dain and Nina had remained longer than usual in their shady retreat. Only Almayer's heavy step on the verandah and his querulous clamour for food decided Mrs. Almayer to lift a warning cry. Maroola leaped lightly over the low bamboo fence, and made his way through the banana plantation down to the muddy shore of the back creek, while Nina walked slowly towards the house to minister to her father's wants, as was her wont every evening. Almayer felt happy enough that evening; the preparations were nearly completed; to-morrow he would launch his boats. In his mind's eye he saw the rich prize in his grasp; and, with tin spoon in his hand, he was forgetting the plateful of rice before him in the fanciful arrangement of some splendid banquet to take place on his arrival in Amsterdam. Nina, reclining in the long chair, listened absently to the few disconnected words escaping from her father's lips. Expedition! Gold! What did she care for all that? But at the name of Maroola mentioned by her father she was all attention. Dain was going down the river with his brig to-morrow to remain away a few days, said Almayer. It was very annoying, this delay. As soon as Dain returned they would have to start without loss of time, for the river was rising. He would not be surprised if a great flood was coming. And he pushed away his plate with an impatient gesture on rising from the table.

But now Nina heard him not. Dain going away! That's why
he had ordered her, with that quiet masterfulness it was
her delight to obey, to meet him at break of day in Bulangi's creek. Was there a paddle in her canoe? she thought.
Was it ready? She would have to start early—at four in the
morning, in a very few hours.

She rose from her chair, thinking she would require rest
before the long pull in the early morning. The lamp was
burning dimly, and her father, tired with the day's labour,
was already in his hammock. Nina put the lamp out and
passed into a large room she shared with her mother on the
left of the central passage. Entering, she saw that Mrs. Almayer had deserted the pile of mats serving her as bed in
one corner of the room, and was now bending over the
opened lid of her large wooden chest. Half a shell of cocoanut filled with oil, where a cotton rag floated for a wick,
stood on the floor, surrounding her with a ruddy halo of
light shining through the black and odorous smoke. Mrs.
Almayer's back was bent, and her head and shoulders hidden in the deep box. Her hands rummaged in the interior,
where a soft clink as of silver money could be heard. She did
not notice at first her daughter's approach, and Nina, standing silently by her, looked down on many little canvas bags
ranged in the bottom of the chest, wherefrom her mother
extracted handfuls of shining guilders and Mexican dollars,
letting them stream slowly back again through her claw-like
fingers. The music of tinkling silver seemed to delight her,
and her eyes sparkled with the reflected gleam of freshly-
minted coins. She was muttering to herself: "And this, and
this, and yet this! Soon he will give more—as much more as
I ask. He is a great Rajah—a Son of Heaven! And she will
be a Ranee—he gave all this for her! Who ever gave anything for me? I am a slave! Am I? I am the mother of a
great Ranee!" She became aware suddenly of her daughter's
presence, and ceased her droning, shutting the lid down
violently; then, without rising from her crouching position,
she looked up at the girl standing by with a vague smile on
her dreamy face.

"You have seen. Have you?" she shouted, shrilly. "That is all mine, and for you. It is not enough! He will have to give more before he takes you away to the southern island where his father is king. You hear me? You are worth more, granddaughter of Rajahs! More! More!"

The sleepy voice of Almayer was heard on the verandah recommending silence. Mrs. Almayer extinguished the light and crept into her corner of the room. Nina lay down on her back on a pile of soft mats, her hands entwined under her head, gazing through the shutterless hole, serving as a window at the stars twinkling on the black sky; she was awaiting the time of start for her appointed meeting-place. With quiet happiness she thought of that meeting in the great forest, far from all human eyes and sounds. Her soul, lapsing again into the savage mood, which the genius of civilization working by the hand of Mrs. Vinck could never destroy, experienced a feeling of pride and of some slight trouble at the high value her worldly-wise mother had put upon her person; but she remembered the expressive glances and words of Dain, and, tranquillized, she closed her eyes in a shiver of pleasant anticipation.

There are some situations where the barbarian and the, so-called, civilized man meet upon the same ground. It may be supposed that Dain Maroola was not exceptionally delighted with his prospective mother-in-law, nor that he actually approved of that worthy woman's appetite for shining dollars. Yet on that foggy morning when Babalatchi, laying aside the cares of state, went to visit his fish-baskets in the Bulangi creek, Maroola had no misgivings, experienced no feelings but those of impatience and longing, when paddling to the east side of the island forming the backwater in question. He hid his canoe in the bushes and strode rapidly across the islet, pushing with impatience through the twigs of heavy undergrowth intercrossed over his path. From motives of prudence he would not take his canoe to the meeting-place, as Nina had done. He had left it in the main stream till his return from the other side of the island. The heavy warm fog was closing rapidly round him, but he managed to catch a fleeting glimpse of a light away to the left, proceeding from Bulangi's house. Then he could see nothing in the thickening vapour, and kept to the path only by a sort of instinct, which also led him to the very point on the opposite shore he wished to reach. A great log had stranded there, at right angles to the bank, forming a kind of jetty against which the swiftly flowing stream broke with a loud ripple. He stepped on it with a quick but steady motion, and in two strides found himself at the outer end, with the rush and swirl of the foaming water at his feet.

Standing there alone, as if separated from the world; the heavens, earth; the very water roaring under him swallowed up in the thick veil of the morning fog, he breathed out the name of Nina before him into the apparently limitless space, sure of being heard, instinctively sure of the nearness of the delightful creature; certain of her being aware of his near presence as he was aware of hers.

The bow of Nina's canoe loomed up close to the log, canted high out of the water by the weight of the sitter in the stern. Maroola laid his hand on the stem and leaped lightly in, giving it a vigorous shove off. The light craft, obeying the new impulse, cleared the log by a hair's breadth, and the river, with obedient complicity, swung it broadside to the current, and bore it off slightly and rapidly between the invisible banks. And once more Dain, at the feet of Nina, forgot the world, felt himself carried away helpless by a great wave of supreme emotion, by a rush of joy, pride, and desire; understood once more with overpowering certitude that there was no life possible without that being he held clasped in his arms with passionate strength in a prolonged embrace.

Nina disengaged herself gently with a low laugh.

"You will overturn the boat, Dain," she whispered.

He looked into her eyes eagerly for a minute and let her go with a sigh, then lying down in the canoe he put his head on her knees, gazing upwards and stretching his arms backwards till his hands met round the girl's waist. She bent over him, and, shaking her head, framed both their faces in the falling locks of her long black hair.

And so they drifted on, he speaking with all the rude elo-

quence of a savage nature giving itself up without restraint
to an overmastering passion, she bending low to catch the
murmur of words sweeter to her than life itself. To those
two nothing existed then outside the gunwales of the narrow
and fragile craft. It was their world, filled with their intense
and all-absorbing love. They took no heed of thickening
mist, or of the breeze dying away before sunrise; they forgot
the existence of the great forests surrounding them, of all
the tropical nature awaiting the advent of the sun in a
solemn and impressive silence.

Over the low river-mist hiding the boat with its freight
of young passionate life and all-forgetful happiness, the stars
paled, and a silvery-grey tint crept over the sky from the east-
ward. There was not a breath of wind, not a rustle of stirring leaf, not a splash of leaping fish to disturb the serene
repose of all living things on the banks of the great river.
Earth, river, and sky were wrapped up in a deep sleep from
which it seemed there would be no waking. All the seething
life and movement of tropical nature seemed concentrated
in the ardent eyes, in the tumultuously beating hearts of the
two beings drifting in the canoe, under the white canopy of
mist, over the smooth surface of the river.

Suddenly a great sheaf of yellow rays shot upwards from
behind the black curtain of trees lining the banks of the
Pantai. The stars went out; the little black clouds of the
zenith glowed for a moment with crimson tints, and the
thick mist, stirred by the gentle breeze, the sigh of waking
nature, whirled round and broke into fantastically torn
pieces, disclosing the wrinkled surface of the river sparkling in the broad light of day. Great flocks of white birds
wheeled screaming above the swaying tree-tops. The sun
had risen on the east coast.

Dain was the first to return to the cares of everyday life.
He rose and glanced rapidly up and down the river. His
eye detected Babalatchi's boat astern, and another small
black speck on the glittering water, which was Taminah's
canoe. He moved cautiously forward, and, kneeling, took
up a paddle; Nina at the stern took hers. They bent their

bodies to the work, throwing up the water at every stroke, and the small craft went swiftly ahead, leaving a narrow wake fringed with a lacelike border of white and gleaming foam. Without turning his head, Dain spoke.

"Somebody behind us, Nina. We must not let him gain. I think he is too far to recognize us."

"Somebody before us also," panted out Nina, without ceasing to paddle.

"I think I know," rejoined Dain. "The sun shines over there, but I fancy it is the girl Taminah. She comes down every morning to my brig to sell cakes—stays often all day. It does not matter; steer more into the bank; we must get under the bushes. My canoe is hidden not far from here."

As he spoke his eyes watched the broad-leaved nipas which they were brushing in their swift and silent course.

"Look out, Nina," he said at last; "there, where the water palms end and the twigs hang down under the leaning tree. Steer for the big green branch."

He stood up attentive, and the boat drifted slowly in shore, Nina guiding it by a gentle and skilful movement of her paddle. When near enough Dain laid hold of the big branch, and leaning back shot the canoe under a low green archway of thickly matted creepers giving access to a miniature bay formed by the caving in of the bank during the last great flood. His own boat was there anchored by a stone, and he stepped into it, keeping his hand on the gunwale of Nina's canoe. In a moment the two little nutshells with their occupants floated quietly side by side, reflected by the black water in the dim light struggling through a high canopy of dense foliage; while above, away up in the broad day, flamed immense red blossoms sending down on their heads a shower of great dew-sparkling petals that descended rotating slowly in a continuous and perfumed stream; and over them, under them, in the sleeping water; all around them in a ring of luxuriant vegetation bathed in the warm air charged with strong and harsh perfumes, the intense work of tropical nature went on: plants shooting upward, entwined, interlaced in inextricable confusion, climbing madly and brutally over each other in the terrible silence of a desperate struggle towards the life-giving sunshine above—as if struck with sudden horror at the seething mass of corruption below, at the death and decay from which they sprang.

"We must part now," said Dain, after a long silence. "You must return at once, Nina. I will wait till the brig drifts down here, and shall get on board then."

"And will you be long away, Dain?" asked Nina, in a low voice.

"Long!" exclaimed Dain. "Would a man willingly remain long in a dark place? When I am not near you, Nina, I am like a man that is blind. What is life to me without light?"

Nina leaned over, and with a proud and happy smile took Dain's face between her hands, looking into his eyes with a fond yet questioning gaze. Apparently she found there the confirmation of the words just said, for a feeling of grateful security lightened for her the weight of sorrow at the hour of parting. She believed that he, the descendant of many great Rajahs, the son of a great chief, the master of life and death, knew the sunshine of life only in her presence. An immense wave of gratitude and love welled forth out of her heart towards him. How could she make an outward and visible sign of all she felt for the man who had filled her heart with so much joy and so much pride? And in the great tumult of passion, like a flash of lightning came to her the reminiscence of that despised and almost forgotten civilization she had only glanced at in her days of restraint, of sorrow, and of anger. In the cold ashes of that hateful and miserable past she would find the sign of love, the fitting expression of the boundless felicity of the present, the pledge of a bright and splendid future. She threw her arms around Dain's neck and pressed her lips to his in a long and burning kiss. He closed his eyes, surprised and frightened at the storm raised in his breast by the strange and to him hitherto unknown contact, and long after Nina had pushed her canoe into the river he remained motionless,

without daring to open his eyes, afraid to lose the sensation
of intoxicating delight he had tasted for the first time.

Now he wanted but immortality, he thought, to be the
equal of gods, and the creature that could open so the gates
of paradise must be his—soon would be his for ever!

He opened his eyes in time to see through the archway of
creepers the bows of his brig come slowly into view, as the
vessel drifted past on its way down the river. He must go
on board now, he thought; yet he was loth to leave the place
where he had learned to know what happiness meant. "Time
yet. Let them go," he muttered to himself; and he closed his
eyes again under the red shower of scented petals, trying
to recall the scene with all its delight and all its fear.

He must have been able to join his brig in time, after
all, and found much occupation outside, for it was in vain
that Almayer looked for his friend's speedy return. The
lower reach of the river where he so often and so impatiently directed his eyes remained deserted, save for the rapid
flitting of some fishing canoe; but down the upper reaches
came black clouds and heavy showers heralding the final
setting in of the rainy season with its thunderstorms and
great floods making the river almost impossible of ascent
for native canoes.

Almayer, strolling along the muddy beach between his
houses, watched uneasily the river rising inch by inch,
creeping slowly nearer to the boats, now ready and hauled
up in a row under the cover of dripping Kajang-mats. Fortune seemed to elude his grasp, and in his weary tramp
backwards and forwards under the steady rain falling from
the lowering sky, a sort of despairing indifference took possession of him. What did it matter? It was just his luck!
Those two infernal savages, Lakamba and Dain, induced
him, with their promises of help, to spend his last dollar
in the fitting out of boats, and now one of them was gone
somewhere, and the other shut up in his stockade would
give no sign of life. No, not even the scoundrelly Babalatchi,
thought Almayer, would show his face near him, now they
had sold him all the rice, brass gongs, and cloth necessary

for his expedition. They had his very last coin, and did not
care whether he went or stayed. And with a gesture of
abandoned discouragement Almayer would climb up slowly
to the verandah of his new house to get out of the rain, and
leaning on the front rail with his head sunk between his
shoulders he would abandon himself to the current of bitter
thoughts, oblivious of the flight of time and the pangs of
hunger, deaf to the shrill cries of his wife calling him to the
evening meal. When, roused from his sad meditations by the
first roll of the evening thunderstorm, he stumbled slowly
towards the glimmering light of his old house, his half-dead
hope made his ears preternaturally acute to any sound on
the river. Several nights in succession he had heard the
splash of paddles and had seen the indistinct form of a boat,
but when hailing the shadowy apparition, his heart bounding with sudden hope of hearing Dain's voice, he was disappointed each time by the sulky answer conveying to him
the intelligence that the Arabs were on the river, bound on
a visit to the home-staying Lakamba. This caused him many
sleepless nights, spent in speculating upon the kind of vil-
lainy those estimable personages were hatching now. At
last, when all hope seemed dead, he was overjoyed on hearing Dain's voice; but Dain also appeared very anxious to see
Lakamba, and Almayer felt uneasy owing to a deep and
ineradicable distrust as to that ruler's disposition towards
himself. Still, Dain had returned at last. Evidently he meant
to keep to his bargain. Hope revived, and that night Almayer slept soundly, while Nina watched the angry river
under the lash of the thunderstorm sweeping onward towards the sea.

CHAPTER 6

Dain was not long in crossing the river after leaving Almayer. He landed at the water-gate of the stockade enclosing the group of houses which composed the residence of
the Rajah of Sambir. Evidently somebody was expected
there, for the gate was open, and men with torches were
ready to precede the visitor up the inclined plane of planks
leading to the largest house where Lakamba actually resided,
and where all the business of state was invariably trans-
acted. The other buildings within the enclosure served only
to accommodate the numerous household and the wives of
the ruler.

Lakamba's own house was a strong structure of solid
planks, raised on high piles, with a verandah of split bamboos surrounding it on all sides; the whole was covered in
by an immensely high-pitched roof of palmleaves, resting on
beams blackened by the smoke of many torches.

The building stood parallel to the river, one of its long
sides facing the water-gate of the stockade. There was a
door in the short side looking up the river, and the inclined
plank-way led straight from the gate to that door. By the
uncertain light of smoky torches, Dain noticed the vague
outlines of a group of armed men in the dark shadows to
his right. From that group Babalatchi stepped forward to
open the door, and Dain entered the audience chamber of
the Rajah's residence. About one-third of the house was
curtained off, by heavy stuff of European manufacture, for
that purpose; close to the curtain there was a big armchair
of some black wood, much carved, and before it a rough
deal table. Otherwise the room was only furnished with

mats in great profusion. To the left of the entrance stood a
rude arm-rack, with three rifles with fixed bayonets in it.
By the wall, in the shadow, the bodyguard of Lakamba—
all friends or relations—slept in a confused heap of brown
arms, legs, and multi-coloured garments, from whence
issued an occasional snore or a subdued groan of some uneasy sleeper. An European lamp with a green shade standing on the table made all this indistinctly visible to Dain.

"You are welcome to your rest here," said Babalatchi,
looking at Dain interrogatively.

"I must speak to the Rajah at once," answered Dain.

Babalatchi made a gesture of assent, and, turning to the
brass gong suspended under the arm-rack, struck two sharp
blows.

The ear-splitting din woke up the guard. The snores
ceased; outstretched legs were drawn in; the whole heap
moved, and slowly resolved itself into individual forms
with much yawning and rubbing of sleepy eyes; behind the
curtains there was a burst of feminine chatter; then the bass
voice of Lakamba was heard.

"Is that the Arab trader?"

"No, Tuan," answered Babalatchi; "Dain has returned at
last. He is here for an important talk, bitcharra—if you
mercifully consent."

Evidently Lakamba's mercy went so far—for in a short
while he came out from behind the curtain—but it did not
go to the length of inducing him to make an extensive toilet.
A short red sarong tightened hastily round his hips was his
only garment. The merciful ruler of Sambir looked sleepy
and rather sulky. He sat in the armchair, his knees well
apart, his elbows on the arm-rests, his chin on his breast,
breathing heavily and waiting malevolently for Dain to
open the important talk.

But Dain did not seem anxious to begin. He directed his
gaze towards Babalatchi, squatting comfortably at the feet
of his master, and remained silent with a slightly bent head
as if in attentive expectation of coming words of wisdom.

Babalatchi coughed discreetly, and, leaning forward,

pushed over a few mats for Dain to sit upon, then lifting up his squeaky voice he assured him with eager volubility of everybody's delight at this long-looked-for return. His heart had hungered for the sight of Dain's face, and his ears were withering for the want of the refreshing sound of his voice. Everybody's hearts and ears were in the same sad predicament, according to Babalatchi, as he indicated with a sweeping gesture the other bank of the river where the settlement slumbered peacefully, unconscious of the great joy awaiting it on the morrow when Dain's presence amongst them would be disclosed. "For"—went on Babalatchi—"what is the joy of a poor man if not the open hand of a generous trader or of a great—"

Here he checked himself abruptly with a calculated embarrassment of manner, and his roving eye sought the floor, while an apologetic smile dwelt for a moment on his misshapen lips. Once or twice during this opening speech an amused expression flitted across Dain's face, soon to give way, however, to an appearance of grave concern. On Lakamba's brow a heavy frown had settled, and his lips moved angrily as he listened to his Prime Minister's oratory. In the silence that fell upon the room when Babalatchi ceased speaking arose a chorus of varied snores from the corner where the body-guard had resumed their interrupted slumbers, but the distant rumble of thunder filling then Nina's heart with apprehension for the safety of her lover passed unheeded by those three men intent each on their own purposes, for life or death.

After a short silence, Babalatchi discarding now the flowers of polite eloquence, spoke again, but in short and hurried sentences and in a low voice. They had been very uneasy. Why did Dain remain so long absent? The men dwelling on the lower reaches of the river heard the reports of big guns and saw a fire-ship of the Dutch amongst the islands of the estuary. So they were anxious. Rumours of a disaster had reached Abdulla a few days ago, and since then they had been waiting for Dain's return under the apprehension of some misfortune. For days they had closed their eyes in fear, and woke up alarmed, and walked abroad trembling, like men before an enemy. And all on account of Dain. Would he not allay their fears for his safety, not for themselves? They were quiet and faithful, and devoted to the great Rajah in Batavia—may his fate lead him ever to victory for the joy and profit of his servants! "And here," went on Babalatchi, "Lakamba my master was getting thin in his anxiety for the trader he had taken under his protection; and so was Abdulla, for what would wicked men not say if perchance—"

"Be silent, fool!" growled Lakamba, angrily.

Babalatchi subsided into silence with a satisfied smile, while Dain, who had been watching him as if fascinated, turned with a sigh of relief towards the ruler of Sambir. Lakamba did not move, and, without raising his head, looked at Dain from under his eyebrows, breathing audibly, with pouted lips, in an air of general discontent.

"Speak! O Dain!" he said at last. "We have heard many rumours. Many nights in succession has my friend Reshid come here with bad tidings. News travels fast along the coast. But they may be untrue; there are more lies in men's mouths in these days than when I was young, but I am not easier to deceive now."

"All my words are true," said Dain, carelessly. "If you want to know what befell my brig, then learn that it is in the hands of the Dutch. Believe me, Rajah," he went on, with sudden energy, "the Orang Blanda have good friends in Sambir, or else how did they know I was coming thence?"

Lakamba gave Dain a short and hostile glance. Babalatchi rose quietly, and, going to the arm-rack, struck the gong violently.

Outside the door there was a shuffle of bare feet; inside, the guard woke up and sat staring in sleepy surprise.

"Yes, you faithful friend of the white Rajah," went on Dain, scornfully, turning to Babalatchi, who had returned to his place, "I have escaped, and I am here to gladden your heart. When I saw the Dutch ship I ran the brig inside the reefs and put her ashore. They did not dare to follow with

the ship, so they sent the boats. We took to ours and tried to
get away, but the ship dropped fireballs at us, and killed
many of my men. But I am left, O Babalatchi! The Dutch
are coming here. They are seeking for me. They're coming
to ask their faithful friend Lakamba and his slave Babalatchi. Rejoice!"

But neither of his hearers appeared to be in a joyful
mood. Lakamba had put one leg over his knee, and went
on gently scratching it with a meditative air, while Babalatchi, sitting cross-legged, seemed suddenly to become
smaller and very limp, staring straight before him vacantly.
The guard evinced some interest in the proceedings, stretching themselves full length on the mats to be nearer the
speaker. One of them got up and now stood leaning against
the arm-rack, playing absently with the fringes of his sword-
hilt.

Dain waited till the crash of thunder had died away in
distant mutterings before he spoke again.

"Are you dumb, O ruler of Sambir, or is the son of a
great Rajah unworthy of your notice? I am come here to
seek refuge and to warn you, and want to know what you in-
tend doing."

"You came here because of the white man's daughter,"
retorted Lakamba, quickly. "Your refuge was with your
father, the Rajah of Bali, the Son of Heaven, the 'Anak
Agong' himself. What am I to protect great princes? Only
yesterday I planted rice in a burnt clearing; to-day you say
I hold your life in my hand."

Babalatchi glanced at his master. "No man can escape
his fate," he murmured piously. "When love enters a man's
heart he is like a child—without any understanding. Be
merciful, Lakamba," he added, twitching the corner of the
Rajah's sarong warningly.

Lakamba snatched away the skirt of the sarong angrily.
Under the dawning comprehension of intolerable embarrass-
ments caused by Dain's return to Sambir he began to lose
such composure as he had been, till then, able to maintain;
and now he raised his voice loudly above the whistling of

the wind and the patter of rain on the roof in the hard squall passing over the house.

"You came here first as a trader with sweet words and great promises, asking me to look the other way while you worked your will on the white man there. And I did. What do you want now? When I was young I fought. Now I am old, and want peace. It is easier for me to have you killed than to fight the Dutch. It is better for me."

The squall had now passed, and, in the short stillness of the lull in the storm, Lakamba repeated softly, as if to himself, "Much easier. Much better."

Dain did not seem greatly discomposed by the Rajah's threatening words. While Lakamba was speaking he had glanced once rapidly over his shoulder, just to make sure that there was nobody behind him, and, tranquillized in that respect, he had extracted a siri-box out of the folds of his waist-cloth, and was wrapping carefully the little bit of betel-nut and a small pinch of lime in the green leaf tendered him politely by the watchful Babalatchi. He accepted this as a peace-offering from the silent statesman—a kind of mute protest against his master's undiplomatic violence, and as an omen of a possible understanding to be arrived at yet. Otherwise Dain was not uneasy. Although recognizing the justice of Lakamba's surmise that he had come back to Sambir only for the sake of the white man's daughter, yet he was not conscious of any childish lack of understanding, as suggested by Babalatchi. In fact, Dain knew very well that Lakamba was too deeply implicated in the gunpowder smuggling to care for an investigation by the Dutch authorities into that matter. When sent off by his father, the independent Rajah of Bali, at the time when the hostilities between Dutch and Malays threatened to spread from Sumatra over the whole archipelago, Dain had found all the big traders deaf to his guarded proposals and above the temptation of the great prices he was ready to give for gunpowder. He went to Sambir as a last and almost hopeless resort, having heard in Macassar of the white man there, and of the regular steamer trading from Singapore—allured also by the fact that there was no Dutch resident on the river, which would make things easier, no doubt. His hopes got nearly wrecked against the stubborn loyalty of Lakamba arising from well-understood self-interest; but at last the young man's generosity, his persuasive enthusiasm, the prestige of his father's great name, overpowered the prudent hesitation of the ruler of Sambir. Lakamba would have nothing to do himself with any illegal traffic. He also objected to the Arabs being made use of in that matter; but he suggested Almayer, saying that he was a weak man easily persuaded, and that his friend, the English captain of the steamer, could be made very useful—very likely even would join in the business, smuggling the powder in the steamer without Abdulla's knowledge. There again Dain met in Almayer an unexpected resistance; Lakamba had to send Babalatchi over with the solemn promise that his eyes would be shut in friendship for the white man. Dain paying for the promise and the friendship in good silver guilders of the hated Orang Blanda. Almayer, at last consenting, said the powder would be obtained, but Dain must trust him with dollars to send to Singapore in payment for it. He would induce Ford to buy and smuggle it in the steamer on board the brig. He did not want any money for himself out of the transaction, but Dain must help him in his great enterprise after sending off the brig. Almayer had explained to Dain that he could not trust Lakamba alone in that matter; he would be afraid of losing his treasure and his life through the cupidity of the Rajah; yet the Rajah had to be told, and insisted on taking a share in that operation, or else his eyes would remain shut no longer. To this Almayer had to submit. Had Dain not seen Nina he would have probably refused to engage himself and his men in the projected expedition to Gunong Mas—the mountain of gold. As it was he intended to return with half of his men as soon as the brig was clear of the reefs, but the persistent chase given him by the Dutch frigate had forced him to run south and ultimately to wreck and destroy his vessel in order to preserve his liberty or perhaps even his life. Yes, he had come back to Sambir

for Nina, although aware that the Dutch would look for
him there, but he had also calculated his chances of safety
in Lakamba's hands. For all his ferocious talk, the merciful
ruler would not kill him, for he had long ago been impressed
with the notion that Dain possessed the secret of the white
man's treasure; neither would he give him up to the Dutch,
for fear of some fatal disclosure of complicity in the trea-
sonable trade. So Dain felt tolerably secure as he sat meditating quietly his answer to the Rajah's bloodthirsty speech.
Yes, he would point out to him the aspect of his position
should he—Dain—fall into the hands of the Dutch and
should he speak the truth. He would have nothing more to
lose then, and he would speak the truth. And if he did return to Sambir, disturbing thereby Lakamba's peace of
mind, what then? He came to look after his property. Did
he not pour a stream of silver into Mrs. Almayer's greedy
lap? He had paid, for the girl, a price worthy of a great
prince, although unworthy of that delightfully maddening
creature for whom his untamed soul longed in an intensity
of desire far more tormenting than the sharpest pain. He
wanted his happiness. He had the right to be in Sambir.

He rose, and, approaching the table, leaned both his
elbows on it; Lakamba responsively edged his seat a little
closer, while Babalatchi scrambled to his feet and thrust his
inquisitive head between his master's and Dain's. They interchanged their ideas rapidly, speaking in whispers into
each other's faces, very close now, Dain suggesting, Lakamba contradicting, Babalatchi conciliating and anxious in
his vivid apprehension of coming difficulties. He spoke most,
whispering earnestly, turning his head slowly from side to
side so as to bring his solitary eye to bear upon each of his
interlocutors in turn. Why should there be strife? said he.
Let Tuan Dain, whom he loved only less than his master,
go trustfully into hiding. There were many places for that.
Bulangi's house away in the clearing was best. Bulangi was
a safe man. In the network of crooked channels no white
man could find his way. White men were strong, but very
foolish. It was undesirable to fight them, but deception was

easy. They were like silly women—they did not know the use of reason, and he was a match for any of them—went on Babalatchi, with all the confidence of deficient experience. Probably the Dutch would seek Almayer. Maybe they would take away their countryman if they were suspicious of him. That would be good. After the Dutch went away Lakamba and Dain would get the treasure without any trouble, and there would be one person less to share it. Did he not speak wisdom? Will Tuan Dain go to Bulangi's house till the danger is over, go at once?

Dain accepted this suggestion of going into hiding with a certain sense of conferring a favour upon Lakamba and the anxious statesman, but he met the proposal of going at once with a decided no, looking Babalatchi meaningly in the eye. The statesman sighed as a man accepting the inevitable would do, and pointed silently towards the other bank of the river. Dain bent his head slowly.

"Yes, I am going there," he said.

"Before the day comes?" asked Babalatchi.

"I am going there now," answered Dain, decisively. "The Orang Blanda will not be here before to-morrow night, perhaps, and I must tell Almayer of our arrangements."

"No, Tuan. No; say nothing," protested Babalatchi. "I will go over myself at sunrise and let him know."

"I will see," said Dain, preparing to go.

The thunderstorm was recommencing outside, the heavy clouds hanging low overhead now. There was a constant rumble of distant thunder punctuated by the nearer sharp crashes, and in the continuous play of blue lightning the woods and the river showed fitfully, with all the elusive distinctness of detail characteristic of such a scene. Outside the door of the Rajah's house Dain and Babalatchi stood on the shaking verandah as if dazed and stunned by the violence of the storm. They stood there amongst the cowering forms of the Rajah's slaves and retainers seeking shelter from the rain, and Dain called aloud to his boatmen, who responded with an unanimous "Ada! Tuan!" while they looked uneasily at the river.

"This is a great flood!" shouted Babalatchi into Dain's ear. "The river is very angry. Look! Look at the drifting logs! Can you go?"

Dain glanced doubtfully on the livid expanse of seething water bounded far away on the other side by the narrow black line of the forests. Suddenly, in a vivid white flash, the low point of land with the bending trees on it and Almayer's house, leaped into view, flickered and disappeared. Dain pushed Babalatchi aside and ran down to the water-gate followed by his shivering boatmen.

Babalatchi backed slowly in and closed the door, then turned round and looked silently upon Lakamba. The Rajah sat still, glaring stonily upon the table, and Babalatchi gazed curiously at the perplexed mood of the man he had served so many years through good and evil fortune. No doubt the one-eyed statesman felt within his savage and much sophisticated breast the unwonted feelings of sympathy with, and perhaps even pity for, the man he called his master. From the safe position of a confidential adviser, he could, in the dim vista of past years, see himself—a casual cut-throat—finding shelter under that man's roof in the modest rice-clearing of early beginnings. Then came a long period of unbroken success, of wise counsels, and deep plottings resolutely carried out by the fearless Lakamba, till the whole east coast from Poulo Laut to Tanjong Batu listened to Babalatchi's wisdom speaking through the mouth of the ruler of Sambir. In those long years how many dangers escaped, how many enemies bravely faced, how many white men successfully circumvented! And now he looked upon the result of so many years of patient toil: the fearless Lakamba cowed by the shadow of an impending trouble. The ruler was growing old, and Babalatchi, aware of an uneasy feeling at the pit of his stomach, put both his hands there with a suddenly vivid and sad perception of the fact that he himself was growing old too; that the time of reckless daring was past for both of them, and that they had to seek refuge in prudent cunning. They wanted peace; they were disposed to reform; they were ready even to retrench so as to have the wherewithal to bribe the evil days away, if bribed away they could be. Babalatchi sighed for the second time that night as he squatted again at his master's feet and tendered him his betel-nut box in mute sympathy. And they sat there in close yet silent communion of betel-nut chewers, moving their jaws slowly, expectorating decorously into the wide-mouthed brass vessel they passed to one another, and listening to the awful din of the battling elements outside.

"There is a very great flood," remarked Babalatchi, sadly.

"Yes," said Lakamba. "Did Dain go?"

"He went, Tuan. He ran down to the river like a man possessed of the Sheitan himself."

There was another long pause.

"He may get drowned," suggested Lakamba at last, with some show of interest.

"The floating logs are many," answered Babalatchi, "but he is a good swimmer," he added languidly.

"He ought to live," said Lakamba; "he knows where the treasure is."

Babalatchi assented with an ill-humoured grunt. His want of success in penetrating the white man's secret as to the locality where the gold was to be found was a sore point with the statesman of Sambir, as the only conspicuous failure in an otherwise brilliant career.

A great peace had now succeeded the turmoil of the storm. Only the little belated clouds, which hurried past overhead to catch up with the main body flashing silently in the distance, sent down short showers that pattered softly with a soothing hiss over the palm-leaf roof.

Lakamba roused himself from his apathy with an appearance of having grasped the situation at last.

"Babalatchi," he called briskly, giving him a slight kick.

"Ada Tuan! I am listening."

"If the Orang Blanda come here, Babalatchi, and take Almayer to Batavia to punish him for smuggling gunpowder, what will he do, you think?"

"I do not know, Tuan."

"You are a fool," commented Lakamba, exultingly. "He

will tell them where the treasure is, so as to find mercy. He will."

Babalatchi looked up at his master and nodded his head with by no means a joyful surprise. He had not thought of this; there was a new complication.

"Almayer must die," said Lakamba, decisively, "to make our secret safe. He must die quietly, Babalatchi. You must do it."

Babalatchi assented, and rose wearily to his feet. "To-morrow?" he asked.

"Yes; before the Dutch come. He drinks much coffee," answered Lakamba, with seeming irrelevancy.

Babalatchi stretched himself yawning, but Lakamba, in the flattering consciousness of a knotty problem solved by his own unaided intellectual efforts, grew suddenly very wakeful.

"Babalatchi," he said to the exhausted statesman, "fetch the box of music the white captain gave me. I cannot sleep."

At this order a deep shade of melancholy settled upon Babalatchi's features. He went reluctantly behind the curtain and soon reappeared carrying in his arms a small hand-organ, which he put down on the table with an air of deep dejection. Lakamba settled himself comfortably in his arm-chair.

"Turn, Babalatchi, turn," he murmured, with closed eyes.

Babalatchi's hand grasped the handle with the energy of despair, and as he turned, the deep gloom on his countenance changed into an expression of hopeless resignation. Through the open shutter the notes of Verdi's music floated out on the great silence over the river and forest. Lakamba listened with closed eyes and a delighted smile; Babalatchi turned, at times dozing off and swaying over, then catching himself up in a great fright with a few quick turns of the handle. Nature slept in an exhausted repose after the fierce turmoil, while under the unsteady hand of the statesman of Sambir the Trovatore fitfully wept, wailed, and bade good-bye to his Leonore again and again in a mournful round of tearful and endless iteration.

the meeting currents of the two branches of the river. Mahmat walked down to the water's edge to examine the rattan moorings of his house just as the sun cleared the trees of the forest on the opposite shore. As he bent over the fastenings he glanced again carelessly at the unquiet tumble of logs and saw there something that caused him to drop his hatchet and stand up, shading his eyes with his hand from the rays of the rising sun. It was something red, and the logs rolled over it, at times closing round it, sometimes hiding it. It looked to him at first like a strip of red cloth. The next moment Mahmat had made it out and raised a great shout.

"Ah ya! There!" yelled Mahmat. "There's a man amongst the logs." He put the palms of his hands to his lips and shouted, enunciating distinctly, his face turned towards the settlement: "There's a body of a man in the river! Come and see! A dead—stranger!"

The women of the nearest house were already outside kindling the fires and husking the morning rice. They took up the cry shrilly, and it travelled so from house to house, dying away in the distance. The men rushed out excited but silent, and ran towards the muddy point where the unconscious logs tossed and ground and bumped and rolled over the dead stranger with the stupid persistency of inanimate things. The woman followed, neglecting their domestic duties and disregarding the possibilities of domestic discontent, while groups of children brought up the rear, warbling joyously, in the delight of unexpected excitement.

Almayer called aloud for his wife and daughter, but receiving no response, stood listening intently. The murmur of the crowd reached him faintly, bringing with it the assurance of some unusual event. He glanced at the river just as he was going to leave the verandah and checked himself at the sight of a small canoe crossing over from the Rajah's landing-place. The solitary occupant (in whom Almayer soon recognized Babalatchi) effected the crossing a little below the house and paddled up to the Lingard jetty in the dead water under the bank. Babalatchi clambered out slowly and went on fastening his canoe with fastidious care,

as if not in a hurry to meet Almayer, whom he saw looking
at him from the verandah. This delay gave Almayer time to
notice and greatly wonder at Babalatchi's official get-up.
The statesman of Sambir was clad in a costume befitting
his high rank. A loudly checkered sarong encircled his waist
and from its many folds peeped out the silver hilt of the
kriss that saw the light only on great festivals or during
official receptions. Over the left shoulder and across the
otherwise unclad breast of the aged diplomatist glistened a
patent leather belt bearing a brass plate with the arms of
Netherlands under the inscription, "Sultan of Sambir."
Babalatchi's head was covered by a red turban, whose
fringed ends falling over the left cheek and shoulder gave
to his aged face a ludicrous expression of joyous recklessness. When the canoe was at last fastened to his satisfaction he straightened himself up, shaking down the folds of
his sarong, and moved with long strides towards Almayer's
house, swinging regularly his long ebony staff, whose gold
head ornamented with precious stones flashed in the morning sun. Almayer waved his hand to the right towards the
point of land, to him invisible, but in full view from the
jetty.

"Oh, Babalatchi! oh!" he called out; "what is the matter
there? can you see?"

Babalatchi stopped and gazed intently at the crowd on
the river bank, and after a little while the astonished Almayer saw him leave the path, gather up his sarong in one
hand, and break into a trot through the grass towards the
muddy point. Almayer, now greatly interested, ran down
the steps of the verandah. The murmur of men's voices
and the shrill cries of women reached him quite distinctly
now, and as soon as he turned the corner of his house he
could see the crowd on the low promontory swaying and
pushing round some object of interest. He could indistinctly
hear Babalatchi's voice, then the crowd opened before the
aged statesman and closed after him with an excited hum,
ending in a loud shout.

As Almayer approached the throng a man ran out and
rushed past him towards the settlement, unheeding his call

to stop and explain the cause of this excitement. On the very outskirts of the crowd Almayer found himself arrested by an unyielding mass of humanity, regardless of his entreaties for a passage, insensible to his gentle pushes as he tried to work his way through it towards the riverside.

In the midst of his gentle and slow progress he fancied suddenly he had heard his wife's voice in the thickest of the throng. He could not mistake very well Mrs. Almayer's high-pitched tones, yet the words were too indistinct for him to understand their purport. He paused in his endeavours to make a passage for himself, intending to get some intelligence from those around him, when a long and piercing shriek rent the air, silencing the murmurs of the crowd and the voices of his informants. For a moment Almayer remained as if turned into stone with astonishment and horror, for he was certain now that he had heard his wife wailing for the dead. He remembered Nina's unusual absence, and maddened by his apprehensions as to her safety, he pushed blindly and violently forward, the crowd falling back with cries of surprise and pain before his frantic advance.

On the point of land in a little clear space lay the body of the stranger just hauled out from amongst the logs. On one side stood Babalatchi, his chin resting on the head of his staff and his one eye gazing steadily at the shapeless mass of broken limbs, torn flesh, and bloodstained rags. As Almayer burst through the ring of horrified spectators, Mrs. Almayer threw her own head-veil over the upturned face of the drowned man, and, squatting by it, with another mournful howl, sent a shiver through the now silent crowd. Mahmat, dripping wet, turned to Almayer, eager to tell his tale.

In the first moment of reaction from the anguish of his fear the sunshine seemed to waver before Almayer's eyes, and he listened to words spoken around him without comprehending their meaning. When, by a strong effort of will, he regained the possession of his senses, Mahmat was saying—

"That is the way, Tuan. His sarong was caught in the

broken branch, and he hung with his head under water. When I saw what it was I did not want it here. I wanted it to get clear and drift away. Why should we bury a stranger in the midst of our houses for his ghost to frighten our women and children? Have we not enough ghosts about this place?"

A murmur of approval interrupted him here. Mahmat looked reproachfully at Babalatchi.

"But the Tuan Babalatchi ordered me to drag the body ashore"—he went on looking round at his audience, but addressing himself only to Almayer—"and I dragged him by the feet; in through the mud I have dragged him, although my heart longed to see him float down the river to strand perchance on Bulangi's clearing—may his father's grave be defiled!"

There was subdued laughter at this, for the enmity of Mahmat and Bulangi was a matter of common notoriety and of undying interest to the inhabitants of Sambir. In the midst of that mirth Mrs. Almayer wailed suddenly again.

"Allah! What ails the woman!" exclaimed Mahmat, angrily. "Here, I have touched this carcass which came from nobody knows where, and have most likely defiled myself before eating rice. By orders of Tuan Babalatchi I did this thing to please the white man. Are you pleased, O Tuan Almayer? And what will be my recompense? Tuan Babalatchi said a recompense there will be, and from you. Now consider. I have been defiled and if not defiled I may be under the spell. Look at his ankles! Who ever heard of a corpse appearing during the night amongst the logs with gold anklets on its legs? There is witchcraft there. However," added Mahmat, after a reflective pause, "I will have the anklet if there is permission, for I have a charm against the ghosts and am not afraid. God is great!"

A fresh outburst of noisy grief from Mrs. Almayer checked the flow of Mahmat's eloquence. Almayer, bewildered, looked in turn at his wife, at Mahmat, at Babalatchi, and at last arrested his fascinated gaze on the body lying on the mud with covered face in a grotesquely unnatural contortion of mangled and broken limbs, one twisted and lacerated arm, with white bones protruding in many places through the torn flesh, stretched out; the hand with outspread fingers nearly touching his foot.

"Do you know who this is?" he asked of Babalatchi, in a low voice.

Babalatchi, staring straight before him, hardly moved his lips, while Mrs. Almayer's persistent lamentations drowned the whisper of his murmured reply intended only for Almayer's ear.

"It was fate. Look at your feet, white man. I can see a ring on those torn fingers which I know well."

Saying this, Babalatchi stepped carelessly forward, putting his foot as if accidentally on the hand of the corpse and pressing it into the soft mud. He swung his staff menacingly towards the crowd, which fell back a little.

"Go away," he said sternly, "and send your women to their cooking fires, which they ought not to have left to run after a dead stranger. This is men's work here. I take him now in the name of the Rajah. Let no man remain here but Tuan Almayer's slaves. Now go!"

The crowd reluctantly began to disperse. The women went first, dragging away the children that hung back with all their weight on the maternal hand. The men strolled slowly after them in ever forming and changing groups that gradually dissolved as they neared the settlement and every man regained his own house with steps quickened by the hungry anticipation of the morning rice. Only on the slight elevation where the land sloped down towards the muddy point a few men, either friends or enemies of Mahmat, remained gazing curiously for some time longer at the small group standing around the body on the river bank.

"I do not understand what you mean, Babalatchi," said Almayer. "What is the ring you are talking about? Whoever he is, you have trodden the poor fellow's hand right into the mud. Uncover his face," he went on, addressing Mrs. Almayer, who, squatting by the head of the corpse, rocked herself to and fro, shaking from time to time her dishevelled grey locks, and muttering mournfully.

"Hai!" exclaimed Mahmat, who had lingered close by. "Look, Tuan; the logs came together so," and here he pressed the palms of his hands together, "and his head must have been between them, and now there is no face for you to look at. There are his flesh and his bones, the nose, and the lips, and maybe his eyes, but nobody could tell the one from the other. It was written the day he was born that no man could look at him in death and be able to say, 'This is my friend's face.'"

"Silence, Mahmat; enough!" said Babalatchi, "and take thy eyes off his anklet, thou eater of pig's flesh. Tuan Almayer," he went on, lowering his voice, "have you seen Dain this morning?"

Almayer opened his eyes wide and looked alarmed. "No," he said quickly; "haven't you seen him? Is he not with the Rajah? I am waiting; why does he not come?"

Babalatchi nodded his head sadly.

"He is come, Tuan. He left last night when the storm was great and the river spoke angrily. The night was very black, but he had within him a light that showed the way to your house as smooth as a narrow backwater, and the many logs no bigger than wisps of dried grass. Therefore he went; and now he lies here." And Babalatchi nodded his head towards the body.

"How can you tell?" said Almayer, excitedly, pushing his wife aside. He snatched the cover off and looked at the formless mass of flesh, hair, and drying mud, where the face of the drowned man should have been. "Nobody can tell," he added, turning away with a shudder.

Babalatchi was on his knees wiping the mud from the stiffened fingers of the outstretched hand. He rose to his feet and flashed before Almayer's eyes a gold ring set with a large green stone.

"You know this well," he said. "This never left Dain's hand. I had to tear the flesh now to get it off. Do you believe now?"

Almayer raised his hands to his head and let them fall listlessly by his side in the utter abandonment of despair.

Babalatchi, looking at him curiously, was astonished to see him smile. A strange fancy had taken possession of Almayer's brain, distracted by this new misfortune. It seemed to him that for many years he had been falling into a deep precipice. Day after day, month after month, year after year, he had been falling, falling, falling; it was a smooth, round, black thing, and the black walls had been rushing upwards with wearisome rapidity. A great rush, the noise of which he fancied he could hear yet; and now, with an awful shock, he had reached the bottom, and behold! he was alive and whole, and Dain was dead with all his bones broken. It struck him as funny. A dead Malay; he had seen many dead Malays without any emotion; and now he felt inclined to weep, but it was over the fate of a white man he knew; a man that fell over a deep precipice and did not die. He seemed somehow to himself to be standing on one side, a little way off, looking at a certain Almayer who was in great trouble. Poor, poor fellow! Why doesn't he cut his throat? He wished to encourage him; he was very anxious to see him lying dead over that other corpse. Why does he not die and end this suffering? He groaned aloud unconsciously and started with affright at the sound of his own voice. Was he going mad? Terrified by the thought he turned away and ran towards his house repeating to himself, "I am not going mad; of course not, no, no, no!" He tried to keep a firm hold of the idea. Not mad, not mad. He stumbled as he ran blindly up the steps repeating fast and ever faster those words wherein seemed to lie his salvation. He saw Nina standing there, and wished to say something to her, but could not remember what, in his extreme anxiety not to forget that he was not going mad, which he still kept repeating mentally as he ran round the table, till he stumbled against one of the armchairs and dropped into it exhausted. He sat staring wildly at Nina, still assuring himself mentally of his own sanity and wondering why the girl shrank from him in open-eyed alarm. What was the matter with her? This was foolish. He struck the table violently with his clenched fist and shouted hoarsely, "Give

me some gin! Run!" Then, while Nina ran off, he remained
in the chair, very still and quiet, astonished at the noise he
had made.

Nina returned with a tumbler half filled with gin, and
found her father staring absently before him. Almayer felt
very tired now, as if he had come from a long journey. He
felt as if he had walked miles and miles that morning and
now wanted to rest very much. He took the tumbler with
a shaking hand, and as he drank his teeth chattered against
the glass which he drained and set down heavily on the
table. He turned his eyes slowly towards Nina standing beside him, and said steadily—

"Now all is over, Nina. He is dead, and I may as well
burn all my boats."

He felt very proud of being able to speak so calmly. Decidedly he was not going mad. This certitude was very com-
forting, and he went on talking about the finding of the
body, listening to his own voice complacently. Nina stood
quietly, her hand resting lightly on her father's shoulder,
her face unmoved, but every line of her features, the attitude of her whole body expressing the most keen and anxious attention.

"And so Dain is dead," she said coldly, when her father
ceased speaking.

Almayer's elaborately calm demeanour gave way in a
moment to an outburst of violent indignation.

"You stand there as if you were only half alive, and talk
to me," he exclaimed angrily, "as if it was a matter of no
importance. Yes, he is dead! Do you understand? Dead!
What do you care? You never cared; you saw me struggle,
and work, and strive, unmoved; and my suffering you could
never see. No, never. You have no heart, and you have no
mind, or you would have understood that it was for you,
for your happiness I was working. I wanted to be rich; I
wanted to get away from here. I wanted to see white men
bowing low before the power of your beauty and your
wealth. Old as I am I wished to seek a strange land, a civilization to which I am a stranger, so as to find a new life
in the contemplation of your high fortunes, of your tri-

umphs, of your happiness. For that I bore patiently the burden of work, of disappointment, of humiliation amongst these savages here, and I had it all nearly in my grasp."

He looked at his daughter's attentive face and jumped to his feet upsetting the chair.

"Do you hear? I had it all there; so; within reach of my hand."

He paused, trying to keep down his rising anger, and failed.

"Have you no feeling?" he went on. "Have you lived without hope?" Nina's silence exasperated him; his voice rose, although he tried to master his feelings.

"Are you content to live in this misery and die in this wretched hole? Say something, Nina; have you no sympathy? Have you no word of comfort for me? I that loved you so."

He waited for a while for an answer, and receiving none shook his fist in his daughter's face.

"I believe you are an idiot!" he yelled.

He looked round for the chair, picked it up and sat down stiffly. His anger was dead within him, and he felt ashamed of his outburst, yet relieved to think that now he had laid clear before his daughter the inner meaning of his life. He thought so in perfect good faith, deceived by the emotional estimate of his motives, unable to see the crookedness of his ways, the unreality of his aims, the futility of his regrets. And now his heart was filled only with a great tenderness and love for his daughter. He wanted to see her miserable, and to share with her his despair; but he wanted it only as all weak natures long for a companionship in misfortune with beings innocent of its cause. If she suffered herself she would understand and pity him; but now she would not, or could not, find one word of comfort or love for him in his dire extremity. The sense of his absolute loneliness came home to his heart with a force that made him shudder. He swayed and fell forward with his face on the table, his arms stretched straight out, extended and rigid. Nina made a quick movement towards her father and stood looking at the grey head, on the broad shoulders shaken convulsively by the violence of feelings that found relief at last in sobs and tears.

Nina sighed deeply and moved away from the table. Her features lost the appearance of stony indifference that had exasperated her father into his outburst of anger and sorrow. The expression of her face, now unseen by her father, underwent a rapid change. She had listened to Almayer's appeal for sympathy, for one word of comfort, apparently indifferent, yet with her breast torn by conflicting impulses raised unexpectedly by events she had not foreseen, or at least did not expect to happen so soon. With her heart deeply moved by the sight of Almayer's misery, knowing it in her power to end it with a word, longing to bring peace to that troubled heart, she heard with terror the voice of her overpowering love commanding her to be silent. And she submitted after a short and fierce struggle of her old self against the new principle of her life. She wrapped herself up in absolute silence, the only safeguard against some fatal admission. She could not trust herself to make a sign, to murmur a word for fear of saying too much; and the very violence of the feelings that stirred the innermost recesses of her soul seemed to turn her person into a stone. The dilated nostrils and the flashing eyes were the only signs of the storm raging within, and those signs of his daughter's emotion Almayer did not see, for his sight was dimmed by self-pity, by anger, and by despair.

Had Almayer looked at his daughter as she leant over the front rail of the verandah he could have seen the expression of indifference give way to a look of pain and that again pass away, leaving the glorious beauty of her face marred by deep-drawn lines of watchful anxiety. The long grass in the neglected courtyard stood very straight before her eyes in the noonday heat. From the river-bank there were voices and a shuffle of bare feet approaching the house; Babalatchi could be heard giving directions to Almayer's men, and Mrs. Almayer's subdued wailing became audible as the small procession bearing the body of the drowned man and headed by that sorrowful matron turned the corner of the house. Babalatchi had taken the broken anklet off the man's leg, and now held it in his hand as he moved by the side of the bearers, while Mahmat lingered behind timidly, in the hopes of the promised reward.

"Lay him there," said Babalatchi to Almayer's men, pointing to a pile of drying planks in front of the verandah. "Lay him there. He was a Kaffir and the son of a dog, and he was the white man's friend. He drank the white man's strong water," he added, with affected horror. "That I have seen myself."

The men stretched out the broken limbs on two planks they had laid level, while Mrs. Almayer covered the body with a piece of white cotton cloth, and after whispering for some time with Babalatchi departed to her domestic duties. Almayer's men, after laying down their burden, dispersed themselves in quest of shady spots wherein to idle the day away. Babalatchi was left alone by the corpse that lay rigid under the white cloth in the bright sunshine.

Nina came down the steps and joined Babalatchi, who put his hand to his forehead, and squatted down with great deference.

"You have a bangle there," said Nina, looking down on Babalatchi's upturned face and into his solitary eye.

"I have, Mem Putih," returned the polite statesman. Then turning towards Mahmat he beckoned him closer, calling out, "Come here!"

Mahmat approached with some hesitation. He avoided looking at Nina, but fixed his eyes on Babalatchi.

"Now, listen," said Babalatchi, sharply. "The ring and the anklet you have seen, and you know they belonged to Dain the trader, and to no other. Dain returned last night in a canoe. He spoke with the Rajah, and in the middle of the night left to cross over to the white man's house. There was a great flood, and this morning you found him in the river."

"By his feet I dragged him out," muttered Mahmat under his breath. "Tuan Babalatchi, there will be a recompense!" he exclaimed aloud.

Babalatchi held up the gold bangle before Mahmat's eyes. "What I have told you, Mahmat, is for all ears. What I give you now is for your eyes only. Take."

Mahmat took the bangle eagerly and hid it in the folds of his waist-cloth. "Am I a fool to show this thing in a house with three women in it?" he growled. "But I shall tell them about Dain the trader, and there will be talk enough."

He turned and went away, increasing his pace as soon as he was outside Almayer's compound.

Babalatchi looked after him till he disappeared behind the bushes. "Have I done well, Mem Putih?" he asked, humbly addressing Nina.

"You have," answered Nina. "The ring you may keep yourself."

Babalatchi touched his lips and forehead, and scrambled to his feet. He looked at Nina, as if expecting her to say something more, but Nina turned towards the house and went up the steps, motioning him away with her hand.

Babalatchi picked up his staff and prepared to go. It was very warm, and he did not care for the long pull to the Rajah's house. Yet he must go and tell the Rajah—tell of the event; of the change in his plans; of all his suspicions. He walked to the jetty and began casting off the rattan painter of his canoe.

The broad expanse of the lower reach, with its shimmering surface dotted by the black specks of the fishing canoes, lay before his eyes. The fishermen seemed to be racing. Babalatchi paused in his work, and looked on with sudden interest. The man in the foremost canoe, now within hail of the first houses of Sambir, laid in his paddle and stood up shouting—

"The boats! the boats! the man-of-war's boats are coming! They are here!"

In a moment the settlement was again alive with people rushing to the riverside. The men began to unfasten their boats, the women stood in groups looking towards the bend down the river. Above the trees lining the reach a slight puff of smoke appeared like a black stain on the brilliant blue of the cloudless sky.

Babalatchi stood perplexed, the painter in his hand. He looked down the reach, then up towards Almayer's house, and back again at the river as if undecided what to do. At last he made the canoe fast again hastily, and ran towards the house and up the steps of the verandah.

"Tuan! Tuan!" he called, eagerly. "The boats are coming. The man-of-war's boats. You had better get ready. The officers will come here, I know."

Almayer lifted his head slowly from the table, and looked at him stupidly.

"Mem Putih!" exclaimed Babalatchi to Nina, "look at him. He does not hear. You must take care," he added meaningly.

Nina nodded to him with an uncertain smile, and was going to speak, when a sharp report from the gun mounted in the bow of the steam launch that was just then coming into view arrested the words on her parted lips. The smile died out, and was replaced by the old look of anxious attention. From the hills far away the echo came back like a long-drawn and mournful sigh, as if the land had sent it in answer to the voice of its masters.

CHAPTER 8

The news as to the identity of the body lying now in Almayer's compound spread rapidly over the settlement. During the forenoon most of the inhabitants remained in the long street discussing the mysterious return and the unexpected death of the man who had become known to them as the trader. His arrival during the northeast monsoon, his long sojourn in their midst, his sudden departure with his brig, and, above all, the mysterious appearance of the body, said to be his, amongst the logs, were subjects to wonder at and to talk over and over again with undiminished interest. Mahmat moved from house to house and from group to group, always ready to repeat his tale: how he saw the body caught by the sarong in a forked log; how Mrs. Almayer coming, one of the first, at his cries, recognized it, even before he had it hauled on shore; how Babalatchi ordered him to bring it out of the water. "By the feet I dragged him in, and there was no head," exclaimed Mahmat, "and how could the white man's wife know who it was? She was a witch, it was well known. And did you see how the white man himself ran away at the sight of the body? Like a deer he ran!" And here Mahmat imitated Almayer's long strides, to the great joy of the beholders. And for all his trouble he had nothing. The ring with the green stone Tuan Babalatchi kept. "Nothing! Nothing!" He spat down at his feet in sign of disgust, and left that group to seek further on a fresh audience.

The news spreading to the furthermost parts of the settlement found out Abdulla in the cold recess of his godown, where he sat overlooking his Arab clerks and the men loading and unloading the up-country canoes. Reshid, who was busy on the jetty, was summoned into his uncle's presence and found him, as usual, very calm and even cheerful, but very much surprised. The rumour of the capture or destruction of Dain's brig had reached the Arab's ears three days before from the sea-fishermen and through the dwellers on the lower reaches of the river. It had been passed upstream from neighbour to neighbour till Bulangi, whose clearing was nearest to the settlement, had brought that news himself to Abdulla whose favour he courted. But rumour also spoke of a fight and of Dain's death on board his own vessel. And now all the settlement talked of Dain's visit to the Rajah and of his death when crossing the river in the dark to see Almayer. They could not understand this. Reshid thought that it was very strange. He felt uneasy and doubtful. But Abdulla, after the first shock of surprise, with the old age's dislike for solving riddles, showed a becoming resignation. He remarked that the man was dead now at all events, and consequently no more dangerous. Where was the use to wonder at the decrees of Fate, especially if they were propitious to the True Believers? And with a pious ejaculation to Allah the Merciful, the Compassionate, Abdulla seemed to regard the incident as closed for the present.

Not so Reshid. He lingered by his uncle, pulling thoughtfully his neatly trimmed beard.

"There are many lies," he murmured. "He has been dead once before, and came to life to die again now. The Dutch will be here before many days and clamour for the man. Shall I not believe my eyes sooner than the tongues of women and idle men?"

"They say that the body is being taken to Almayer's compound," said Abdulla. "If you want to go there you must go before the Dutch arrive here. Go late. It should not be said that we have been seen inside that man's enclosure lately."

Reshid assented to the truth of this last remark and left his uncle's side. He leaned against the lintel of the big doorway and looked idly across the courtyard through the open gate on to the main road of the settlement. It lay empty, straight, and yellow under the flood of light. In the hot noontide the smooth trunks of palm trees, the outlines of the houses, and away there at the other end of the road the roof of Almayer's house visible over the bushes on the dark background of forest, seemed to quiver in the heat radiating from the steaming earth. Swarms of yellow butterflies rose, and settled to rise again in short flights before Reshid's half-closed eyes. From under his feet arose the dull hum of insects in the long grass of the courtyard. He looked on sleepily.

From one of the side paths amongst the houses a woman stepped out on the road, a slight girlish figure walking under the shade of a large tray balanced on its head. The consciousness of something moving stirred Reshid's half-sleeping senses into a comparative wakefulness. He recognized Taminah, Bulangi's slave-girl, with her tray of cakes for sale—an apparition of daily recurrence and of no im-

portance whatever. She was going towards Almayer's house.
She could be made useful. He roused himself up and ran
towards the gate calling out, "Taminah O!" The girl
stopped, hesitated, and came back slowly. Reshid waited,
signing to her impatiently to come nearer.

When near Reshid Taminah stood with downcast eyes.
Reshid looked at her a while before he asked—

"Are you going to Almayer's house? They say in the
settlement that Dain the trader, he that was found drowned
this morning, is lying in the white man's campong."

"I have heard this talk," whispered Taminah; "and this
morning by the riverside I saw the body. Where it is now I
do not know."

"So you have seen it?" asked Reshid, eagerly. "Is it
Dain? You have seen him many times. You would know
him."

The girl's lips quivered and she remained silent for a
while breathing quickly.

"I have seen him, not a long time ago," she said at last.
"The talk is true; he is dead. What do you want from me,
Tuan? I must go."

Just then the report of the gun fired on board the steam
launch was heard, interrupting Reshid's reply. Leaving the
girl he ran to the house, and met in the courtyard Abdulla
coming towards the gate.

"The Orang Blanda are come," said Reshid, "and now
we shall have our reward."

Abdulla shook his head doubtfully. "The white men's
rewards are long in coming," he said. "White men are
quick in anger and slow in gratitude. We shall see."

He stood at the gate stroking his grey beard and listening to the distant cries of greeting at the other end of the
settlement. As Taminah was turning to go he called her
back.

"Listen, girl," he said: "there will be many white men in
Almayer's house. You shall be there selling your cakes to
the men of the sea. What you see and what you hear you
may tell me. Come here before the sun sets and I will give

you a blue handkerchief with red spots. Now go, and forget not to return."

He gave her a push with the end of his long staff as she was going away and made her stumble.

"This slave is very slow," he remarked to his nephew, looking after the girl with great disfavour.

Taminah walked on, her tray on the head, her eyes fixed on the ground. From the open doors of the houses were heard, as she passed, friendly calls inviting her within for business purposes, but she never heeded them, neglecting her sales in the preoccupation of intense thinking. Since the very early morning she had heard much, she had also seen much that filled her heart with a joy mingled with great suffering and fear. Before the dawn, before she left Bulangi's house to paddle up to Sambir she had heard voices outside the house when all in it but herself were asleep. And now, with her knowledge of the words spoken in the darkness, she held in her hand a life and carried in her breast a great sorrow. Yet from her springy step, erect figure, and face veiled over by the every-day look of apathetic indifference, nobody could have guessed of the double load she carried under the visible burden of the tray piled up high with cakes manufactured by the thrifty hands of Bulangi's wives. In that supple figure straight as an arrow, so graceful and free in its walk, behind those soft eyes that spoke of nothing but of unconscious resignation, there slept all feelings and all passions, all hopes and all fears, the curse of life and the consolation of death. And she knew nothing of it all. She lived like the tall palms amongst whom she was passing now, seeking the light, desiring the sunshine, fearing the storm, unconscious of either. The slave had no hope, and knew of no change. She knew of no other sky, no other water, no other forest, no other world, no other life. She had no wish, no hope, no love, no fear, except of a blow, and no vivid feeling but that of occasional hunger, which was seldom, for Bulangi was rich and rice was plentiful in the solitary house in his clearing. The absence of pain and hunger was her happiness, and when she felt unhappy she was simply tired, more than usual, after the day's labour. Then in the hot nights of the south-west monsoon she slept dreamlessly under the bright stars on the platform built outside the house and over the river. Inside they slept too: Bulangi by the door; his wives further in; the children with their mothers. She could hear their breathing; Bulangi's sleepy voice; the sharp cry of a child soon hushed with tender words. And she closed her eyes to the murmur of the water below her, to the whisper of the warm wind above, ignorant of the never-ceasing life of that tropical nature that spoke to her in vain with the thousand faint voices of the near forest, with the breath of tepid wind; in the heavy scents that lingered around her head; in the white wraiths of morning mist that hung over her in the solemn hush of all creation before the dawn.

Such had been her existence before the coming of the brig with the strangers. She remembered well that time; the uproar in the settlement, the never-ending wonder, the days and nights of talk and excitement. She remembered her own timidity with the strange men, till the brig moored to the bank became in a manner part of the settlement, and the fear wore off in the familiarity of constant intercourse. The call on board then became part of her daily round. She walked hesitatingly up the slanting planks of the gang-way amidst the encouraging shouts and more or less decent jokes of the men idling over the bulwarks. There she sold her wares to those men that spoke so loud and carried themselves so free. There was a throng, a constant coming and going; calls interchanged, orders given and executed with shouts; the rattle of blocks, the flinging about of coils of rope. She sat out of the way under the shade of the awning, with her tray before her, the veil drawn well over her face, feeling shy amongst so many men. She smiled at all buyers, but spoke to none, letting their jests pass with stolid unconcern. She heard many tales told around her of far-off countries, of strange customs, of events stranger still. Those men were brave; but the most fearless of them spoke of their chief with fear. Often the man they called their master passed before her, walking erect and indifferent, in the pride of youth, in the flash of rich dress, with a tinkle of gold ornaments, while everybody stood aside, watching anxiously for a movement of his lips, ready to do his bidding. Then all her life seemed to rush into her eyes, and from under her veil she gazed at him, charmed yet fearful to attract attention. One day he noticed her and asked, "Who is that girl?" "A slave, Tuan! A girl that sells cakes," a dozen voices replied together. She rose in terror to run on shore, when he called her back; and as she stood trembling with head hung down before him, he spoke kind words, lifting her chin with his hand and looking into her eyes with a smile. "Do not be afraid," he said. He never spoke to her any more. Somebody called out from the river-bank; he turned away and forgot her existence. Taminah saw Almayer standing on the shore with Nina on his arm. She heard Nina's voice calling out gaily, and saw Dain's face brighten with joy as he leaped on shore. She hated the sound of that voice ever since.

After that day she left off visiting Almayer's compound, and passed the noon hours under the shade of the brig awning. She watched for his coming with heart beating quicker and quicker, as he approached, into a wild tumult of newly-aroused feelings of joy and hope and fear that died away with Dain's retreating figure, leaving her tired out, as if after a struggle, sitting still for a long time, in dreamy languor. Then she paddled home slowly in the afternoon, often letting her canoe float with the lazy stream in the quiet backwater of the river. The paddle hung idle in the water as she sat in the stern, one hand supporting her chin, her eyes wide open, listening intently to the whispering of her heart that seemed to swell at last into a song of extreme sweetness. Listening to that song she husked the rice at home; it dulled her ears to the shrill bickerings of Bulangi's wives, to the sound of angry reproaches addressed to herself. And when the sun was near its setting she walked to the bathing-place and heard it as she stood on the tender grass of the low bank, her robe at her feet, and looked at the reflection of her figure on the glass-like surface of the creek. Listening to it she walked slowly back, her wet hair hanging over

her shoulders; lying down to rest under the bright stars, she
closed her eyes to the murmur of the water below, of the
warm wind above; to the voice of nature speaking through
the faint noises of the great forest, and to the song of her own
heart.

She heard, but did not understand, and drank in the
dreamy joy of her new existence without troubling about
its meaning or its end, till the full consciousness of life came
to her through pain and anger. And she suffered horribly
the first time she saw Nina's long canoe drift silently past
the sleeping house of Bulangi, bearing the two lovers into
the white mist of the great river. Her jealousy and rage
culminated into a paroxysm of physical pain that left her
lying panting on the river-bank in the dumb agony of a
wounded animal. But she went on moving patiently in the
enchanted circle of slavery, going through her task day
after day with all the pathos of the grief she could not express, even to herself, locked within her breast. She shrank
from Nina as she would have shrunk from the sharp blade
of a knife cutting into her flesh, but she kept on visiting
the brig to feed her dumb, ignorant soul on her own despair.
She saw Dain many times. He never spoke, he never looked.
Could his eyes see only one woman's image? Could his ears
hear only one woman's voice? He never noticed her; not
once.

And then he went away. She saw him and Nina for the
last time on that morning when Babalatchi, while visiting
his fish baskets, had his suspicions of the white man's daughter's love affair with Dain confirmed beyond the shadow of
doubt. Dain disappeared, and Taminah's heart, where lay
useless and barren the seeds of all love and of all hate, the
possibilities of all passions and of all sacrifices, forgot its
joys and its sufferings when deprived of the help of the
senses. Her half-formed, savage mind, the slave of her
body—as her body was the slave of another's will—forgot
the faint and vague image of the ideal that had found its
beginning in the physical promptings of her savage nature.
She dropped back into the torpor of her former life and
found consolation—even a certain kind of happiness—in

the thought that now Nina and Dain were separated, probably for ever. He would forget. This thought soothed the last pangs of dying jealousy that had nothing now to feed upon, and Taminah found peace. It was like the dreary tranquillity of a desert, where there is peace only because there is no life.

And now he had returned. She had recognized his voice calling aloud in the night for Bulangi. She had crept out after her master to listen closer to the intoxicating sound. Dain was there, in a boat, talking to Bulangi. Taminah, listening with arrested breath, heard another voice. The maddening joy, that only a second before she thought herself incapable of containing within her fast-beating heart, died out, and left her shivering in the old anguish of physical pain that she had suffered once before at the sight of Dain and Nina. Nina spoke now, ordering and entreating in turns, and Bulangi was refusing, expostulating, at last consenting. He went in to take a paddle from the heap lying behind the door. Outside the murmur of two voices went on, and she caught a word here and there. She understood that he was fleeing from white men, that he was seeking a hiding-place, that he was in some danger. But she heard also words which woke the rage of jealousy that had been asleep for so many days in her bosom. Crouching low on the mud in the black darkness amongst the piles, she heard the whisper in the boat that made light of toil, of privation, of danger, of life itself, if in exchange there could be but a short moment of close embrace, a look from the eyes, the feel of light breath, the touch of soft lips. So spoke Dain as he sat in the canoe holding Nina's hands while waiting for Bulangi's return; and Taminah, supporting herself by the slimy pile, felt as if a heavy weight was crushing her down, down into the black oily water at her feet. She wanted to cry out; to rush at them and tear their vague shadows apart; to throw Nina into the smooth water, cling to her close, hold her to the bottom where that man could not find her. She could not cry, she could not move. Then footsteps were heard on the bamboo platform above her head; she saw Bulangi get into his smallest canoe and take the lead, the other boat following, paddled by Dain and Nina. With a slight splash of the paddles dipped stealthily into the water, their indistinct forms passed before her aching eyes and vanished in the darkness of the creek.

She remained there in the cold and wet, powerless to move, breathing painfully under the crushing weight that the mysterious hand of Fate had laid so suddenly upon her slender shoulders, and shivering, she felt within a burning fire, that seemed to feed upon her very life. When the breaking day had spread a pale golden ribbon over the black outline of the forests, she took up her tray and departed towards the settlement, going about her task purely from the force of habit. As she approached Sambir she could see the excitement and she heard with momentary surprise of the finding of Dain's body. It was not true, of course. She knew it well. She regretted that he was not dead. She should have liked Dain to be dead, so as to be parted from that woman —from all women. She felt a strong desire to see Nina, but without any clear object. She hated her, and feared her, and she felt an irresistible impulse pushing her towards Almayer's house to see the white woman's face, to look close at those eyes, to hear again that voice, for the sound of which Dain was ready to risk his liberty, his life even. She had seen her many times; she had heard her voice daily for many months past. What was there in her? What was there in that being to make a man speak as Dain had spoken, to make him blind to all other faces, deaf to all other voices?

She left the crowd by the riverside, and wandered aimlessly among the empty houses, resisting the impulse that pushed her towards Almayer's campong to seek there in Nina's eyes the secret of her own misery. The sun mounting higher, shortened the shadows and poured down upon her a flood of light and of stifling heat as she passed on from shadow to light, from light to shadow amongst the houses, the bushes, the tall trees, in her unconscious flight from the pain in her own heart. In the extremity of her distress she could find no words to pray for relief, she knew of no heaven to send her prayer to, and she wandered on with tired feet in the dumb surprise and terror at the injustice of the suffering inflicted upon her without cause and without redress.

The short talk with Reshid, the proposal of Abdulla steadied her a little and turned her thoughts into another channel. Dain was in some danger. He was hiding from white men. So much she had overheard last night. They all thought him dead. She knew he was alive, and she knew of his hiding-place. What did the Arabs want to know about the white men? The white men want with Dain? Did they wish to kill him? She could tell them all—no, she would say nothing, and in the night she would go to him and sell him his life for a word, for a smile, for a gesture even, and be a slave in far-off countries, away from Nina. But there were dangers. The one-eyed Babalatchi who knew everything; the white man's wife!—she was a witch. Perhaps they would tell. And then there was Nina. She must hurry on and see.

In her impatience she left the path and ran towards Almayer's dwelling through the undergrowth between the palm trees. She came out at the back of the house, where a narrow ditch, full of stagnant water that overflowed from the river, separated Almayer's campong from the rest of the settlement. The thick bushes growing on the bank were hiding from her sight the large courtyard with its cooking shed. Above them rose several thin columns of smoke, and from behind the sound of strange voices informed Taminah that the Men of the Sea belonging to the warship had already landed and were camped between the ditch and the house. To the left one of Almayer's slave-girls came down to the ditch and bent over the shiny water, washing a kettle. To the right the tops of the banana plantation, visible above the bushes, swayed and shook under the touch of invisible hands gathering the fruit. On the calm water several canoes moored to a heavy stake were crowded together, nearly bridging the ditch just at the place where Taminah stood. The voices in the courtyard rose at times into an outburst of calls, replies, and laughter, and then died away into a silence that soon was broken again by a fresh clamour. Now and again the thin blue smoke rushed out thicker and blacker, and drove in odorous masses over the creek, wrapping her for a moment in a suffocating veil; then, as the fresh wood caught well alight, the smoke vanished in the bright sunlight, and only the scent of aromatic wood drifted afar, to leeward of the crackling fires.

Taminah rested her tray on a stump of a tree, and remained standing with her eyes turned towards Almayer's house, whose roof and part of a whitewashed wall were visible over the bushes. The slave-girl finished her work, and after looking for a while curiously at Taminah, pushed her way through the dense thicket back to the courtyard. Round Taminah there was now a complete solitude. She threw herself down on the ground, and hid her face in her hands. Now when so close she had no courage to see Nina. At every burst of louder voices from the courtyard she shivered in the fear of hearing Nina's voice. She came to the resolution of waiting where she was till dark, and then going straight to Dain's hiding-place. From where she was she could watch the movements of white men, of Nina, of all Dain's friends, and of all his enemies. Both were hateful alike to her, for both would take him away beyond her reach. She hid herself in the long grass to wait anxiously for the sunset that seemed so slow to come.

On the other side of the ditch, behind the bush, by the clear fires, the seamen of the frigate had encamped on the hospitable invitation of Almayer. Almayer, roused out of his apathy by the prayers and importunity of Nina, had managed to get down in time to the jetty so as to receive the officers at their landing. The lieutenant in command accepted his invitation to his house with the remark that in any case their business was with Almayer—and perhaps not very pleasant, he added. Almayer hardly heard him. He shook hands with them absently and led the way towards the house. He was scarcely conscious of the polite words of welcome he greeted the strangers with, and afterwards repeated several times over again in his efforts to appear at ease. The agitation of their host did not escape the officer's eyes, and the chief confided to his subordinate, in a low voice, his doubts as to Almayer's sobriety. The young sub-lieutenant laughed and expressed in a whisper the hope that the white man was not intoxicated enough to neglect the offer of some refreshments. "He does not seem very danger-ous," he added, as they followed Almayer up the steps of the verandah.

"No, he seems more of a fool than a knave; I have heard of him," returned the senior.

They sat around the table. Almayer with shaking hands made gin cocktails, offered them all round, and drank him-self, with every gulp feeling stronger, steadier, and better able to face all the difficulties of his position. Ignorant of the fate of the brig he did not suspect the real object of the officer's visit. He had a general notion that something must have leaked out about the gunpowder trade, but appre-hended nothing beyond some temporary inconvenience. After emptying his glass he began to chat easily, lying back in his chair with one of his legs thrown negligently over the arm. The lieutenant astride on his chair, a glowing cheroot in the corner of his mouth, listened with a sly smile from behind the thick volumes of smoke that escaped from his compressed lips. The young sub-lieutenant, leaning with both elbows on the table, his head between his hands, looked on sleepily in the torpor induced by fatigue and the gin. Almayer talked on—

"It is a great pleasure to see white faces here. I have lived here many years in great solitude. The Malays, you understand, are not company for a white man; moreover they are not friendly; they do not understand our ways. Great rascals they are. I believe I am the only white man on the east coast that is a settled resident. We get visitors from Macassar or Singapore sometimes—traders, agents, or explorers, but they are rare. There was a scientific explorer here a year or more ago. He lived in my house: drank from morning to night. He lived joyously for a few months, and when the liquor he brought with him was gone he returned to Batavia with a report on the mineral wealth of the in-terior. Ha, ha, ha! Good, is it not?"

He ceased abruptly and looked at his guests with a meaningless stare. While they laughed he was reciting to himself the old story: "Dain dead, all my plans destroyed. This is the end of all hope and of all things." His heart sank within him. He felt a kind of deadly sickness.

"Very good. Capital!" exclaimed both officers.

Almayer came out of his despondency with another burst of talk.

"Eh! what about the dinner? You have got a cook with you. That's all right. There is a cooking shed in the other courtyard. I can give you a goose. Look at my geese—the only geese on the east coast—perhaps on the whole island. Is that your cook? Very good. Here, Ali, show this Chinaman the cooking place and tell Mem Almayer to let him have room there. My wife, gentlemen, does not come out; my daughter may. Meantime have some more drink. It is a hot day."

The lieutenant took the cigar out of his mouth, looked at the ash critically, shook it off and turned towards Almayer.

"We have a rather unpleasant business with you," he said.

"I am sorry," returned Almayer. "It can be nothing very serious, surely."

"If you think an attempt to blow up forty men at least, not a serious matter you will not find many people of your opinion," retorted the officer sharply.

"Blow up! What? I know nothing about it," exclaimed Almayer. "Who did that, or tried to do it?"

"A man with whom you had some dealings," answered the lieutenant. "He passed here under the name of Dain Maroola. You sold him the gunpowder he had in that brig we captured."

"How did you hear about the brig?" asked Almayer. "I know nothing about the powder he may have had."

"An Arab trader of this place has sent the information about your goings on here to Batavia, a couple of months ago," said the officer. "We were waiting for the brig outside, but he slipped past us at the mouth of the river, and we had to chase the fellow to the southward. When he sighted us he ran inside the reefs and put the brig ashore. The crew escaped in boats before we could take possession.

As our boats neared the craft it blew up with a tremendous explosion; one of the boats being too near got swamped. Two men drowned—that is the result of your speculation, Mr. Almayer. Now we want this Dain. We have good grounds to suppose he is hiding in Sambir. Do you know where he is? You had better put yourself right with the authorities as much as possible by being perfectly frank with me. Where is this Dain?"

Almayer got up and walked towards the balustrade of the verandah. He seemed not to be thinking of the officer's question. He looked at the body lying straight and rigid under its white cover on which the sun, declining amongst the clouds to the westward, threw a pale tinge of red. The lieutenant waited for the answer, taking quick pulls at his half-extinguished cigar. Behind them Ali moved noiselessly laying the table, ranging solemnly the ill-assorted and shabby crockery, the tin spoons, the forks with broken prongs, and the knives with saw-like blades and loose handles. He had almost forgotten how to prepare the table for white men. He felt aggrieved; Mem Nina would not help him. He stepped back to look at his work admiringly, feeling very proud. This must be right; and if the master afterwards is angry and swears, then so much the worse for Mem Nina. Why did she not help? He left the verandah to fetch the dinner.

"Well, Mr. Almayer, will you answer my question as frankly as it is put to you?" asked the lieutenant, after a long silence.

Almayer turned round and looked at his interlocutor steadily. "If you catch this Dain what will you do with him?" he asked.

The officer's face flushed. "This is not an answer," he said, annoyed.

"And what will you do with me?" went on Almayer, not heeding the interruption.

"Are you inclined to bargain?" growled the other. "It would be bad policy, I assure you. At present I have no orders about your person, but we expected your assistance in catching this Malay."

"Ah!" interrupted Almayer, "just so: you can do nothing without me, and I, knowing the man well, am to help you in finding him."

"This is exactly what we expect," assented the officer. "You have broken the law, Mr. Almayer, and you ought to make amends."

"And save myself?"

"Well, in a sense yes. Your head is not in any danger," said the lieutenant, with a short laugh.

"Very well," said Almayer, with decision, "I shall deliver the man up to you."

Both officers rose to their feet quickly, and looked for their side-arms which they had unbuckled. Almayer laughed harshly.

"Steady, gentlemen!" he exclaimed. "In my own time and in my own way. After dinner, gentlemen, you shall have him."

"This is preposterous," urged the lieutenant. "Mr. Almayer, this is no joking matter. The man is a criminal. He deserves to hang. While we dine he may escape; the rumour of our arrival—"

Almayer walked towards the table. "I give you my word of honour, gentlemen, that he shall not escape; I have him safe enough."

"The arrest should be effected before dark," remarked the young sub.

"I shall hold you responsible for any failure. We are ready, but can do nothing just now without you," added the senior, with evident annoyance.

Almayer made a gesture of assent. "On my word of honour," he repeated vaguely. "And now let us dine," he added briskly.

Nina came through the doorway and stood for a moment holding the curtain aside for Ali and the old Malay woman bearing the dishes; then she moved towards the three men by the table.

"Allow me," said Almayer pompously. "This is my daughter. Nina, these gentlemen, officers of the frigate outside, have done me the honour to accept my hospitality."

Nina answered the low bows of the two officers by a slow inclination of the head and took her place at the table opposite her father. All sat down. The coxswain of the steam launch came up carrying some bottles of wine.

"You will allow me to have this put upon the table?" said the lieutenant to Almayer.

"What! Wine! You are very kind. Certainly. I have none myself. Times are very hard."

The last words of his reply were spoken by Almayer in a faltering voice. The thought that Dain was dead recurred to him vividly again, and he felt as if an invisible hand was gripping his throat. He reached for the gin bottle while they were uncorking the wine and swallowed a big gulp. The lieutenant, who was speaking to Nina, gave him a quick glance. The young sub began to recover from the astonishment and confusion caused by Nina's unexpected appearance and great beauty. "She was very beautiful and imposing," he reflected, "but after all a half-caste girl." This thought caused him to, pluck up heart and look at Nina sideways. Nina, with composed face, was answering in a low, even voice the elder officer's polite questions as to the country and her mode of life. Almayer pushed his plate away and drank his guest's wine in gloomy silence.

CHAPTER 9

"Can I believe what you tell me? It is like a tale for men that listen only half awake by the camp fire, and it seems to have run off a woman's tongue."

"Who is there here for me to deceive, O Rajah?" answered Babalatchi. "Without you I am nothing. All I have told you I believe to be true. I have been safe for many years in the hollow of your hand. This is no time to harbour suspicions. The danger is very great. We should advise and act at once, before the sun sets."

"Right. Right," muttered Lakamba, pensively.

They had been sitting for the last hour together in the audience chamber of the Rajah's house, for Babalatchi, as soon as he had witnessed the landing of the Dutch officers, had crossed the river to report to his master the events of the morning, and to confer with him upon the line of conduct to pursue in the face of altered circumstances. They were both puzzled and frightened by the unexpected turn the events had taken. The Rajah, sitting crosslegged on his chair, looked fixedly at the floor; Babalatchi was squatting close by in an attitude of deep dejection.

"And where did you say he is hiding now?" asked Lakamba, breaking at last the silence full of gloomy forebodings in which they both had been lost for a long while.

"In Bulangi's clearing—the furthest one, away from the house. They went there that very night. The white man's daughter took him there. She told me so herself, speaking to me openly, for she is half white and has no decency. She said she was waiting for him while he was here; then, after a long time, he came out of the darkness and fell at her feet exhausted. He lay like one dead, but she brought him back to life in her arms, and made him breathe again with her own breath. That is what she said, speaking to my face, as I am speaking now to you, Rajah. She is like a white woman and knows no shame."

He paused, deeply shocked. Lakamba nodded his head. "Well, and then?" he asked.

"They called the old woman," went on Babalatchi, "and he told them all—about the brig, and how he tried to kill many men. He knew the Orang Blanda were very near, although he had said nothing to us about that; he knew his great danger. He thought he had killed many, but there were only two dead, as I have heard from the men of the sea that came in the warship's boats."

"And the other man, he that was found in the river?" interrupted Lakamba.

"That was one of his boatmen. When his canoe was overturned by the logs those two swam together, but the other man must have been hurt. Dain swam, holding him up. He left him in the bushes when he went up to the house. When they all came down his heart had ceased to beat; then the old woman spoke; Dain thought it was good. He took off his anklet and broke it, twisting it round the man's foot. His ring he put on that slave's hand. He took off his sarong and clothed that thing that wanted no clothes, the two women holding it up meanwhile, their intent being to deceive all eyes and to mislead the minds in the settlement, so that they could swear to the thing that was not, and that there could be no treachery when the white men came. Then Dain and the white woman departed to call up Bulangi and find a hiding-place. The old woman remained by the body."

"Hai!" exclaimed Lakamba. "She has wisdom."

"Yes, she has a Devil of her own to whisper counsel in her ear," assented Babalatchi. "She dragged the body with great toil to the point where many logs were stranded. All these things were done in the darkness after the storm had passed away. Then she waited. At the first sign of daylight she battered the face of the dead with a heavy stone, and she pushed him amongst the logs. She remained near, watching. At sunrise Mahmat Banjer came and found him. They all believed; I myself was deceived, but not for long. The white man believed, and, grieving, fled to his house. When we were alone, I, having doubts, spoke to the woman, and she, fearing my anger and your might, told me all, asking for help in saving Dain."

"He must not fall into the hands of the Orang Blanda," said Lakamba; "but let him die, if the thing can be done quietly."

"It cannot, Tuan! Remember there is that woman who, being half white, is ungovernable, and would raise a great outcry. Also the officers are here. They are angry enough already. Dain must escape; he must go. We must help him now for our own safety."

"Are the officers very angry?" inquired Lakamba, with interest.

"They are. The principal chief used strong words when speaking to me—to me when I salaamed in your name. I do not think," added Babalatchi, after a short pause and looking very worried—"I do not think I saw a white chief so angry before. He said we were careless or even worse. He told me he would speak to the Rajah, and that I was of no account."

"Speak to the Rajah!" repeated Lakamba, thoughtfully. "Listen, Babalatchi: I am sick, and shall withdraw; you cross over and tell the white men."

"Yes," said Babalatchi, "I am going over at once; and as to Dain?"

"You get him away as you can best. This is a great trouble in my heart," sighed Lakamba.

Babalatchi got up, and, going close to his master, spoke earnestly.

"There is one of our praus at the southern mouth of the river. The Dutch warship is to the northward watching the main entrance. I shall send Dain off to-night in a canoe, by the hidden channels, on board the prau. His father is a great prince, and shall hear of our generosity. Let the prau take him to Ampanam. Your glory shall be great, and your reward in powerful friendship. Almayer will no doubt deliver the dead body as Dain's to the officers, and the foolish white men shall say, 'This is very good; let there be peace.' And the trouble shall be removed from your heart, Rajah."

"True! true!" said Lakamba.

"And, this being accomplished by me who am your slave, you shall reward with a generous hand. That I know! The white man is grieving for the lost treasure, in the manner of white men who thirst after dollars. Now, when all other things are in order, we shall perhaps obtain the treasure from the white man. Dain must escape, and Almayer must live."

"Now go, Babalatchi, go!" said Lakamba, getting off his chair. "I am very sick, and want medicine. Tell the white chief so."

But Babalatchi was not to be got rid of in this summary

manner. He knew that his master, after the manner of the great, liked to shift the burden of toil and danger on to his servants' shoulders, but in the difficult straits in which they were now the Rajah must play his part. He may be very sick for the white men, for all the world if he liked, as long as he would take upon himself the execution of part at least of Babalatchi's carefully thought-of plan. Babalatchi wanted a big canoe manned by twelve men to be sent out after dark towards Bulangi's clearing. Dain may have to be overpowered. A man in love cannot be expected to see clearly the path of safety if it leads him away from the object of his affections, argued Babalatchi, and in that case they would have to use force in order to make him go. Would the Rajah see that trusty men manned the canoe? The thing must be done secretly. Perhaps the Rajah would come himself, so as to bring all the weight of his authority to bear upon Dain if he should prove obstinate and refuse to leave his hiding-place. The Rajah would not commit himself to a definite promise, and anxiously pressed Babalatchi to go, being afraid of the white men paying him an unexpected visit. The aged statesman reluctantly took his leave and went into the courtyard.

Before going down to his boat Babalatchi stopped for a while in the big open space where the thick-leaved trees put black patches of shadow which seemed to float on a flood of smooth, intense light that rolled up to the houses and down to the stockade and over the river, where it broke and sparkled in thousands of glittering wavelets, like a band woven of azure and gold edged with the brilliant green of the forests guarding both banks of the Pantai. In the perfect calm before the coming of the afternoon breeze the irregularly jagged line of tree-tops stood unchanging, as if traced by an unsteady hand on the clear blue of the hot sky. In the space sheltered by the high palisades there lingered the smell of decaying blossoms from the surrounding forest, a taint of drying fish; with now and then a whiff of acrid smoke from the cooking fires when it eddied down from under the leafy boughs and clung lazily about the burnt-up grass.

As Babalatchi looked up at the flagstaff overtopping a group of low trees in the middle of the courtyard the tri-colour flag of the Netherlands stirred slightly for the first time since it had been hoisted that morning on the arrival of the man-of-war boats. With a faint rustle of trees the breeze came down in light puffs, playing capriciously for a time with this emblem of Lakamba's power, that was also the mark of his servitude; then the breeze freshened in a sharp gust of wind, and the flag flew out straight and steady above the trees. A dark shadow ran along the river, rolling over and covering up the sparkle of declining sunlight. A big white cloud sailed slowly across the darkening sky, and hung to the westward as if waiting for the sun to join it there. Men and things shook off the torpor of the hot after-noon and stirred into life under the first breath of the sea breeze.

Babalatchi hurried down to the water-gate; yet before he passed through it he paused to look round the courtyard, with its light and shade, with its cheery fires, with the groups of Lakamba's soldiers and retainers scattered about. His own house stood amongst the other buildings in that en-closure, and the statesman of Sambir asked himself with a sinking heart when and how would it be given him to return to that house. He had to deal with a man more dangerous than any wild beast of his experience: a proud man, a man wilful after the manner of princes, a man in love. And he was going forth to speak to that man words of cold and worldly wisdom. Could anything be more ap-palling? What if that man should take umbrage at some fancied slight to his honour or disregard of his affections and suddenly "amok"? The wise adviser would be the first victim, no doubt, and death would be his reward. And un-derlying the horror of this situation there was the danger of those meddlesome fools, the white men. A vision of com-fortless exile in far-off Madura rose up before Babalatchi. Wouldn't that be worse than death itself? And there was that half-white woman with threatening eyes. How could he tell what an incomprehensible creature of that sort would or would not do? She knew so much that she made

the killing of Dain an impossibility. That much was certain.
And yet the sharp, rough-edged kriss is a good and discreet
friend, thought Babalatchi, as he examined his own lovingly,
and put it back in the sheath, with a sigh of regret, before
unfastening his canoe. As he cast off the painter, pushed
out into the stream, and took up his paddle, he realized
vividly how unsatisfactory it was to have women mixed
up in state affairs. Young women, of course. For Mrs.
Almayer's mature wisdom, and for the easy aptitude in intrigue that comes with years to the feminine mind, he felt
the most sincere respect.

He paddled leisurely, letting the canoe drift down as he
crossed towards the point. The sun was high yet, and nothing pressed. His work would commence only with the coming of darkness. Avoiding the Lingard jetty, he rounded
the point, and paddled up the creek at the back of Almayer's
house. There were many canoes lying there, their noses all
drawn together, fastened all to the same stake. Babalatchi
pushed his little craft in amongst them and stepped on
shore. On the other side of the ditch something moved in
the grass.

"Who's that hiding?" hailed Babalatchi. "Come out and
speak to me."

Nobody answered. Babalatchi crossed over, passing from
boat to boat, and poked his staff viciously in the suspicious
place. Taminah jumped up with a cry.

"What are you doing here?" he asked, surprised. "I have
nearly stepped on your tray. Am I a Dyak that you should
hide at my sight?"

"I was weary, and—I slept," whispered Taminah, confusedly.

"You slept! You have not sold anything to-day, and you
will be beaten when you return home," said Babalatchi.

Taminah stood before him abashed and silent. Babalatchi
looked her over carefully with great satisfaction. Decidedly
he would offer fifty dollars more to that thief Bulangi. The
girl pleased him.

"Now you go home. It is late," he said sharply. "Tell
Bulangi that I shall be near his house before the night is

half over, and that I want him to make all things ready for
a long journey. You understand? A long journey to the
southward. Tell him that before sunset, and do not forget
my words."

Taminah made a gesture of assent, and watched Babalatchi recross the ditch and disappear through the bushes
bordering Almayer's compound. She moved a little further
off the creek and sank in the grass again, lying down on
her face, shivering in dry-eyed misery.

Babalatchi walked straight towards the cooking shed
looking for Mrs. Almayer. The courtyard was in a great
uproar. A strange Chinaman had possession of the kitchen
fire and was noisily demanding another saucepan. He
hurled objurgations, in the Canton dialect and bad Malay,
against the group of slave-girls standing a little way off,
half frightened, half amused, at his violence. From the
camping fires round which the seamen of the frigate were
sitting came words of encouragement, mingled with laughter and jeering. In the midst of this noise and confusion
Babalatchi met Ali, an empty dish in his hand.

"Where are the white men?" asked Babalatchi.

"They are eating on the front verandah," answered Ali.
"Do not stop me, Tuan. I am giving the white men their
food and am busy."

"Where's Mem Almayer?"

"Inside the passage. She is listening to the talk."

Ali grinned and passed on; Babalatchi ascended the
plankway to the rear verandah, and beckoning out Mrs.
Almayer, engaged her in earnest conversation. Through
the long passage, closed at the further end by the red curtain, they could hear from time to time Almayer's voice
mingling in conversation with an abrupt loudness that made
Mrs. Almayer look significantly at Babalatchi.

"Listen," she said. "He has drunk much."

"He has," whispered Babalatchi. "He will sleep heavily
to-night."

Mrs. Almayer looked doubtful.

"Sometimes the devil of strong gin makes him keep
awake, and he walks up and down the verandah all night,

cursing; then we stand afar off," explained Mrs. Almayer, with the fuller knowledge born of twenty odd years of married life.

"But then he does not hear, nor understand, and his hand, of course, has no strength. We do not want him to hear to-night."

"No," assented Mrs. Almayer, energetically, but in a cautiously subdued voice. "If he hears he will kill."

Babalatchi looked incredulous.

"Hai Tuan, you may believe me. Have I not lived many years with that man? Have I not seen death in that man's eyes more than once when I was younger and he guessed at many things? Had he been a man of my own people I would not have seen such a look twice; but he—"

With a contemptuous gesture she seemed to fling unutterable scorn on Almayer's weak-minded aversion to sudden bloodshed.

"If he has the wish but not the strength, then what do we fear?" asked Babalatchi, after a short silence during which they both listened to Almayer's loud talk till it subsided into the murmur of general conversation. "What do we fear?" repeated Babalatchi again.

"To keep the daughter whom he loves he would strike into your heart and mine without hesitation," said Mrs. Almayer. "When the girl is gone he will be like the devil unchained. Then you and I had better beware."

"I am an old man and fear not death," answered Babalatchi, with a mendacious assumption of indifference. "But what will you do?"

"I am an old woman, and wish to live," retorted Mrs. Almayer. "She is my daughter also. I shall seek safety at the feet of our Rajah, speaking in the name of the past when we both were young, and he—"

Babalatchi raised his hand.

"Enough. You shall be protected," he said soothingly.

Again the sound of Almayer's voice was heard, and again interrupting their talk, they listened to the confused but loud utterance coming in bursts of unequal strength, with unexpected pauses and noisy repetitions that made some

words and sentences fall clear and distinct on their ears out
of the meaningless jumble of excited shoutings emphasized
by the thumping of Almayer's fist upon the table. On the
short intervals of silence, the high complaining note of
tumblers, standing close together and vibrating to the
shock, lingered, growing fainter, till it leapt up again into
tumultuous ringing, when a new idea started a new rush of
words and brought down the heavy hand again. At last the
quarrelsome shouting ceased, and the thin plaint of disturbed glass died away into reluctant quietude.

Babalatchi and Mrs. Almayer had listened curiously, their
bodies bent and their ears turned towards the passage. At
every louder shout they nodded at each other with a ridiculous affectation of scandalized propriety, and they remained
in the same attitude for some time after the noise had
ceased.

"This is the devil of gin," whispered Mrs. Almayer. "Yes;
he talks like that sometimes when there is nobody to hear
him."

"What does he say?" inquired Babalatchi, eagerly. "You
ought to understand."

"I have forgotten their talk. A little I understood. He
spoke without any respect of the white ruler in Batavia,
and of protection, and said he had been wronged; he said
that several times. More I did not understand. Listen! Again
he speaks!"

"Tse! tse! tse!" clicked Babalatchi, trying to appear
shocked, but with a joyous twinkle of his solitary eye.
"There will be great trouble between those white men. I
will go round now and see. You tell your daughter that
there is a sudden and a long journey before her, with much
glory and splendour at the end. And tell her that Dain
must go, or he must die, and that he will not go alone."

"No, he will not go alone," slowly repeated Mrs. Almayer, with a thoughtful air, as she crept into the passage
after seeing Babalatchi disappear round the corner of the
house.

The statesman of Sambir, under the impulse of vivid
curiosity, made his way quickly to the front of the house,

but once there he moved slowly and cautiously as he crept step by step up the stairs of the verandah. On the highest step he sat down quietly, his feet on the steps below, ready for flight should his presence prove unwelcome. He felt pretty safe so. The table stood nearly endways to him, and he saw Almayer's back; at Nina he looked full face, and had a side view of both officers; but of the four persons sitting at the table only Nina and the younger officer noticed his noiseless arrival. The momentary dropping of Nina's eyelids acknowledged Babalatchi's presence; she then spoke at once to the young sub, who turned towards her with attentive alacrity, but her gaze was fastened steadily on her father's face while Almayer was speaking uproariously.

". . . disloyalty and unscrupulousness! What have you ever done to make me loyal? You have no grip on this country. I had to take care of myself, and when I asked for protection I was met with threats and contempt, and had Arab slander thrown in my face. I! a white man!"

"Don't be violent, Almayer," remonstrated the lieutenant; "I have heard all this already."

"Then why do you talk to me about scruples? I wanted money, and I gave powder in exchange. How could I know that some of your wretched men were going to be blown up? Scruples! Pah!"

He groped unsteadily amongst the bottles, trying one after another, grumbling to himself the while. "No more wine," he muttered discontentedly.

"You have had enough, Almayer," said the lieutenant, as he lighted a cigar. "Is it not time to deliver to us your prisoner? I take it you have that Dain Maroola stowed away safely somewhere. Still we had better get that business over, and then we shall have more drink. Come! don't look at me like this."

Almayer was staring with stony eyes, his trembling fingers fumbling about his throat.

"Gold," he said with difficulty. "Hem! A hand on the windpipe, you know. Sure you will excuse. I wanted to say —a little gold for a little powder. What's that?"

"I know, I know," said the lieutenant soothingly.

"No! You don't know. Not one of you knows!" shouted Almayer. "The government is a fool, I tell you. Heaps of gold. I am the man that knows; I and another one. But he won't speak. He is—"

He checked himself with a feeble smile, and, making an unsuccessful attempt to pat the officer on the shoulder, knocked over a couple of empty bottles.

"Personally you are a fine fellow," he said very distinctly, in a patronizing manner. His head nodded drowsily as he sat muttering to himself.

The two officers looked at each other helplessly.

"This won't do," said the lieutenant, addressing his junior. "Have the men mustered in the compound here. I must get some sense out of him. Hi! Almayer! Wake up, man. Redeem your word. You gave your word. You gave your word of honour, you know."

Almayer shook off the officer's hand with impatience, but his ill-humour vanished at once, and he looked up, putting his forefinger to the side of his nose.

"You are very young; there is time for all things," he said, with an air of great sagacity.

The lieutenant turned towards Nina, who, leaning back in her chair, watched her father steadily.

"Really I am very much distressed by all this for your sake," he exclaimed. "I do not know," he went on, speaking with some embarrassment, "whether I have any right to ask you anything, unless, perhaps, to withdraw from this painful scene, but I feel that I must—for your father's good— suggest that you should—I mean if you have any influence over him you ought to exert it now to make him keep the promise he gave me before he—before he got into this state."

He observed with discouragement that she seemed not to take any notice of what he said, sitting still with half-closed eyes.

"I trust—" he began again.

"What is the promise you speak of?" abruptly asked Nina, leaving her seat and moving towards her father.

"Nothing that is not just and proper. He promised to deliver to us a man who in time of profound peace took the lives of innocent men to escape the punishment he deserved for breaking the law. He planned his mischief on a large scale. It is not his fault if it failed, partially. Of course you have heard of Dain Maroola. Your father secured him, I understand. We know he escaped up this river. Perhaps you—"

"And he killed white men!" interrupted Nina.

"I regret to say they were white. Yes, two white men lost their lives through that scoundrel's freak."

"Two only!" exclaimed Nina.

The officer looked at her in amazement.

"Why! why! You—" he stammered, confused.

"There might have been more," interrupted Nina. "And when you get this—this scoundrel, will you go?"

The lieutenant, still speechless, bowed his assent.

"Then I would get him for you if I had to seek him in a burning fire," she burst out with intense energy. "I hate the sight of your white faces. I hate the sound of your gentle voices. That is the way you speak to women, dropping sweet words before any pretty face. I have heard your voices before. I hoped to live here without seeing any other white face but this," she added in a gentler tone, touching lightly her father's cheek.

Almayer ceased his mumbling and opened his eyes. He caught hold of his daughter's hand and pressed it to his face, while Nina with the other hand smoothed his rumpled grey hair, looking defiantly over her father's head at the officer, who had now regained his composure and returned her look with a cool, steady stare. Below, in front of the verandah, they could hear the tramp of seamen mustering there according to orders. The sub-lieutenant came up the steps, while Babalatchi stood up uneasily and, with finger on lip, tried to catch Nina's eye.

"You are a good girl," whispered Almayer, absently, dropping his daughter's hand.

"Father! father!" she cried, bending over him with passionate entreaty. "See those two men looking at us. Send them away. I cannot bear it any more. Send them away. Do what they want and let them go."

She caught sight of Babalatchi and ceased speaking suddenly, but her foot tapped the floor with rapid beats in a paroxysm of nervous restlessness. The two officers stood close together looking on curiously.

"What has happened? What is the matter?" whispered the younger man.

"Don't know," answered the other, under his breath. "One is furious, and the other is drunk. Not so drunk, either. Queer this. Look!"

Almayer had risen, holding on to his daughter's arm. He hesitated a moment, then he let go his hold and lurched half-way across the verandah. There he pulled himself together, and stood very straight, breathing hard and glaring round angrily.

"Are the men ready?" asked the lieutenant.

"All ready, sir."

"Now, Mr. Almayer, lead the way," said the lieutenant.

Almayer rested his eyes on him as if he saw him for the first time.

"Two men," he said thickly. The effort of speaking seemed to interfere with his equilibrium. He took a quick step to save himself from a fall, and remained swaying backwards and forwards. "Two men," he began again, speaking with difficulty. "Two white men—men in uniform —honourable men. I want to say—men of honour. Are you?"

"Come! None of that," said the officer impatiently. "Let us have that friend of yours."

"What do you think I am?" asked Almayer, fiercely.

"You are drunk, but not so drunk as not to know what you are doing. Enough of this tomfoolery," said the officer sternly, "or I will have you put under arrest in your own house."

"Arrest!" laughed Almayer, discordantly. "Ha! ha! ha! Arrest! Why, I have been trying to get out of this infernal place for twenty years, and I can't. You hear, man! I can't, and never shall! Never!"

He ended his words with a sob, and walked unsteadily down the stairs. When in the courtyard the lieutenant approached him, and took him by the arm. The sub-lieutenant and Babalatchi followed close.

"That's better, Almayer," said the officer encouragingly. "Where are you going to? There are only planks there. Here," he went on, shaking him slightly, "do we want the boats?"

"No," answered Almayer, viciously. "You want a grave."

"What? Wild again! Try to talk sense."

"Grave!" roared Almayer, struggling to get himself free. "A hole in the ground. Don't you understand? You must be drunk. Let me go! Let go, I tell you!"

He tore away from the officer's grasp, and reeled towards the planks where the body lay under its white cover; then he turned round quickly, and faced the semicircle of interested faces. The sun was sinking rapidly, throwing long shadows of house and trees over the courtyard, but the light lingered yet on the river, where the logs went drifting past in midstream, looking very distinct and black in the pale red glow. The trunks of the trees in the forest on the east bank were lost in gloom while their highest branches swayed gently in the departing sunlight. The air felt heavy and cold in the breeze, expiring in slight puffs that came over the water.

Almayer shivered as he made an effort to speak, and again with an uncertain gesture he seemed to free his throat from the grip of an invisible hand. His bloodshot eyes wandered aimlessly from face to face.

"There!" he said at last. "Are you all there? He is a dangerous man."

He dragged at the cover with hasty violence, and the body rolled stiffly off the planks and fell at his feet in rigid helplessness.

"Cold, perfectly cold," said Almayer, looking round with a mirthless smile. "Sorry can do no better. And you can't hang him, either. As you observe, gentlemen," he added gravely, "there is no head, and hardly any neck."

The last ray of light was snatched away from the tree-tops, the river grew suddenly dark, and in the great stillness the murmur of the flowing water seemed to fill the vast expanse of grey shadow that descended upon the land.

"This is Dain," went on Almayer to the silent group that surrounded him. "And I have kept my word. First one hope, then another, and this is my last. Nothing is left now. You think there is one dead man here? Mistake, I sure you. I am much more dead. Why don't you hang me?" he suggested suddenly, in a friendly tone, addressing the lieutenant. "I assure, assure you it would be a mat—matter of form altog—altogether."

These last words he muttered to himself, and walked zig-zagging towards his house. "Get out!" he thundered at Ali, who was approaching timidly with offers of assistance. From afar, scared groups of men and women watched his devious progress. He dragged himself up the stairs by the banister, and managed to reach a chair into which he fell heavily. He sat for awhile panting with exertion and anger, and look-ing round vaguely for Nina; then making a threatening gesture towards the compound, where he had heard Baba-latchi's voice, he overturned the table with his foot in a great crash of smashed crockery. He muttered yet menac-ingly to himself, then his head fell on his breast, his eyes closed, and with a deep sigh he fell asleep.

That night—for the first time in its history—the peaceful and flourishing settlement of Sambir saw the lights shining about "Almayer's Folly." These were the lanterns of the boats hung up by the seamen under the verandah where the two officers were holding a court of inquiry into the truth of the story related to them by Babalatchi. Babalatchi had regained all his importance. He was eloquent and per-suasive, calling Heaven and Earth to witness the truth of his statements. There were also other witnesses. Mahmat Banjer and a good many others underwent a close examina-tion that dragged its weary length far into the evening. A messenger was sent for Abdulla, who excused himself from coming on the score of his venerable age, but sent Reshid. Mahmat had to produce the bangle, and saw with rage and mortification the lieutenant put it in his pocket as one of the proofs of Dain's death, to be sent in with the official report of the mission. Babalatchi's ring was also impounded for the same purpose, but the experienced statesman was resigned to that loss from the very beginning. He did not mind as long as he was sure that the white men believed. He put that question to himself earnestly as he left, one of the last, when the proceedings came to a close. He was not certain. Still, if they believed only for a night, he would put Dain beyond their reach and feel safe himself. He walked away fast, looking from time to time over his shoulder in the fear of being followed, but he saw and heard nothing.

"Ten o'clock," said the lieutenant, looking at his watch and yawning. "I shall hear some of the captain's complimentary remarks when we get back. Miserable business, this."

"Do you think all this is true?" asked the younger man.

"True! It is just possible. But if it isn't true what can we do? If we had a dozen boats we could patrol the creeks; and that wouldn't be much good. That drunken madman was right; we haven't enough hold on this coast. They do what they like. Are our hammocks slung?"

"Yes, I told the coxswain. Strange couple over there," said the sub, with a wave of his hand towards Almayer's house.

"Hem! Queer, certainly. What have you been telling her? I was attending to the father most of the time."

"I assure you I have been perfectly civil," protested the other warmly.

"All right. Don't get excited. She objects to civility, then, from what I understand. I thought you might have been tender. You know we are on service."

"Well, of course. Never forget that. Coldly civil. That's all."

They both laughed a little, and not feeling sleepy began to pace the verandah side by side. The moon rose stealthily above the trees, and suddenly changed the river into a stream of scintillating silver. The forest came out of the black void and stood sombre and pensive over the sparkling water. The breeze died away into a breathless calm.

Seamanlike, the two officers tramped measuredly up and down without exchanging a word. The loose planks rattled rhythmically under their steps with obtrusive dry sound in the perfect silence of the night. As they were wheeling round again the younger man stood attentive.

"Did you hear that?" he asked.

"No!" said the other. "Hear what?"

"I thought I heard a cry. Ever so faint. Seemed a woman's voice. In that other house. Ah! Again! Hear it?"

"No," said the lieutenant, after listening awhile. "You young fellows always hear women's voices. If you are going to dream you had better get into your hammock. Goodnight."

The moon mounted higher, and the warm shadows grew smaller and crept away as if hiding before the cold and cruel light.

CHAPTER 10

"It has set at last," said Nina to her mother pointing towards the hills behind which the sun had sunk. "Listen, mother, I am going now to Bulangi's creek, and if I should never return—"

She interrupted herself, and something like doubt dimmed for a moment the fire of suppressed exaltation that had glowed in her eyes and had illuminated the serene impassiveness of her features with a ray of eager life during all that long day of excitement—the day of joy and anxiety, of hope and terror, of vague grief and indistinct delight. While the sun shone with that dazzling light in which her love was born and grew till it possessed her whole being, she was kept firm in her unwavering resolve by the mysterious whisperings of desire which filled her heart with impatient longing for the darkness that would mean the end of danger and strife, the beginning of happiness, the fulfilling of love, the completeness of life. It had set at last! The short tropical twilight went out before she could draw the long breath of relief; and now the sudden darkness seemed to be full of menacing voices calling upon her to rush headlong into the unknown; to be true to her own impulses to give herself up to the passion she had evoked and shared. He was waiting! In the solitude of the secluded clearing, in the vast silence of the forest he was waiting alone, a fugitive in fear of his life. Indifferent to his danger he was waiting for her. It was for her only that he had come; and now as the time approached when he should have his reward, she asked herself with dismay what meant that chilling doubt of her own will and of her own desire? With an effort she shook off the fear of the passing weakness. He should have his reward. Her woman's love and her woman's honour overcame the faltering distrust of that unknown future waiting for her in the darkness of the river.

"No, you will not return," muttered Mrs. Almayer, prophetically. "Without you he will not go, and if he remains here—" She waved her hand towards the lights of "Almayer's Folly," and the unfinished sentence died out in a threatening murmur.

The two women had met behind the house, and now were walking slowly together towards the creek where all the canoes were moored. Arrived at the fringe of bushes they stopped by a common impulse, and Mrs. Almayer, laying her hand on her daughter's arm, tried in vain to look close into the girl's averted face. When she attempted to speak her first words were lost in a stifled sob that sounded strangely coming from that woman who, of all human passions, seemed to know only those of anger and hate.

"You are going away to be a great Ranee," she said at last, in a voice that was steady enough now, "and if you be wise you shall have much power that will endure many

days, and even last into your old age. What have I been? A
slave all my life, and I have cooked rice for a man who had
no courage and no wisdom. Hai! I! even I, was given in
gift by a chief and a warrior to a man that was neither.
Hai! Hai!"

She wailed to herself softly, lamenting the lost possibilities of murder and mischief that could have fallen to her
lot had she been mated with a congenial spirit. Nina bent
down over Mrs. Almayer's slight form and scanned attentively, under the stars that had rushed out on the black sky
and now hung breathless over that strange parting, her
mother's shrivelled features, and looked close into the
sunken eyes that could see into her own dark future by the
light of a long and a painful experience. Again she felt herself fascinated, as of old, by her mother's exalted mood and
by the oracular certainty of expression which, together with
her fits of violence, had contributed not a little to the reputation for witchcraft she enjoyed in the settlement.

"I was a slave, and you shall be a queen," went on Mrs.
Almayer, looking straight before her; "but remember men's
strength and their weakness. Tremble before his anger, so
that he may see your fear in the light of day; but in your
heart you may laugh, for after sunset he is your slave."

"A slave! He! The master of life! You do not know him,
mother."

Mrs. Almayer condescended to laugh contemptuously.

"You speak like a fool of a white woman," she exclaimed.
"What do you know of men's anger and of men's love?
Have you watched the sleep of men weary of dealing
death? Have you felt about you the strong arm that could
drive a kriss deep into a beating heart? Yah! you are a white
woman, and ought to pray to a woman god!"

"Why do you say this? I have listened to your words so
long that I have forgotten my old life. If I was white would
I stand here, ready to go? Mother, I shall return to the
house and look once more at my father's face."

"No!" said Mrs. Almayer, violently. "No, he sleeps now
the sleep of gin; and if you went back he might awake and

see you. No, he shall never see you. When the terrible old man took you away from me when you were little, you remember—"

"It was such a long time ago," murmured Nina.

"I remember," went on Mrs. Almayer, fiercely. "I wanted to look at your face again. He said no! I heard you cry and jumped into the river. You were his daughter then; you are my daughter now. Never shall you go back to that house; you shall never cross this courtyard again. No! no!"

Her voice rose almost to a shout. On the other side of the creek there was a rustle in the long grass. The two women heard it, and listened for a while in startled silence.

"I shall go," said Nina, in a cautious but intense whisper. "What is your hate or your revenge to me?"

She moved towards the house, Mrs. Almayer clinging to her and trying to pull her back.

"Stop, you shall not go!" she gasped.

Nina pushed away her mother impatiently and gathered up her skirts for a quick run, but Mrs. Almayer ran forward and turned round, facing her daughter with outstretched arms.

"If you move another step," she exclaimed, breathing quickly, "I shall cry out. Do you see those lights in the big house? There sit two white men, angry because they cannot have the blood of the man you love. And in those dark houses," she continued, more calmly as she pointed towards the settlement, "my voice could wake up men that would lead the Orang Blanda soldiers to him who is waiting—for you."

She could not see her daughter's face, but the white figure before her stood silent and irresolute in the darkness. Mrs. Almayer pursued her advantage.

"Give up your old life! Forget!" she said in entreating tones. "Forget that you ever looked at a white face; forget their words; forget their thoughts. They speak lies. And they think lies because they despise us that are better than they are, but not so strong. Forget their friendship and their contempt; forget their many gods. Girl, why do you want to remember the past when there is a warrior and a chief ready to give many lives—his own life—for one of your smiles?"

While she spoke she pushed gently her daughter towards the canoes, hiding her own fear, anxiety, and doubt under the flood of passionate words that left Nina no time to think and no opportunity to protest, even if she had wished it. But she did not wish it now. At the bottom of that passing desire to look again at her father's face there was no strong affection. She felt no scruples and no remorse at leaving suddenly that man whose sentiment towards herself she could not understand, she could not even see. There was only an instinctive clinging to old life, to old habits, to old faces; that fear of finality which lurks in every human breast and prevents so many heroisms and so many crimes. For years she had stood between her mother and her father, the one so strong in her weakness, the other so weak where he could have been strong. Between those two beings so dissimilar, so antagonistic, she stood with mute heart wondering and angry at the fact of her own existence. It seemed so unreasonable, so humiliating to be flung there in that settlement and to see the days rush by into the past, without a hope, a desire, or an aim that would justify the life she had to endure in ever-growing weariness. She had little belief and no sympathy for her father's dreams; but the savage ravings of her mother chanced to strike a responsive chord, deep down somewhere in her despairing heart; and she dreamed dreams of her own with the persistent absorption of a captive thinking of liberty within the walls of his prison cell. With the coming of Dain she found the road to freedom by obeying the voice of the new-born impulses, and with surprised joy she thought she could read in his eyes the answer to all the questionings of her heart. She understood now the reason and the aim of life; and in the triumphant unveiling of that mystery she threw away disdainfully her past with its sad thoughts, its bitter feelings and its faint affections, now withered and dead in contact with her fierce passion.

Mrs. Almayer unmoored Nina's own canoe and, straight-ening herself painfully, stood, painter in hand, looking at her daughter.

"Quick," she said; "get away before the moon rises, while the river is dark. I am afraid of Abdulla's slaves. The wretches prowl in the night often, and might see and follow you. There are two paddles in the canoe."

Nina approached her mother and touched lightly with her lips the wrinkled forehead. Mrs. Almayer snorted contemptuously in protest against that tenderness which she, nevertheless, feared could be contagious.

"Shall I ever see you again, mother?" murmured Nina.

"No," said Mrs. Almayer, after a short silence. "Why should you return here where it is my fate to die? You will live far away in splendour and might. When I hear of white men driven from the islands, then I shall know that you are alive, and that you remember my words."

"I shall always remember," returned Nina, earnestly; "but where is my power, and what can I do?"

"Do not let him look too long in your eyes, nor lay his head on your knees without reminding him that men should fight before they rest. And if he lingers, give him his kriss yourself and bid him go, as the wife of a mighty prince should do when the enemies are near. Let him slay the white men that come to us to trade, with prayers on their lips and loaded guns in their hands. Ah"—she ended with a sigh—"they are on every sea, and on every shore; and they are very many!"

She swung the bow of the canoe towards the river, but did not let go the gunwale, keeping her hand on it in irresolute thoughtfulness. Nina put the point of the paddle against the bank, ready to shove off into the stream.

"What is it, mother?" she asked, in a low voice. "Do you hear anything?"

"No," said Mrs. Almayer, absently. "Listen, Nina," she continued, abruptly, after a slight pause, "in after years there will be other women—"

A stifled cry in the boat interrupted her, and the paddle rattled in the canoe as it slipped from Nina's hands, which

she put out in a protesting gesture. Mrs. Almayer fell on
her knees on the bank and leaned over the gunwale so as
to bring her own face close to her daughter's.

"There will be other women," she repeated firmly; "I tell
you that, because you are half white, and may forget that
he is a great chief, and that such things must be. Hide your
anger, and do not let him see on your face the pain that will
eat your heart. Meet him with joy in your eyes and wisdom
on your lips, for to you he will turn in sadness or in doubt.
As long as he looks upon many women your power will last,
but should there be one, one only with whom he seems to
forget you, then—"

"I could not live," exclaimed Nina, covering her face
with both her hands. "Do not speak so, mother; it could not
be."

"Then," went on Mrs. Almayer, steadily, "to that woman, Nina, show no mercy."

She moved the canoe down towards the stream by the
gunwale, and gripped it with both her hands, the bow pointing into the river.

"Are you crying?" she asked sternly of her daughter, who
sat still with covered face. "Arise, and take your paddle, for
he has waited long enough. And remember, Nina, no mercy;
and if you must strike, strike with a steady hand."

She put out all her strength, and swinging her body over
the water, shot the light craft far into the stream. When she
recovered herself from the effort she tried vainly to catch a
glimpse of the canoe that seemed to have dissolved suddenly into the white mist trailing over the heated waters of
the Pantai. After listening for a while intently on her
knees, Mrs. Almayer rose with a deep sigh, while two tears
wandered slowly down her withered cheeks. She wiped
them off quickly with a wisp of her grey hair as if ashamed
of herself, but could not stifle another loud sigh, for her
heart was heavy and she suffered much, being unused to
tender emotions. This time she fancied she had heard a faint
noise, like the echo of her own sigh, and she stopped, strain-
ing her ears to catch the slightest sound, and peering ap-
prehensively towards the bushes near her.

"Who is there?" she asked, in an unsteady voice, while her imagination peopled the solitude of the riverside with ghost-like forms. "Who is there?" she repeated faintly.

There was no answer: only the voice of the river murmuring in sad monotone behind the white veil seemed to swell louder for a moment, to die away again in a soft whisper of eddies washing against the bank.

Mrs. Almayer shook her head as if in answer to her own thoughts, and walked quickly away from the bushes, looking to the right and left watchfully. She went straight towards the cooking shed, observing that the embers of the fire there glowed more brightly than usual, as if somebody had been adding fresh fuel to the fires during the evening. As she approached, Babalatchi, who had been squatting in the warm glow, rose and met her in the shadow outside.

"Is she gone?" asked the anxious statesman, hastily.

"Yes," answered Mrs. Almayer. "What are the white men doing? When did you leave them?"

"They are sleeping now, I think. May they never wake!" exclaimed Babalatchi, fervently. "Oh! but they are devils, and made much talk and trouble over that carcass. The chief threatened me twice with his hand, and said he would have me tied up to a tree. Tie me up to a tree! Me!" he repeated, striking his breast violently.

Mrs. Almayer laughed tauntingly.

"And you salaamed and asked for mercy. Men with arms by their side acted otherwise when I was young."

"And where are they, the men of your youth? You mad woman!" retorted Babalatchi, angrily. "Killed by the Dutch. Aha! But I shall live to deceive them. A man knows when to fight and when to tell peaceful lies. You would know that if you were not a woman."

But Mrs. Almayer did not seem to hear him. With bent body and outstretched arm she appeared to be listening to some noise behind the shed.

"There are strange sounds," she whispered, with evident alarm. "I have heard in the air the sounds of grief, as of a sigh and weeping. That was by the riverside. And now again I heard—"

"Where?" asked Babalatchi, in an altered voice. "What did you hear?"

"Close here. It was like a breath long drawn. I wish I had burnt the paper over the body before it was buried."

"Yes," assented Babalatchi. "But the white men had him thrown into a hole at once. You know he found his death on the river," he added cheerfully, "and his ghost may hail the canoes, but would leave the land alone."

Mrs. Almayer, who had been craning her neck to look round the corner of the shed, drew back her head.

"There is nobody there," she said, reassured. "Is it not time for the Rajah war-canoe to go to the clearing?"

"I have been waiting for it here, for I myself must go," explained Babalatchi. "I think I will go over and see what makes them late. When will you come? The Rajah gives you refuge."

"I shall paddle over before the break of day. I cannot leave my dollars behind," muttered Mrs. Almayer.

They separated. Babalatchi crossed the courtyard towards the creek to get his canoe, and Mrs. Almayer walked slowly to the house, ascended the plankway, and passing through the back verandah entered the passage leading to the front of the house; but before going in she turned in the doorway and looked back at the empty and silent courtyard, now lit up by the rays of the rising moon. No sooner she had disappeared, however, than a vague shape flitted out from amongst the stalks of the banana plantation, darted over the moonlit space, and fell in the darkness at the foot of the verandah. It might have been the shadow of a driving cloud, so noiseless and rapid was its passage, but for the trail of disturbed grass, whose feathery heads trembled and swayed for a long time in the moonlight before they rested motionless and gleaming, like a design of silver sprays embroidered on a sombre background.

Mrs. Almayer lighted the cocoanut lamp, and lifting cautiously the red curtain, gazed upon her husband, shading the light with her hand. Almayer, huddled up in the chair, one of his arms hanging down, the other thrown across the lower part of his face, as if to ward off an invisible enemy, his legs stretched straight out, slept heavily, unconscious of the unfriendly eyes that looked upon him in disparaging criticism. At his feet lay the overturned table, amongst a wreck of crockery and broken bottles. The appearance as of traces left by a desperate struggle was accentuated by the chairs, which seemed to have been scattered violently all over the place, and now lay about the verandah with a lamentable aspect of inebriety in their helpless attitudes. Only Nina's big rocking-chair, standing black and motionless on its high runners, towered above the chaos of demoralized furniture, unflinchingly dignified and patient, waiting for its burden.

With a last scornful look towards the sleeper, Mrs. Almayer passed behind the curtain into her own room. A couple of bats, encouraged by the darkness and the peaceful state of affairs, resumed their silent and oblique gambols above Almayer's head, and for a long time the profound quiet of the house was unbroken, save for the deep breathing of the sleeping man and the faint tinkle of silver in the hands of the woman preparing for flight. In the increasing light of the moon that had risen now above the night mist, the objects on the verandah came out strongly outlined in black splashes of shadow with all the uncompromising ugliness of their disorder, and a caricature of the sleeping Almayer appeared on the dirty whitewash of the wall behind him in a grotesquely exaggerated detail of attitude and feature enlarged to a heroic size. The discontented bats departed in quest of darker places, and a lizard came out in short, nervous rushes, and, pleased with the white tablecloth, stopped on it in breathless immobility that would have suggested sudden death had it not been for the melodious call he exchanged with a less adventurous friend hiding amongst the lumber in the courtyard. Then the boards in the passage creaked, the lizard vanished, and Almayer stirred uneasily with a sigh: slowly, out of the senseless annihilation of drunken sleep, he was returning, through the land of dreams, to waking consciousness. Almayer's head rolled from shoulder to shoulder in the oppression of his dream; the heavens had descended upon him like a

heavy mantle, and trailed in starred folds far under him.
Stars above, stars all around him; and from the stars under his
feet rose a whisper full of entreaties and tears, and sorrowful faces flitted amongst the clusters of light filling the infinite space below. How escape from the importunity of
lamentable cries and from the look of staring, sad eyes in
the faces which pressed round him till he gasped for breath
under the crushing weight of worlds that hung over his aching shoulders? Get away! But how? If he attempted to move
he would step off into nothing, and perish in the crashing
fall of that universe of which he was the only support. And
what were the voices saying? Urging him to move! Why?
Move to destruction! Not likely! The absurdity of the thing
filled him with indignation. He got a firmer foothold and
stiffened his muscles in heroic resolve to carry his burden
to all eternity. And ages passed in the superhuman labour,
amidst the rush of circling worlds; in the plaintive murmur
of sorrowful voices urging him to desist before it was too
late—till the mysterious power that had laid upon him the
giant task seemed at last to seek his destruction. With terror
he felt an irresistible hand shaking him by the shoulder,
while the chorus of voices swelled louder into an agonized
prayer to go, go before it is too late. He felt himself slipping,
losing his balance, as something dragged at his legs, and he
fell. With a faint cry he glided out of the anguish of perish-
ing creation into an imperfect waking that seemed to be
still under the spell of his dream.

"What? What?" he murmured sleepily, without moving or
opening his eyes. His head still felt heavy, and he had not
the courage to raise his eyelids. In his ears there still lingered the sound of entreating whisper.—"Am I awake?—
Why do I hear the voices?" he argued to himself, hazily.—
"I cannot get rid of the horrible nightmare yet.—I have
been very drunk.—What is that shaking me? I am dreaming yet.—I must open my eyes and be done with it. I am
only half awake, it is evident."

He made an effort to shake off his stupor and saw a face
close to his, glaring at him with staring eyeballs. He closed
his eyes again in amazed horror and sat up straight in the

chair, trembling in every limb. What was this apparition?—
His own fancy, no doubt.—His nerves had been much tried
the day before—and then the drink! He would not see it
again if he had the courage to look.—He would look directly.—Get a little steadier first.—So.—Now.

He looked. The figure of a woman standing in the steely
light, her hands stretched forth in a suppliant gesture, confronted him from the far-off end of the verandah; and in
the space between him and the obstinate phantom floated
the murmur of words that fell on his ears in a jumble of
torturing sentences, the meaning of which escaped the
utmost efforts of his brain. Who spoke the Malay words?
Who ran away? Why too late—and too late for what? What
meant those words of hate and love mixed so strangely together, the ever-recurring names falling on his ears again
and again—Nina, Dain; Dain, Nina? Dain was dead, and
Nina was sleeping, unaware of the terrible experience
through which he was now passing. Was he going to be tormented for ever, sleeping or waking, and have no peace
either night or day? What was the meaning of this?

He shouted the last words aloud. The shadowy woman
seemed to shrink and recede a little from him towards the
doorway, and there was a shriek. Exasperated by the incomprehensible nature of his torment, Almayer made a rush
upon the apparition, which eluded his grasp, and he
brought up heavily against the wall. Quick as lightning he
turned round and pursued fiercely the mysterious figure
fleeing from him with piercing shrieks that were like fuel
to the flames of his anger. Over the furniture, round the
overturned table, and now he had it cornered behind Nina's
chair. To the left, to the right they dodged, the chair rocking madly between them, she sending out shriek after shriek
at every feint, and he growling meaningless curses through
his hard-set teeth. Oh! the fiendish noise that split his head
and seemed to choke his breath.—It would kill him.—It
must be stopped! An insane desire to crush that yelling
thing induced him to cast himself recklessly over the chair
with a desperate grab, and they came down together in a
cloud of dust amongst the splintered wood. The last shriek

Joseph Conrad

died out under him in a faint gurgle, and he had secured the relief of absolute silence.

He looked at the woman's face under him. A real woman. He knew her. By all that is wonderful; Taminah! He jumped up ashamed of his fury and stood perplexed, wiping his forehead. The girl struggled to a kneeling posture and embraced his legs in a frenzied prayer for mercy.

"Don't be afraid," he said, raising her. "I shall not hurt you. Why do you come to my house in the night? And if you had to come, why not go behind the curtain where the women sleep?"

"The place behind the curtain is empty," gasped Taminah, catching her breath between the words. "There are no women in your house any more, Tuan. I saw the old Mem go away before I tried to wake you. I did not want your women, I wanted you."

"Old Mem!" repeated Almayer. "Do you mean my wife?" She nodded her head.

"But of my daughter you are not afraid?" said Almayer.

"Have you not heard me?" she exclaimed. "Have I not spoken for a long time when you lay there with eyes half open? She is gone too."

"I was asleep. Can you not tell when a man is sleeping and when awake?"

"Sometimes," answered Taminah in a low voice; "sometimes the spirit lingers close to a sleeping body and may hear. I spoke a long time before I touched you, and I spoke softly for fear it would depart at a sudden noise and leave you sleeping for ever. I took you by the shoulder only when you began to mutter words I could not understand. Have you not heard, then, and do you know nothing?"

"Nothing of what you said. What is it? Tell again if you want me to know."

He took her by the shoulder and led her unresisting to the front of the verandah into a stronger light. She wrung her hands with such an appearance of grief that he began to be alarmed.

"Speak," he said. "You made noise enough to wake even dead men. And yet nobody living came," he added to himself in an uneasy whisper. "Are you mute? Speak!" he repeated.

In a rush of words which broke out after a short struggle from her trembling lips she told him the tale of Nina's love and her own jealousy. Several times he looked angrily into her face and told her to be silent; but he could not stop the sounds that seemed to him to run out in a hot stream, swirl about his feet, and rise in scalding waves about him, higher, higher, drowning his heart, touching his lips with a feel of molten lead, blotting out his sight in scorching vapour, closing over his head, merciless and deadly. When she spoke of the deception as to Dain's death of which he had been the victim only that day, he glanced again at her with terrible eyes, and made her falter for a second, but he turned away directly, and his face suddenly lost all expression in a stony stare far away over the river. Ah! the river! His old friend and his old enemy, speaking always with the same voice as he runs from year to year bringing fortune or disappointment, happiness or pain, upon the same varying but unchanged surface of glancing currents and swirling eddies. For many years he had listened to the passionless and soothing murmur that sometimes was the song of hope, at times the song of triumph, of encouragement; more often the whisper of consolation that spoke of better days to come. For so many years! So many years! And now to the accompaniment of that murmur he listened to the slow and painful beating of his heart. He listened attentively, wondering at the regularity of its beats. He began to count mechanically. One, two. Why count? At the next beat it must stop. No heart could suffer so and beat so steadily for long. Those regular strokes as of a muffled hammer that rang in his ears must stop soon. Still beating unceasing and cruel. No man can bear this: and is this the last, or will the next one be the last?—How much longer? O God! how much longer? His hand weighed heavier unconsciously on the girl's shoulder, and she spoke the last words of her story crouching at his feet with tears of pain and shame and anger. Was her revenge to fail her? This white man was like a senseless stone. Too late! Too late!

"And you saw her go?" Almayer's voice sounded harshly above her head.

"Did I not tell you?" she sobbed, trying to wriggle gently out from under his grip. "Did I not tell you that I saw the witchwoman push the canoe? I lay hidden in the grass and heard all the words. She that we used to call the white Mem wanted to return to look at your face, but the witchwoman forbade her, and—"

She sank lower yet on her elbow, turning half round under the downward push of the heavy hand, her face lifted up to him with spiteful eyes.

"And she obeyed," she shouted out in a half-laugh, half-cry of pain. "Let me go, Tuan. Why are you angry with me? Hasten, or you will be too late to show your anger to the deceitful woman."

Almayer dragged her up to her feet and looked close into her face while she struggled, turning her head away from his wild stare.

"Who sent you here to torment me?" he asked violently. "I do not believe you. You lie."

He straightened his arm suddenly and flung her across the verandah towards the doorway, where she lay immobile and silent, as if she had left her life in his grasp, a dark heap, without a sound or a stir.

"Oh! Nina!" whispered Almayer, in a voice in which reproach and love spoke together in pained tenderness. "Oh! Nina! I do not believe."

A light draught from the river ran over the courtyard in a wave of bowing grass and, entering the verandah, touched Almayer's forehead with its cool breath, in a caress of infinite pity. The curtain in the women's doorway blew out and instantly collapsed with startling helplessness. He stared at the fluttering stuff.

"Nina!" cried Almayer. "Where are you, Nina?"

The wind passed out of the empty house in a tremulous sigh, and all was still.

Almayer hid his face in his hands as if to shut out a loathsome sight. When, hearing a slight rustle, he uncovered his eyes, the dark heap by the door was gone.

CHAPTER 11

In the middle of a shadowless square of moonlight, shining on a smooth and level expanse of young rice-shoots, a little shelter-hut perched on high posts, the pile of brushwood near by and the glowing embers of a fire with a man stretched before it, seemed very small and as if lost in the pale green iridescence reflected from the ground. On three sides of the clearing, appearing very far away in the deceptive light, the big trees of the forest, lashed together with manifold bonds by a mass of tangled creepers, looked down at the growing young life at their feet with the sombre resignation of giants that had lost faith in their strength. And in the midst of them the merciless creepers clung to the big trunks in cable-like coils, leaped from tree to tree, hung in thorny festoons from the lower boughs, and, sending slender tendrils on high to seek out the smallest branches, carried death to their victims in an exulting riot of silent destruction.

On the fourth side, following the curve of the bank of that branch of the Pantai that formed the only access to the clearing, ran a black line of young trees, bushes, and thick second growth, unbroken save for a small gap chopped out in one place. At that gap began the narrow footpath leading from the water's edge to the grass-built shelter used by the night watchers when the ripening crop had to be protected from the wild pigs. The pathway ended at the foot of the piles on which the hut was built, in a circular space covered with ashes and bits of burnt wood. In the middle of that space, by the dim fire, lay Dain.

He turned over on his side with an impatient sigh, and, pillowing his head on his bent arm, lay quietly with his face to the dying fire. The glowing embers shone redly in a small circle, throwing a gleam into his wide-open eyes. His body was weary with the exertion of the past few days, his mind more weary still with the strain of solitary waiting for his fate. Never before had he felt so helpless. He had heard the report of the gun fired on board the launch, and he knew that his life was in untrustworthy hands, and that his enemies were very near.

During the slow hours of the afternoon he had roamed about on the edge of the forest, or, hiding in the bushes, watched the creek with unquiet eyes for some sign of danger. He feared not death, yet he desired ardently to live, for life to him was Nina. She had promised to come, to follow him, to share his danger and his splendour. But with her by his side he cared not for danger, and without her there could be no splendour and no joy in existence. Crouching in his shady hiding-place, he closed his eyes, trying to evoke the gracious and charming image of the white figure that for him was the beginning and the end of life. With eyes shut tight, his teeth hard set, he tried in a great effort of passionate will to keep his hold on that vision of supreme delight. In vain! His heart grew heavy as the figure of Nina faded away to be replaced by another vision this time—a vision of armed men, of angry faces, of glittering arms—and he seemed to hear the hum of excited and triumphant voices as they discovered him in his hiding-place. Startled by the vividness of his fancy, he would open his eyes, and, leaping out into the sunlight, resume his aimless wanderings around the clearing. As he skirted in his weary march the edge of the forest he glanced now and then into its dark shade, so enticing in its deceptive appearance of coolness, so repellent with its unrelieved gloom, where lay, entombed and rotting, countless generations of trees, and where their successors stood as if mourning, in dark green foliage, immense and helpless, awaiting their turn. Only the parasites seemed to live there in a sinuous rush upwards into the air and sunshine, feeding on the dead and the dying alike, and crowning their victims with pink and blue flowers that gleamed amongst the boughs, incongruous and cruel, like a strident and mocking note in the solemn harmony of the doomed trees.

A man could hide there, thought Dain, as he approached a place where the creepers had been torn and hacked into an archway that might have been the beginning of a path. As he bent down to look through he heard angry grunting, and a sounder of wild pig crashed away in the undergrowth. An acrid smell of damp earth and of decaying leaves took him by the throat, and he drew back with a scared face, as if he had been touched by the breath of Death itself. The very air seemed dead in there—heavy and stagnating, poisoned with the corruption of countless ages. He went on, staggering on his way, urged by the nervous restlessness that made him feel tired yet caused him to loathe the very idea of immobility and repose. Was he a wild man to hide in the woods and perhaps be killed there—in the darkness —where there was no room to breathe? He would wait for his enemies in the sunlight, where he could see the sky and feel the breeze. He knew how a Malay chief should die. The sombre and desperate fury, that peculiar inheritance of his race, took possession of him, and he glared savagely across the clearing towards the gap in the bushes by the riverside. They would come from there. In imagination he saw them now. He saw the bearded faces and the white jackets of the officers, the light on the levelled barrels of the rifles. What is the bravery of the greatest warrior before the firearms in the hand of a slave? He would walk towards them with a smiling face, with his hands held out in a sign of submission till he was very near them. He would speak friendly words—come nearer yet—yet nearer—so near that they could touch him with their hands and stretch them out to make him a captive. That would be the time; with a shout and a leap he would be in the midst of them, kriss in hand, killing, killing, killing, and would die with the shouts of his enemies in his ears, their warm blood spurting before his eyes.

Carried away by his excitement, he snatched the kriss hidden in his sarong, and, drawing a long breath, rushed forward, struck at the empty air, and fell on his face. He lay as if stunned in the sudden reaction from his exaltation, thinking that, even if he died thus gloriously, it would have to be before he saw Nina. Better so. If he saw her again he felt that death would be too terrible. With horror he, the descendant of Rajahs and of conquerors, had to face the doubt of his own bravery. His desire of life tormented him in a paroxysm of agonizing remorse. He had not the courage to stir a limb. He had lost faith in himself, and there was nothing else in him of what makes a man. The suffering remained, for it is ordered that it should abide in the human body even to the last breath, and fear remained. Dimly he could look into the depths of his passionate love, see its strength and its weakness, and felt afraid.

The sun went down slowly. The shadow of the western forest marched over the clearing, covered the man's scorched shoulders with its cool mantle, and went on hurriedly to mingle with the shadows of other forests on the eastern side. The sun lingered for a while amongst the light tracery of the higher branches, as if in friendly reluctance to abandon the body stretched in the green paddy-field. Then Dain, revived by the cool of the evening breeze, sat up and stared round him. As he did so the sun dipped sharply, as if ashamed of being detected in a sympathizing attitude, and the clearing, which during the day was all light, became suddenly all darkness, where the fire gleamed like an eye. Dain walked slowly towards the creek, and, divesting himself of his torn sarong, his only garment, entered the water cautiously. He had nothing to eat that day, and had not dared show himself in daylight by the water-side to drink. Now, as he swam silently, he swallowed a few mouthfuls of water that lapped about his lips. This did him good, and he walked with greater confidence in himself and others as he returned towards the fire. Had he been betrayed by Lakamba all would have been over by this. He made up a big blaze, and while it lasted dried himself, and then lay down by the embers. He could not sleep, but he felt a great numbness in all his limbs. His restlessness was gone, and he was content to lie still, measuring the time by watching the stars that arose in endless succession above the forest, while the slight puffs of wind under the cloudless sky seemed to fan their twinkle into a greater brightness. Dreamily he assured himself over and over again that she would come, till the certitude crept into his heart and filled him with a great peace. Yes, when the next day broke, they would be together on the great blue sea that was like life—away from the forests that were like death. He murmured the name of Nina into the silent space with a tender smile: this seemed to break the spell of stillness, and far away by the creek a frog croaked loudly as if in answer. A chorus of loud roars and plaintive calls rose from the mud along the line of bushes. He laughed heartily; doubtless it was their love-song. He felt affectionate towards the frogs and listened, pleased with the noisy life near him.

When the moon peeped above the trees he felt the old impatience and the old restlessness steal over him. Why was she so late? True, it was a long way to come with a single paddle. With what skill and what endurance could those small hands manage a heavy paddle! It was very wonderful —such small hands, such soft little palms that knew how to touch his cheek with a feel lighter than the fanning of a butterfly's wing. Wonderful! He lost himself lovingly in the contemplation of this tremendous mystery, and when he looked at the moon again it had risen a hand's breadth above the trees. Would she come? He forced himself to lie still, overcoming the impulse to rise and rush round the clearing again. He turned this way and that; at last, quivering with the effort, he lay on his back, and saw her face among the stars looking down on him.

The croaking of frogs suddenly ceased. With the watchfulness of a hunted man Dain sat up, listening anxiously, and heard several splashes in the water as the frogs took rapid headers into the creek. He knew that they had been alarmed by something, and stood up suspicious and attentive. A slight grating noise, then the dry sound as of two pieces of wood struck against each other. Somebody was about to land! He took up an armful of brushwood, and, without taking his eyes from the path, held it over the embers of his fire. He waited, undecided, and saw something

gleam amongst the bushes; then a white figure came out of
the shadows and seemed to float towards him in the pale
light. His heart gave a great leap and stood still, then went
on shaking his frame in furious beats. He dropped the
brushwood upon the glowing coals, and had an impression
of shouting her name—of rushing to meet her; yet he
emitted no sound, he stirred not an inch, but he stood silent
and motionless like chiselled bronze under the moonlight
that streamed over his naked shoulders. As he stood still,
fighting with his breath, as if bereft of his senses by the intensity of his delight, she walked up to him with quick, resolute steps, and, with the appearance of one about to leap
from a dangerous height, threw both arms round his neck
with a sudden gesture. A small blue gleam crept amongst
the dry branches, and the crackling of reviving fire was the
only sound as they faced each other in the speechless emotion of that meeting; then the dry fuel caught at once, and a
bright hot flame shot upwards in a blaze as high as their
heads, and in its light they saw each other's eyes.

Neither of them spoke. He was regaining his senses in a
slight tremor that ran upwards along his rigid body and
hung about his trembling lips. She drew back her head and
fastened her eyes on his in one of those long looks that are
a woman's most terrible weapon; a look that is more stirring than the closest touch, and more dangerous than the
thrust of a dagger, because it also whips the soul out of the
body, but leaves the body alive and helpless, to be swayed
here and there by the capricious tempests of passion and
desire; a look that enwraps the whole body, and that pene-
trates into the innermost recesses of the being, bringing
terrible defeat in the delirious uplifting of accomplished
conquest. It has the same meaning for the man of the forests and the sea as for the man threading the paths of the
more dangerous wilderness of houses and streets. Men that
have felt in their breasts the awful exultation such a look
awakens become mere things of to-day—which is paradise;
forget yesterday—which was suffering; care not for to-morrow—which may be perdition. They wish to live under that
look for ever. It is the look of woman's surrender.

He understood, and, as if suddenly released from his invisible bonds, fell at her feet with a shout of joy, and, embracing her knees, hid his head in the folds of her dress, murmuring disjointed words of gratitude and love. Never before had he felt so proud as now, when at the feet of that woman that half belonged to his enemies. Her fingers played with his hair in an absent-minded caress as she stood absorbed in thought. The thing was done. Her mother was right. The man was her slave. As she glanced down at his kneeling form she felt a great pitying tenderness for that man she used to call—even in her thoughts—the master of life. She lifted her eyes and looked sadly at the southern heavens under which lay the path of their lives—her own, and that man's at her feet. Did he not say himself that she was the light of his life? She would be his light and his wisdom; she would be his greatness and his strength; yet hidden from the eyes of all men she would be, above all, his only and lasting weakness. A very woman! In the sublime vanity of her kind she was thinking already of moulding a god from the clay at her feet. A god for others to worship. She was content to see him as he was now, and to feel him quiver at the slightest touch of her light fingers. And while her eyes looked sadly at the southern stars a faint smile seemed to be playing about her firm lips. Who can tell in the fitful light of a camp fire? It might have been a smile of triumph, or of conscious power, or of tender pity, or perhaps, of love.

She spoke softly to him, and he rose to his feet, putting his arm round her in quiet consciousness of his ownership; she laid her head on his shoulder with a sense of defiance to all the world in the encircling protection of that arm. He was hers with all his qualities and his faults. His strength and his courage, his recklessness and his daring, his simple wisdom and his savage cunning—all were hers. As they passed together out of the red light of the fire into the silver shower of rays that fell upon the clearing he bent his head over her face, and she saw in his eyes the dreamy intoxication of boundless felicity from the close touch of her slight figure clasped to his side. With a rhythmical swing of their

bodies they walked through the light towards the outlying
shadows of the forests that seemed to guard their happiness
in solemn immobility. Their forms melted in the play of
light and shadow at the foot of the big trees, but the murmur of tender words lingered over the empty clearing, grew
faint, and died out. A sigh as of immense sorrow passed
over the land in the last effort of the dying breeze, and in
the deep silence which succeeded, the earth and the heavens
were suddenly hushed up in the mournful contemplation of
human love and human blindness.

They walked slowly back to the fire. He made for her a
seat out of the dry branches, and, throwing himself down at
her feet, lay his head in her lap and gave himself up to the
dreamy delight of the passing hour. Their voices rose and
fell, tender or animated as they spoke of their love and of
their future. She, with a few skilful words spoken from time
to time, guided his thoughts, and he let his happiness
flow in a stream of talk passionate and tender, grave or
menacing, according to the mood which she evoked. He
spoke to her of his own island, where the gloomy forests
and the muddy rivers were unknown. He spoke of its ter-
raced fields, of the murmuring clear rills of sparkling water
that flowed down the sides of great mountains, bringing life
to the land and joy to its tillers. And he spoke also of the
mountain peak that rising lonely above the belt of trees
knew the secrets of the passing clouds, and was the dwell-
ing-place of the mysterious spirit of his race, of the guardian genius of his house. He spoke of vast horizons swept by
fierce winds that whistled high above the summits of burning mountains. He spoke of his forefathers that conquered
ages ago the island of which he was to be the future ruler.
And then as, in her interest, she brought her face nearer
to his, he, touching lightly the thick tresses of her long hair,
felt a sudden impulse to speak to her of the sea he loved so
well; and he told her of its never-ceasing voice, to which he
had listened as a child, wondering at its hidden meaning
that no living man has penetrated yet; of its enchanting
glitter; of its senseless and capricious fury; how its surface

was for ever changing, and yet always enticing, while its depths were for ever the same, cold and cruel, and full of the wisdom of destroyed life. He told her how it held men slaves of its charm for a lifetime, and then, regardless of their devotion, swallowed them up, angry at their fear of its mystery, which it would never disclose, not even to those that loved it most. While he talked, Nina's head had been gradually sinking lower, and her face almost touched his now. Her hair was over his eyes, her breath was on his forehead, her arms were about his body. No two beings could be closer to each other, yet she guessed rather than understood the meaning of his last words that came out after a slight hesitation in a faint murmur, dying out imperceptibly into a profound and significant silence: "The sea, O Nina, is like a woman's heart."

She closed his lips with a sudden kiss, and answered in a steady voice—

"But to the men that have no fear, O master of my life, the sea is ever true."

Over their heads a film of dark, thread-like clouds, looking like immense cobwebs drifting under the stars, darkened the sky with the presage of the coming thunderstorm. From the invisible hills the first distant rumble of thunder came in a prolonged roll which, after tossing about from hill to hill, lost itself in the forests of the Pantai. Dain and Nina stood up, and the former looked at the sky uneasily.

"It is time for Babalatchi to be here," he said. "The night is more than half gone. Our road is long, and a bullet travels quicker than the best canoe."

"He will be here before the moon is hidden behind the clouds," said Nina. "I heard a splash in the water," she added. "Did you hear it too?"

"Alligator," answered Dain shortly, with a careless glance towards the creek. "The darker the night," he continued, "the shorter will be our road, for then we could keep in the current of the main stream, but if it is light—even no more than now—we must follow the small channels of sleeping water, with nothing to help our paddles."

"Dain," interposed Nina, earnestly, "it was no alligator. I heard the bushes rustling near the landing-place."

"Yes," said Dain, after listening awhile. "It cannot be Babalatchi, who would come in a big war canoe, and openly. Those that are coming, whoever they are, do not wish to make much noise. But you have heard, and now I can see," he went on quickly. "It is but one man. Stand behind me, Nina. If he is a friend he is welcome; if he is an enemy you shall see him die."

He laid his hand on his kriss, and waited the approach of his unexpected visitor. The fire was burning very low, and small clouds—precursors of the storm—crossed the face of the moon in rapid succession, and their flying shadows darkened the clearing. He could not make out who the man might be, but he felt uneasy at the steady advance of the tall figure walking on the path with a heavy tread, and hailed it with a command to stop. The man stopped at some little distance, and Dain expected him to speak, but all he could hear was his deep breathing. Through a break in the flying clouds a sudden and fleeting brightness descended upon the clearing. Before the darkness closed in again Dain saw a hand holding some glittering object extended towards him, heard Nina's cry of "Father!" and in an instant the girl was between him and Almayer's revolver. Nina's loud cry woke up the echoes of the sleeping woods, and the three stood still as if waiting for the return of silence before they would give expression to their various feelings. At the appearance of Nina, Almayer's arm fell by his side, and he made a step forward. Dain pushed the girl gently aside.

"Am I a wild beast that you should try to kill me suddenly and in the dark, Tuan Almayer?" said Dain, breaking the strained silence. "Throw some brushwood on the fire," he went on, speaking to Nina, "while I watch my white friend, lest harm should come to you or to me, O delight of my heart!"

Almayer ground his teeth and raised his arm again. With a quick bound Dain was at his side: there was a short scuffle, during which one chamber of the revolver went off harmlessly, then the weapon, wrenched out of Almayer's hand, whirled through the air and fell in the bushes. The two men stood close together, breathing hard. The replenished fire threw out an unsteady circle of light and shone on the terrified face of Nina, who looked at them with outstretched hands.

"Dain!" she cried out warningly, "Dain!"

He waved his hand towards her in a reassuring gesture, and, turning to Almayer, said with great courtesy—

"Now we may talk, Tuan. It is easy to send out death, but can your wisdom recall the life? She might have been harmed," he continued, indicating Nina. "Your hand shook much; for myself I was not afraid."

"Nina!" exclaimed Almayer, "come to me at once. What is this sudden madness? What bewitched you? Come to your father, and together we shall try to forget this horrible nightmare!"

He opened his arms with the certitude of clasping her to his breast in another second. She did not move. As it dawned upon him that she did not mean to obey he felt a deadly cold creep into his heart, and pressing the palms of his hands to his temples, he looked down on the ground in mute despair. Dain took Nina by the arm and led her towards her father.

"Speak to him in the language of his people," he said. "He is grieving—as who would not grieve at losing thee, my pearl! Speak to him the last words he shall hear spoken by that voice, which must be very sweet to him, but is all my life to me."

He released her, and, stepping back a few paces out of the circle of light, stood in the darkness looking at them with calm interest. The reflection of a distant flash of lightning lit up the clouds over their heads, and was followed after a short interval by the faint rumble of thunder, which mingled with Almayer's voice as he began to speak.

"Do you know what you are doing? Do you know what is waiting for you if you follow that man? Have you no pity for yourself? Do you know that you shall be at first his play-thing and then a scorned slave, a drudge, and a servant of some new fancy of that man?"

She raised her hand to stop him, and turning her head slightly, asked—

"You hear this Dain! Is it true?"

"By all the gods!" came the impassioned answer from the darkness—"by heaven and earth, by my head and thine I swear: this is a white man's lie. I have delivered my soul into your hands for ever; I breathe with your breath, I see with your eyes, I think with your mind, and I take you into my heart for ever."

"You thief!" shouted the exasperated Almayer.

A deep silence succeeded this outburst, then the voice of Dain was heard again.

"Nay, Tuan," he said in a gentle tone, "that is not true also. The girl came of her own will. I have done no more but to show her my love like a man; she heard the cry of my heart, and she came, and the dowry I have given to the woman you call your wife."

Almayer groaned in his extremity of rage and shame. Nina laid her hand lightly on his shoulder, and the contact, light as the touch of a falling leaf, seemed to calm him. He spoke quickly, and in English this time.

"Tell me," he said—"tell me, what have they done to you, your mother and that man? What made you give your-self up to that savage? For he is a savage. Between him and you there is a barrier that nothing can remove. I can see in your eyes the look of those who commit suicide when they are mad. You are mad. Don't smile. It breaks my heart. If I were to see you drowning before my eyes, and I without the power to help you, I could not suffer a greater torment. Have you forgotten the teaching of so many years?"

"No," she interrupted, "I remember it well. I remember how it ended also. Scorn for scorn, contempt for contempt, hate for hate. I am not of your race. Between your people and me there is also a barrier that nothing can remove.

You ask why I want to go, and I ask you why I should stay."

He staggered as if struck in the face, but with a quick, unhesitating grasp she caught him by the arm and steadied him.

"Why you should stay!" he repeated slowly, in a dazed manner, and stopped short, astounded at the completeness of his misfortune.

"You told me yesterday," she went on again, "that I could not understand or see your love for me: it is so. How can I? No two human beings understand each other. They can understand but their own voices. You wanted me to dream your dreams, to see your own visions—the visions of life amongst the white faces of those who cast me out from their midst in angry contempt. But while you spoke I listened to the voice of my own self; then this man came, and all was still; there was only the murmur of his love. You call him a savage! What do you call my mother, your wife?"

"Nina!" cried Almayer, "take your eyes off my face."

She looked down directly, but continued speaking only a little above a whisper.

"In time," she went on, "both our voices, that man's and mine, spoke together in a sweetness that was intelligible to our ears only. You were speaking of gold then, but our ears were filled with the song of our love, and we did not hear you. Then I found that we could see through each other's eyes: that he saw things that nobody but myself and he could see. We entered a land where no one could follow us, and least of all you. Then I began to live."

She paused. Almayer sighed deeply. With her eyes still fixed on the ground she began speaking again.

"And I mean to live. I mean to follow him. I have been rejected with scorn by the white people, and now I am a Malay! He took me in his arms, he laid his life at my feet. He is brave; he will be powerful, and I hold his bravery and his strength in my hand, and I shall make him great. His name shall be remembered long after both our bodies are laid in the dust. I love you no less than I did before, but I shall never leave him, for without him I cannot live."

"If he understood what you have said," answered Al-mayer, scornfully, "he must be highly flattered. You want him as a tool for some incomprehensible ambition of yours. Enough, Nina. If you do not go down at once to the creek, where Ali is waiting with my canoe, I shall tell him to re-turn to the settlement and bring the Dutch officers here. You cannot escape from this clearing, for I have cast adrift your canoe. If the Dutch catch this hero of yours they will hang him as sure as I stand here. Now go."

He made a step towards his daughter and laid hold of her by the shoulder, his other hand pointing down the path to the landing-place.

"Beware!" exclaimed Dain; "this woman belongs to me!"

Nina wrenched herself free and looked straight at Al-mayer's angry face.

"No, I will not go," she said with desperate energy. "If he dies I shall die too!"

"You die?" said Almayer, contemptuously. "Oh, no! You shall live a life of lies and deception till some other vaga-bond comes along to sing; how did you say that? The song of love to you! Make up your mind quickly."

He waited for a while, and then added meaningly—

"Shall I call out to Ali?"

"Call out," she answered in Malay, "you that cannot be true to your own countrymen. Only a few days ago you were selling the powder of their destruction; now you want to give up to them the man that yesterday you called your friend. Oh, Dain," she said, turning towards the motionless but attentive figure in the darkness, "instead of bringing you life I bring you death, for he will betray unless I leave you for ever!"

Dain came into the circle of light, and, throwing his arm around Nina's neck, whispered in her ear—

"I can kill him where he stands, before a sound can pass his lips. For you it is to say yes or no. Babalatchi cannot be far now."

He straightened himself up, taking his arm off her shoul-der, and confronted Almayer, who looked at them both with an expression of concentrated fury.

There was no answer. She did not even turn her head, which was pressed close to Dain's breast.

He made a movement as if to leave them and stopped. By the dim glow of the burning-out fire he saw their two motionless figures. The woman's back turned to him with the long black hair streaming down over the white dress, and Dain's calm face looking at him above her head.

"I cannot," he muttered to himself. After a long pause he spoke again a little lower, but in an unsteady voice, "It would be too great a disgrace. I am a white man." He broke down completely there, and went on tearfully, "I am a white man, and of good family. Very good family," he repeated, weeping bitterly. "It would be a disgrace . . . all over the island, . . . the only white man on the east coast. No, it cannot be . . . white men finding my daughter with this Malay. My daughter!" he cried aloud, with a ring of despair in his voice.

He recovered his composure after a while and said distinctly—

"I will never forgive you, Nina—never! If you were to come back to me now, the memory of this night would poison all my life. I shall try to forget. I have no daughter. There used to be a half-caste woman in my house, but she is going even now. You, Dain, or whatever your name may be, I shall take you and that woman to the island at the mouth of the river myself. Come with me."

He led the way, following the bank as far as the forest. Ali answered to his call, and, pushing their way through the dense bush, they stepped into the canoe hidden under the overhanging branches. Dain laid Nina in the bottom, and sat holding her head on his knees. Almayer and Ali each took up a paddle. As they were going to push out Ali hissed warningly. All listened.

In the great stillness before the bursting out of the thunderstorm they could hear the sound of oars working regularly in their row-locks. The sound approached steadily, and Dain, looking through the branches, could see the faint shape of a big white boat. A woman's voice said in a cautious tone—

"There is the place where you may land, white men; a little higher—there!"

The boat was passing them so close in the narrow creek that the blades of the long oars nearly touched the canoe.

"Way enough! Stand by to jump on shore! He is alone and unarmed," was the quiet order in a man's voice, and in Dutch.

Somebody else whispered: "I think I can see a glimmer of a fire through the bush." And then the boat floated past them, disappearing instantly in the darkness.

"Now," whispered Ali, eagerly, "let us push out and paddle away."

The little canoe swung into the stream, and as it sprung forward in response to the vigorous dig of the paddles they could hear an angry shout.

"He is not by the fire. Spread out, men, and search for him!"

Blue lights blazed out in different parts of the clearing, and the shrill voice of a woman cried in accents of rage and pain—

"Too late! O senseless white men! He has escaped!"

CHAPTER 12

"That is the place," said Dain, indicating with the blade of his paddle a small islet about a mile ahead of the canoe—"that is the place where Babalatchi promised that a boat from the prau would come for me when the sun is overhead. We will wait for that boat there."

Almayer, who was steering, nodded without speaking, and by a slight sweep of his paddle laid the head of the canoe in the required direction.

They were just leaving the southern outlet of the Pantai,

which lay behind them in a straight and long vista of water
shining between two walls of thick verdure that ran down-
wards and towards each other, till at last they joined and
sank together in the far-away distance. The sun, rising
above the calm waters of the Straits, marked its own path
by a streak of light that glided upon the sea and darted up
the wide reach of the river, a hurried messenger of light
and life to the gloomy forests of the coast; and in this radi-
ance of the sun's pathway floated the black canoe heading
for the islet which lay bathed in sunshine, the yellow sands
of its encircling beach shining like an inlaid golden disc
on the polished steel of the unwrinkled sea. To the north
and south of it rose other islets, joyous in their brilliant colouring of green and yellow, and on the main coast the sombre line of mangrove bushes ended to the southward in the
reddish cliffs of Tanjong Mirrah, advancing into the sea,
steep and shadowless under the clear light of the early
morning.

The bottom of the canoe grated upon the sand as the
little craft ran upon the beach. Ali leaped on shore and
held on while Dain stepped out carrying Nina in his arms,
exhausted by the events and the long travelling during the
night. Almayer was the last to leave the boat, and together
with Ali ran it higher up on the beach. Then Ali, tired out
by the long paddling, lay down in the shade of the canoe,
and incontinently fell asleep. Almayer sat sideways on the
gunwale, and with his arms crossed on his breast, looked
to the southward upon the sea.

After carefully laying Nina down in the shade of the
bushes growing in the middle of the islet, Dain threw himself beside her and watched in silent concern the tears that
ran down from under her closed eyelids, and lost themselves
in that fine sand upon which they both were lying face to
face. These tears and this sorrow were for him a profound
and disquieting mystery. Now, when the danger was past,
why should she grieve? He doubted her love no more than
he would have doubted the fact of his own existence, but as
he lay looking ardently in her face, watching her tears, her
parted lips, her very breath, he was uneasily conscious of

something in her he could not understand. Doubtless she had the wisdom of perfect beings. He sighed. He felt something invisible that stood between them, something that would let him approach her so far, but no farther. No desire, no longing, no effort of will or length of life could destroy this vague feeling of their difference. With awe but also with great pride he concluded that it was her own incomparable perfection. She was his, and yet she was like a woman from another world. His! His! He exulted in the glorious thought; nevertheless her tears pained him.

With a wisp of her own hair which he took in his hand with timid reverence he tried in an access of clumsy tenderness to dry the tears that trembled on her eyelashes. He had his reward in a fleeting smile that brightened her face for the short fraction of a second, but soon the tears fell faster than ever, and he could bear it no more. He rose and walked towards Almayer, who still sat absorbed in his contemplation of the sea. It was a very, very long time since he had seen the sea—that sea that leads everywhere, brings everything, and takes away so much. He had almost forgotten why he was there, and dreamily he could see all his past life on the smooth and boundless surface that glittered before his eyes.

Dain's hand laid on Almayer's shoulder recalled him with a start from some country very far away indeed. He turned round, but his eyes seemed to look rather at the place where Dain stood than at the man himself. Dain felt uneasy under the unconscious gaze.

"What do you want?" asked Almayer.

"She is crying," murmured Dain, softly.

"She is crying! Why?" asked Almayer, indifferently.

"I came to ask you. My Ranee smiles when looking at the man she loves. It is the white woman that is crying now. You would know."

Almayer shrugged his shoulders and turned away again towards the sea.

"Go, Tuan Putih," urged Dain. "Go to her; her tears are more terrible to me than the anger of gods."

"Are they? You will see them more than once. She told

me she could not live without you," answered Almayer, speaking without the faintest spark of expression in his face, "so it behoves you to go to her quick, for fear you may find her dead."

He burst into a loud and unpleasant laugh which made Dain stare at him with some apprehension, but got off the gunwale of the boat and moved slowly towards Nina, glancing up at the sun as he walked.

"And you go when the sun is overhead?" he said.

"Yes, Tuan. Then we go," answered Dain.

"I have not long to wait," muttered Almayer. "It is most important for me to see you go. Both of you. Most important," he repeated, stopping short and looking at Dain fixedly.

He went on again towards Nina, and Dain remained behind. Almayer approached his daughter and stood for a time looking down on her. She did not open her eyes, but hearing footsteps near her, murmured in a low sob, "Dain."

Almayer hesitated for a minute and then sank on the sand by her side. She, not hearing a responsive word, not feeling a touch, opened her eyes—saw her father, and sat up suddenly with a movement of terror.

"Oh, father!" she murmured faintly, and in that word there was expressed regret and fear and dawning hope.

"I shall never forgive you, Nina," said Almayer, in a dispassionate voice. "You have torn my heart from me while I dreamt of your happiness. You have deceived me. Your eyes that for me were like truth itself lied to me in every glance—for how long? You know that best. When you were caressing my cheek you were counting the minutes to the sunset that was the signal for your meeting with that man—there!"

He ceased, and they both sat silent side by side, not looking at each other, but gazing at the vast expanse of the sea. Almayer's words had dried Nina's tears, and her look grew hard as she stared before her into the limitless sheet of blue that shone limpid, unwaving, and steady like heaven itself. He looked at it also, but his features had lost all expression, and life in his eyes seemed to have gone out. The face was a blank, without a sign of emotion, feeling, reason, or even knowledge of itself. All passion, regret, grief, hope, or anger —all were gone, erased by the hand of fate, as if after this last stroke everything was over and there was no need for any record. Those few who saw Almayer during the short period of his remaining days were always impressed by the sight of that face that seemed to know nothing of what went on within: like the blank wall of a prison enclosing sin, regrets, and pain, and wasted life, in the cold indifference of mortar and stones.

"What is there to forgive?" asked Nina, not addressing Almayer directly, but more as if arguing with herself. "Can I not live my own life as you have lived yours? The path you would have wished me to follow has been closed to me by no fault of mine."

"You never told me," muttered Almayer.

"You never asked me," she answered, "and I thought you were like the others and did not care. I bore the memory of my humiliation alone, and why should I tell you that it came to me because I am your daughter? I knew you could not avenge me."

"And yet I was thinking of that only," interrupted Almayer, "and I wanted to give you years of happiness for the short day of your suffering. I only knew of one way."

"Ah! but it was not my way!" she replied. "Could you give me happiness about life? Life!" she repeated with sudden energy that sent the word ringing over the sea. "Life that means power and love," she added in a low voice.

"That!" said Almayer, pointing his finger at Dain standing close by and looking at them in curious wonder.

"Yes, that!" she replied, looking her father full in the face and noticing for the first time with a slight gasp of fear the unnatural rigidity of his features.

"I would have rather strangled you with my own hands," said Almayer, in an expressionless voice which was such a contrast to the desperate bitterness of his feelings that it surprised even himself. He asked himself who spoke, and, after looking slowly round as if expecting to see somebody, turned again his eyes towards the sea.

"You say that because you do not understand the meaning of my words," she said sadly. "Between you and my mother there never was any love. When I returned to Sambir I found the place which I thought would be a peaceful refuge for my heart, filled with weariness and hatred—and mutual contempt. I have listened to your voice and to her voice. Then I saw that you could not understand me; for was I not part of that woman? Of her who was the regret and shame of your life? I had to choose—I hesitated. Why were you so blind? Did you not see me struggling before your eyes? But, when he came, all doubt disappeared, and I saw only the light of the blue and cloudless heaven—"

"I will tell you the rest," interrupted Almayer: "when that man came I also saw the blue and the sunshine of the sky. A thunderbolt has fallen from that sky, and suddenly all is still and dark around me for ever. I will never forgive you, Nina; and to-morrow I shall forget you! I shall never forgive you," he repeated with mechanical obstinacy while she sat, her head bowed down as if afraid to look at her father.

To him it seemed of the utmost importance that he should assure her of his intention of never forgiving. He was convinced that his faith in her had been the foundation of his hopes, the motive of his courage, of his determination to live and struggle, and to be victorious for her sake. And now his faith was gone, destroyed by her own hands; destroyed cruelly, treacherously, in the dark; in the very moment of success. In the utter wreck of his affections and of all his feelings, in the chaotic disorder of his thoughts, above the confused sensation of physical pain that wrapped him up in a sting as of a whiplash curling round him from his shoulders down to his feet, only one idea remained clear and definite—not to forgive her; only one vivid desire—to forget her. And this must be made clear to her—and to himself—by frequent repetition. That was his idea of his duty to himself—to his race—to his respectable connections; to the whole universe unsettled and shaken by this frightful catastrophe of his life. He saw it clearly and believed he was a strong man. He had always prided himself upon his unflinching firmness. And yet he was afraid. She had been all in all to him. What if he should let the memory of his love for her weaken the sense of his dignity? She was a re-markable woman; he could see that; all the latent greatness of his nature—in which he honestly believed—had been transfused into that slight, girlish figure. Great things could be done! What if he should suddenly take her to his heart, forget his shame, and pain, and anger, and—follow her! What if he changed his heart if not his skin and made her life easier between the two loves that would guard her from any mischance? His heart yearned for her. What if he should say that his love for her was greater than . . .

"I will never forgive you, Nina!" he shouted, leaping up madly in the sudden fear of his dream.

This was the last time in his life that he was heard to raise his voice. Henceforth he spoke always in a monoto-nous whisper like an instrument of which all the strings but one are broken in a last ringing clamour under a heavy blow.

She rose to her feet and looked at him. The very violence of his cry soothed her in an intuitive conviction of his love, and she hugged to her breast the lamentable remnants of that affection with the unscrupulous greediness of women who cling desperately to the very scraps and rags of love, any kind of love, as a thing that of right belongs to them and is the very breath of their life. She put both her hands on Almayer's shoulders, and looking at him half tenderly, half playfully, she said—

"You speak so because you love me."

Almayer shook his head.

"Yes, you do," she insisted softly; then after a short pause she added, "and you will never forget me."

Almayer shivered slightly. She could not have said a more cruel thing.

"Here is the boat coming now," said Dain, his arm out-stretched towards a black speck on the water between the coast and the islet.

They all looked at it and remained standing in silence till the little canoe came gently on the beach and a man landed and walked towards them. He stopped some distance off and hesitated.

"What news?" asked Dain.

"We have had orders secretly and in the night to take off from this islet a man and a woman. I see the woman. Which of you is the man?"

"Come, delight of my eyes," said Dain to Nina. "Now we go, and your voice shall be for my ears only. You have spoken your last words to the Tuan Putih, your father. Come."

She hesitated for a while, looking at Almayer, who kept his eyes steadily on the sea, then she touched his forehead in a lingering kiss, and a tear—one of her tears—fell on his cheek and ran down his immovable face.

"Good-bye," she whispered, and remained irresolute till he pushed her suddenly into Dain's arms.

"If you have any pity for me," murmured Almayer, as if repeating some sentence learned by heart, "take that woman away."

He stood very straight, his shoulders thrown back, his head held high, and looked at them as they went down the beach to the canoe, walking enlaced in each other's arms. He looked at the line of their footsteps marked in the sand. He followed their figures moving in the crude blaze of the vertical sun, in that light violent and vibrating, like a triumphal flourish of brazen trumpets. He looked at the man's brown shoulders, at the red sarong round his waist; at the tall, slender, dazzling white figure he supported. He looked at the white dress, at the falling masses of the long black hair. He looked at them embarking, and at the canoe growing smaller in the distance, with rage, despair, and regret in his heart, and on his face a peace as that of a carved image of oblivion. Inwardly he felt himself torn to pieces, but Ali who—now aroused—stood close to his master, saw on his features the blank expression of those who live in that hopeless calm which sightless eyes only can give.

The canoe disappeared, and Almayer stood motionless with his eyes fixed on its wake. Ali from under the shade of his hand examined the coast curiously. As the sun de-clined, the sea-breeze sprang up from the northward and shivered with its breath the glassy surface of the water.

"Dapat!" exclaimed Ali, joyously. "Got him, master! Got prau! Not there! Look more Tanah Mirrah side. Ah! That way! Master, see? Now plain. See?"

Almayer followed Ali's forefinger with his eyes for a long time in vain. At last he sighted a triangular patch of yellow light on the red background of the cliffs of Tanjong Mirrah. It was the sail of the prau that had caught the sunlight and stood out, distinct with its gay tint, on the dark red of the cape. The yellow triangle crept slowly from cliff to cliff, till it cleared the last point of land and shone brilliantly for a fleeting minute on the blue of the open sea. Then the prau bore up to the southward: the light went out of the sail, and all at once the vessel itself disappeared, vanishing in the shadow of the steep headland that looked on, patient and lonely, watching over the empty sea.

Almayer never moved. Round the little islet the air was full of the talk of the rippling water. The crested wavelets ran up the beach audaciously, joyously, with the lightness of young life, and died quickly, unresistingly, and graciously, in the wide curves of transparent foam on the yellow sand. Above the white clouds sailed rapidly southwards as if intent upon overtaking something. Ali seemed anxious.

"Master," he said timidly, "time to go house now. Long way off to pull. All ready, sir."

"Wait," whispered Almayer.

Now she was gone his business was to forget, and he had a strange notion that it should be done systematically and in order. To Ali's great dismay he fell on his hands and knees, and, creeping along the sand, erased carefully with his hands all traces of Nina's footsteps. He piled up small heaps of sand, leaving behind him a line of miniature graves right down to the water. After burying the last slight imprint of Nina's slipper he stood up, and, turning his face towards the headland where he had last seen the prau, he made an effort to shout out loud again his firm resolve to never forgive. Ali watching him uneasily saw only his lips move, but heard no sound. He brought his foot down with a stamp. He was a firm man—firm as a rock. Let her go. He never had a daughter. He would forget. He was forgetting already.

Ali approached him again, insisting on immediate departure, and this time he consented, and they went together towards their canoe, Almayer leading. For all his firmness he looked very dejected and feeble as he dragged his feet slowly through the sand on the beach; and by his side—invisible to Ali—stalked that particular fiend whose mission it is to jog the memories of men, lest they should forget the meaning of life. He whispered into Almayer's ear a childish prattle of many years ago. Almayer, his head bent on one side, seemed to listen to his invisible companion, but his face was like the face of a man that has died struck from behind—a face from which all feelings and all expression are suddenly wiped off by the hand of unexpected death.

They slept on the river that night, mooring their canoe under the bushes and lying down in the bottom side by side, in the absolute exhaustion that kills hunger, thirst, all feeling and all thought in the overpowering desire for that deep sleep which is like the temporary annihilation of the tired body. Next day they started again and fought doggedly with the current all the morning, till about midday they reached the settlement and made fast their little craft to the jetty of Lingard and Co. Almayer walked straight to the house, and Ali followed, paddles on shoulder, thinking that he would like to eat something. As they crossed the front courtyard they noticed the abandoned look of the place. Ali looked in at the different servants' houses: all were empty. In the back courtyard there was the same absence of sound and life. In the cooking shed the fire was out and the black embers were cold. A tall, lean man came stealthily out of the banana plantation, and went away rapidly across the open space looking at them with big, frightened eyes over his shoulder. Some vagabond without a master; there were many such in the settlement, and they looked upon Almayer as their patron. They prowled about his premises and picked their living there, sure that nothing worse could befall them than a shower of curses when they got in the way of the white man, whom they trusted and liked, and called a fool amongst themselves. In the house, which Almayer entered through the back verandah, the only living thing that met his eyes was his small monkey, which hungry and unnoticed for the last two days, began to cry and complain in monkey language as soon as it caught sight of the familiar face. Almayer soothed it with a few words and ordered Ali to bring in some bananas, then while Ali was gone to get them he stood in the doorway of the front verandah looking at the chaos of overturned furniture. Finally he picked up the table and sat on it while the monkey let itself down from the roof-stick by its chain and perched on his shoulder. When the bananas came they had their breakfast together; both hungry, both eating greedily and showering the skins round them recklessly, in the trusting silence of perfect friendship. Ali went away, grumbling, to cook some rice himself, for all the women about the house had disappeared; he did not know where. Almayer did not seem to care, and, after he finished eating, he sat on the table swinging his legs and staring at the river as if lost in thought.

After some time he got up and went to the door of a room on the right of the verandah. That was the office. The office of Lingard and Co. He very seldom went in there. There was no business now, and he did not want an office. The door was locked, and he stood biting his lower lip, trying to think of the place where the key could be. Suddenly he remembered: in the women's room hung upon a nail. He went over to the doorway where the red curtain hung down in motionless folds, and hesitated for a moment before pushing it aside with his shoulder as if breaking down some solid obstacle. A great square of sunshine entering through the window lay on the floor. On the left he saw Mrs. Almayer's big wooden chest, the lid thrown back, empty; near it the brass nails of Nina's European trunk shone in the large initials N.A. on the cover. A few of Nina's dresses hung on wooden pegs, stiffened in a look of offended dignity at their abandonment. He remembered making the pegs himself and noticed that they were very good pegs.

Where was the key? He looked round and saw it near the door where he stood. It was red with rust. He felt very much annoyed at that, and directly afterwards wondered at his own feeling. What did it matter? There soon would be no key—no door—nothing! He paused, key in hand, and asked himself whether he knew well what he was about. He went out again on the verandah and stood by the table thinking. The monkey jumped down, and, snatching a banana skin, absorbed itself in picking it to shreds industriously.

"Forget!" muttered Almayer, and that word started before him a sequence of events, a detailed programme of things to do. He knew perfectly well what was to be done now. First this, then that, and then forgetfulness would come easy. Very easy. He had a fixed idea that if he should not forget before he died he would have to remember to all eternity. Certain things had to be taken out of his life, stamped out of sight, destroyed, forgotten. For a long time he stood in deep thought, lost in the alarming possibilities of unconquerable memory, with the fear of death and eternity before him. "Eternity!" he said aloud, and the sound of that word recalled him out of his reverie. The monkey started, dropped the skin, and grinned up at him amicably.

He went towards the office door and with some difficulty managed to open it. He entered in a cloud of dust that rose under his feet. Books open with torn pages bestrewed the floor; other books lay about grimy and black, looking as if they had never been opened. Account books. In those books he had intended to keep day by day a record of his rising fortunes. Long time ago. A very long time. For many years there had been no record to keep on the blue and red ruled pages! In the middle of the room the big office desk, with one of its legs broken, careened over like the hull of a stranded ship; most of the drawers had fallen out, disclosing heaps of paper yellow with age and dirt. The revolving office chair stood in its place, but he found the pivot set fast when he tried to turn it. No matter. He desisted, and his eyes wandered slowly from object to object. All those things had cost a lot of money at the time. The desk, the paper, the torn books, and the broken shelves, all under a thick coat of dust. The very dust and bones of a dead and gone business. He looked at all these things, all that was left after so many years of work, of strife, of weariness, of discouragement, conquered so many times. And all for what? He stood thinking mournfully of his past life till he heard distinctly the clear voice of a child speaking amongst all this wreck, ruin, and waste. He started with a great fear in his heart, and feverishly began to rake in the papers scattered on the floor, broke the chair into bits, splintered the drawers by banging them against the desk, and made a big heap of all that rubbish in one corner of the room.

He came out quickly, slammed the door after him, turned the key, and, taking it out, ran to the front rail of the verandah, and, with a great swing of his arm, sent the key whizzing into the river. This done he went back slowly to the table, called the monkey down, unhooked its chain, and induced it to remain quiet in the breast of his jacket. Then he sat again on the table and looked fixedly at the door of the room he had just left. He listened also intently. He heard a dry sound of rustling sharp cracks as of dry wood snapping; a whirr like that of a bird's wings when it rises suddenly, and then he saw a thin stream of smoke come through the keyhole. The monkey struggled under his coat. Ali appeared with his eyes starting out of his head.

"Master! House burn!" he shouted.

Almayer stood up holding by the table. He could hear the yells of alarm and surprise in the settlement. Ali wrung his hands, lamenting aloud.

"Stop this noise, fool!" said Almayer, quietly. "Pick up my hammock and blankets and take them to the other house. Quick, now!"

The smoke burst through the crevices of the door, and Ali, with the hammock in his arms, cleared in one bound the steps of the verandah.

"It has caught well," muttered Almayer to himself. "Be quiet, Jack," he added, as the monkey made a frantic effort to escape from its confinement.

The door split from top to bottom, and a rush of flame and smoke drove Almayer away from the table to the front rail of the verandah. He held on there till a great roar overhead assured him that the roof was ablaze. Then he ran down the steps of the verandah, coughing, half choked with the smoke that pursued him in bluish wreaths curling about his head.

On the other side of the ditch, separating Almayer's courtyard from the settlement, a crowd of the inhabitants of Sambir looked at the burning house of the white man. In the calm air the flames rushed up on high, coloured pale brick-red, with violet gleams in the strong sunshine. The thin column of smoke ascended straight and unwavering till it lost itself in the clear blue of the sky, and in the great empty space between the two houses the interested spectators could see the tall figure of the Tuan Putih, with bowed head and dragging feet, walking slowly away from the fire towards the shelter of "Almayer's Folly."

In that manner did Almayer move into his new house. He took possession of the new ruin, and in the undying folly of his heart set himself to wait in anxiety and pain for that forgetfulness which was so slow to come. He had done all he could. Every vestige of Nina's existence had been destroyed; and now with every sunrise he asked himself whether the longed-for oblivion would come before sunset, whether it would come before he died? He wanted to live only long enough to be able to forget, and the tenacity of his memory filled him with dread and horror of death; for should it come before he could accomplish the purpose of his life he would have to remember for ever! He also longed for loneliness. He wanted to be alone. But he was not. In the dim light of the rooms with their closed shutters, in the bright sunshine of the verandah, wherever he went, whichever way he turned, he saw the small figure of a little maiden with pretty olive face, with long black hair, her little pink robe slipping off her shoulders, her big eyes looking up at him in the tender trustfulness of a petted child. Ali did not see anything, but he also was aware of the presence of a child in the house. In his long talks by the

evening fires of the settlement he used to tell his intimate
friends of Almayer's strange doings. His master had turned
sorcerer in his old age. Ali said that often when Tuan Putih
had retired for the night he could hear him talking to something in his room. Ali thought that it was a spirit in the
shape of a child. He knew his master spoke to a child from
certain expressions and words his master used. His master
spoke in Malay a little, but mostly in English, which he,
Ali, could understand. Master spoke to the child at times
tenderly, then he would weep over it, laugh at it, scold it,
beg of it to go away; curse it. It was a bad and stubborn
spirit. Ali thought his master had imprudently called it up,
and now could not get rid of it. His master was very brave;
he was not afraid to curse this spirit in the very Presence;
and once he fought with it. Ali had heard a great noise as of
running about inside the room and groans. His master
groaned. Spirits do not groan. His master was brave, but
foolish. You cannot hurt a spirit. Ali expected to find his
master dead next morning, but he came out very early, looking much older than the day before, and had no food all
day.

So far Ali to the settlement. To Captain Ford he was
much more communicative, for the good reason that Captain Ford had the purse and gave orders. On each of Ford's
monthly visits to Sambir Ali had to go on board with a
report about the inhabitant of "Almayer's Folly." On his
first visit to Sambir, after Nina's departure, Ford had taken
charge of Almayer's affairs. They were not cumbersome.
The shed for the storage of goods was empty, the boats had
disappeared, appropriated—generally in night-time—by
various citizens of Sambir in need of means of transport.
During a great flood the jetty of Lingard and Co. left the
bank and floated down the river, probably in search of more
cheerful surroundings; even the flock of geese—"the only
geese on the east coast"—departed somewhere, preferring
the unknown dangers of the bush to the desolation of their
old home. As time went on the grass grew over the black
patch of ground where the old house used to stand, and

nothing remained to mark the place of the dwelling that had sheltered Almayer's young hopes, his foolish dream of splendid future, his awakening, and his despair.

Ford did not often visit Almayer, for visiting Almayer was not a pleasant task. At first he used to respond listlessly to the old seaman's boisterous inquiries about his health; he even made efforts to talk, asking for news in a voice that made it perfectly clear that no news from this world had any interest for him. Then gradually he became more silent —not sulkily—but as if he was forgetting how to speak. He used also to hide in the darkest rooms of the house where Ford had to seek him out guided by the patter of the monkey galloping before him. The monkey was always there to receive and introduce Ford. The little animal seemed to have taken complete charge of its master, and whenever it wished for his presence on the verandah it would tug perseveringly at his jacket, till Almayer obediently came out into the sunshine, which he seemed to dislike so much.

One morning Ford found him sitting on the floor of the verandah, his back against the wall, his legs stretched stiffly out, his arms hanging by his side. His expressionless face, his eyes open wide with immobile pupils, and the rigidity of his pose, made him look like an immense man-doll broken and flung there out of the way. As Ford came up the steps he turned his head slowly.

"Ford," he murmured from the floor, "I cannot forget."

"Can't you?" said Ford, innocently, with an attempt at joviality: "I wish I was like you. I am losing my memory— age, I suppose; only the other day my mate—"

He stopped, for Almayer had got up, stumbled, and steadied himself on his friend's arm.

"Hallo! You are better to-day. Soon be all right," said Ford, cheerfully, but feeling rather scared.

Almayer let go his arm and stood very straight with his head up and shoulders thrown back, looking stonily at the multitude of suns shining in ripples of the river. His jacket and his loose trousers flapped in the breeze on his thin limbs.

"Let her go!" he whispered in a grating voice. "Let her go. To-morrow I shall forget. I am a firm man, . . . firm as a . . . rock, . . . firm. . . ."

Ford looked at his face—and fled. The skipper was a tolerably firm man himself—as those who had sailed with him could testify—but Almayer's firmness was altogether too much for his fortitude.

Next time the steamer called in Sambir Ali came on board early with a grievance. He complained to Ford that Jim-Eng the Chinaman had invaded Almayer's house, and actually had lived there for the last month.

"And they both smoke," added Ali.

"Phew! Opium, you mean?"

Ali nodded, and Ford remained thoughtful; then he muttered to himself, "Poor devil! The sooner the better now." In the afternoon he walked up to the house.

"What are you doing here?" he asked of Jim-Eng, whom he found strolling about on the verandah.

Jim-Eng explained in bad Malay, and speaking in that monotonous, uninterested voice of an opium smoker pretty far gone, that his house was old, the roof leaked, and the floor was rotten. So, being an old friend for many, many years, he took his money, his opium, and two pipes, and came to live in this big house.

"There is plenty of room. He smokes, and I live here. He will not smoke long," he concluded.

"Where is he now?" asked Ford.

"Inside. He sleeps," answered Jim-Eng, wearily.

Ford glanced in through the doorway. In the dim light of the room he could see Almayer lying on his back on the floor, his head on a wooden pillow, the long white beard scattered over his breast, the yellow skin of the face, the half-closed eyelids showing the whites of the eye only. . . .

He shuddered and turned away. As he was leaving he noticed a long strip of faded red silk, with some Chinese letters on it, which Jim-Eng had just fastened to one of the pillars.

"What's that?" he asked.

"That," said Jim-Eng, in his colourless voice, "that is the

name of the house. All the same like my house. Very good name."

Ford looked at him for awhile and went away. He did not know what the crazy-looking maze of the Chinese inscription on the red silk meant. Had he asked Jim-Eng, that patient Chinaman would have informed him with proper pride that its meaning was: "House of heavenly delight."

In the evening of the same day Babalatchi called on Captain Ford. The captain's cabin opened on deck, and Babalatchi sat astride on the high step, while Ford smoked his pipe on the settee inside. The steamer was leaving next morning, and the old statesman came as usual for a last chat.

"We had news from Bali last moon," remarked Babalatchi. "A grandson is born to the old Rajah, and there is great rejoicing."

Ford sat up interested.

"Yes," went on Babalatchi, in answer to Ford's look. "I told him. That was before he began to smoke."

"Well, and what?" asked Ford.

"I escaped with my life," said Babalatchi, with perfect gravity, "because the white man is very weak and fell as he rushed upon me." Then, after a pause, he added, "She is mad with joy."

"Mrs. Almayer, you mean?"

"Yes, she lives in our Rajah's house. She will not die soon. Such women live a long time," said Babalatchi, with a slight tinge of regret in his voice. "She has dollars, and she has buried them, but we know where. We had much trouble with those people. We had to pay a fine and listen to threats from the white men, and now we have to be careful." He sighed and remained silent for a long while. Then with energy:

"There will be fighting. There is a breath of war on the islands.

"Shall I live long enough to see? . . . Ah, Tuan!" he went on, more quietly, "the old times were best. Even I have sailed with Lanun men, and boarded in the night silent ships

with white sails. That was before an English Rajah ruled
in Kuching. Then we fought amongst ourselves and were
happy. Now when we fight with you we can only die!"

He rose to go. "Tuan," he said, "you remember the girl
that man Bulangi had? Her that caused all the trouble?"

"Yes," said Ford. "What of her?"

"She grew thin and could not work. Then Bulangi, who
is a thief and a pig-eater, gave her to me for fifty dollars.
I sent her amongst my women to grow fat. I wanted to hear
the sound of her laughter, but she must have been bewitched, and . . . she died two days ago. Nay, Tuan. Why
do you speak bad words? I am old—that is true—but why
should I not like the sight of a young face and the sound
of a young voice in my house?" He paused, and then added
with a little mournful laugh, "I am like a white man talking
too much of what is not men's talk when they speak to
one another."

And he went off looking very sad.

The crowd massed in a semicircle before the steps of
"Almayer's Folly," swayed silently backwards and forwards,
and opened out before the group of white-robed and tur-
baned men advancing through the grass towards the house.
Abdulla walked first, supported by Reshid and followed by
all the Arabs in Sambir. As they entered the lane made by
the respectful throng there was a subdued murmur of voices,
where the word "Mati" was the only one distinctly audible.
Abdulla stopped and looked round slowly.

"Is he dead?" he asked.

"May you live!" answered the crowd in one shout, and
then there succeeded a breathless silence.

Abdulla made a few paces forward and found himself
for the last time face to face with his old enemy. Whatever he might have been once he was not dangerous now,
lying stiff and lifeless in the tender light of the early day.
The only white man on the east coast was dead, and his
soul, delivered from the trammels of his earthly folly, stood
now in the presence of Infinite Wisdom. On the upturned
face there was that serene look which follows the sudden

relief from anguish and pain, and it testified silently before the cloudless heaven that the man lying there under the gaze of indifferent eyes had been permitted to forget before he died.

Abdulla looked down sadly at this Infidel he had fought so long and had bested so many times. Such was the reward of the Faithful! Yet in the Arab's old heart there was a feeling of regret for that thing gone out of his life. He was leaving fast behind him friendships, and enmities, successes, and disappointments—all that makes up a life; and before him was only the end. Prayer would fill up the remainder of the days allotted to the True Believer! He took in his hand the beads that hung at his waist.

"I found him here, like this, in the morning," said Ali, in a low and awed voice.

Abdulla glanced coldly once more at the serene face.

"Let us go," he said, addressing Reshid.

And as they passed through the crowd that fell back before them, the beads in Abdulla's hand clicked, while in a solemn whisper he breathed out piously the name of Allah! The Merciful! The Compassionate!

THE
LAGOON

The Lagoon

The white man, leaning with both arms over the roof
of the little house in the stern of the boat, said to the steersman—

"We will pass the night in Arsat's clearing. It is late."

The Malay only grunted, and went on looking fixedly at
the river. The white man rested his chin on his crossed
arms and gazed at the wake of the boat. At the end of the
straight avenue of forests cut by the intense glitter of the
river, the sun appeared unclouded and dazzling, poised
low over the water that shone smoothly like a band of
metal. The forests, sombre and dull, stood motionless and
silent on each side of the broad stream. At the foot of big,
towering trees, trunkless nipa palms rose from the mud of
the bank, in bunches of leaves enormous and heavy, that
hung unstirring over the brown swirl of eddies. In the stillness of the air every tree, every leaf, every bough, every
tendril of creeper and every petal of minute blossoms
seemed to have been bewitched into an immobility perfect
and final. Nothing moved on the river but the eight paddles that rose flashing regularly, dipped together with a
single splash; while the steersman swept right and left with
a periodic and sudden flourish of his blade describing a
glinting semicircle above his head. The churned-up water
frothed alongside with a confused murmur. And the white
man's canoe, advancing upstream in the short-lived disturbance of its own making, seemed to enter the portals of a
land from which the very memory of motion had forever
departed.

The white man, turning his back upon the setting sun,

looked along the empty and broad expanse of the sea-reach. For the last three miles of its course the wandering, hesitating river, as if enticed irresistibly by the freedom of an open horizon, flows straight into the sea, flows straight to the east—to the east that harbours both light and darkness. Astern of the boat the repeated call of some bird, a cry discordant and feeble, skipped along over the smooth water and lost itself, before it could reach the other shore, in the breathless silence of the world.

The steersman dug his paddle into the stream, and held hard with stiffened arms, his body thrown forward. The water gurgled aloud; and suddenly the long straight reach seemed to pivot on its centre, the forests swung in a semicircle, and the slanting beams of sunset touched the broadside of the canoe with a fiery glow, throwing the slender and distorted shadows of its crew upon the streaked glitter of the river. The white man turned to look ahead. The course of the boat had been altered at right-angles to the stream, and the carved dragon-head of its prow was pointing now at a gap in the fringing bushes of the bank. It glided through, brushing the overhanging twigs, and disappeared from the river like some slim and amphibious creature leaving the water for its lair in the forests.

The narrow creek was like a ditch: tortuous, fabulously deep; filled with gloom under the thin strip of pure and shining blue of the heaven. Immense trees soared up, invisible behind the festooned draperies of creepers. Here and there, near the glistening blackness of the water, a twisted root of some tall tree showed amongst the tracery of small ferns, black and dull, writhing and motionless, like an arrested snake. The short words of the paddlers reverberated loudly between the thick and sombre walls of vegetation. Darkness oozed out from between the trees, through the angled maze of the creepers, from behind the great fantastic and unstirring leaves; the darkness, mysterious and invincible; the darkness scented and poisonous of impenetrable forests.

The men poled in the shoaling water. The creek broadened, opening out into a wide sweep of a stagnant lagoon.

The forests receded from the marshy bank, leaving a level strip of bright green, reedy grass to frame the reflected blueness of the sky. A fleecy pink cloud drifted high above, trailing the delicate colouring of its image under the floating leaves and the silvery blossoms of the lotus. A little house, perched on high piles, appeared black in the distance. Near it, two tall nibong palms, that seemed to have come out of the forests in the background, leaned slightly over the ragged roof, with a suggestion of sad tenderness and care in the droop of their leafy and soaring heads.

The steersman, pointing with his paddle, said, "Arsat is there. I see his canoe fast between the piles."

The polers ran along the sides of the boat glancing over their shoulders at the end of the day's journey. They would have preferred to spend the night somewhere else than on this lagoon of weird aspect and ghostly reputation. Moreover, they disliked Arsat, first as a stranger, and also because he who repairs a ruined house, and dwells in it, proclaims that he is not afraid to live amongst the spirits that haunt the places abandoned by mankind. Such a man can disturb the course of fate by glances or words; while his familiar ghosts are not easy to propitiate by casual wayfarers upon whom they long to wreak the malice of their human master. White men care not for such things, being unbelievers and in league with the Father of Evil, who leads them unharmed through the invisible dangers of this world. To the warnings of the righteous they oppose an offensive pretence of disbelief. What is there to be done?

So they thought, throwing their weight on the end of their long poles. The big canoe glided on swiftly, noiselessly, and smoothly, towards Arsat's clearing, till, in a great rattling of poles thrown down, and the loud murmurs of "Allah be praised!" it came with a gentle knock against the crooked piles below the house.

The boatmen with uplifted faces shouted discordantly, "Arsat! O Arsat!" Nobody came. The white man began to climb the rude ladder giving access to the bamboo platform before the house. The juragan of the boat said sulkily, "We will cook in the sampan, and sleep on the water."

"Pass my blankets and the basket," said the white man, curtly.

He knelt on the edge of the platform to receive the bundle. Then the boat shoved off, and the white man, standing up, confronted Arsat, who had come out through the low door of his hut. He was a man young, powerful, with broad chest and muscular arms. He had nothing on but his sarong. His head was bare. His big, soft eyes stared eagerly at the white man, but his voice and demeanour were composed as he asked, without any words of greeting—

"Have you medicine, Tuan?"

"No," said the visitor in a startled tone. "No. Why? Is there sickness in the house?"

"Enter and see," replied Arsat, in the same calm manner, and turning short round, passed again through the small doorway. The white man, dropping his bundles, followed.

In the dim light of the dwelling he made out on a couch of bamboos a woman stretched on her back under a broad sheet of red cotton cloth. She lay still, as if dead; but her big eyes, wide open, glittered in the gloom, staring upwards at the slender rafters, motionless and unseeing. She was in a high fever, and evidently unconscious. Her cheeks were sunk slightly, her lips were partly open, and on the young face there was the ominous and fixed expression—the absorbed, contemplating expression of the unconscious who are going to die. The two men stood looking down at her in silence.

"Has she been long ill?" asked the traveller.

"I have not slept for five nights," answered the Malay, in a deliberate tone. "At first she heard voices calling her from the water and struggled against me who held her. But since the sun of to-day rose she hears nothing—she hears not me. She sees nothing. She sees not me—me!"

He remained silently for a minute, then asked softly—

"Tuan, will she die?"

"I fear so," said the white man, sorrowfully. He had known Arsat years ago, in a far country in times of trouble and danger, when no friendship is to be despised. And since his Malay friend had come unexpectedly to dwell in the hut on the lagoon with a strange woman, he had slept many times there, in his journeys up and down the river. He liked the man who knew how to keep faith in council and how to fight without fear by the side of his white friend. He liked him—not so much perhaps as a man likes his favourite dog—but still he liked him well enough to help and ask no questions, to think sometimes vaguely and hazily in the midst of his own pursuits, about the lonely man and the long-haired woman with audacious face and triumphant eyes, who lived together hidden by the forests—alone and feared.

The white man came out of the hut in time to see the enormous conflagration of sunset put out by the swift and stealthy shadows that, rising like a black and impalpable vapour above the tree-tops, spread over the heaven, extinguishing the crimson glow of floating clouds and the red brilliance of departing daylight. In a few moments all the stars came out above the intense blackness of the earth and the great lagoon gleaming suddenly with reflected lights resembled an oval patch of night sky flung down into the hopeless and abysmal night of the wilderness. The white man had some supper out of the basket, then collecting a few sticks that lay about the platform, made up a small fire, not for warmth, but for the sake of the smoke, which would keep off the mosquitos. He wrapped himself in the blankets and sat with his back against the reed wall of the house, smoking thoughtfully.

Arsat came through the doorway with noiseless steps and squatted down by the fire. The white man moved his outstretched legs a little.

"She breathes," said Arsat in a low voice, anticipating the expected question. "She breathes and burns as if with a great fire. She speaks not; she hears not—and burns!"

He paused for a moment, then asked in a quiet, incurious tone—

"Tuan . . . will she die?"

The white man moved his shoulders uneasily and muttered in a hesitating manner—

"If such is her fate."

"No, Tuan," said Arsat, calmly. "If such is my fate. I hear, I see, I wait. I remember . . . Tuan, do you remember the old days? Do you remember my brother?"

"Yes," said the white man. The Malay rose suddenly and went in. The other, sitting still outside, could hear the voice in the hut. Arsat said: "Hear me! Speak!" His words were succeeded by a complete silence. "O Diamelen!" he cried, suddenly. After that cry there was a deep sigh. Arsat came out and sank down again in his old place.

They sat in silence before the fire. There was no sound within the house, there was no sound near them; but far away on the lagoon they could hear the voices of the boatmen ringing fitful and distinct on the calm water. The fire in the bows of the sampan shone faintly in the distance with a hazy red glow. Then it died out. The voices ceased. The land and the water slept invisible, unstirring and mute. It was as though there had been nothing left in the world but the glitter of stars streaming, ceaseless and vain, through the black stillness of the night.

The white man gazed straight before him into the darkness with wide-open eyes. The fear and fascination, the inspiration and the wonder of death—of death, near, unavoidable, and unseen, soothed the unrest of his race and stirred the most indistinct, the most intimate of his thoughts. The ever-ready suspicion of evil, the gnawing suspicion that lurks in our hearts, flowed out into the stillness round him —into the stillness profound and dumb, and made it appear untrustworthy and infamous, like the placid and impenetrable mask of an unjustifiable violence. In that fleeting and powerful disturbance of his being the earth enfolded in the starlight peace became a shadowy country of inhuman strife, a battle-field of phantoms terrible and charming, august or ignoble, struggling ardently for the possession of our helpless hearts. An unquiet and mysterious country of inextinguishable desires and fears.

A plaintive murmur rose in the night; a murmur saddening and startling, as if the great solitudes of surrounding woods had tried to whisper into his ear the wisdom of their immense and lofty indifference. Sounds hesitating and vague floated in the air round him, shaped themselves slowly into words; and at last flowed on gently in a murmuring stream of soft and monotonous sentences. He stirred like a man waking up and changed his position slightly. Arsat, motionless and shadowy, sitting with bowed head under the stars, was speaking in a low and dreamy tone—

"... for where can we lay down the heaviness of our trouble but in a friend's heart? A man must speak of war and of love. You, Tuan, know what war is, and you have seen me in time of danger seek death as other men seek life! A writing may be lost; a lie may be written; but what the eye has seen is truth and remains in the mind!"

"I remember," said the white man, quietly. Arsat went on with mournful composure—

"Therefore I shall speak to you of love. Speak in the night. Speak before both night and love are gone—and the eye of day looks upon my sorrow and my shame; upon my blackened face; upon my burnt-up heart."

A sigh, short and faint, marked an almost imperceptible pause, and then his words flowed on, without a stir, without a gesture.

"After the time of trouble and war was over and you went away from my country in the pursuit of your desires, which we, men of the islands, cannot understand, I and my brother became again, as we had been before, the sword-bearers of the Ruler. You know we were men of family, belonging to a ruling race, and more fit than any to carry on our right shoulder the emblem of power. And in the time of prosperity Si Dendring showed us favour, as we, in time of sorrow, had showed to him the faithfulness of our courage. It was a time of peace. A time of deer-hunts and cock-fights; of idle talks and foolish squabbles between men whose bellies are full and weapons are rusty. But the sower watched the young rice-shoots grow up without fear, and the traders came and went, departed lean and returned fat into the river of peace. They brought news, too. Brought lies and truth mixed together, so that no man knew when to rejoice and when to be sorry. We heard from

them about you also. They had seen you here and had seen
you there. And I was glad to hear, for I remembered the
stirring times, and I always remembered you, Tuan, till the
time came when my eyes could see nothing in the past, because they had looked upon the one who is dying there—in
the house."

He stopped to exclaim in an intense whisper, "O Mara
bahia! O Calamity!" then went on speaking a little louder:

"There's no worse enemy and no better friend than a
brother, Tuan, for one brother knows another, and in perfect knowledge is strength for good or evil. I loved my
brother. I went to him and told him that I could see nothing but one face, hear nothing but one voice. He told me:
'Open your heart so that she can see what is in it—and
wait. Patience is wisdom. Inchi Midah may die or our Ruler
may throw off his fear of a woman!' . . . I waited! . . . You
remember the lady with the veiled face, Tuan, and the fear
of our Ruler before her cunning and temper. And if she
wanted her servant, what could I do? But I fed the hunger
of my heart on short glances and stealthy words. I loitered
on the path to the bath-houses in the daytime, and when
the sun had fallen behind the forest I crept along the jas-
mine hedges of the women's courtyard. Unseeing, we spoke
to one another through the scent of flowers, through the
veil of leaves, through the blades of long grass that stood
still before our lips; so great was our prudence, so faint
was the murmur of our great longing. The time passed
swiftly . . . and there were whispers amongst women—and
our enemies watched—my brother was gloomy, and I began to think of killing and of a fierce death. . . . We are of a
people who take what they want—like you whites. There
is a time when a man should forget loyalty and respect.
Might and authority are given to rulers, but to all men is
given love and strength and courage. My brother said, 'You
shall take her from their midst. We are two who are like
one.' And I answered, 'Let it be soon, for I find no warmth
in sunlight that does not shine upon her.' Our time came
when the Ruler and all the great people went to the mouth
of the river to fish by torchlight. There were hundreds of

boats, and on the white sand, between the water and the forests, dwellings of leaves were built for the households of the Rajah. The smoke of cooking-fires was like a blue mist of the evening, and many voices rang in it joyfully. While they were making the boats ready to beat up the fish, my brother came to me and said, 'To-night!' I looked to my weapons, and when the time came our canoe took its place in the circle of boats carrying the torches. The lights blazed on the water, but behind the boats there was darkness. When the shouting began and the excitement made them like mad we dropped out. The water swallowed our fire, and we floated back to the shore that was dark with only here and there the glimmer of embers. We could hear the talk of slave-girls amongst the sheds. Then we found a place deserted and silent. We waited there. She came. She came running along the shore, rapid and leaving no trace, like a leaf driven by the wind into the sea. My brother said gloomily, 'Go and take her; carry her into our boat.' I lifted her in my arms. She panted. Her heart was beating against my breast. I said, 'I take you from those people. You came to the cry of my heart, but my arms take you into my boat against the will of the great!' 'It is right,' said my brother. 'We are men who take what we want and can hold it against many. We should have taken her in daylight.' I said, 'Let us be off'; for since she was in my boat I began to think of our Ruler's many men. 'Yes. Let us be off,' said my brother. 'We are cast out and this boat is our country now—and the sea is our refuge.' He lingered with his foot on the shore, and I entreated him to hasten, for I remembered the strokes of her heart against my breast and thought that two men cannot withstand a hundred. We left, paddling downstream close to the bank; and as we passed by the creek where they were fishing, the great shouting had ceased, but the murmur of voices was loud like the humming of insects flying at noonday. The boats floated, clustered together, in the red light of torches, under a black roof of smoke; and men talked of their sport. Men that boasted, and praised, and jeered—men that would have been our friends in the morning, but on that night were already our enemies. We paddled swiftly past. We had no more friends in the country of our birth. She sat in the middle of the canoe with covered face; silent as she is now; unseeing as she is now—and I had no regret at what I was leaving because I could hear her breathing close to me—as I can hear her now."

He paused, listened with his ear turned to the doorway, then shook his head and went on:

"My brother wanted to shout the cry of challenge—one cry only—to let the people know we were freeborn robbers who trusted our arms and the great sea. And again I begged him in the name of our love to be silent. Could I not hear her breathing close to me? I knew the pursuit would come quick enough. My brother loved me. He dipped his paddle without a splash. He only said, 'There is half a man in you now—the other half is in that woman. I can wait. When you are a whole man again, you will come back with me here to shout defiance. We are sons of the same mother.' I made no answer. All my strength and all my spirit were in my hands that held the paddle—for I longed to be with her in a safe place beyond the reach of men's anger and of women's spite. My love was so great, that I thought it could guide me to a country where death was unknown, if I could only escape from Inchi Midah's fury and from our Ruler's sword. We paddled with haste, breathing through our teeth. The blades bit deep into the smooth water. We passed out of the river; we flew in clear channels amongst the shallows. We skirted the black coast; we skirted the sand beaches where the sea speaks in whispers to the land; and the gleam of white sand flashed back past our boat, so swiftly she ran upon the water. We spoke not. Only once I said, 'Sleep, Diamelen, for soon you may want all your strength.' I heard the sweetness of her voice, but I never turned my head. The sun rose and still we went on. Water fell from my face like rain from a cloud. We flew in the light and heat. I never looked back, but I knew that my brother's eyes, behind me, were looking steadily ahead, for the boat went as straight as a bushman's dart, when it leaves the end of the sumpitan. There was no better paddler, no better steersman than my brother. Many times, together, we had won races in that canoe. But we never had put out our strength as we did then—then, when for the last time we paddled together! There was no braver or stronger man in our country than my brother. I could not spare the strength to turn my head and look at him, but every moment I heard the hiss of his breath getting louder behind me. Still he did not speak. The sun was high. The heat clung to my back like a flame of fire. My ribs were ready to burst, but I could no longer get enough air into my chest. And then I felt I must cry out with my last breath, 'Let us rest!' . . . 'Good!' he answered; and his voice was firm. He was strong. He was brave. He knew not fear and no fatigue . . . My brother!"

A murmur powerful and gentle, a murmur vast and faint; the murmur of trembling leaves, of stirring boughs, ran through the tangled depths of the forests, ran over the starry smoothness of the lagoon, and the water between the piles lapped the slimy timber once with a sudden splash. A breath of warm air touched the two men's faces and passed on with a mournful sound—a breath loud and short like an uneasy sigh of the dreaming earth.

Arsat went on in an even, low voice.

"We ran our canoe on the white beach of a little bay close to a long tongue of land that seemed to bar our road; a long wooded cape going far into the sea. My brother knew that place. Beyond the cape a river has its entrance, and through the jungle of that land there is a narrow path. We made a fire and cooked rice. Then we lay down to sleep on the soft sand in the shade of our canoe, while she watched. No sooner had I closed my eyes than I heard her cry of alarm. We leaped up. The sun was halfway down the sky already, and coming in sight in the opening of the bay we saw a prau manned by many paddlers. We knew it at once; it was one of our Rajah's praus. They were watching the shore, and saw us. They beat the gong, and turned the head of the prau into the bay. I felt my heart become weak within my breast. Diamelen sat on the sand and covered her face. There was no escape by sea. My brother laughed. He had the gun you had given him, Tuan, before you went away, but there was only a handful of powder. He spoke to me quickly: 'Run with her along the path. I shall keep them back, for they have no firearms, and landing in the face of a man with a gun is certain death for some. Run with her. On the other side of that wood there is a fisherman's house—and a canoe. When I have fired all the shots I will follow. I am a great runner, and before they can come up we shall be gone. I will hold out as long as I can, for she is but a woman—that can neither run nor fight, but she has your heart in her weak hands.' He dropped behind the canoe. The prau was coming. She and I ran, and as we rushed along the path I heard shots. My brother fired—once—twice—and the booming of the gong ceased. There was silence behind us. That neck of land is narrow. Before I heard my brother fire the third shot I saw the shelving shore, and I saw the water again; the mouth of a broad river. We crossed a grassy glade. We ran down to the water. I saw a low hut above the black mud, and a small canoe hauled up. I heard another shot behind me. I thought, 'That is his last charge.' We rushed down to the canoe; a man came running from the hut, but I leaped on him, and we rolled together in the mud. Then I got up, and he lay still at my feet. I don't know whether I had killed him or not. I and Diamelen pushed the canoe afloat. I heard yells behind me, and I saw my brother run across the glade. Many men were bounding after him, I took her in my arms and threw her into the boat, then leaped in myself. When I looked back I saw that my brother had fallen. He fell and was up again, but the men were closing round him. He shouted, 'I am coming!' The men were close to him. I looked. Many men. Then I looked at her. Tuan, I pushed the canoe! I pushed it into deep water. She was kneeling forward looking at me, and I said, 'Take your paddle,' while I struck the water with mine. Tuan, I heard him cry. I heard him cry my name twice; and I heard voices shouting, 'Kill! Strike!' I never turned back. I heard him calling my name again with a great shriek, as when life is going out together with the voice—and I never turned my head.

My own name! . . . My brother! Three times he called—
but I was not afraid of life. Was she not there in that
canoe? And could I not with her find a country where
death is forgotten—where death is unknown!"

The white man sat up. Arsat rose and stood, an indistinct
and silent figure above the dying embers of the fire. Over
the lagoon a mist drifting and low had crept, erasing slowly
the glittering images of the stars. And now a great expanse
of white vapour covered the land: it flowed cold and gray
in the darkness, eddied in noiseless whirls round the tree-
trunks and about the platform of the house, which seemed
to float upon a restless and impalpable illusion of a sea.
Only far away the tops of the trees stood outlined on the
twinkle of heaven, like a sombre and forbidding shore—a
coast deceptive, pitiless and black.

Arsat's voice vibrated loudly in the profound peace.

"I had her there! I had her! To get her I would have
faced all mankind. But I had her—and—"

His words went out ringing into the empty distances.
He paused, and seemed to listen to them dying away very
far—beyond help and beyond recall. Then he said quietly—

"Tuan, I loved my brother."

A breath of wind made him shiver. High above his head,
high above the silent sea of mist the drooping leaves of the
palms rattled together with a mournful and expiring sound.
The white man stretched his legs. His chin rested on his
chest, and he murmured sadly without lifting his head—

"We all love our brothers."

Arsat burst out with an intense whispering violence—

"What did I care who died? I wanted peace in my own
heart."

He seemed to hear a stir in the house—listened—then
stepped in noiselessly. The white man stood up. A breeze
was coming in fitful puffs. The stars shone paler as if they
had retreated into the frozen depths of immense space.
After a chill gust of wind there were a few seconds of perfect calm and absolute silence. Then from behind the black
and wavy line of the forests a column of golden light shot
up into the heavens and spread over the semicircle of the

eastern horizon. The sun had risen. The mist lifted, broke into drifting patches, vanished into thin flying wreaths; and the unveiled lagoon lay, polished and black, in the heavy shadows at the foot of the wall of trees. A white eagle rose over it with a slanting and ponderous flight, reached the clear sunshine and appeared dazzlingly brilliant for a moment, then soaring higher, became a dark and motionless speck before it vanished into the blue as if it had left the earth forever. The white man, standing gazing upwards before the doorway, heard in the hut a confused and broken murmur of distracted words ending with a loud groan. Suddenly Arsat stumbled out with outstretched hands, shivered and stood still for some time with fixed eyes. Then, he said—

"She burns no more."

Before his face the sun showed its edge above the tree-tops rising steadily. The breeze freshened; a great brilliance burst upon the lagoon, sparkled on the rippling water. The forests came out of the clear shadows of the morning, became distinct, as if they had rushed nearer—to stop short in a great stir of leaves, of nodding boughs, of swaying branches. In the merciless sunshine the whisper of unconscious life grew louder, speaking in an incomprehensible voice round the dumb darkness of that human sorrow. Arsat's eyes wandered slowly, then stared at the rising sun.

"I can see nothing," he said half aloud to himself.

"There is nothing," said the white man, moving to the edge of the platform and waving his hand to his boat. A shout came faintly over the lagoon and the sampan began to glide towards the abode of the friend of ghosts.

"If you want to come with me, I will wait all the morning," said the white man, looking away upon the water.

"No, Tuan," said Arsat, softly. "I shall not eat or sleep in this house, but I must first see my road. Now I can see nothing—see nothing! There is no light and no peace in the world; but there is death—death for many. We are sons of the same mother—and I left him in the midst of enemies; but I am going back now."

He drew a long breath and went on in a dreamy tone:

"In a little while I shall see clear enough to strike—to strike. But she has died, and ... now ... darkness."

He flung his arms wide open, let them fall along his body, then stood still with unmoved face and stony eyes, staring at the sun. The white man got down into his canoe. The polers ran smartly along the sides of the boat, looking over their shoulders at the beginning of a weary journey. High in the stern, his head muffled up in white rags, the juragan sat moody, letting his paddle trail in the water. The white man, leaning with both arms over the grass roof of the little cabin, looked back at the shining ripple of the boat's wake. Before the sampan passed out of the lagoon into the creek he lifted his eyes. Arsat had not moved. He stood lonely in the searching sunshine; and he looked beyond the great light of a cloudless day into the darkness of a world of illusions.

DELL LAUREL EDITIONS

The world's greatest literature in its
most inexpensive form. Among the world-famous
novels in Dell Laurel Editions:

SIX GREAT MODERN SHORT NOVELS James Joyce: *The
Dead;* Herman Melville: *Billy Budd,
Foretopman;* Katherine Anne Porter: *Noon Wine;*
Gogol: *The Overcoat;* Glenway Wescott: *The Pilgrim
Hawk;* William Faulkner: *The Bear* 60c

WUTHERING HEIGHTS Emily Brontë 50c

CRIME AND PUNISHMENT Dostoyevsky 75c

BRIDESHEAD REVISITED Evelyn Waugh 75c

THE RETURN OF THE NATIVE Thomas Hardy 60c

JANE EYRE Charlotte Brontë 50c

DOMBEY AND SON Charles Dickens 95c

THE AMBASSADORS Henry James 60c

THE WEB AND THE ROCK Thomas Wolfe 95c

TRISTRAM SHANDY Laurence Sterne 75c

MADAME BOVARY Gustave Flaubert 50c

MOLL FLANDERS Daniel Defoe 50c

GULLIVER'S TRAVELS Jonathan Swift 50c

MOBY DICK Herman Melville 75c

*Other outstanding volumes in the
Dell Reference Library*

THE COLUMBIA-VIKING DESK ENCYCLOPEDIA

The biggest bargain ever in paperback—the completely revised and up-to-date portable encyclopedia that sold over a million and a half copies in hardcover.
2,016 pages. $1.95

WHITNEY'S PARLIAMENTARY PROCEDURE
Byrl A. Whitney

A practical, easy-to-use manual for group decision-making, with a complete chart of parliamentary motions, glossary of terms and index.   50c

MODERN AMERICAN DICTIONARY

Prepared by the editorial staff of the American College Dictionary. With 640 pages and 46,000 entries.   75c

CORRECT SPELLING MADE EASY   Norman Lewis

A 60-day guide to expert spelling by the author of *Better English*.   50c

NEW WAYS TO GREATER WORD POWER
Roger B. Goodman and David Lewin

The complete book of vocabulary-improvement, covering all phases of speaking and writing.   40c

DELL BOOKS

Other Volumes in

THE LAUREL JOSEPH CONRAD

LORD JIM   50c
The tale of a young sailing mate's lifelong efforts to atone for one moment's cowardice, often considered Conrad's masterpiece.

THE NIGGER OF THE NARCISSUS
and THE END OF THE TETHER   50c
Conrad captures the mood and mystery of the sea in two of his most famous adventure novels.

NOSTROMO   75c
Conrad turns from his characteristic settings of sea and jungle to paint a vivid picture of South American revolution.

AN OUTCAST OF THE ISLANDS   50c
Passion, betrayal and deterioration in the tropics: an outstanding novel on a major Conrad theme.